VILLAIN'S ASSISTANT

The Villain's Trilogy + Book One

VILLAIN'S ASSISTANT

CARLEY HIBBERT

EMBER PUBLISHING

Cover design and artwork by Katrina Jorgensen
Interior design by Keith Nerdin

ISBN-10: 0-692-49631-9

ISBN-13: 978-0-692-49631-2

Ember Publishing

*For all my friends and family
that nudged me along the way,
but especially for my husband,
who never let me quit.*

PROLOGUE

Benjamin bent over a shiny gold coin lying on the dusty road. His mother had already walked ahead of him to the market, impatient to talk to a vendor. No one was in sight. Benjamin picked the coin up. Sunlight glinted over King Aldo's face as Benjamin turned the coin over and over in his small hand. *Beautiful,* he thought. He never had a coin of his own before. He could give it to his mother as a present the next time she got sad. He closed his hand around the coin and squeezed. He heard two girls quarrelling on the road ahead of him and he looked up, clutching the coin to his chest.

"I must have dropped it when I pulled the string out of my pocket."

Two young girls, wearing tattered peasant dresses, walked from the market toward Benjamin, scanning the ground. The taller girl pulled a sweat-stained scarf from her mousy hair and began twisting it. She scowled at the younger one, who looked about Benjamin's age.

The younger one rubbed at a grease spot on her skirt and fingered her thin braid.

"I knew this would happen," the taller girl said. "If Mama ever lets us go to market again, *I'll* hold the money."

The little sister wiped her nose with the back of her hand, leaving a dirt smudge on her nose. Tears welled up in her eyes, as she went back to rubbing the spot on her dress.

"We've just got to find it." The little sister sniffed and turned her empty pockets out again.

Benjamin glanced down at his hand and felt sick. He scanned the road. A group of raggedy women approached, their dingy skirts swaying in unison as they gossiped over news from the market. They weren't watching. He squeezed his hand around the coin until its hard edges cut into his palm. He swallowed hard against the burning in his throat as he waited for the sisters to notice him. The younger sister paused and tugged her braid as she made eye contact. Benjamin stepped forward and opened his hand, revealing his precious find for her to see. The young girl's eyes widened as she lunged at Benjamin.

"You found it!" The little girl wrapped both of her grimy hands around his and grinned. She was missing a tooth. "Thank you." She turned and raised the lost coin over her head like a trophy. The older girl smirked at Benjamin as her sister dropped the coin in her hand.

"Who gives up a free coin?" the older girl asked, shaking her head.

The girls burst into harsh laughter and scampered past the women to spend their newly acquired coin.

Benjamin felt something cold and heavy hit his stomach when his mother's cold blue eyes met his. She shoved one of the gossiping women aside, her dark braid trailing behind. The women stopped to stare in silence as she grabbed his arm, nearly yanking it from its socket. She dragged him back to their home in a silent rage. Prickly shrubs cut through his thin pants and into his legs as she pulled him across country to their house. He'd spend the rest of the day picking stickers from his socks for sure.

As soon as Benjamin's mother slammed the front door, one of the shutters broke free of its hinges, letting light into their one-room hovel. She finally released his arm. He rubbed his throbbing arm while examining the multiple knots that kept his laces intact and began counting burrs.

"Great Wolves! How could you have embarrassed me like that?" His mother paced back and forth, pressing her hands over her face as if trying to block out her son's offense. "No villain ever gives up free coin! I set that whole thing up to prove to my friends that you're pure villain like your father. Who taught you to do good deeds? Not me!" She paused to stare at Benjamin, her deep blue eyes glinting with moisture. "How will you ever be the greatest villain's assistant on the Thieves' Plain if you do things like give money to poor people for no good reason? I'm just glad your father isn't around to see that! We should both be thankful that he's *dead*."

Benjamin counted twelve burrs in his laces, but then he couldn't remember which number came next, so he swallowed and looked at his mother. She closed her eyes and slapped a hand over her mouth to stifle a sob.

An ache built in Benjamin's chest. He pressed his wet face into her skirt and wrapped his arms around her legs. "I'm sorry, Mother! Please don't cry! I'll never do it again. Just please don't cry," he pleaded. His mother clutched his shoulder, pushing him away from her. She guided him to his chair in the corner, wiped the tears off her face, and clenched her jaw.

"You're right, no more crying," she said, turning to stare out the window. "If you want something done right, you have to do it yourself."

ONE

From his splintery chair on the stage, Benjamin watched students, faculty, and parents settle uneasily into their assigned seats. He resisted the urge to bounce his knee up and down, since the stage creaked loudly and it would give away his nerves, but his heart pounded loudly in his chest anyway. Under the heat of the afternoon sun, family members blistered below on shaky wooden benches in the stone courtyard while the students and faculty melted on the temporary stage. Everyone scowled at their neighbors and eyed the exits in case the graduation ceremony turned ugly, which was a viable risk with so many villains gathered in one spot.

Benjamin glared at the sun, wiping away an errant trickle of sweat from his temple. The sweltering heat only added to the tension among the feuding villains who came to watch future generations join their ranks. Despite the graduation pact each attendee signed before entering the Villains' Academy grounds, some blood was always spilled. It was too tempting to settle old scores and bump off rivals.

Benjamin scanned the crowd. Sweat trailed down their dusty faces, leaving clean streaks behind.

When Headmaster Greely stood, all eyes flicked to him. Benjamin glanced over his shoulder at the boys sitting behind him. He had no intention of getting stabbed in the back. There was a very limited amount of decent employment opportunities for fresh graduates, and taking out the top graduate would open the door for a lesser villain, but they just grinned foolishly at each other and waved at their families. An ache spread through Benjamin's chest as he gazed at the crowd below. He didn't have any living family. In fact, he didn't know any living person outside the academy's walls.

His father, the famous Black-Eyed Barnaby, had perished before Benjamin was born. His mother's death, mere weeks before school had started, finalized Benjamin's decision to attend the Villains' Academy. He imagined her sitting in an aisle seat close to the back. She would have been smirking, and her indigo eyes would have glowed with plans for his future, knowing that only half his journey was done. However, instead of his mother, some jittery gentleman with a goat's beard sat fiddling with the knives he had illegally smuggled in to the graduation ceremony under his sleeves.

Benjamin shifted his disappointed gaze to the back of Headmaster Greely's head as he mumbled along in a strained way at the podium. Benjamin tugged on his sleeve, his fingers brushing against his own secret knife. It was rumored that an assassination attempt on Greely's life had been foiled just this very morning. *Ah, well.*

"We would like to acknowledge the students unable to attend these ceremonies due to a truly ill-timed outbreak of influenza," Greely said with a straight face, "and others who failed to follow the points of the graduation pact that we all signed."

Got caught, you mean. Benjamin smirked at the three empty seats between him and the podium. Considering it was a school intended for the most promising villains on the Thieves' Plain, Benjamin felt his peers were fairly inept. Everyone seemed to either get caught or killed a little too easily. Most of the traps his peers set for him were tripped before Benjamin even had to worry about springing them. *He* had never been caught. However, he tried to stay humble about his prowess; spouting off about your successes usually got you killed.

Benjamin surveyed the area around him. Sunlight glinted on tripwires around his chair. He glanced back over his shoulder. A few thug-sized boys glared back. Sven, the one with the biggest biceps, drew his long finger across his throat. Benjamin slid his knife out with a sigh and easily dismantled their booby traps. After all, he had expected some reprisals for being named valedictorian.

A rare breeze brushed across Benjamin's damp forehead. Before it could die, he slid a small envelope out of his other sleeve and drew a deep breath. He raised his hand in a mock scratch to his ear and released a fine powder on the breeze while holding his breath. Nothing serious, just something to cloud the plotting minds behind him. Everyone would be in a stupor just long enough for him to make a clean getaway after his speech. He slipped the envelope back up his sleeve and slowly exhaled.

"Our original valedictorian is among those unable to attend," said Headmaster Greely, barely intelligible. "We thank Benjamin Black who has graciously prepared a *short* last-minute address in his place. Benjamin?"

Benjamin stood up and checked the audience and graduates behind him for sudden movements or furtive glances. His fellow graduates already seemed safely befuddled in a fog bank. The parents and other villains were too busy looking over their own shoulders to be a threat. Benjamin shook Greely's offered hand—after checking the headmaster's palms for poisons first, of course.

Greely threatened him through clenched teeth, "And by short I mean *short*, or there may not be any survivors."

Point taken. Benjamin swallowed dryly as he examined the dart that had just struck the side of podium. It was most likely poisoned. Looking up, he locked eyes, as it were, with a one-eyed man sitting dead center in the front row. The man's eye patch glistened in the shadow of his hood while iron hair drizzled down his pale face to his shoulders. Unsettled by such straightforward attention, Benjamin choked over his introduction and skipped straight to the end line. "If we survive today, we *can* conquer tomorrow!"

This was met with general cheers from the audience and a few slurred outbursts from the graduates behind him. One dazed boy fell onto his neighbor and was then reflexively shoved to the floor, sparking a scuffle on the stage.

Benjamin took advantage of the confusion and slinked past the graduates, sidestepping a few poorly aimed fists and knives. Some graduates were crawling under chairs. Benjamin crouched at the back of the stage to cast a cautious glance behind him. The cloaked man watched Benjamin as families scrambled to the exits. *An assassin?* A knot tightened in Benjamin's chest, but the man did not move. The idea of an assassin coming after him was incredibly unlikely; no one else knew who his father was, not even Greely.

Benjamin slid down the back side of the stage, scraping his spine on the exposed wood. He winced as he checked under the stage, his back still throbbing. He saw no one lurking among the wooden supports. All was clear. Benjamin staggered through the cobbled courtyard where the students had gathered earlier to mount the stage. There were a few grubby packs tucked away in the corners, but days before, Benjamin had stashed his pack outside the walls of the academy. No sense in taking chances now. Benjamin sneaked through the gates just as a scream sent a chill through him.

TWO

A few days later, Benjamin sprang out of bed, too restless to stay in bed any longer, though the sun had barely come up. He fumbled with his crisp, new black suit as he wadded it up, wrapped it in the dusty rug from the floor, and jumped on it. He dressed in the now-rumpled suit and rubbed chalk strategically on his elbows and knees. No one wanted to hire someone who was afraid to get dirty. He closed the wardrobe door and glanced into the mirror. Benjamin looked small for his sixteen years, and therefore, people often underestimated him. Their mistake.

Benjamin wished once more that his warm, brown eyes held just a speck of the cold intensity of his mother's stormy blue eyes. He closed his eyes and took a deep breath. *I can do this. I will do this!* He shook the tension out of his hands. His interview today was just another step on the path to becoming the greatest villain's assistant the Thieves' Plain had ever known, just like his father, Black-Eyed Barnaby.

His late father had assisted the archvillain Shreb the First to tame the lesser villains of the plain. No one stole a turnip without Shreb the First's permission, because Black-Eyed Barnaby made sure there were consequences otherwise. That kind of order had not existed on the Thieves' Plain before or since Benjamin's father reigned beside the archvillain First. Now it was up to Benjamin to continue his father's work.

He shoved an apple into the pocket of his jacket for his breakfast later; for once he wasn't hungry. He plucked a sleek black eye patch off the kitchen table and hesitated. Eye patches could look pathetic if they weren't done right; he'd seen obvious fakes before. So he shoved it in his pocket and headed outside.

Benjamin locked the door to his hideout and tucked the key into a knothole above the door. He then stepped back and surveyed the small house where he spent his early days with his mother. A broken shutter leaned from the front window. It was as sun-bleached and shabby as the rest of the shack. He turned to hurry past the front gate that lay broken to the side, nearly grown over with crisp weeds. This place had always been more of a hideout than a home, but it was his. It was someplace he could return if things got bad.

Benjamin's heart pounded in his throat as he picked his way through the overgrown path to the road. Branches pricked at his jacket and scraped his scalp. He rarely used this path anymore. He'd resided at the Villains' Academy for the last five years, except on holidays when he returned here to eat toast and hard cheese alone. And now he was going to a job interview with Shreb II, the son of the archvillain his own father had worked for.

He was now well on the way to following in his father's dark footsteps, like his mother had always wished. No one seemed to know much about Black-Eyed Barnaby besides his exploits for the great archvillain Shreb the First, including Benjamin's mother. She seemed unable or unwilling to answer even simple questions like what his favorite cheese had been. *That won't help you become a better villain, she would say.*

"I can't believe I'm finally going," Benjamin said, smiling to himself.

Benjamin's excitement fell as his feet hit the dust of the main road. A man with gray streaks in his dark hair stood in the road, staring at the Sunrise Mountains that marked the boundary of the Thieves' Plain from the rest of the kingdom of Lam. The boundary had been made by King Aldo's father, King Zavier, in order to dispel the corruption and filth that had infected his kingdom and threatened his crown. Usurpers and villains were pushed to the Thieves' Plain and left to the mercy of the archvillain's rule. The plain began drying into a dustbowl the day after Lam was split in half, so life was hard, and people had to steal and kill just to survive.

"Interview with Shreb?" the old man asked over his shoulder.

"Uh, the *Mighty* Shreb? Yes." Benjamin glanced quickly around. There was no one else on the road. "He doesn't like to be…" He stopped himself. Why should he be handing out free advice? Let the nosy old man find out the hard way how Shreb II liked to be addressed.

"That's where I'm headed too. Safety in numbers." The man turned to face him, revealing a black eye patch encrusted with small rubies.

Benjamin took a step back and was relieved that he hadn't chosen to wear his eye patch. He took a step toward Shreb's fortress, not knowing what to do and hoping it didn't show. Maybe he could outpace the old man and leave him behind. Unfortunately, the old man didn't take the hint and stepped in beside him.

"Good day for an interview. This your first one?" The old man traced the edge of his eye patch with a grimy finger.

Benjamin turned and tripped over his own feet, kicking up a sizable dust cloud that sent him into a hard coughing fit. The villain waited until Benjamin's coughs stopped to continue talking.

"How did I know this is your first time? And that you're going to Shreb's?" The old man chuckled and steered clear of the dust cloud around Benjamin. "As easily as you can tell that I've been at this for a while. Besides, that's the only place anyone's going."

"You don't look like the type who would be looking for employment." Benjamin hacked a few more times as he examined the man's faded black suit.

"Worried about a little competition?" The old villain chuckled. "No worries. Let's say I'm more curious than serious."

Benjamin stopped to eye the one-eyed man. "You're spying for your employer, then?"

The old villain walked on silently, not answering the question. Benjamin trailed behind. The old man tugged at the strap wrapped around his head and glanced behind them toward the mountains and then back to the road ahead, turning his head slightly to study Benjamin.

Maybe the old man will need to rest soon, and then I can ditch him.

"What position are you trying for, entry-level grunt work?" the villain asked, trying not to sound too interested and failing.

Heat bloomed in Benjamin's cheeks. Why did everyone assume he was an incapable, just because he was young? He didn't have time for grunt work. "I'm trying for villain's assistant."

The old man rubbed his chin as he stole a few sideways glances at Benjamin. "Well, you *are* ambitious."

The villain slipped into a thoughtful silence. Benjamin tried to look unconcerned. So, of course, he felt self-conscious of every step he took and how he held his head and where he looked. The scoundrel probably wasn't truly interested in him. Still, Benjamin felt there was something off with him. What if he wanted to steal Benjamin from the Mighty Shreb? He was the only employer acceptable to him right now. Benjamin slowly increased his pace.

The villain pulled out a flask and drank, and then tucked it back into his pocket. *A flask! Why didn't I think of that?* Benjamin's mouth felt like a dry riverbed. There was a well along the road, but a good VA drank from a flask to avoid poisoning. His life and job depended on it.

"I'd offer you my flask, but we both know that's not going to happen. Don't worry, there's a well around the corner."

Benjamin nodded.

"So why the VA position?"

"It's the timing. I just graduated valedictorian from my class at the Villains' Academy." *And my dad used to work for his dad.* Benjamin shrugged. "I can handle it. Plus, it's what I want to do."

"Sort of like fate, huh?"

Benjamin nodded and clutched the eye patch in his pocket.

"Fate can be a cruel taskmaster, kid. You still have other choices."

"I'm not a kid," Benjamin snipped. "I'm *sixteen*."

The villain adjusted his eye patch but didn't respond.

"Wait. Is that some sort of job offer, or are you just trying to get me out of the way?" Benjamin asked.

He stopped and faced the villain, who seemed to be considering how to answer.

"Navigating these interviews can be tricky. It's nice to have someone to watch your back." The villain's good eye, a pale-brown one, flicked away for a moment before burrowing into Benjamin. "I want you to know that if you need help, you can trust me."

Benjamin stiffened. Trust was a loaded word around here. The villain stepped back slowly while maintaining eye contact, and then turned and walked off toward Shreb's Fortress alone. Benjamin stood and watched the villain's suit until the man was a dark smudge on the road.

Benjamin tapped his foot in the fine road dust and pulled out his apple and crunched into it, while he decided what to do next. The juices were not as satisfying as he had hoped, but it was all he had.

"Good riddance," he said, peering up the empty road ahead of him. But the cold lump in his chest said otherwise. This wasn't school anymore. He just might need help. He picked up his pace so he could keep the old man in sight. Benjamin had never witnessed a successful alliance in school, but here in the real world, there were no points handed out for the best betrayal. He shoved his apple back into his pocket and scrambled to catch up.

THREE

Benjamin bent over, gasping for air, his head throbbing in the heat. The gates to Shreb's fortress were still closed, so the interviews hadn't started yet. He trudged off the road to where several clumps of sweaty villains sat waiting. The head of this troupe was known only as the Villain, and at the moment, he sat under a sickly shade tree. He waved Benjamin over, and the young man collapsed next to him, thankful for the sliver of shade. He scanned the scowling crowd around him as he swabbed the sweat off his face. He was surprised to find several death glares aimed in his general direction, but then, there weren't any other shady spots to sit. Benjamin pulled his knees into his chest and examined the Villain, who was only concerned with the apple he had started peeling.

"I'm guessing that some of these guys know you?" Benjamin asked, taking count of visible knives and weapons.

The Villain chuckled. "Don't think of trying to start a friendly conversation with any of them. Trust me; you're safer here."

Benjamin had no intention of going anywhere at that moment. A large man with matted arm hair watched them, fingering a sparkling knife. Sweat dripped down the crease between his prickly eyebrows and into the bush of chest hair that crawled up from his open leather vest. Benjamin might be young and inexperienced, but he wasn't stupid. Sitting here with the Villain marked him as an associate. Whatever unsettled scores these thugs might have with the old man they would now have with Benjamin as well. He swallowed the hard lump that was building in his throat. Benjamin would be considered collateral damage if anyone wanted to take out the one-eyed man.

"Is that because they're dangerous?" Benjamin asked under his breath, "or is that because you're dangerous?"

Directly in front of them, just a knife's throw away, the hairy thug fidgeted against a large rock. Under the scalding sun, that boulder must have been a miserable resting place. Benjamin tucked his elbows in, drawing his knees tighter into his chest. Their shady spot must have looked like a place worth killing for.

The Villain glanced at Benjamin and asked, "Do you have any plans to deal with him?"

Benjamin grazed the pommel of the knife hidden under his sleeve with his thumb, determining how accurate a throw he could make from where he sat.

"My *plan* was to slide through unnoticed." Benjamin said through stiff lips, watching the hairy man's knife. "Plus I think he's looking murderously at you, not me."

Benjamin could hear the academy gossip already. *Did you hear about Benjamin Black? He didn't even make it a week...killed at his first interview...we all had such high hopes...thankfully, his father isn't around to see this.*

"You know, I think you're right," The Villain said as he finished peeling the apple, allowing a single strip of peel to fall into his lap. Then he looked up.

The hairy man hesitated for a full second under the gaze of the one-eyed man, but that was all the time the veteran needed. He threw his knife into the hairy man's muscled shoulder. The man's eyes popped as he clutched his arm with a screech. The impatient grumbling of the crowd was cut off by the time the injured man's knife hit the ground.

The Villain stood up, tossed his peel, and bit into his apple. Then he strolled over and pressed his boot into the man's wooly chest, causing the thug to howl. He pulled his knife out, and then directed, with a simple nod of his head, where the dirty man should go if he didn't want worse. The thug crept past the wide eyes of his neighbors, leaving only an indentation in the dirt and a few drops of blood. The Villain settled next to Benjamin.

"That brute didn't have subtlety, and it nearly killed him." The Villain pulled out a red rag from his pocket and cleaned his blade. "Subtlety is a skill you need to develop or else your every movement screams your intent."

The Villain replaced his rag and turned to whittling a piece of wood, ignoring the sea of eyes that followed every stroke of his knife. Benjamin blinked at the silent men who surrounded him. He was now invisible to everyone. Of course, there were worse things to be than invisible at the moment—like *gutted*.

A couple of guys elbowed each other and signaled it was time to move on. After a few more small groups left, Benjamin began to wonder what the Villain's leverage was. He couldn't see what the old man was doing, so he readjusted his position to watch. At the slightest narrowing of the Villain's eye, four young men stood and walked away.

Who was this scoundrel? There had to be more to him than a steely gaze. This man must be somebody, possibly an archvillain. How could Benjamin not know who he was? He went over the list from school—Cyril the Insane had just fled the plain when his men turned on him. Mantis hadn't had a following in decades. Tendenham had laid low since he lost his hand. There wasn't anyone else so formidable. Benjamin was out of the loop—and that could be a dangerous place to be.

Soon there were only a few interviewees left. One guy lay against a tall rock, his hat tipped over his face. He was the only person not completely engrossed in the silent battle raging around the old man. Two other thugs stared intently at the Villain. Benjamin flicked his eyes between the old man and the thugs, who had an obvious physical advantage. They were sweating pure malice. The Villain stood and tipped his hat to them with a smile. The thugs turned their glares at each other, each suspecting the other of being allied with the old man. They charged one another.

The Villain walked around them and slid his knife in its sheath, looking satisfied with his handiwork. The napper sat up, pushed his hat back, and grinned, revealing a mouth full of gold.

The color drained from the old man's face, and his knuckles went white around his knife. Judging by their icy glares, both men knew each other. There was no professional admiration, only loathing. The Villain slid his eye to Benjamin, his jaw muscles flexing, and then gestured with his head to follow. And Benjamin, like everyone else that day, obeyed. The Villain's eye had said, "*If you want to live, follow me.*" Benjamin realized he wanted to live more than he wanted his dream job.

FOUR

"That was an unfortunate twist of fate," the Villain said, rubbing at a spot on the back of his head. His stride was purposeful and tense as he quickly covered ground.

Benjamin shook his head as if that would put his thoughts into some kind of order. He was incapable of matching the old man's pace, since he still couldn't breathe. Did he really just walk away from his life's master plan? Being VA to the second Shreb was all Benjamin had ever thought about while in school, and now, in one second, it was all over! Benjamin pressed a fist against his chest, imploring his lungs to breathe. He wasn't sure how his feet were moving; he couldn't feel them.

Occasionally the old man cast a look over his shoulder that caused Benjamin to jump and catch up. Soon the Villain and Benjamin were at a crossroads. The Villain took the road that led away from Benjamin's hideout,: the place he was supposed to go when things didn't go as planned. Benjamin hesitated a moment. One road led to uncertainty, and the other led to someplace he'd already been. *I am alive*, he reminded himself. There was always a chance for better opportunities if he kept moving down new paths. His heart pounded against his eardrums as he trailed after his new employer.

They walked until the shadows got long and Benjamin's throat scratched with dust. The old man sat on a rock to rest, scrutinizing Benjamin for several seconds before scooting over. "You look like you need to sit down."

The Villain pulled out his flask. He drank and handed it over to Benjamin. The water was warm and metallic tasting, but it soothed his burning throat. Benjamin thanked him, trying not to sound ungrateful for the most unsettling day of his life. Nothing had gone according to plan. Even his worst-case scenarios couldn't have predicted this. *But it could have been worse,* he reminded himself, *so much worse.* He remembered the nightmarish gold smile that ruined his life, and he shivered.

"So what do I call you?"

"The Lieutenant," the old man said, studying Benjamin from the corner of his eye.

"What about the gold-mouth guy? It seems like I would have heard about him, but then I've never heard of the Lieutenant either."

"Well, he wouldn't be on any lists."

"Too new?"

"No, too dead—a long time dead." The Lieutenant stared across the brush. "I suppose the devil wouldn't take him."

Dead? Benjamin thought over his history courses. *I have passed over to the land of the weird.*

"I don't remember any gold teeth."

"That part is new and not an improvement to his personality at all. Surely you've heard of Old Mouthrot?"

Benjamin gasped.

"Ah, I see that you have."

"But he was just…just a story." Benjamin remembered the whispers that drifted through the dormitories at night.

"Well, no one knew much about him. Mouthrot preferred to be thought of as a ghost, and this little resurrection doesn't bode well for any of us, especially not the *Mighty* Shreb." There was mocking in the Lieutenant's tone. "Mouthrot should have replaced the first Shreb as archvillain, except that Mouthrot also died, or nearly died, fourteen years ago."

"Hmm…impressive," Benjamin muttered, his head buzzing with the idea of a villain more formidable than the Mighty Shreb. "That would be a crowning achievement for Mouthrot to get the VA position with the current archvillain. Shreb would have to be fairly gullible, though, wouldn't he? It's not like Mouthrot looks like the type who takes orders."

"What did you say?" The jewels in the old man's eye patch glinted in the failing light.

"Shreb would have to be quite—"

"No, no, not that…I said it was a *crowning* achievement."

With that, the old man stood up and reached for his flask. Benjamin gulped as much as he dared before tossing back the flask.

"Come on; we've got work to do."

The Lieutenant took off down the road refreshed, while Benjamin dragged behind. He wouldn't sleep in his bed anytime soon, though there was nothing he wanted more. Benjamin fought off his desire to lie down and lick his inner wounds, but instead he picked up speed. The thought of getting lost and sleeping in the dark outdoors propelled him forward. Besides, the brush looked prickly.

They approached a two-story shack, bleached white from the sun. A lantern was lit outside the door, casting shadows in the fading light. The Lieutenant warned Benjamin to stand back before he knocked.

Benjamin studied the open area around him, noting a pile of firewood and a well. The door flew open, and a girl with tattered yellow braids appeared at the door, wrapped in a shawl. The man muttered something to her and then gestured toward Benjamin.

"I brought a lad back with me," he said. The Lieutenant waved Benjamin over.

The girl looked not much older than Benjamin. She glared at him and stepped aside, pulling her faded skirt back to expose a pair of well-worn boots.

Benjamin ducked his head as he slipped past her. "He told me to come."

"Of course he did," she growled and slammed the door.

"I trust him." The Lieutenant shrugged.

"Oh, really? That's new."

The Lieutenant put his hands on her shoulder, pushing her yellow braids back, and looked her in the eye. "*Mouthrot* saw us together."

"Mouthrot?" The girl's face went slack, her gray eyes widening. "But he's *dead*. You killed him. You *said* that you killed him." The girl pulled away and started pacing, shoving a chair into a kitchen table.

"We never found the body when he fell into that ravine." The Lieutenant looked past the girl as he rubbed the back of his head. "We should have known better. *I* should have known better."

The girl shook her head as her chest heaved violently. She dodged the Lieutenant's outreached arms and ran.

"Rebecca!" the Lieutenant cried, his head falling in defeat as she pounded up the stairs and slammed a door.

Benjamin rocked back and forth silently on his feet as he studied the road dust on the tops of his boots. After an awkward silence passed, the Lieutenant set a plate of cheese and bread on the planks that made up the kitchen table. The heavy wood bench screeched across floor as Benjamin sat down and tried to swallow the tasteless food.

The old villain creaked up the stairs and then returned with a thin pad and blanket. He pushed back a curtain behind Benjamin, revealing a pantry, and dropped the bedding on the floor. The Lieutenant nodded a silent good night and slipped back up the stairs.

Benjamin woke the next morning on a dusty floor pad with a small, grimy blanket twisted around him. He pressed the heels of his hands into his eyes, wishing the previous day had just been a nightmare. He wondered if he was truly with allies, but as he had never had allies before, he wasn't sure.

They hadn't tied Benjamin up, locked him away, or mistreated him. They certainly hadn't interrogated him, at least not yet. In fact, the girl had barely acknowledged his existence last night.

Benjamin poked his head through the curtain that separated his pantry "bedroom" from the kitchen. He hadn't heard any noises yet. He stoked the fire in the stove and then headed outside to cut firewood.

Benjamin had just unloaded the wood next to the stove when the teenage girl from the night before came into the kitchen. He didn't remember her name. She pinched her lips together. Hard muscle stood out on her arm as she handed him an empty bucket without a word and pointed him outside. Benjamin hurried out the door, hiding his scowl. She was taller than he was as well, he noticed. He returned with a bucket full of water and set it down next to the wood he'd brought in earlier.

"I don't expect the Lieutenant will be up for a while. No doubt, he was up all night planning," the girl said, finally breaking her silence.

Benjamin noticed she had dark circles under her eyes. "Were you up helping him?"

She turned her back to him and grew silent once again.

He sat at the table and pulled out a small book. He crossed out "Shamelessly impress Mighty Shreb" and "Gloat after becoming the youngest VA ever" from his to-do list with a thick pencil. It might have been easier to just tear out all the pages, but he hated to waste the paper. It looked as though he would have to start from scratch to find his way back in Shreb's potential employment. He pressed his knuckles into his forehead as he stared at the scribbled page and then glanced at the girl over his shoulder. The stove hissed as she filled a pot with water. He then wrote: *Make friends with hostiles.*

How naïve he'd been yesterday! He never stood a chance against those thugs. He really was lucky to have made it out alive, he had to admit. Organizational skills were not, as it turned out, the most crucial qualification for a career in villainy (or at least not when starting out). He closed his book and hid it in his jacket pocket, promising himself a planning session later.

The girl sat down with her own book, her fine features twisted in an unpleasant grimace while she read. Scabs dotted her knuckles. Benjamin realized—too late—that he'd been staring when her gray eyes flared at him.

"Yes?" she growled. She planted an elbow in the middle of her book to mark her place. The muscles in her forearm tightened. "Haven't you seen a person read before? Or maybe never a *girl?*" She puffed at a loose strand of yellow hair that fell over one eye. "Any more questions?"

"Yes...I don't...or no?"

She narrowed her eyes at him. "Well, what is it? Do you *have* a question or not?"

"Y-yes, I do, but I never actually asked one before—earlier." He smiled nervously. This was the first girl he'd ever had to deal with besides the occasional maid at school, and so far, he didn't like it much.

She rolled her eyes. "What?"

"My name is B—"

The scary girl lifted her hand to silence him, cocked her head to the side, and took a deep breath (and possibly counted to ten). "No! We don't use our real names here. You can call me Rebecca. I've already got one for you." Rebecca slammed her book down. "It's 'Hey You.' Breakfast will be ready in ten minutes. Don't talk to me until then." Fire burned behind her eyes.

He nodded, drew his lips tightly together, and then got up and padded around the room. A heavy knot tightened in his chest as he struggled to ignore the two fears screaming inside him: he was now unemployable, and this girl who called herself Rebecca was probably going to stab him in the back.

Benjamin couldn't organize a single thought, so he stopped trying. Instead, he admired the neat stacks of dishes arranged by size on the shelves. When Rebecca cleared her throat, he jumped out of her way. She filled two bowls with gruel and placed them on the table.

"Hey You, while you let that cool, fill that bucket again so I can clean the kitchen."

Benjamin, now officially dubbed Hey You, slunk out to the well.

After breakfast, he went outside with yet another bucket of cold water and dunked his head, hoping to rinse away the frustrations of the last twenty-four hours. After drying off a little, Benjamin returned inside to announce that he would like to see the Lieutenant.

"Now," he demanded.

Rebecca stopped scrubbing a frying pan, looked quizzically in his direction, and then continued scrubbing. At a loss, Benjamin turned to march up the stairs but stumbled to a stop. The Lieutenant sat at the kitchen table, leafing through some papers. His steel-speckled hair gleamed in the morning light.

"You don't have to sleep in there again," he said. "We can clear out the room at the bottom of the stairs." He then looked at Benjamin with his good eye, a smile barely perceptible at the corners of his mouth.

Rebecca stomped up the stairs in protest. The Villain picked up his papers and stacked them neatly beside a plate of food. "Please, sit down. We need to talk." The Lieutenant smiled tightly.

"Yes, we do. Don't ever leave me alone with her again. It's cruel." Benjamin fiddled with his damp collar. A room full of plotting young men he could handle, but a prickly girl was something else entirely.

The Lieutenant looked over his shoulder and up the stairs. "Sorry about that. I never know what to expect with her. But you, I think, bring the worst out in her," he said and then chuckled nervously. "Should I cut to the chase? You can't go out there now. Mouthrot will hunt you down if he thinks you're with me. You're welcome to work with me—with us. I think the job you were after is now filled. Mouthrot gets what he goes after. So…now he's got your job. The end."

"Oh? You want me to work with you?" Benjamin perked up at the thought of being wanted. *Any* employment would be a step in the right direction.

"Nothing flashy, but things are about to pick up around here, and I'll need an assistant." He gave Benjamin a look that lifted the hair on the back of his neck. "It would be a lot less messy for you."

Benjamin watched the Lieutenant as he cut the sausage on his plate. He discreetly checked the kitchen for any stray breakfast meats but didn't see any lying around. As a young villain, Benjamin did need a job. He could always sneak away and start over, if he needed to. *Nothing was permanent, right?*

"Do I get to talk to your employer?" Benjamin asked, wondering where the Lieutenant was on the chain of command.

"Oh, no, my boss shall remain faceless and nameless. As far as you're concerned, I *am* the boss."

A nameless boss? Benjamin rubbed at the two hairs that had sprouted on his chin. It had been three days since he'd shaved. Benjamin bit his lip. He didn't like not knowing, but he wasn't sure he had much of a choice. Opportunity had found him; it would seem silly not to let things play out. Benjamin nodded.

The Lieutenant gave him a sharp nod back and took another bite of sausage. "So, your name?"

"Oh, it's B—"

The Lieutenant held up a hand cutting Benjamin off. "Are you sure you want to use your real name? Lots of villain's assistants use nicknames, in case things end badly. Your real identity is your life."

Benjamin watched the sausage on the Lieutenant's plate disappear one bite at a time.

The Lieutenant chewed as he batted around some possible nicknames. Juices glinted on his thick stubble. "Pork…Pen…Toad…Patch. I like Patch," he said, as he opened his mouth for the last bite of sausage. "Yeah, let's try that one for a while."

"Patch?" Benjamin sat blinking, the sausage forgotten. "That's not a villainous name."

"Exactly." The Lieutenant smiled and then drank from his cup.

Patch? I think I prefer Hey You, he thought wryly.

"Don't worry about Rebecca." The old man waved Benjamin's concerns off. "Once she realizes you're not a threat to her, she'll calm down."

"I think I'll stick with Benjamin, thanks."

The Lieutenant ripped a piece of bread in half and shrugged as he mopped the juices off his plate.

FIVE

*A*fter several mornings of filling water buckets and chopping firewood, Benjamin decided it was time to stop tiptoeing around Rebecca. She enjoyed ordering him around too much, and he needed to find his place within the organization. He didn't want to become her permanent drudge. He suspected that even the Lieutenant was a little scared of her, and *he* was the one in charge. If Benjamin wanted to do more than grunt work, he'd have to win her over. He took a deep breath as he unrolled his sleeves, noting that they were still damp after washing dishes and scrubbing the floor.

"So…" he started with what he hoped sounded like a semblance of confidence, "how long have you been working for the Lieutenant?"

"Hmm." Rebecca seemed to consider her answer a few seconds too long. Perhaps that was classified.

"Uh, how did you meet?"

Rebecca coughed and went to stir the simmering pot on the stove, focusing her attention on it instead of Benjamin. A heavy ball sunk into his stomach. *Was everything a secret with these two?*

"What do you do around here?"

Rebecca coughed again and nearly dropped her spoon into the pot. The heavy ball grew in his stomach as she carefully skimmed bubbles off the top of the boiling liquid.

"Is there anything that you *can* tell me?"

He stepped beside her. Rebecca dropped her hands and grimaced at him. A yellow piece of hair had slipped from one of her braids, skimming her eyelashes.

"Listen, I could make up lies or I could tell you nothing. Which would you prefer?"

Benjamin hooted, searching for the humor of the situation. "Wow! And people say *I* have trust issues!" He attempted a smile to lighten the mood but saw that his efforts weren't helping. "Never mind."

He breathed in and closed his eyes, and then he laughed again. *This whole situation is ridiculous.* Perhaps he could learn something from this. He whipped out his notebook, but as nothing came to mind, he shoved it back into his pocket.

Rebecca chewed on her bottom lip as she gazed out the window, her arms wrapped tightly around her. Then she squeezed her eyes closed, as if that alone would keep her secrets safely locked away.

Benjamin threw his hands in the air and turned to head outside. The Lieutenant, who had been leaning against the doorframe, followed him. Benjamin pulled the axe out of the chopping block.

"I should have had a better story prepared," the Lieutenant said, tugging at his eye patch.

"Story? I get that everyone has their secrets, but I can't even have a conversation because *everything* here is secret." He looked up in time to see just a hint of Rebecca's skirt twirl out of sight. He sighed. "Maybe that's why she's so angry." He slammed the axe back into the cutting block.

The old man nodded. "You're probably right, but sometimes there just isn't any other way. Secrets keep you alive."

"They also suffocate you!" Benjamin walked over to the well and jerked on the chain. "They just kill you more slowly."

Silence filled the space between them. When Benjamin looked up, the Lieutenant was rubbing the back of his head and kicking at the dirt. The villain opened his mouth wordlessly several times before he was finally able to speak. "I'll have Rebecca show you the drop box. You can start checking that for us." The Lieutenant adjusted his eye patch and returned inside.

Benjamin blinked at the space where the old man had just stood. He'd been expecting a little more than that. Yes, he'd just climbed one more rung on the trust ladder, but who knew how many more he needed to climb before he saw any light. Right now, he was completely baffled by these two. All gangs had secrets but this felt different. It felt dangerous, and not the Villains' Academy kind of dangerous. He yanked the axe out of the cutting block and slammed it deep into the wood, trying to split it wide open but failing. He tugged and tugged at the axe but was unable to pull it out by himself—and there was no way he was asking the Lieutenant or Rebecca for help.

SIX

Rebecca followed the boy at a distance. His size suggested he was just a boy, but his mouth said otherwise. He was probably close to her age. She'd just turned seventeen this spring, and she'd guessed him to be fifteen or sixteen. He'd been careful to keep a buffer between them all day, and she could hardly blame him. She'd been a beast since he arrived. What was the Lieutenant thinking, dragging some random kid from the plain into all this? Life was dangerous enough. She yanked on the straps of her pack, letting the air cool her shoulders for a moment. She tried to remember the grass being any other shade besides yellow or brown and couldn't. She glanced at the mountain range over her shoulder. Just on the other side, green things sprouted. Forests grew thick enough to nearly block out all sunlight. And the law of the king held the people together. It had been so long since she'd seen any of it, she wasn't sure if it was still there. Rain didn't fall on this side of the Sunrise Mountains, except just enough to keep everything from burning—or so it had been the last eight years she'd lived here.

The boy stopped and swiped his brown locks from his eyes to scan for the dead tree she had described to him earlier. This was the closest drop box where they exchanged news with couriers. Her charge glanced back at her, his light-brown eyes searching her face for hints. Rebecca had no problem keeping her face blank. He was supposed to find this on his own. Lieutenant's orders.

She tapped her foot on the goat path. A painful hole was growing in her chest every day. No amount of crying or screaming filled that black pit either; in fact, both only made her feel it more keenly. She wished she could talk openly to someone about everything. The Lieutenant preferred not to discuss the past. "The past is safely buried in the past," he'd say. But she could feel her secrets pressing hard inside her as she hunted for an escape. Fortunately, she didn't know very many people or she wouldn't have any secrets left.

When Rebecca glanced back, the boy had climbed onto a rock to get another foot and a half of perspective. *How different his childhood must have been,* she thought, *without a life of secrets weighing him down.* She wondered if he'd had enough to eat when he was young. It didn't look like it. The boy grinned at Rebecca and then pointed in the right direction. She waved him on to check it out. A puff of dust erupted as he hit the ground and ran. He really looked excited. Once the dust settled, she picked up her pace to keep him in sight. When was the last time she'd been excited about anything?

The tree wasn't really a tree anymore. It was bleached white and so dry that it had deep fractures running down its sides. Bees floated in and out of the cracks. The boy glared at her. She rolled her eyes.

"This better not be some kind of sick trick you play on the new guy, because I swear I will personally tell Mouthrot where you all live!" the boy shouted.

"Just be careful," Rebecca called as she approached.

The problem with working with this new boy was that she found herself wanting to explain herself to him. *Like why I'm such a raging mess,* she thought, *but that would be dangerous.* So she kept her distance, but the weight of her life tugged on her all the more when she was with this person who might want to listen to her splintered story. *Or I could just invent a happy tale about myself to tell this peasant boy,* she mused, *one where I knew all the answers. That might be a nice change.* But the mere thought of more lies only weighed her heart down more, so much so that she couldn't take another step until she dismissed the idea. She squeezed the locket that hung under her blouse and stumbled on.

The boy circled the tree, examining it as close as he dared until he found the burnt-out pit. His eyes glowed like amber with this small victory. He studied her a moment before putting his hand in to fetch the message that might be hidden inside. She tried to look uninterested.

A few bees circled him as he skittered back from the tree, waving a leather tube in the air. He handed it over to Rebecca. As she opened the tube, the boy swatted at the bees that were already returning to the tree. She exchanged the incoming message with an outgoing message the Lieutenant had written this morning about Shreb and Mouthrot. Personally, she thought he had waited too long, but he had first wanted to review some of the reports he'd received in the previous month. The Lieutenant liked to be thorough. She dropped the tube back into the tree and slid the sealed message into her pack.

She sat down for a moment in the narrow slice of shade the burnt-out tree provided. The boy mopped his wet face with his sleeve, slicking his wet strands away from his pale face. She thought about this morning and the simple questions she wasn't allowed to answer. She felt words building in her chest, and she opened her mouth to let a few out. *Surely,* a *few couldn't hurt,* she thought.

"I've known the Lieutenant nearly all my life," she said, rifling through her pack to find her waterskin.

"Really?" The boy raised his eyebrows.

"I don't know much more about him than you do, though." Rebecca smiled in apology. Nothing she could say could explain how a person could live with someone for nearly fifteen years and not know or understand him. "So, Patch, where did you work before?"

The boy cringed at the terrible nickname. "Benjamin, please. Well, I guess you could say I'm straight out of school." He deflated a little. "This is my first job."

Rebecca nodded at Benjamin. This wasn't his first choice of employment. He had walked into something he had no way to prepare for. She knew she hadn't been ready for this life.

"The Lieutenant isn't your father, is he?"

"Um…no."

She shook her head. *If I had a father, I would never have stepped foot on this cursed plain.*

"I didn't think so. The Lieutenant doesn't seem like the fatherly type."

Rebecca thought that was enough conversation. She repacked her bag and announced it was time to head back. As she led them, she tried not to think of the ghosts who lived in her past. They dragged her to a cold, damp place from which it was hard to escape. Any thoughts of the future sent waves of ice and flame through her veins, so she focused on each step she took, the sound of Benjamin breathing behind her, and the feeling of the sun scorching her skin. It was the only tolerable way for her to live.

The sun was dipping into late afternoon angles. She shifted her heavy braids away from her steaming neck. This trip always took ages, but today it took even longer with Benjamin. It took time to let people figure things out for themselves. Sometimes too long. She paused to check on Benjamin and was surprised to see him watching her. He glanced at the sun to mark their time and drank from his waterskin.

She was going to have to start dinner when they got back, but she didn't have the energy to think about it. She fanned her face as she caught her breath. She had to admit, she preferred thinking of him as Benjamin over "Patch" or "Hey You." It felt real. *I need more real in my life.*

"Benjamin, do you cook at all?" She rubbed her arm over her forehead, pressing loose strands of hair out of her face.

"I can boil water," he said, blushing.

She nodded at this. "That's where all cooking starts."

That was what the Lieutenant had said when he first handed the cooking over to her.

SEVEN

*A*s they neared the hideout, Rebecca raised a hand to slow Benjamin down. The Lieutenant always had her stop and approach with caution. "The places where you feel safest are where you are the most vulnerable," he often said.

Benjamin began to scan the area around them. Rebecca traced the outline of the prickly bushes that framed their hideout. Nothing moved. Her eyes fell on the empty woodblock. Benjamin had been chopping wood. Had he forgotten to put the axe back in the block?

Rebecca turned to make eye contact with Benjamin. "Where did you leave the axe?"

He glanced around, took her arm, and dragged her behind a prickly bush. "The axe is gone. I left it in the wood block," he said as he glanced around the edge of the bush toward the shack. "The back door is open too."

The Lieutenant could be testing them. He did that sort of thing. Rebecca peered over the bush. The door was ajar. The lamp was not lit, but it wasn't quite dark yet. They could wait to see if the Lieutenant came out to light it. Maybe he forgot something.

"Let's wait a minute. This isn't quite right." Rebecca glanced at Benjamin, who had already started crawling closer to the woodpile.

When she caught up to him, he was peering over the pile and scrutinizing the area outside the hideout.

"I don't see any signs of a struggle out here," Benjamin said. "Was the Lieutenant planning on going out? Did he follow us?"

They both checked behind them. She didn't think so, but who knew with the Lieutenant? She suspected that while he didn't really like Rebecca out wandering by herself, he'd wanted some time alone. Was that why he'd sent both of them to check the drop box?

"No, he was planning on staying here." She twisted the end of her braid around her finger. "He would have put the bucket out on the back porch to let me know."

Benjamin rubbed his chin with the back of his finger as he listened. "What are the procedures for something like this?"

"We should treat it like it's real, even if we suspect it's a test. We would meet—"

A squat man shoved the back door open with the missing axe. His thick silhouette blocked their view inside the dark house. They heard glass crashing inside as the stranger walked over to the woodpile and slammed the axe down, jamming it into a log just above Benjamin's head. Rebecca pressed both hands over her mouth to keep from screaming.

"Told you no one was out here," the thickset stranger called to the door. "No one's coming. Let's get out of here."

"Well, Mouthrot said there was some kid with old One-Eye. Keep looking." A tall, thin man stepped out the door. He took off his grimy cap, wiped his forehead, and ducked back inside.

Benjamin tugged on Rebecca's skirt as he crawled toward the bushes. She grimaced as she watched the man pull out a knife and grudgingly patrol around the house. She clenched her jaw as she followed Benjamin's lead. She felt something between a sob and scream building in her throat. What if she cracked?

The Lieutenant's voice pierced through her swarming panic: *Focus on your breathing. People forget to breathe when they're scared.* She leaned back and inhaled.

There was a loud clatter, and then the tall man stepped outside again. His eyebrows gathered low over his eyes. His patience with this task was running out. Rebecca met Benjamin's eyes as he beckoned her to leave. Shadows were growing around them.

She turned from Benjamin to watch the tall man hunt after his companion. She closed her eyes and took another breath to clear her swarming thoughts. In many ways, the Lieutenant had been her prison guard, but he'd also been her guardian and sole companion over the years. She would not consider the option that he was dead. Rebecca pressed her locket against her chest. She knew how many close calls the Lieutenant had survived, but Benjamin didn't know. *The Lieutenant is alive,* she reassured herself. She knew he was alive. *Right?*

A yank on Rebecca's skirt jerked her back into the moment. Benjamin watched her, waiting for her to take the lead. They needed to get out of there to regroup so the Lieutenant could find them. Rebecca gripped her head between her cold hands. Once the tall man rounded the corner, she ran. She then burrowed into the tall grass, waiting until she could think clearly. Benjamin was close behind her. She grabbed Benjamin's hand as she found her feet and sprinted again. Benjamin gripped her hand without a word, following her. He must have believed she knew where she was going. Too bad for him.

EIGHT

Rebecca ran blindly as branches and blades of grass whipped across her face and her arms. *Please, not again.* She was certain she smelled smoke as she pulled Benjamin behind her. She glanced behind her but didn't see any smoke or flames. Rebecca and Benjamin's shared panting faded under the remembered sounds of crackling fire, screams, and the clanging of swords from a time long ago. On that panicked night, she'd run for her life into a black forest with her nurse. She swallowed a scream. Without the Lieutenant, what did she have? Was she on her own now? *No, I have the boy.* She felt the shadows of memories darken her thoughts.

"Shhh, shhh." She drew comfort from the memory of her nurse whimpering in her ear. *"We can't let them find us."* Before, so long ago, she had run through a cursed forest to escape. This time, however, she was running through dry grass.

Rebecca tried not to think of the Lieutenant, who could be possibly unconscious and bleeding right now. Her stomach recoiled at the thought. *He is not dead. No one could kill him. Maybe he escaped.* The Lieutenant knew a thousand ways to escape ropes and chains, and he'd shown her some of them. He'd also taught her how to use a knife. He could take down two large men with or without a weapon. She believed the few stories that he'd told. He didn't need to embellish anything. He had lived hidden among the king's greatest enemies for years. If anything, he had understated the danger and left the ugliest parts out.

Mouthrot could not defeat him. No one could. It was impossible. *Impossible.* But Mouthrot had come back from the dead. That was one impossibility. That scum villain certainly wasn't going to get two impossibilities. Not in this borrowed second life; not even if he bartered all of his new gold teeth.

Rebecca scowled at the grass to keep her tears from falling as she ran through the growing darkness. Benjamin's hand slipped from hers to grab a fistful of skirt, but still he followed her. She pressed her now-empty hand to her chest to calm her panicking heart. Dark pressed in without mercy as they stumbled along.

Benjamin tugged on Rebecca's skirt as he hissed, "Stop!"

As she turned to face him, Rebecca set her face into a glare to hide her fear from him.

"Do you know where we are?" Benjamin leaned in closer than she would have liked. "We're going to need to find somewhere to hide."

"We have a safe house, but it's north. We ran south," she panted. "I think."

Rebecca couldn't make out Benjamin's exact expression, but she guessed by the way he fingered his sleeve that he wasn't happy.

"Well, we shouldn't sleep on top of a hill for all the world to see." He kicked into the dirt. "We need a low spot or someplace hidden. Bushes would be nice."

Rebecca scanned the area around them. They were standing on a hill. Out this far, there was only yellowed grass and rocks just big enough to trip over: no place offered shelter. They were going to have to sleep in the open, under the stars, and in a bed of dust.

Benjamin sighed. "Down here, before we lose the light." He grabbed her arm and towed her behind him.

✝ ✝ ✝

Rebecca woke up stiff and exhausted, the gifts of too much hiking and sleeping on hard dirt. Benjamin moaned as he rolled over to drink from his half-empty waterskin. She threw an arm over her eyes and rolled onto her back. The pain in her hips screamed almost as loudly as the pain in her throat. As she reached for her own waterskin, it felt as if someone was stabbing her calf.

"Cramp! Cramp!" she yelled, rubbing her leg.

Benjamin scrambled over to her. "Straighten it out. Where is it?"

"My calf! This one!"

"Stand up and straighten it out."

He wrapped an arm around her waist, pulling her against him to support her weight. She glanced down at him, but he was focused on her leg.

"Too much walking and not enough water."

The pain dulled as they walked, but her calf was still stiff and tender.

"I thought you said I'd walked too much." Rebecca tried to hide her wince. She didn't want him to think she couldn't keep up because she was a girl. She could be tough.

"C'mon." He stepped slowly, waiting for her as she limped along.

"I thought we were under attack when I heard you scream," he said, yawning.

"Sorry. There wasn't someone here to cut my throat," she said through gritted teeth. "I really need some water."

Benjamin nodded and helped her sit on a stump. "I'll get it." He shook his head as he retrieved her waterskin from her pack. He handed it to her and stared in the general direction of the hideout.

Rebecca felt a moment of gratitude that Benjamin was with her. Rebecca wasn't sure if she would have been able to get up by herself. She drank greedily. It was hard not to. They needed to get more water; her waterskin was nearly empty. She watched the brittle grass bobbing in the morning breeze.

"What now?" Benjamin asked. "Do you think they're watching the house?"

She shrugged as she took a last sip. She closed her eyes and stretched her calf out, unable to think of anything beyond her fatigue and pain.

"I would," he said as he sat beside her and scanned the area around him.

"Well, I wouldn't be surprised if the Lieutenant found us by lunchtime," she said, pounding the stopper back into her waterskin.

Even as Rebecca said it, she felt an uneasy fluttering in her stomach. However, she refused to give up completely on the idea that the Lieutenant was safe. He was the type to defy all odds. She fiddled with her waterskin and looked at Benjamin, who was pressing a knuckle against his lip in thought.

"You think he escaped?" Benjamin asked.

"*You* think he was kidnapped?" She glared.

"Yes, I do—and I think Mouthrot left those two behind to search the place."

She clenched her fist and hit her waterskin. *The Lieutenant was fine. He had to be fine.*

"I suppose it's possible he escaped, though unlikely. Mouthrot probably oversaw his capture personally." Benjamin frowned and shook his head.

"We need to get down there." She stood up to pick up her pack.

"What for? Just to get caught? You think the Lieutenant would go back?"

"We've got to do something!" The words burned through her throat. "What if he's injured? What if they left him for dead?"

Her fingers fumbled numbly as she tried to shove her waterskin back into her pack. Frustrated when she couldn't work the tie on her pack, she flung it down, a tear escaping down her cheek. She rubbed it away and then picked up her pack again with a glare.

"We need more food and water," he said. "Your leg is stiff right now. Could you run if you needed to?"

She bit her lip and squeezed her eyes closed. *Great Wolves! He's right. We can't go back.* She shook her head. She could hear Benjamin walk toward her.

"Is there anywhere else we can go? Anyone you know who would help us?"

She opened her eyes, causing Benjamin to take two steps back. Something clicked in Rebecca's head. A calm washed over her. Here was a boy who knew how villains thought, probably as well as the Lieutenant did.

"That depends." She took a moment to catch her breath. "Will you help me rescue him...if he needs to be rescued?"

Benjamin's eyebrows shot up. He took another step back. He rubbed the back of his neck, grimacing. She watched as he pushed ideas through his head. She wouldn't let the Lieutenant die. Benjamin would help her. He had to.

"We need to take care of ourselves first."

She smiled. *I'll take that as a yes.*

"We can go to Denny's. He and his brothers have worked with us for years. It's not far from Shreb's, and the Lieutenant might go there."

Benjamin nodded at this as he rifled through his pack. He pulled out his knife and an apple, cutting it in half. He handed Rebecca half and bit into his. The juices cooled her parched throat. Yes, she was glad Benjamin was here.

She rebraided her hair, smoothing it down in the back as much as possible, while Benjamin sucked on his apple core. He was flipping through a small book, scribbling and crossing things out. He closed it and slid it into his jacket pocket with a sigh. She stretched her sore leg and rubbed it before shrugging her pack on and limping ahead. At first, her calf complained, but after a few minutes, it relaxed. It felt better to be moving, to be doing something. Anything. Much better than sitting idle, waiting for someone to tell her what was going on.

NINE

*H*is hands and knees raw and scratched, Benjamin crawled behind Rebecca. As they approached Denny's farm, fatigue gutted him. All he wanted was food and a bed, but the ground was looking more welcoming all the time.

"Are you purposely picking the worst possible way to go?" Benjamin stopped to pull a sticker out of his hand.

"You're the one who said that Denny's place is probably being watched, right? And didn't *you* suggest that we watch them before we contact them?" She turned to scowl at him. He remained silent. "And you don't want them to hear us, right?"

Benjamin rolled his eyes. He hated it when she was right. He would just have to put up with the thousand cuts, slices, and thorns ravishing his flesh. He'd never really worked in tandem with anyone before, especially not a girl, and he wasn't sure he liked it.

They came to a halt on the fringe of undergrowth. From their vantage point, they could see a squat building with a patchy roof and a large but slightly crooked barn. A broken cart sat propped against the barn, and a goat slept under it. Between the two buildings was an open space of compacted dirt with a covered well.

Rebecca smiled. "That's probably why we haven't seen them for a while." She pointed to the broken wheel on the cart.

Obediently, Benjamin looked over and shrugged, trying to keep his skepticism in check. He moved next to her to get a better look at the yard. Nothing but the goat was visible, but a rumble in the barn drew their attention. A giant youth, a few years older than Benjamin and with short, mousy hair, came out of the barn carrying a few items bent at odd angles. He sat down next to the goat in the shade. The youth reached behind the goat and pulled out a box of tools. He then proceeded to straighten and untangle several pieces of metal. Benjamin raised an eyebrow at Rebecca.

"He's one of Denny's brothers," she whispered. "Odie."

"One?"

"He has two brothers, Odie and Baldo. Odie can fix anything and is an excellent fighter. He's beaten the Lieutenant at swords a few times. Baldo is a clever little guy. Always planning something. You remind me of him, now that I think about it."

Benjamin frowned. Rebecca obviously underestimated him. He was the *valedictorian* of his class. "Are they all that big?"

"No, just Odie." She smiled. "Baldo is tiny. Denny is tall, but not nearly as large as Odie. Denny does all the talking."

A lean stripling stepped out of the house, and his golden hair gleamed in the sun. "Dinner's ready!" he yelled.

The smell of root vegetables and meat wafted toward them.

"I never thought Denny's rabbit stew could smell so good," Rebecca said, leaning forward.

Benjamin salivated and rested a hand on Rebecca's shoulder. She leaned back. The goat stood while the larger brother worked on silently. Denny watched with a wry smile as the goat trotted over to him and bleated.

"Where do you think you're going?" he said, patting the goat on the head and leading it to the barn. "Odie, you've spoiled this goat. Rina thinks she's a pet—or a person. I doubt she knows she's a goat."

Odie didn't acknowledge his brother as he untwisted the metal strips as if they were mere wire. Denny tapped his brother on the head, and Odie jumped. Denny motioned to the house, and they both went inside.

"So how long do we have to sit here and watch before we decide to talk to him?" Rebecca whispered.

Benjamin thought about that for a minute. It was tempting to think that perhaps they could just knock on the door and get some stew and a good place to sleep. The brothers seemed innocent enough. But then they needed to remember who they were dealing with. Someone must have told Mouthrot where to find the Lieutenant. The goat bleated from inside the barn.

"What if they're being watched?"

She rolled her eyes. "But they're just kids, hardly a threat to Mouthrot or Shreb. That's why the Lieutenant used them."

"Would they have talked about where the Lieutenant lived?" Rebecca's face scrunched in skepticism, but she gave his idea a fair chance before she flatly rejected it.

Benjamin saw movement in the tall grass near the barn. *A perfect hiding place*, he thought. He pulled Rebecca down. A small hare sprinted to the barn and disappeared.

Benjamin released Rebecca's arm and stifled a yawn. She rubbed her arm and rolled her eyes. Fatigue seeped through him as he closed his eyes. Rebecca was probably right. The brothers were undoubtedly safe, and he was hungry. She jarred Benjamin out of his self-pity with an elbow to his ribs. Rebecca stared wide-eyed down the road toward the sound of an approaching horse's hooves.

The two thugs they saw yesterday slid off their horses. Rebecca squeezed Benjamin's arm so tightly he thought she'd snap it in two. The thugs approached the house while looking over their shoulders at the barn.

Benjamin gasped when Denny exploded out of the little house. The men jumped back, startled. Rebecca twisted Benjamin's sleeve. His cheeks burned. Thankfully, Denny was yelling so loudly no one would have heard his faint outburst.

"What do you want?" Denny scowled at them.

The tall man lifted his chin, not caring that he wasn't wanted there. The thickset man sneered at the young man, amused. "We came to see if you've finished mending our gear," said the tall man.

"Hmm. That garbage?" Denny strode to the barn, kicking up a small cloud of dust behind him. He returned with a heavy burlap sack, pulled out a few harnesses, and shoved them back into the bag.

The short one snatched the sack and inspected the harnesses. Benjamin recognized the dull look in the henchmen's eyes. *Idiots.* He'd seen enough of their type. These fools wouldn't have lasted a single day at the academy.

The short idiot nodded, and the tall one handed Denny some coins. Denny counted the coins and weighed them in his hand. The men nodded curtly and mounted their horses. Odie peered out the door, unresponsive to the men's jibes. The thugs rode off, leaving a trail of dust behind them.

Smiling, Rebecca turned to look at Benjamin, who couldn't help but smile back. Mutual loathing was a good sign. Mouthrot's men were obviously ill at ease here and too stupid to suspect anything.

Benjamin suggested they wait until the brothers had cooled off before approaching, but Rebecca just rolled her eyes at him and climbed out of the bramble.

"I've humored your paranoia long enough. Let's go while dinner's still warm."

Knowing they were so close to real food, his resolve quickly crumbled away. His stomach pulled him toward the door, but he stood behind Rebecca as she knocked. Swear words erupted. The door opened. Denny raised an axe over his head and then froze.

Rebecca's face went white, and Benjamin was very glad he was so very dehydrated. "We should have waited," Benjamin muttered into Rebecca's ear.

Denny stood there gaping like a fish, unable to speak.

Odie appeared, wielding knives.

"D-Denny, it's me," Rebecca said.

The brothers took a collective breath and lowered their weapons but then moved their curious eyes toward Benjamin, meeting their gaze to prove he wasn't scared out of his mind.

"Is the Lieutenant here?" Rebecca asked.

That snapped the hulking figures from their shock. They stepped back, letting the two refugees in. Benjamin hesitated at the door until Denny placed his axe on the ground. Denny blinked silently and rubbed his hands through his hair before he could look Rebecca in the face.

"I thought I was seeing a ghost." Denny let out a long, ragged breath. "We heard rumors of a prisoner matching the Lieutenant's description at Shreb's."

Rebecca collapsed onto a bench and dropped her head on the kitchen table. Benjamin melted into the bench beside Rebecca. With a glance, Denny measured the distance between Rebecca and Benjamin and then rubbed his face.

"I wasn't really worried about this *Mighty* Shreb before. He seemed like a bit of fluff." He shook his head in disbelief. "What happened?"

"Well, it was actually Mouthrot, his assistant." Benjamin nearly choked over Denny's hostile look. Benjamin refused to be intimidated; he sat up straighter. "We think his men took the Lieutenant while we were out."

At the mention of Mouthrot, Denny went ashen. He looked at Rebecca, who could only nod a confirmation. She clenched her skirt in both fists. The room went silent. Benjamin wondered why Denny would consider him a threat. *Does my evil genius show?*

"Well, this is bad." Denny paced next to the table where the pot of stew sat steaming. "The first thing we need to do is get you far away from here."

"What? I'm not going anywhere. The Lieutenant is sitting in a dungeon right now, not far from here. I'm not going to run away, and I'm not going to sit around waiting for something horrible to happen." Rebecca stood up in an attempt to look Denny and his large brother in the eyes.

"Move her?" Benjamin chimed in. "They'll be searching the roads for sure. Staying close for a while might be the safest thing." He eyed the pot hopefully and wondered if he could shift the conversation toward dinner yet.

"Who is this guy?"

"Benjamin. He's just some kid the Lieutenant picked up right before this all happened."

"Really?"

Rebecca turned and looked at Benjamin for a moment with new eyes. She obviously never thought to suspect him, but at Denny's suggestion, it seemed obvious, even to Benjamin.

"Hi. Listen, I'm trying to help her—"

Denny grabbed a fistful of his shirt. His eyes flicked between Rebecca and Benjamin.

"When was it Benji showed up again?" Denny pressed his face so close to Benjamin's that they were breathing the same air. Denny's blue eyes blazed.

"The Lieutenant met him on the way to check out the interviews Shreb had announced a few weeks ago. He felt sorry for him."

"Well, isn't that *convenient.*" Denny folded his arms across his chest and squeezed his sizable biceps.

"No, actually it wasn't," Benjamin said through gritted teeth, holding Denny's gaze. "He *completely* sabotaged my chances for the villain's assistant position."

"Really? Interviewing for the enemy?" Denny looked at his brother, who gripped a rope in his mallet-like fists. "Well, that *is* interesting."

TEN

*B*enjamin could barely breathe. The ropes that bound him to his chair were excruciatingly tight around his chest. His hands were tied down to his knees. *Odie was handy with rope and knots,* Benjamin observed, *as well as metal.* Benjamin was too tired and hungry to think himself out of this one. He looked imploringly at Rebecca. She frowned.

No one said anything. The brothers looked back and forth between Benjamin and Rebecca. Benjamin's stomach growled. Finally, Rebecca began to ask questions.

"Why *did* the Lieutenant bring you back with him?"

"I'm pretty sure he told you. Mouthrot saw me with him. I was as good as dead. So he offered to bring me home with him to keep me safe…like I am now," he added, nodding to his bound hands.

"Yeah? Why were you seen with him, huh?" Denny leaned in, and Rebecca nodded enthusiastically.

"He *hijacked* me along the road and tormented me the whole walk there. But I don't think he was expecting to see Mouthrot, so he offered me a job."

Rebecca glared at him and then looked at Denny and Odie.

"Well," Denny seemed to consider his story. "It actually does sound like something the Lieutenant would do. But a job? Did you bump into him on the road?"

"He was waiting for me on the road." Benjamin cleared his throat. "And considering that I just graduated *head* of my class at the Villains' Academy, a job offer seems completely likely to me."

Denny gasped. "Did you know that? He grad—from Vill—"

Denny and Odie exchanged looks. They gathered around the table and discussed him. Benjamin used an incredible amount of self-control to keep from rolling his eyes at all this. Yes, he had to admit that it was perfectly logical to suspect him, but he hadn't forced himself into this party or even gained anything from this venture.

Meanwhile, he just sat quietly, hoping that he might at least convince them to loosen his ropes so that he could take a decent breath of air. *It wasn't much,* he thought, *but it's good to have goals.* He focused on shallow breaths to keep the ropes from pinching. An occasional glance was thrown his way, but he just looked ahead, trying to forget about the hunger gnawing in his gut. They broke from their conference to address him.

"Rebecca said that you helped her avoid capture and that for some reason, the Lieutenant trusted you. But I do have one more question for you: have you ever met the Lieutenant before? Think about it. Perhaps he was disguised?"

"No, I'm pretty sure I've never met him before. Look, could you loosen the ropes enough so that I could breathe or possibly eat something?"

Denny nodded to Odie, and with that, he was set free. Two bowls of rabbit stew were placed on the table. Both brothers watched every bite of food that he took. Obviously, they weren't completely convinced, but at the moment, he didn't care.

He was eating.

ELEVEN

The stew was warm, if a bit bland, but that didn't slow Benjamin down. He only looked up once to judge if it was safe to ask for seconds. He sipped at his apple cider after sniffing for poisons and then dared a glance at Rebecca. She did not meet his gaze, choosing instead to remain intent on her own bowl. The brothers continued to take turns watching him as they ate their dinner. No seconds were offered, but his tumbler was filled a number of times.

After dinner, the brothers worked on fixing this or that while taking turns playing old tunes on a battered flute. Benjamin drooped in his chair and looked for a comfortable corner to lie down in. There were a few doors off the kitchen, but he dared not even think of a bed. He stood up and stretched, noticing that Rebecca was nodding off in her chair too. Denny also noticed.

"Rebecca, you're about to fall out of that chair. If you want, you can have Odie's room." Denny glanced at Odie, who nodded as he put his tools away. "He sleeps out in the barn with Rina anyway."

"What about Baldo?" she yawned.

The brothers dropped their eyes and started kicking at loose floorboards, as Denny muttered something unintelligible about his taking a job. Rebecca didn't notice as she stumbled to Odie's door.

Benjamin wondered where Baldo worked. Obviously, somewhere that the brothers weren't comfortable admitting. Was Baldo working for the king? The bedroom door clicked shut behind Rebecca.

Denny glared at Benjamin. "Pushed her a little hard, didn't you? I hope you didn't forget that you're traveling with a lady." Odie joined his brother's glare.

"She's safe, isn't she?" Heat throbbed in Benjamin's cheeks.

The brothers frowned, unsatisfied.

"*No one* could force *her* to go slower or faster than she wants!"

Denny shoved him against the door, his face inches from Benjamin's. "You can sleep in the barn with Odie. He'll keep an eye on you," he said in a low voice that chilled Benjamin's bones. "And Rina will let us know if you decide to so much as pee too far from the barn. Got it?"

"It's nice to know I've got someone to keep an eye on me. I'll sleep soundly tonight." Benjamin choked the words out, holding Denny's icy-blue stare. "But who'll keep an eye on you?"

Denny dropped him, sending a shudder through his body as he hit the ground. Denny stepped back so Odie could usher Benjamin to the barn. Benjamin smoothed out his jacket and met Denny's glare with a shrug. He refused to be rattled.

He followed Odie's hulking white shirt to the barn, his heart pounding in his ears. Odie threw him a dirty saddle blanket and pointed out his pile of straw. It wasn't cold yet, and the straw was itchy, so Benjamin threw the blanket on top of the straw and lay on top of it. He sighed and watched the giant boy and the goat snuggle around each other before settling for the night. Rina rested her chin on top of Odie's knees so she could stare at him through heavy eyes.

Odie was far noisier asleep than awake. Incredibly, not a single snore was alike, the unpredictable pattern making the ruckus impossible to ignore. As a result, Benjamin spent the night never wholly asleep. Halfway through the night, Rina nuzzled into him, pinning his arms against his chest.

As bright pinks and oranges pushed the purple from the sky, Odie finally rolled over into silent slumber. The goat got up, stretched her legs, and wandered back to her friend. The new quiet weighed Benjamin down and quickly dragged him into sleep.

He jerked awake when Denny called, "Breakfast!"

Odie shuffled off to eat, but Benjamin was far more tired than hungry. He rolled over, pulling the filthy saddle blanket over his head.

Rina butted him in the back. Benjamin ignored her through gritted teeth and even tried to shove her away, but the abuse stubbornly continued. He finally sat up and opened his eyes. Rina bleated happily and sat. As soon as his heavy eyes sagged shut, a hard head bumped against his leg. Soon she pressed him into a standing position and out into the daylight. He flinched and wrapped his arms around his head to block the sun. Who would have thought that goats were such morning animals? He stumbled half-blindly toward the house, under the guard of a goat.

Benjamin slouched into the kitchen table. Rebecca eyed him oddly. The brothers seemed uninterested, as if someone always fell asleep at their table first thing in the morning.

When the gnawing in Benjamin's stomach finally woke him, his face was stuck to the table, a little puddle of saliva dribbling from his mouth. He sat up and wiped it away with his sleeve. Rebecca was muttering quietly with Denny, so thankfully they hadn't seen him drooling.

He rubbed his sore neck and glanced over at the tools and rope hanging on the wall. Stacks of buckets were piled in one corner. A pile of dirty clothes was shoved behind the front door. The murmuring stopped as Rebecca and Denny looked at him.

"I kept some breakfast for you," Rebecca said.

She dished something into a bowl, set it down on the table, and then went back to her conversation. After a few minutes, his head cleared enough to feed himself.

"Didn't you get enough sleep? Or wasn't the straw soft enough?" Denny sneered.

Benjamin blinked a few times at Denny's glowering face. He was too tired to care about Denny's suspicions right now. He spooned the mush into his mouth, eating the overly thick breakfast thankfully. It was still a little warm. A mug of milk was set down next to his bowl, and he sniffed the creamy milk instinctively before pouring it over his breakfast, hoping to thin it enough to swallow. He licked the spoon clean and looked for more. He was a growing boy, after all. Rebecca and Denny were watching him.

"Thank you for breakfast," he said, unable to keep his eyes from drifting to the pot on the stove.

Rebecca just rolled her eyes and refilled his bowl. He smiled. He would try to think more kindly of Rebecca in the future. The food helped strip him of the fog that he'd woken with. When he finished that bowl, Rebecca scraped the pot clean for him.

"Finish the last of this so we can come up with a brilliant plan that will convince Denny to help us." Rebecca set another partially full bowl in front of him, pouring more milk over it.

"Help us?" Benjamin mumbled through sticky bites.

"Rescue the Lieutenant, of course."

"You want me to spit out a plan right now? This very second?" He looked from Rebecca to Denny, scratching his head. "I was hoping to get a little more information first."

"Ah, the first smart thing you've said." Denny nodded approvingly. "Fortunately or unfortunately, Baldo has taken a job inside Shreb's fortress. I can talk to him, if you like."

"Baldo is working for Shreb?" Rebecca asked, nearly dropping her pitcher of milk.

Denny frowned and picked at a spot on the table.

"Just honest work," he said. "Clever Baldo can do anything. I think he was a little bored around here."

Rebecca shook her head. Benjamin scanned the dingy shack again. He could see *himself* bored here. Denny went on explaining what he knew about the fortress. Benjamin scrawled the details in his book.

Shreb's men came and went at all hours, but they let merchants and farmers inside to do business in the mornings. The traffic had surged in the last month. Denny thought they were probably stockpiling weapons in the armory.

"Now that they've got the Lieutenant, we need to send a courier to King Aldo." Denny sighed as he raked through his pale hair. "Warn him, if nothing else."

"The king?" Benjamin laughed and closed his book, marking his spot with his finger. "What does the king care about the Thieves' Plain? That's why there *is* a Thieves' Plain in the first place. We scheme and plot over here, and he leaves us alone."

"He cares about the Lieutenant!" Rebecca slammed her hand on the table. "Plus, with Mouthrot involved, that changes the usual business into something else altogether, don't you think?"

"Why would King Aldo care about Mouthrot or the Lieutenant?"

Benjamin tapped his book on the table, no longer able to hide his impatience. He wasn't optimistic about this planning session.

Rebecca bit her lip as she exchanged a look with Denny. She closed her eyes, steeling herself. "Mouthrot is a nobleman—or *was*. A distant cousin of Aldo's."

Benjamin raised his eyebrows, impressed.

Rebecca glanced at Denny again, who nodded. She took a deep breath and locked eyes with Benjamin. "You're wrong about the king not minding what goes on here. What do you think the Lieutenant does, exactly? He could be anywhere doing anything, but he's here in this dust hole *spying* for the king." Rebecca leaned forward, her gray eyes widening.

"Wha-?" Benjamin's little black book tumbled to the table. The blood drained from his head and into his burning stomach. The room grew dim. Outrage bubbled up from deep in his chest. *What?* "Wait!"

Denny looked at Rebecca. Benjamin tried to stand but fell back into his chair, his legs failing him. He gripped the table and rubbed his thumb against its gouged surface. Benjamin glanced between Rebecca and Denny. *They must be lying.* But he only saw earnest pleading in their eyes.

"So…so…I've been…working…for *the king*?" Benjamin raised a hand as if to fend off her information. "Villains don't work for the king." *Especially,* he thought as raw outrage surged within, *a king who had banished all villains and crooks to this wolf-forsaken plain.*

Rebecca dipped her head. Denny flexed his jaw and nodded as well. His muscled arms tightened across his chest. *Where is Odie?* Benjamin didn't see him in the shack. *Is he outside making sure I don't run?* Rebecca watched him expectantly. *What is she waiting for?* Indignation sizzled through Benjamin's veins. He slammed his fist on the table.

"Give me a moment to absorb!" He blinked at his crumpled notebook next to his empty bowl. "Lies! All the lies! I thought 'the good guys' were into truth and honesty. This is worse than finals at the academy." Benjamin reached out and scooped up his book, the only thing that seemed real in the room. *Good guys? My left hand!* "At least with villains, you know you're being lied to and that they're planning to stab you in the back. By the Great Wolves!"

Benjamin stared into the fireplace, squeezing his notebook, feeling the leather bend in his hands. The king was spying? Was that really a surprise? The real question was what else was King Aldo up to? Benjamin's dreams of the World's Greatest Villain's Assistant title had turned to ash and now rested in that very grate. How had this happened? This was the opposite of everything that he'd been working for his whole life. What did that leave him with? He averted his gaze from the fireplace. It was too close a representation of his life. He put his notebook back in his pocket.

Then, for the first time, he thought he saw Rebecca look contrite, if only for a moment. Something clicked inside him. *That might make the whole crazy caper worth it*, he decided. *Maybe I can find a way to make this work for me.*

Benjamin stared at the ash-filled hearth again as he let the new information trickle into his brain. No wonder Denny and Odie reacted so severely last night. Benjamin shook his head. How had he missed this? He reviewed his conversations with the Lieutenant. The old man was probably the best liar he'd ever met. He simply omitted the most important detail: he wasn't a villain. Benjamin could learn a few things from him yet.

Denny ran his fingers through his hair, flashing worried glances at Rebecca. His arms tightened with tension. She ignored him and kept her eyes fixed on Benjamin. Benjamin wasn't quite able to look directly at her.

What would be more villainous than turning against the biggest archvillain of the day? Benjamin smiled. *Taking down two?* Never mind that destroying Shreb and Mouthrot might save his life as well.

"I'll need to know how many men are behind those walls. Schedules and movements." There was no reason he shouldn't benefit from this situation.

Denny, noticeably relaxed, now wrapped an arm around Rebecca. She breathed a sigh of relief and slid into a chair. They needed his help. He could solve this puzzle.

"They're preparing to defend against a big army, but not a needle prick." *Benjamin Black's name will be known across the plain yet,* he thought as cool blood rushed through his veins. "How long would it take for a message to get to the king and for him to respond? Because that's how much time we have to rescue the Lieutenant and prepare to defeat this massing army of thieves." He smiled wider.

I will find my way, he challenged fate, *one way or another.*

TWELVE

*D*enny rested his hand on the back of Rebecca's chair, scraping his thumbnail into the wood before he answered. "Listen, the king isn't going to send an army into the depths of the Thieves' Plain. His father, King Zavier, created it to be a safe haven for villains, so the rest of Lam could heal without their filth clogging up his good works. He promised to leave them alone if they left Lam alone. If Aldo brings an army here, he'd risk starting a war that might never end. He'd send Lam back to where it was before his father forced a bloody peace on the nobility."

"Yes, yes." Benjamin swiped his hair out of his face, dropping his smile. "He couldn't send a small force of some sort? Unofficially, of course?"

Rebecca paced around the table, wringing her fingers. "He'd need undeniable proof that either Shreb or Mouthrot was massing an army to overthrow the throne."

They all stared silently at the gnarled leg of the kitchen table when Benjamin's eyes popped. A stream of light entered his brain. He strode around the room, almost running into Rebecca. He stopped a few times and drew lines in the air to connect his rambling thoughts. He knew what would happen; it was obvious if you were a villain with a past. Finally he looked at them. "But that's exactly what's going on here: two villains planning to overthrow King Aldo." Benjamin smiled appreciatively. "Shreb the First ruled all of the Thieves' Plain, so his son would want to surpass his father's ambition." *That's what I would do.* "Mouthrot's ambitions were very nearly stamped out by the king, right? By tradition, he would feel obligated to go after the king himself, to seek revenge for his defeat and pick up where he left off."

Rebecca slumped in her seat, silently twisting a knot in her skirt. Denny stared at the floor, his hair disheveled.

"That's exactly why he's working for the 'Mighty' Shreb. He's hiding under Shreb's cape until he can strike against the king. The Lieutenant said Mouthrot liked to be thought of as a ghost." Benjamin began pacing again. "Except the Lieutenant ruined that by spotting him."

Rebecca looked up, her face like marble. Both Denny and Benjamin looked at her. *She knows something,* Benjamin surmised.

There was a fear in her eyes that came from knowing an awful truth. She tugged at a braid. "He wants to be king. He's already removed all the direct lines of inheritance," she said, covering her face with her hands.

"Oh!" Denny leaned forward, clutching a chair. "Prince Evan and his wife died in a fire. I think they had a child as well. Everyone thought it was a freak accident."

"And a few cousins? Lord Amsby and Lady Remba, as well," Rebecca said through her hands. "Amsby died of some strange withering illness. Poor Lady Remba went slowly mad before throwing herself out a window."

When she removed her hands, Rebecca was a sick pallor.

"I can't imagine how he can go further than that. How do you know he was involved?" Benjamin sat down facing Rebecca.

"That was why the Lieutenant hunted him down." She twisted a yellow braid around her finger. "He saw him at the prince's castle as it burned."

Benjamin rubbed his face. "So who else would be in danger besides the king? Who's next in the line of succession?"

"The king was to name Prince Evan's child as his successor, but no one seems to know if the child survived or not." Denny shrugged. "Plus, I heard the king was thinking of remarrying. Not a lot of royal news out here."

Rebecca shifted in her seat but remained silent, and that was perfect as far as Benjamin was concerned. "Well, there's only one thing to do now. Do you have paper and ink? I think we need to compose a letter to the king." He stood. "Then the rescue."

"Who's going to deliver it, eh?" Denny asked.

"What's Odie up to? Any plans *he* could break?" Benjamin smiled to himself, thinking that a quiet night's sleep was nearly within his grasp.

THIRTEEN

Rebecca dried her hands on her skirt and heaved a big sigh, hoping to release the tightness building in her chest. She had set things in motion. She hoped the Lieutenant would be proud of her. It was a risk to spill most of their cover to Benjamin. She glanced at him and wondered how he could be comfortable bent over the table like that. Benjamin fidgeted at the table, fussing over the folding of the letter. Rebecca had repeatedly assured Benjamin it was fine. He wanted another opinion and held it up for Denny and Odie's approval as they passed through.

Denny dug out the sealing wax and stamp hidden under a floorboard in the pantry. He set it down for Benjamin and helped Odie scavenge food for his trip.

"Farmer Demsey delivers his wool across the border this time of year. He usually waits for Odie to deliver it, even if he has to wait a month."

Odie chewed on a piece of dried meat as he stuffed food into his pack.

"In fact, he usually lets Odie take it alone." Denny looked at his brother, who adjusted his cap. Odie put another piece of meat into his mouth and gave a firm nod. "It might take longer, but no one would think to question Odie."

Odie shoved more food and an extra waterskin into his pack. He slipped a few daggers under his belt and hid them under a ragged cloak. Benjamin set the letter delicately in his large hand. Odie slipped the letter into his vest, avoiding direct eye contact with everyone but Denny. In a few minutes, he was down the road and out of sight.

Rebecca plunged a rag into the scalding dishwater as Denny cleared off the table. She started to scrub at the table, but Denny waved her off. He grabbed a piece of charcoal from the fireplace to sketch a rough outline of Shreb's fortress on the table, marking the entrances and watchtowers. Denny pointed out things he had observed from the outside. Rebecca pushed in between Benjamin and Denny so that she could study the map as well. Heat rushed up her neck as Denny rested his hand on her back as he made room for her.

"Since Shreb Jr. showed up, men have been making their way here from all over." Denny twirled the charcoal in his slender fingers. "Like someone finally got the word out that something big was about to happen. There are guards all over the place, around the clock. Mouthrot knows how to keep his men disciplined. One fight and that was it. Rumor has it that he made sure all the men involved were left with a visible mark, as a warning to others."

Goose bumps prickled down Rebecca's arms, and she cinched her wrap tightly around her shoulders, fighting off the images of scarred and branded men. Denny hesitated, his azure eyes asking if she was okay. She smiled and he continued.

"The place is a meandering mess. You're more likely to get lost than find anything you're looking for." Denny rubbed his chin, leaving a black smudge just under his lips. "I can talk to Baldo. He's been there long enough to know the ins and outs of the place."

Benjamin nodded. "A more detailed map would be nice, something that will get us to the Lieutenant and out again. Any extra information Baldo could supply would be helpful."

Rebecca traced the rough charcoaled lines with her eyes and imagined herself in Shreb's fortress. Mouthrot had already seen Benjamin with the Lieutenant. Denny had been in the fortress to visit Baldo in the kitchens; the staff might recognize him. She was the only one who hadn't been seen by any of Shreb's men. It would make sense for her to go, though the Lieutenant would not be happy about it. He had always gone out of his way to keep her from anything that smelled of danger, even while preparing her to fight herself out of it, but she knew she could do this.

Denny smudged his chin again. "I agree. I'll talk with him, but I won't put Baldo into any danger. He's only twelve, and I should never have let him go there in the first place. Maybe we can get him home now."

"Absolutely." Rebecca wiped Denny's chin with the edge of her wrap, surprised to feel stubble.

Denny dropped his charcoal into the ashes and grabbed for a pack. "I might as well leave now. You two will need to hide out. I don't want to have to explain why I've got two extras at home. Got it?" He stuffed some apples, dried meat, and a blanket into the small pack.

"Sure." Benjamin eyed the bedrooms behind Denny.

Denny found some scraps of paper and another piece of charcoal and added them to his bag. What was she supposed to do, sweep and mop? Rebecca found two waterskins and a pack in the pantry.

"I'm coming with you. Benjamin has been seen, not me." She stared Denny down. "A second pair of eyes is always a good idea," she added in a tone that reminded her of the Lieutenant.

Denny flinched. "Yes, but the Lieutenant would come back from the dead and kill me if anything happened to you!"

She waved off the distasteful idea. "Nothing will happen. We're just going to visit your brother. I can be your girlfriend. People would believe that."

She stuffed her pack with food from the pantry, poking her head out to confirm with Benjamin. "Right?"

Benjamin smiled as he glanced at Denny, who looked away. "Right! Anything that guarantees me some sleep."

She rolled her eyes at him.

The smile slid off Benjamin's face. "Have you ever slept with a goat?"

She relented and sighed. "Sleep in my room. It's the one on the left."

Denny's head whipped around at this. "Are you sure we can leave him on his own? Can we trust him?"

Benjamin pushed past them toward Rebecca's bed. "You can trust me to sleep. Rebecca will be fine." He yawned and rubbed his eyes. "She's probably better trained than you are anyway."

Denny chewed on his bottom lip, studying Benjamin.

Rebecca didn't see how this was his choice. She had already decided. "See? C'mon, let's go!" She flung the door open and stepped out into the blinding sun, not knowing if Denny was following until she heard the door close and his steps on the wooden porch. "I didn't realize that you were so slow!" Rebecca called over her shoulder. "We need to get there with the other merchants and farmers."

"So exactly how long have you been my girlfriend?" Denny grinned and wagged his eyebrows.

"It's *just* part of the cover." She laughed. "I don't know, a couple of months, at least."

"Okay. Do you think we have a future together?"

"Oh, please."

"I'm going over our cover. Someone might want to know."

She shoved him, but he didn't even falter, instead, he just wrapped an arm around her and drew her closer. The hard lines of his body pressed against her, and she became aware of all his masculine features as his blue eyes bore into hers. A lock fell over one eye, and she smiled lamely.

"Someone might be watching," he said and winked.

"I think couples can walk side by side like normal people." She pulled herself loose so she could breathe and then giggled as she felt heat glowing in her cheeks.

"How about we hold hands?"

She rolled her eyes. She was sure that the Lieutenant wouldn't have approved of walking into the wolf's den like this, but this flirtation could easily get her locked away behind castle walls in no time. Why had she suggested this as a cover? At the time, it had seemed the safest choice, but now she wasn't so sure.

She glanced sideways at Denny, who not-so-casually checked out the scenery around them. She fiddled with her braid and kept her eyes on the road ahead. A breeze rolled across the plain, bending the long-dead grass over the road.

Rebecca cleared her throat and asked, "What does Baldo do for Shreb anyway?" Rebecca thought it was best to change the subject.

"Kitchen boy. It's way beneath him, but he insisted that he wanted to help the Lieutenant too. I don't like him being surrounded by such filth. Mom and Dad wouldn't have liked it."

Denny frowned. None of the brothers had really recovered from their parents' deaths. Not that anyone really does. A dark well opened in Rebecca's heart, but she quickly covered it. She wanted to put her hand on his shoulder but had thought about it a little too long. "Did the Lieutenant know?"

"No. Baldo didn't ask for permission—he just went." Denny shrugged. "He's always been independent. And when he makes up his mind—"

She nodded. She understood perfectly.

"Well, it's turned out to be very helpful." She scanned the main road as they joined it. The Sunrise Mountains stood in the distance, marking part of the boundary between the Thieves' Plain and the rest of Lam. Aldo's castle lay just on the other side, pressed into the Sunset side of the mountain range.

She could see a few carts on the road ahead of them. A heavy square structure rose up from the faded plain. A ravine butted against the back. It was a strange place to build a fortress, but no one could attack from the back. But then, it offered little in the way of escape as well.

Rebecca and Denny passed through the front gates along with a wagon full of protesting chickens. Peddlers wearing heavy packs strapped to their backs pushed through as well. Rebecca stayed close to Denny and shyly peeked around at the guards. When one winked at her, she grabbed Denny's arm and feigned embarrassment. Denny pulled her in a little closer as he glared at the guard.

As they made their way to the kitchens, she made note of where the merchants flowed and where Shreb's soldiers stalked. They weren't the usual scoundrels. They actually had uniforms, of a sort. They each wore an armband with two trumpeting black swans on it. The men moved with some purpose en route to various designated areas. It was clear that they were not just slouching around. A sinking feeling hit her when she quickly surmised that this wasn't quite the chaotic operation of halfwits she had anticipated.

A large woman nodded at Denny as they entered the kitchen. She pointed them in Baldo's general direction with a large wooden spoon. She returned to her pot and wiped her hands on a filthy apron.

"He's probably peeling potatoes in the back," Denny murmured in Rebecca's ear, his lips grazing her ear. A butterfly fluttered in her chest. She stepped back to follow Denny, and he grabbed her hand.

She walked wide-eyed with a gaping mouth, playing the part of a country girl. She had a feeling that Denny enjoyed it. He made a point of placing his hand at the small of her back to guide her through the maze of people. He was a natural at playing the boyfriend. Lack of proximity was probably the only thing keeping the girls away. His duties with the Lieutenant didn't usually involve girls.

Baldo looked up from a potato. His dark eyes bulged in his pale face. He closed a book and tucked it under his stool.

"You remember my *girlfriend*, Rebecca?" Denny smiled tightly.

Baldo lifted an eyebrow to this but played along. He pushed back a lock of mousy hair, revealing dirt smudges around his small wrists. He glanced behind them and assured them it was safe to speak.

"Have you heard? The Lieutenant has been taken by Mouthrot's men," Denny said.

"Mouthrot?" Baldo shook his head.

"He works here. I guess he'd probably use a different name." Rebecca leaned closer to Baldo to lower her voice. "He's got gold teeth now."

"Chessman? But he just started working for Shreb last week," Baldo murmured.

"We think he's trying to use Shreb as a cover to amass enough strength to go after the king." Denny pulled out a bag of food and a few scraps of paper for his little brother. "Can you sketch us a map of the fortress? We'll need it to plan a rescue for the Lieutenant."

"You're planning a rescue?" Baldo wrapped his thin arms around the offering.

"Well, not us. Benjamin actually," Rebecca said.

"*Benjamin?*" Baldo's eyes narrowed.

"He's brilliant—or so he says. Claims he graduated the top of his class at the Villains' Academy. Trust me, this is right up his alley."

Baldo stared vacantly, his dirty clothes hanging loosely over his shoulders as he took it all in. Rebecca didn't remember him being quite so thin. He set his new items under his chair on top of his book after Denny offered to help him store the stuff in the corner of the pantry where he slept. Rebecca helped peel potatoes as Baldo quizzed them about the Lieutenant's capture and their newest recruit. His thirst for information was nearly insatiable.

Finally, Baldo spread the papers on the floor and crouched over them to sketch some rough maps but then shook his head. "I've got some already made up and a few other helpful things set aside." He folded the papers back up and tucked them in the back of his pants.

"I don't want you to put yourself in any danger," Denny said as he placed his hand on Baldo's shoulder.

Baldo stepped back and waved his brother off. "No danger. I'll fetch the maps after I drop off Shreb's lunch. Meet me in the courtyard."

Rebecca grinned at Denny's little brother. He nodded back and darted past them to the kitchens. Denny raked his fingers through his hair. He wrapped his arm around her waist to lead her around the fortress. She could feel the hard cords of his tense muscles press into her back. She wrapped her arm around his waist and squeezed reassuringly.

"He'll be fine," she whispered in his ear.

Even though he smiled at her, his blue eyes searched for Baldo.

FOURTEEN

*B*enjamin opened the door for Denny and Rebecca. Denny managed a nod before he slid into a chair. Rebecca shuffled in and collapsed at the table.

"What a horrible place," Denny sighed. "To think of my own flesh and blood living there. He's always been thin, but—" He rubbed his face roughly.

Benjamin tried to imagine what Denny's definition of *thin* might be. He fanned out his jacket and sat up taller. He didn't want to know what word they would use to describe him.

Rebecca sat up. "It wasn't that bad. Baldo was very helpful. We couldn't have planned a better setup." She opened her waterskin and drank deeply. "I'm starving." She hobbled into the pantry.

"Baldo certainly put himself in the middle of things. I wouldn't be surprised if he knew everything that went on in that castle. Modest, that Baldo, even though he's easily the most brilliant kid around."

Benjamin bristled at this and brought the conversation to a more relevant point. "So he gave us some useful information?"

"Yeah, you could say that."

Rebecca hooted at Denny's comment as she returned carrying a ham and a basket of eggs.

Denny stood up and pulled out a couple rolls of paper and slammed them on the table, followed by the clang of keys. Benjamin's jaw nearly came unhinged.

"Told you Baldo can do anything." Denny shook his head. He was obviously impressed by his youngest brother as well. "It's a real shame he's stuck there. I don't see that going anyplace good."

"You never know." Benjamin said. "It got me here."

Denny didn't look comforted. He emptied his pack and hung it on the wall. He ran his fingers over a flute that rested on the mantle. Rebecca frowned and stoked the coals in the stove.

Benjamin smoothed the crumpled pages that Denny left on the table next to a set of heavy keys. His breath caught in his throat. There in front of him were sketched maps, which, while not *exactly* to scale, were full of immense detail. Guard schedules and rotations were scrawled on the sides, along with bad habits of some guards and all sorts of useful tidbits. Benjamin looked up, shaking his head.

"Did he spend the whole time drawing this out? It must have taken hours and hours. And the keys? These might be missed. Surely they're not *his*?"

"No, of course not. Baldo's too smart for that. He pulled them off a dead guy weeks ago. That whole storm blew over long ago. Baldo works in the kitchen. No one even thinks to look his way. These maps he drew out in his spare time. He keeps them in the pantry and works on them while he's watching the roasting spit." Denny grinned. "He knows how to be useful."

"He certainly does." Benjamin tapped the map.

Rebecca poured cider into mugs. "I suppose *he* probably already knows how to get the Lieutenant out, and we can skip all the genius planning sessions?"

"If he had, I'm sure the Lieutenant would be sitting gift-wrapped right here at this table." Benjamin glared at her.

"Well, Baldo did have some suggestions but said we'd have to do it ourselves." Denny scooped up a mug. "He couldn't be seen anywhere near the dungeons. You know, a kitchen boy."

"Right." Benjamin pulled his book out of his jacket pocket and flipped to an empty page.

"He thought the best time to come in would be late morning." Denny sipped his cider. "The place is completely packed by noon."

"So we could bring in a cart of whatever without having to do too much talking." Benjamin had to admit that was an excellent idea but tried to look skeptical as he wrote *noon* in his book and circled it.

"The merchants usually pull in here." Denny jabbed the map with a finger. "And are directed to the kitchens or stables as needed. We could make it as far as the guards' mess hall for a drink before we'd get challenged. From there we could take any of these three routes toward the dungeons."

"Why those three and not others?" Benjamin pointed out other routes not marked on the map.

"Those three bypass many checkpoints within the fortress and will take us past the laziest guards."

"Hmmm. Well, we're going to need either a distraction or a really good disguise to get a smelly prisoner out of the dungeons. Do you know any good drinking songs, buddy?"

Denny scowled. Rebecca chuckled over the sizzling eggs and ham. Benjamin paused a moment to appreciate the aroma of cooked ham before writing down "distraction."

"Well, we'll put that on the back burner," Benjamin said, peering back at Denny. "Did you have time to walk around and see any of this personally?"

"Oh yeah, we walked through the kitchens and then wandered through the dining hall, courtyard, and stables. Apparently, Mouthrot and his men were out, so we took advantage of it. No one seemed to mind. Everyone was busy taking a breather, if you know what I mean." Denny winked before continuing. "Baldo said it would be best to wait a day, though. Mouthrot will still be out collecting taxes around the plain and border lands. He's not expected for days."

"Having him gone would be ideal." Benjamin deflated into his chair, tucking his book back into his pocket. "We could do without his sharp eyes."

"You're not *actually* disappointed, are you?" Rebecca frowned over Denny's shoulder at him and set two plates on the table.

"No, not *exactly*. I was expecting there to be a little more to work out is all. Baldo has definitely saved us time and worry."

"It will be difficult enough," Denny added before popping some ham in his mouth. "I suppose you were hoping to show us how brilliant you are?"

I am brilliant, he thought somewhat petulantly, *but there's no point in arguing the point. You will all see soon enough.* He got his own plate and sat down forcefully.

I am brilliant.

+ + +

Benjamin glanced up from Baldo's maps as Rebecca finished scrubbing the kitchen. As Denny grabbed the bucket of grimy water from her to dump outside, his hands grazed hers. She nodded her thanks and pulled her hands into her chest, a faint blush on her

11

cheeks. She pulled the broom out from behind a pile of buckets in the corner. Her sweeping kicked up a lot of dust. Rebecca stopped and studied Benjamin when he coughed.

"What?" he asked over the maps.

"Do you think you should be going in there?" Rebecca stomped the broom into the floor. "Someone might recognize you."

Benjamin crossed his arms and scowled. "Mouthrot will be gone for days." No way was he missing this moment to shine if he wanted to make a name for himself.

Rebecca scoffed as she swept under a bench set against the wall. Gobs of twine, wires, and dust flittered out. "You're ready to take that risk, are you?" She stabbed the broom into the pile of debris. "Denny and I are the only ones Mouthrot or his men aren't looking for."

Benjamin slammed the maps down on the table, his heart hammering behind his ears. No way was she going to decide what his role would be. "You took a class on picking locks and got the fastest record, did you?"

Rebecca dropped her broom, her eyes burning back at him as she pressed her fists into her hips.

"We have keys, idiot!"

The front door opened. Denny froze to examine the scene.

"What?"

"Benjamin thinks he'll be running this rescue all on his own." Rebecca pointed a sharp finger in his direction.

Denny flexed his jaws and closed the door. He blinked at the ceiling, his chest expanding and contracting as he listened.

"*She* wants to go." Benjamin jerked his head toward Rebecca. "She thinks she can worm her way into the dungeons."

"Rebecca, *no* way! The Lieutenant would have my head on a pike if he knew I already took you to the fortress." Denny's Adam's apple jumped as he swallowed. "You know he would never allow you to put yourself in danger."

"But it's the Lieutenant! I can help!"

Denny pressed his lips into a straight line as he shook his head.

"Benjamin, you said I was probably better trained than Denny." She flicked a braid behind her shoulder and scowled at the boys. "Is this because I'm a girl?"

"Yes," Benjamin said.

Denny shot a warning look at Benjamin, but it was too late. Rebecca screeched and kicked the broom.

"No! No!" Denny stumbled forward. "You're the Lieutenant's ward. He has always insisted on keeping you out of things. I can't go against his wishes."

"Even if it means his death?" She crossed her arms, waiting for Denny's answer.

Denny glanced at Benjamin, as if he could help him out of this. Benjamin shrugged. She'd have a valid point, if Benjamin weren't convinced that she'd make everything more difficult. She would probably try to sabotage him just to watch him sweat. Denny raked his fingers through his hair and scrubbed the back of his neck.

"I think the Lieutenant would probably agree with Benjamin." Denny glanced up and frowned. "I agree with Benjamin too. I think you should stay here."

Rebecca screamed and slammed herself behind her bedroom door. Denny groaned and collapsed in a chair. "There's just no winning with her." Benjamin shook his head and moved to sit closer to Denny. Benjamin tried to go over the plan with him. It took a good twenty minutes before Denny stopped staring at the bedroom door.

FIFTEEN

A few mornings later, Benjamin helped Denny load the cart in a show of solidarity. They both stood united against Rebecca; there was no way she was coming on this rescue trip. The Lieutenant would skin them all—or worse. Yesterday had been the tensest day Benjamin remembered in his life, with doors and pots constantly slamming banging and crashing. Benjamin and Denny eventually went to the barn to finish their plans, keeping the front door of the shack in view.

Rebecca, meanwhile, stormed through the shack in a cleaning frenzy. Dust poured out of the door and windows. She beat the rugs with such ferocity that Denny stepped further into the barn to hide. He didn't look happy to have Rebecca this angry with him, but he held to his decision. She knew perfectly well the Lieutenant would not want her going into that place.

If she wanted to be a part of the team, she needed to start suppressing a few of her death glares. How was it that the Lieutenant hadn't dumped her earlier? Benjamin was beginning to suspect that maybe the old man went willingly to Shreb's dungeons for a holiday. Perhaps Benjamin could offer to exchange places with him when he got there. It might be safer.

He scanned through his notes and checked the heavy keys in his pocket. They were still wrapped in rags to muffle any sound. Denny went back to loading the wagon. He stuffed an extra cloak in by the cider and then tied a tarp over the hay.

At least no one was going to fight Benjamin over going down into the dungeons. Denny wanted to keep an eye out for Baldo and create a distraction to cover their exit, so he could hide the Lieutenant in the cart.

When Denny refused to go over the plan again, Benjamin decided it was time to go. Denny cast a worried glance toward the quiet shack. Benjamin could hardly believe that he was about to walk into Shreb's fortress—the place he had wanted to work only weeks earlier—and snatch a man from its bowels. *This would be legendary!* He smiled and helped steer the cart down the dusty road that would lead to his destiny.

After a half mile, Benjamin was sure that even *he* wouldn't recognize his own face covered in all the road dust kicked up by the carts. He caught up to Denny, whose stride was much longer than his. Benjamin grabbed the waterskin. "I don't remember it being this dry and hot," he said.

Denny set the cart down and took a drink himself before answering, "They say that when the first archvillain took residence in the fortress, the rain dared not fall without *his* permission. But when Shreb took over, the flames of hell raged all the stronger and dried the rain up forever." He shrugged and placed the waterskin in the cart.

"All this talk of curses over the land should have died off by now." Benjamin dropped back to help push. Their departure time was well calculated. Several others would arrive at the same time; it would help mask any unplanned difficulties. *If there's one thing I've learned about putting schemes into action in real life,* Benjamin thought, *it's that things rarely go as planned.*

As the road grew more congested, their sparse conversation died completely. Benjamin focused on the travelers who steadily filled the road as they approached the fortress.

First they passed an old, crusty farmer with a slight limp, pulling a skinny cow, followed by a small group of women wearing tattered skirts with bundles strapped to their shoulders. In front of them was a large wagon filled with giant barrels of mead or ale, which was easily the most prized item to sell to a stronghold full of troublesome men. The ale merchants were probably the most familiar with the inside workings of the fortress. Benjamin and Denny could follow them in if they needed to.

Small clusters of men and women followed behind them. Dust clouds floated up further down the road, nearly veiling the mountains at their backs. There must have been even more people far behind them, allowing them to easily blend in when they departed.

Benjamin glanced at Denny, who raised his eyebrows and directed Benjamin's gaze to the stone fortress. For as far as Benjamin could see, nothing but dusty roads surrounded it. He hunted out the lone tree that he had shared with the Lieutenant not so long ago and then shoved the thought away and focused on pushing the cart.

When they arrived at the gate, the line was backed up. Overwhelmed red-faced guards barely glanced at packs and wagons, with almost no attention to any exiting merchant or farmer. The odor was stifling as the smell of hot animals and people baking in the heat merged into one foul stench. *Well, at least my mission is in the dungeons,* Benjamin reflected gratefully as he stifled a gag, *far away from the heat and masses of people. That was something to look forward to anyway.*

As they neared the gate, one guard merely glanced at them as he wiped his brow, while the other half-heartedly prodded the hay in the wagon before waving them through. The courtyard inside was organized chaos with loose lines merging and then drifting apart as groups were directed to the appropriate areas.

"You'd think they've never done this before," Benjamin said, leaning into Denny, who nodded in frustration. In fact, fatigue and frustration lay on everyone's faces. They were directed to the stables, where they were given an unfair price for their wares.

"I know we're not here for profit, but still," Denny mumbled when they were out of earshot.

"Okay, on to the dining hall?" Benjamin tried to draw Denny away from the stables. "Well, you should at least be able to buy a few penny ales with that. Enough to lubricate the mood inside."

"Right." Denny lowered his voice and added, "You go through the laundry, and I'll go in the main entrance."

They nodded and mingled with separate crowds.

Fortunately, not much laundry was being done—not a big surprise in the domain of evil, really. An old woman slept in a sea of shredded rags propped against a giant cauldron on the other side of the courtyard. Benjamin weaved through a few sheets hanging randomly across the space. Benjamin prodded the contents of the tub with a paddle as he passed by and let the paddle drop back into the metal tub. The old woman snorted and sat up, blinking at the limp sheets hanging on the line.

Benjamin hurried inside and through a dark hallway, following the sound of weak conversation. Wilted merchants and farmers propped themselves up against tables and walls as they drank tepid, watered-down ale and cider. Unfortunately, the odor here wasn't much better than in the stables. He saw Denny buying penny ale at the far end of the hall. Denny then found a table that had the best view and set his mugs down next to a farmer and his boy. He turned on his charm and quickly had a few servant girls chatting and pushing the farmer to another table. He looked at Benjamin and rubbed his ear—their signal to move.

The heat proved to be the best distraction, as the first two guards he passed were dozing. Standing in heavy uniforms proved too much for even the most vigilant on such a hot day. Some of the soldiers looked more ill than intimidating and barely noticed anyone walking by. One did ask Benjamin where he was going, but before he was able to give his prepared answer, the guard waved him off and returned to his mug. Benjamin slipped by quickly. No one followed him or questioned him further. The stool next to the dungeon entrance was empty. The remains of a meal that smelled suspicious lay next to the stool. *Baldo?* Benjamin twisted his cloak in frustration. *Why didn't I think of drugging the guards?*

He hurried down the stairs, hoping to remove the Lieutenant before the sick guard was able to return to his station. He peeked around the corner. A form was bent over a lock on one of the doors. Benjamin squeezed the keys between his fingers as he stalked down the hallway.

"This better not be Baldo," he whispered under his breath.

The startled figure turned.

Rebecca stood, chagrined. As she removed a bent tool from the lock, she actually blushed. He felt his own cheeks heat to a deep flush as well, but not because he was embarrassed. She silently stepped back as he slid into her former spot. He shoved a key in the door, his arms shaking as he unlocked the door with near silence.

A moan echoed down the stairs toward them. The missing guard must have returned to his post. Benjamin dragged a muffled but defiant Rebecca around the nearest corner. After wrestling silently with her, she dug her nails into his hand until he let go and hissed, "Keys."

Benjamin peered around the corner. The light from the guard's lantern fell on the keys dangling from the lock in the door. A sweaty, gray-faced guard slumped against the wall and groaned. They both flung themselves against the wall and looked at each other. There was only a narrow, straight tunnel to hide in. *Great! Two stringy teenagers were going to have to silently take out a guard. This was* not *part of the plan for a reason.*

Another moan sent the guard scampering back toward the stairs and a bucket. Benjamin peeked around the corner.

They sprang from their dark corner to the Lieutenant's door. The keys were gone, and the door was locked. Benjamin peered through the slot in the door. The dim light from the passageway parted the darkness of the room. A black form huddled in one of the corners. Benjamin pulled out a candle from his pocket, lit it on one of the torches, and handed it to Rebecca to hold.

"How do we know this is the Lieutenant?" Benjamin asked, pulling his black notebook out of his pocket.

"All the others were empty."

Benjamin nodded and scribbled: *tie up girl* before *leaving without her*. He pressed his lips together, narrowed his eyes at Rebecca, and then slid his book back into his pocket. He was not going to walk away from this with much hope for employment anywhere if he failed now.

He held out his hand to Rebecca, who hesitated before handing over a small roll of tools. "I *can* do it," she said.

"Right, but this isn't about *you*."

Benjamin silently unrolled the cloth and motioned for Rebecca to lower the candle. He took a deep breath to erase the fear of the guard returning, grabbed the sturdiest tool in the pile, and grinned when he heard the click of the lock. A dark mass sprang out of the door, knocking him onto the cold stone floor.

"Lieutenant?" Rebecca gasped.

The mass froze and peered up at Rebecca. The Lieutenant slid off Benjamin's chest and awkwardly wrapped his filthy arms around his ward. Rebecca grimaced and waved off the dungeon stench.

"Rebecca, what are you doing here?" The Lieutenant's voice was strained. When he turned his pale face to Benjamin, his eye patch had lost its glimmer. Benjamin clutched his tools over his pounding heart, rigid as a possum playing dead.

"Do you think we were just going to leave you here?" Rebecca wiped a tear away.

"But Mouthrot—"

"He's gone for the next few days," Benjamin said as he forced himself off the floor.

The Lieutenant slumped in relief. Benjamin propped him up, while Rebecca threw her cloak over the Lieutenant's shoulders. "You still shouldn't have risked coming down here." He shot an accusing glare at both Rebecca and Benjamin.

"Not my idea," Benjamin muttered as they stumbled forward.

The old man was weak and unsteady, having lived off a prisoner's scant rations for a week. Of course, it might have been much worse than that. There was bruising around his wrists.

"We'll talk about this later, Rebecca," the old man warned, pressing his hand to his head as they struggled to the stairs. "I'm assuming you have a plan to get past the guards."

"Of course," Benjamin said.

When Rebecca was able to support the Lieutenant alone, Benjamin checked the pathway in front of them. At the top of the stairs, a guard was retching on the floor. They slunk past unnoticed.

Benjamin leaned over the bent Lieutenant. "If anyone asks, our *dad* isn't feeling well and we were trying to find a quick exit but got lost," he whispered.

Rebecca nodded, straining under the Lieutenant's weight.

They passed a few empty posts. One guard lay in a puddle of filth. Soon enough, they could hear voices in the hall. Benjamin slowed them down just as they cleared the corner. A few men were lying face down over the tables, but what turned Benjamin's stomach was the sight of Mouthrot scowling over the dining hall. People were clearing out.

Benjamin threw his hood over his head. He pulled the Lieutenant closer to shield him from view, hoping his hood covered his scruffy face. "We're going out the back."

Denny stood up from his table, his eyes wide at seeing Rebecca. He paralleled their stumbling steps in an attempt to block Mouthrot's view of them and then bumped into a serving girl, knocking her tray to the ground. She screamed. He then stepped back and kicked over a bucket. The woman who was scrubbing the floor erupted into colorful language, drawing eyes to her. Both women took turns fuming at each other and then at Denny, who stopped to apologize and pick up broken pieces of pottery.

Just as Benjamin reached the exit, the Lieutenant lost his footing. Rebecca lunged forward to help steady him. Benjamin cast a glance behind him as he pulled them through the doorway. Mouthrot was looking in their direction, gaping. Benjamin checked the Lieutenant's hood, but it still covered his face.

"He sees us."

"Oh no!" Rebecca gasped.

They hurried past the old woman, who had hung more sheets in Benjamin's absence. They tucked themselves behind one. Footsteps clattered in the hallway and then stopped. From behind the rippling cloth, Benjamin could see Mouthrot frantically searching for them. A large basin sat just within view. Benjamin patted his pockets and realized that he had lost the keys. Rebecca nudged him impatiently. He looked at the basin again, attempting to judge its distance.

The Lieutenant handed him a small rock. "Here, I was kneeling on this."

He pitched the rock. A deep ringing filled the small courtyard. The washwoman jumped so violently that she upset the tub of water onto the men. Mouthrot howled at the shaking woman as he frantically untangled wet sheets from his feet.

They dashed to the stables, where Denny had the cart waiting. He frowned at Rebecca but rushed over to help the old man into the cart. The Lieutenant dragged Rebecca into the cart with him. Only the intensity of the old man's eye suppressed her arguing. Denny and Benjamin threw their cloaks over them and tied down the tarp.

"I'll walk out ahead of you." Benjamin ran from the stables, grabbing a cast-off hat.

He dragged the palms of his hands against the grimy walls and wiped them on his face and the back of his neck. He stumbled against a gaggle of women complaining about prices and snatched a strip of fabric to tie loosely around his neck. The women barely altered their conversation as they pushed him out of the way.

He walked through the gates, mixing with others. Benjamin passed several groups before he stopped to look back. He watched Denny pull the wagon through the gate. The guard held a farmer back to allow them through. A wet and angry Mouthrot scanned the crowds, his gold teeth flashing as he bellowed orders. The guards stopped the outflow of merchants. A group of wet men walked past Denny's cart to look more closely at the women who had just left.

They're looking for a girl? Benjamin observed in confusion. *Not the Lieutenant or me?*

Denny nodded, tight-lipped, as he passed by. Benjamin nodded back. He glanced toward to the fortress to see if they were being followed. No one took an interest in Denny or his cart. Benjamin took out his waterskin and scanned the road. The sun was beginning to descend, but the day was nowhere near cooling off. He peered down the road again; Mouthrot and a few men were on horseback, stopping women. He strolled quickly to catch up to Denny.

"Mouthrot is on the road," Benjamin said, leaning into the cart.

"Should I get out and help push?" Rebecca peeked out of the cloaks that covered her and the Lieutenant.

"No! He is looking for *you*," Benjamin growled.

"What?" Rebecca and Denny said together while the Lieutenant just groaned.

Horses pounded by, but Mouthrot didn't even glance at the two boys. Dust covered them as their enemy tore past.

When the riders were out of sight, Benjamin slipped his waterskin under the cloaks. All color had drained from Rebecca's face. Her guardian placed a weary hand on her shoulder and pulled the cloak tightly over both of them. Benjamin glanced at Denny, who stared bewildered back at him. Benjamin shrugged and helped Denny push. Then something occurred to him.

How could Mouthrot recognize a girl he'd never seen before?

SIXTEEN

*D*usk hung around the little house by the time they arrived. They had taken the long way back to make sure they weren't followed. Rina greeted them as they settled the cart by the barn. Exhaustion seeped into Benjamin's legs as he collapsed against the barn.

He took a moment to let his frustration grind itself away as he pressed the back of his head into the rough wood. Denny's face was like cold stone as he helped Rebecca and the Lieutenant out of the wagon and into his house. Benjamin wasn't the only one who didn't know about Rebecca's connection to Mouthrot.

Benjamin waited outside, watching the house fade into the deepening darkness as his chest grew heavy. He knew he should plan their next move, but all he could do was question why he was still here. He should just go back to his hideout and forget these people. He didn't need them. Rebecca and the Lieutenant said they wanted his help, but they held him at arm's length, keeping important information from him. They didn't trust him, and he didn't trust them. Rina trotted up to him and butted his leg.

"Oww!" he howled. "Dumb goat!"

Benjamin hopped on one leg, taking in the absurdity of the moment. There was only one way to sort this. He hobbled inside to find some answers. He untied the rag from his neck and wiped the grime from his face and hands.

The Lieutenant sat at the table, a plate in front of him. He silently sipped from a mug. Denny consoled Rebecca with awkward pats on her back. Her eyes and nose were swollen and her face blotchy. Benjamin wished he had seen the Lieutenant finally put Rebecca in her place. *It was about time.*

The old man looked over at Benjamin and pointed to the bench across from him. He sat down, taken aback by the authority used to command him. The Lieutenant's eye patch was scuffed, the jewels scraped off. But on the whole, he looked unscathed, just exhausted. Benjamin waited for the explanations due him, as King Aldo's spy chewed his bread. Benjamin noticed no one offered *him* food and was about to get some when the Lieutenant cleared his throat.

"Denny and Rebecca told me about how you freed me and sent for the king. I'll leave the king's response to the king." The Lieutenant's knuckles whitened around his mug. "Your first response should have been to get yourselves out of danger, not diving headfirst into a hornets' nest. Rebecca should *not* have been allowed anywhere near that fortress."

The Lieutenant's face was twisted into hard lines. He was obviously not happy with anyone in the room. *Wait a minute,* Benjamin thought with no small taint of bitterness. *We just successfully rescued you…and you're disappointed?* Benjamin clenched his fists as his heart pounded behind his ears. Was the old man actually *reprimanding*

Benjamin for saving his life—or for not knowing that Mouthrot would recognize Rebecca?

The Lieutenant stabbed a finger into the table. "You set up a scenario that Rebecca could not pass up, even at your *strong* insistence that she stay home. Did it not occur to you that I already sent a message to the king about Mouthrot being alive and well?"

Benjamin stood up, knocking the bench to the floor. "I did the best I could with the information I had!" He focused on the spy's one good eye. Fire flared in Benjamin's chest. He wasn't the type for emotional outbursts, but he could feel one coming and had no intention of stopping it.

"The few snippets of your personal history with Mouthrot that I *did have* painted a horrific picture if you were left in his grasp." He leaned over the table, and the Lieutenant flexed his jaw. Benjamin slapped the tabletop hard enough that his hand burned. A painful silence filled the room. "And if Rebecca hasn't learned to follow orders, that would be *your* fault, wouldn't it? Yet, I was still able to rescue you *despite* her *and all your precious secrets.*"

He strode toward the pantry, his hand and head throbbing. Any mistakes were on the Lieutenant's head, not his. "Now, I'm going to get something to eat." He wrestled items off the shelves and shoved them into his pack. He couldn't be expected to work in total darkness. He'd given the Lieutenant a chance to explain himself—and he'd failed miserably. "Then I'm going out to the barn to sleep. And tomorrow? Well, don't worry about that. I'll remove myself from the shadow of your disappointment."

Benjamin yanked his pack on and glared at each person. Rebecca snuffled into a handkerchief, and Denny peeked up through his gold strands. The Lieutenant sat rigid in his chair, his muscles standing out like ridges on his neck.

"I was hijacked, misled, and manipulated. Even if I can only get grunt work, I'll be a villain. Better than working with you people. Good night."

He swung a jug onto his shoulder and stomped off to the barn, making sure *everyone* could hear where he was going.

SEVENTEEN

*A*fter the Lieutenant dismissed her, Rebecca slammed into her bed and screamed into her pillow. She was not going to be able to sleep anytime soon. He just wanted her out of the way, like always. *If she would just stay in her bedroom, like a good girl—oh, except to cook dinner and do laundry.* Her eyes burned. She tried to hold back her tears as she stared at the lit candle by her bed. Her head was beginning to throb, which only added to her frustration.

Denny had tried to reason with the Lieutenant, but really Denny was just trying to protect her like everyone else. She could do that for herself.

Neither the Lieutenant nor Denny wanted to see her hurt or even exposed to potential pain. It was annoying. Didn't they know *they* were hurting her? She felt as if she had been holding her breath for years. A mysterious plan was used to dictate her life to her. She beat her heavy pillow into a more yielding shape and adjusted her blankets, which only reminded her how dusty and grimy they were.

"Looks like I'll be doing laundry tomorrow! What else are they going to let me do?" she screamed.

She hoped that made the Lieutenant feel bad, but it probably wouldn't. She kicked her heels into the bed, filling the room with the scent of Odie and goat. Doing laundry would at least get her out of the house. "At least that will make ignoring those stupid boys much easier," she growled. She sat up, hoping it would make something make sense.

Her lack of "good judgment" today was construed as irrational and an act of sabotage—but she just wanted to help with the rescue. Benjamin analyzed every step. They could still be there waiting for him to alphabetize all the potential ways to unlock a dungeon door. *And they needed my help!* No one had considered that the Lieutenant would be so weak and unsteady after being locked away for a week on prison rations.

She *would* take charge of her life. It was *hers*, wasn't it? If she wasn't going to sleep, she should at least start planning, shouldn't she?

She pulled out a knife from her boot and threw it into a dark knothole next to the door with a scream.

Mouthrot saw me! Oh Great Wolves! He knows who I am! He knows I'm alive!

She staggered under the weight of the realization. The devil who had killed her parents and burned down her home recognized her. Would he come looking for her to finish the job now? This was why the Lieutenant and the king kept her hidden away where no villain would look for her. This was why she had never breathed free air.

She strode over to the door and pulled her knife out of the knothole. As she turned back to the bed, a hazy mirror caught her eye. She wiped the dust off. She didn't remember her mother, and the Lieutenant refused to speak about his sister, but he had finally confessed one thing tonight. She lifted the candle to examine her tear-streaked face and her straw-colored hair. She stared at the sharp lines of her nose and cheekbones, trying to imagine she was looking at her mother. *What a strange way to find out what my mother looked like!*

She set the candle down and stood by the bed. She threw her knife into the knothole again; it hit dead center with a satisfying thump. She then wrenched the knife out of the wall. *If they send me to the castle, they're likely to lock me into the dungeons for my own safety.*

She squeezed the knife, wishing she could cut her way out of the bonds tightening around her. She had to get out. She would lose her mind if she were forced to hide in the palace for the rest of her life. She closed her eyes and breathed the dusty air of the room. Somewhere in this world, there *was* air that wasn't stale with dust. Somewhere there were places where no one cared about the politics of Lam. Places where no one had heard of the lost Princess Reyna Brynn Rae Ulmer; places where no one cared if she were alive or dead.

EIGHTEEN

Something knocked Benjamin from his fitful sleep. As he sat up, a small loaf of bread rolled down his chest and fell in his lap. He blinked up at Rebecca.

She leaned over him, her fists pressed into her hips and her brows pressed together. "Breakfast," she said. "Come on."

He tore off a chunk of bread with his teeth and grabbed his pack, shoving Rina off of him. The sun was up, but the morning was still quiet. Everyone else must have still been in bed. Benjamin stumbled out of the barn after Rebecca and prepared for an argument.

Rebecca signaled for him to be quiet. She led him to the spot where they had spied on the brothers and then plunged into the brush. Benjamin halted. Surely she didn't want Benjamin to follow her somewhere? Those days were long gone. He tore another piece of bread off with his teeth, refusing to take another step.

Noticing that no one was following, Rebecca turned around. He watched the memory of yesterday roll over her face. She looked awkward for a moment before she crossed her arms in defiance.

"I'm not sure if you remember, but *we*," he said, gesturing between the two of them, "are not on favorable terms at the moment. So if you think that *we* are going anywhere together, you are crazy."

She tilted her head, unfazed.

He went on. "If you are going that way, well, I'm going to go this way."

"That way? Shreb's castle?" She lifted an eyebrow.

"It's a fortress. And no, probably a little more over there." He moved his arm, indicating the area behind the barn. "Just so long as it's far from you. Besides, aren't you staying here so the Lieutenant can whisk you off to safety?"

"I've come up with my own plans."

"Excuse me, but so have I, and they purposely do not involve you." Benjamin hitched his pack onto his back and checked the shack for signs of life.

Rebecca huffed at this.

"Plus, you're with the Lieutenant. You have obligations and responsibilities," he said.

"Excuse me, but aren't you a villain?" Rebecca flung a yellow braid behind her shoulder. "What do you care about obligations and responsibilities?"

"Good point, but I still have *my* evil plans."

"Fine, you lead then." Rebecca unlocked her arms and scowled.

"Wait a minute. Are you suggesting that you want to be my henchman?" Incredulous, Benjamin shook his head. "No way. How do you think I got to the top of my class?"

"Oh, I don't know." She rolled her eyes. "You're really smart, I suppose?"

"No! Well, yes. But mostly everyone else made the stupid mistake of aligning with *other* people. It always ends badly," he fidgeted with his pack. "Dante was poisoned, Fievel was smothered in bed, and, well, no one knows what happened to Arlo exactly, but we do know that he was dead. Each killed by their allies. I went on my own, thereby being both alive and the smartest."

Benjamin stomped off past the barn, since he'd never been that direction before. Thankfully, Rina was still asleep. He didn't want his exit to be a parade.

"These allies? Weren't they expelled?" Rebecca asked cheerfully, running up behind him.

"Well, yes. If you're caught killing, even in the Villains' Academy, you still get expelled. It's sloppy."

He walked blindly forward. Rebecca followed after him, unperturbed. Resisting the urge to run, he marched briskly. He kept his eyes on the dry brush and grass ahead. The Sunrise Mountains stood pale in the morning light. If he kept going in this direction, he would end up back at his hideout. Maybe he could think about his future there. He clenched his fists. Alone.

By the time they had reached the road, Benjamin had serious concerns about Rebecca abandoning her crusade. Surely the Lieutenant would have noticed her missing by now. They would be out looking for her and notice the angry villain was missing too. Great Wolves! There was no happy ending to this. The little harpy would not be happy until she saw him strung up and tortured. He needed to take her back. He stopped at a fork in the road, pretending to read the sign posted there.

"Shrubshire is a pleasant enough place. Shops, inns, and marketplaces," Rebecca said. "We'd blend into the crowd."

"Right, so we're going this way." He pointed in the general direction not far off from where they just came. "Pig's Hollow."

"What? Pig's Hollow? Are you crazy? We just came from that way!"

"I-I know a guy there."

Her eyes narrowed at this, but she followed. Benjamin scanned the roads. Fortunately, it was early enough that no one was out on the roads yet, but they would be soon. He couldn't be seen with someone who worked for the king, especially if the Lieutenant or Denny came looking for Rebecca.

"So why this sudden desire to stretch your legs? I'm sure the Lieutenant would be thrilled to take you on a world tour at the moment." Benjamin decided it was best to keep her talking.

"Hmmpff. Not likely. He'd probably just take me to the king."

"And have you locked up?"

"Ha ha. No, I was headed that way anyway. Apparently everyone thinks it's time I was taught to be a *proper* lady."

"What?" Benjamin froze midstride, not daring to look at Rebecca. *A lady with connections to the king? Not good.*

Rebecca took a few more steps before she stopped and looked at him wide-eyed. She had just let something slip.

Panic twisted his stomach and he felt sick. "You're a noble?" he whispered.

Benjamin walked faster, trying to guess at the fastest path back to Denny's. He kept his face blank. He needed to keep her talking. If she rambled, she might not notice.

"Um, no. Lady's maid. Do I look like a royal?"

"Royal! You're a royal!" Benjamin gasped, as though someone had just punched him in the stomach. He could see images of the royal gallows. His cool demeanor shattered. He felt sweat prick under his arms as visions of dark dungeons lit only with the glow of red-hot irons loomed in his mind. He needed to get her back or his future would not be good.

Benjamin nearly burst into a run, his heart galloping against his ribs. He forced his steps to slow with a rattled breath. He needed to think. Panic shuts a person's brain off, and he needed *his* to work at full speed right now.

"No, no, no. Don't be silly. You think *I* could be a noblewoman?"

Benjamin decided to not answer that question. There was no safe answer. Since she was dressed in peasant clothes, she did not look like the refined ruling class to him. Still, it would explain some of the Lieutenant's anger last night and why he might rather die than risk Rebecca going anywhere near Mouthrot. It also explained why she was such a—*Oh!* Swallowing hard to keep his breakfast down, Benjamin stopped to stare at her, clenching his jaw so that it wouldn't fall open.

"You're the lost princess, aren't you?"

Rebecca opened and closed her mouth like a wide-eyed fish, silenced by the understanding in his gaze, and then her sharp features screwed up and her eyes reddened. She hugged herself and turned to the mountains behind them. Meanwhile, Benjamin braced himself for the truth.

"I was supposed to go to the castle months ago," Rebecca said, battling tears. "But then the Lieutenant decided to wait until things settled down."

"Surely there are other places you could go?" Benjamin smiled and gathered his strength. "Doesn't the Lieutenant have someplace a little more...stately...tucked away?"

Rebecca looked uncomfortable with that question. She obviously didn't want to reveal any more. Benjamin forced his breathing to slow. He not only needed to *look* calm; he needed to *be* calm. He needed to get the princess back to her protector immediately or he was dead where he stood.

"I mean, if he's the guardian of a princess, he'd have *some* resources." Benjamin focused on keeping his voice light as his head spun. He filled his lungs with air to keep himself from floating away.

"Oh, the Lieutenant has lands and estates. I'm just not sure that he really wants them anymore. He's been living this other life for so long, he's afraid to let it go."

Benjamin nodded. *She hadn't denied it.* The princess whose parents were killed by Mouthrot and who no one was sure was still alive was walking side by side with the most recent valedictorian of the Villains' Academy. Benjamin had personally stood back and let *her* enter Mouthrot's domain.

"I suppose with a plot to kill all the heirs to the throne, the Lieutenant has had to invest a lot of himself to your protection."

"I didn't ask for it!"

Rebecca's eyes popped open nearly as wide as her mouth. Both hands slapped over her mouth. He hooked his arm through one of hers, and she followed Benjamin in shock. He couldn't get back fast enough. Benjamin didn't feel like being hunted down and hanged like a rat today. She hung her head and let him guide her.

Benjamin corralled his racing thoughts. They hadn't been gone long. There was still hope for leniency. Maybe he would run into Denny first, who would probably just kill Benjamin. The Lieutenant, on the other hand, probably knew how to inflict worse punishments. Could Benjamin live with only one eye? Maybe he would have a chance to explain before he was condemned. An ugly image of the Lieutenant tying him to a pyre popped into his mind.

"They've begun to draw up lists of potential husbands," Rebecca said, tears in her voice.

"Poor chumps."

She shoved him soundly, but he recovered with a sly smile. She rolled her eyes at him but smiled back. Benjamin felt the ice around his heart melt a little.

"You people are sure to be the death of me." Benjamin glanced up quickly, judging how close they were to Denny's.

"'You people'? You talk as if we were common pickpockets or thugs."

"If only I was so lucky. No, you're worse. You're the aristocracy. No...you're the very people I will avoid in the future."

"Well, if you're going to set up shop anywhere in Lam, that might be hard to do."

Benjamin stopped abruptly and turned to face his foe. "But I'm not planning to set up shop in this kingdom." His fingers shook. He wasn't sure what emotions he was feeling anymore.

"But I thought you were bent on villainy." Rebecca lifted an eyebrow as she slid a yellow braid behind a shoulder.

"Oh, yes, but certainly not here. We have our own little grapevine, you know."

"So where exactly do you plan to set up your dastardly business?"

He leaned toward Rebecca as she twisted a braid. "Anyplace in the whole world, known or unknown, where you will *not* be, Your Highness." He gathered up all of his courage and turned his back on her. He had to keep walking, no matter what. There was a familiar cluster of prickly brush ahead. He focused on each step and listened for Rebecca. He shoved his way through, scratching his face.

"Ah, just in time." Benjamin stepped to the side so she could see where they were.

"We're back at Denny's?" Rebecca said, her shoulders drooping.

They had popped out of the clump of bushes in front of the brothers' house just as Denny stepped out onto the porch. He eyed the two of them, shook his head, and opened the door. "Never mind," he called inside, "she's out here arguing with Benjamin. You two can just as easily argue indoors as out." Denny eyed the space between Rebecca and Benjamin.

Rebecca screamed and then stomped inside. She slammed her bedroom door and wasn't seen again for the rest of the morning.

Benjamin strode into the hovel and dropped his pack. He sat across from the Lieutenant, who was sipping something warm. Benjamin examined the dark circles under the old man's eyes as he thought about exposing his big secret to the light.

"We'll be getting our own breakfast this morning, then?" the Lieutenant said casually over his shoulder.

Denny sighed and went to the pantry.

"I think that we need to talk about *her*." Benjamin tipped his head toward Rebecca's door. "You know, the p—"

The old man slammed his mug down, silencing Benjamin. Steaming liquid splashed over the Lieutenant's scabbed knuckles and onto the table. The spy didn't flinch; his one visible eye bulged into a threat. He glanced over to the pantry door.

"*She* is not your concern," he whispered through his bared teeth.

"Really?" Benjamin folded his arms across his chest, jamming his knuckles into his arms until it hurt. "She just tried to follow me off into the world for a little adventure. Apparently, she's not so happy with her lot here."

The Lieutenant fumbled his mug as he tried taking another sip.

"Don't think that was *my* idea. I brought her back here." Benjamin stabbed a finger into the table.

The old man examined the ashes in the fireplace. Denny glared at Benjamin as he carried a basket of eggs to the stove.

"I don't know what your plans are, but she is ready to take charge of her life. Someday she'll go, and there won't be anybody to bring her back."

No reply was forthcoming. Benjamin glanced at Denny, who was sulking over a pan of sizzling eggs and bacon. Benjamin nodded a quick good-bye and walked to the door.

"Where are you going?" The Lieutenant pushed his chair back.

"Not here."

"You're not going to finish the job?"

Benjamin felt as if he'd been slapped. Did no one get that he was angry? He had every right to storm off and never look back. "What! Aren't you finished destroying me yet?" Benjamin flung back. "Because I am."

The Lieutenant scrubbed the back of his neck. Benjamin raised his eyebrows in expectation of the Lieutenant's words. "We all have questions that we need to have answered before we can truly move on with our lives. If you leave based on my stupidity, we might both regret it."

Benjamin blinked, unsure what those words meant. The Lieutenant tightened the blanket around his shoulders. His outer fatigue and his inner strength wrestled a moment.

"Regardless of my angry words last night, I recognize that I'm here—and that Rebecca is safely planning our deaths in that room, so *thank you*."

Benjamin returned to his bench, his fingers finding a worn spot on the table's surface while he digested the old man's words. He looked up into the one pale-brown eye of the Lieutenant.

"Ah, and now we come to the truth, almost."

The Lieutenant raised his eyebrow but said nothing.

"You think it might be worth me sticking around?"

The Lieutenant confirmed with a short nod.

"Then you need to answer a question: Why me? Why did you pick me up along the road?"

The Lieutenant stared at the fireplace again. The old man smiled faintly before he turned his gaze back to Benjamin. "I needed a buffer. You were dressed for an interview." The old man shrugged. "There was a possibility that Shreb and some of his men might recognize me."

Benjamin glowered at this. He wasn't buying that. "Does everyone but me know who you are?"

"Well, I used to be very big in this area many years ago."

"Undercover? Or your naturally villainous self?"

"Undercover," he said with a smile. "I'm not sure there's any natural self left after all these years."

Benjamin met the Lieutenant's eye again. His scuffed eye patch looked sadly back at him. This man wanted him here but refused to say why. He should walk away, but there was a part of him that wanted to see how this would play out. Was it possible the Lieutenant just recognized his greatness? Or was there a bigger connection?

"That's probably as close to the truth as I'm going to get, isn't it?" Benjamin leaned back. "So what now?"

"Well, we need to notify the king that Rebecca and I are safe. Denny informed me of the basics of the first letter. I agree that Mouthrot is the more dangerous of the two and is still plotting to kill the entire royal family, but Shreb is very much a danger on his own. They're both plotting independently of each other. Shreb is not quite the trusting imbecile we previously thought. He knows that Mouthrot is not to be fully trusted. I think his aspirations are not much different than Mouthrot's."

The Lieutenant shook his head and returned to sipping from his mug. Benjamin rubbed at the worn spot, trying to take in the ambition of the two archvillains' plans. What if he could help unravel their plans? He grinned. It was almost villainous.

Denny set a couple of plates of slightly burnt bacon and eggs in front of them. "Sorry, nearly forgot about breakfast."

Benjamin prodded an egg yolk with his charred bacon, thankful someone finally remembered him. He watched the golden juice ooze onto his plate, wishing for some of the bread that Rebecca had thrown at his head earlier this morning.

"We could use those two against each other," Benjamin said. "Just the right spark could send the whole thing into flames."

"Set a wildfire loose across the plains and right into the king's castle?" The Lieutenant frowned.

"Not necessarily. They haven't got any momentum yet. Except for Mouthrot's men, the men at the fortress don't seem eager. They're just happy to have a job and some food, I think. They're bored and probably not *too* committed."

The Lieutenant nodded in agreement.

"Their plots are twisted around each other," Benjamin said. "We take down Shreb; we take down Mouthrot, and vice versa. Or at least force one into a tenuous position?"

"Or rouse a hornets' nest." The Lieutenant poked at his bacon. "Either way, it's up to King Aldo. We have only to wait for his decision."

"Watch and wait, then?" Benjamin slurped his eggs.

The Lieutenant nodded, satisfied, and then glanced at Rebecca's bedroom door as he chewed his bacon.

NINETEEN

"Ah, bliss," Benjamin said, exhaling and then biting into a piece of jerky. He'd been camped out and camouflaged as a prickly bush for a few days, silently overlooking Shreb's fortress and taking note of the comings and goings. Mouthrot was definitely not taking the Lieutenant's escape well. He appeared to be in an organized panic.

Benjamin pulled out a spyglass to examine the guards on top of the battlements. He couldn't help but imagine himself standing next to the guards, scheming. He sighed. It would be an exciting but dangerous time. *Anything could happen.* He smirked to himself and then pushed the thought aside. He wasn't inside plotting; he was outside plotting—a sort of villainy for hire, but backward. He shook his head.

He had volunteered for this task. It was all he could do to keep himself from jumping up and down, waving his hand in the air, and screaming, "Pick me! Me! Me! Me!" He smiled at the blue sky. It was nice to be alone for once and safe from Rebecca's death glares and rabid broom.

Not far off, Rina bleated. A hulking figure in a dirty cloak slipped gently through the tall grass and sat on the rock next to Benjamin. Odie looked around and tugged his hood to ensure his face was shadowed.

"Odie?" The goat stepped on Benjamin's hand. "Rina."

Odie dangled a fresh skin of water in front of Benjamin.

Benjamin juggled it for a moment, too stunned to use his hands properly. "You're back? The king?"

Odie shrugged and motioned for Benjamin to follow him.

The steps it took to get to Denny's must have doubled since Benjamin went on duty. Was the king sending an army? Surely a king didn't handle these things personally. Just as well; having his face known by the highest authority in the land would definitely end his career, if not his life. He wished that Odie would just tell him, but Odie wouldn't answer any questions.

"O Great Wolves! Why, oh why don't we have a horse?" Benjamin shook his fist at the empty sky.

TWENTY

*B*enjamin arrived, a sweaty heap of dust. He sat in the shade of the porch, only to find himself staring at a horse tied up in front of the barn with the saddle resting on the cart. Denny came out of the barn carrying a bucket of grain for the horse, who eagerly nosed it. Odie hung his cloak on a peg and strode to the horse to take the bucket. Rina nervously watched from under the cart, while Odie rubbed at the white blaze under the horse's forelock, gazing fondly into the horse's eyes.

"Where did *that* come from?" Benjamin sloshed the water in his waterskin as he squinted toward the horse.

Denny leaned against the porch post. "The king's man gave Odie a horse," he said, his expression pinched. "He was bad enough with a goat." He nodded for them to go inside.

The Lieutenant was bent over a map, rubbing his chin. All the clutter and dirt had been removed. The wood surfaces looked naked and vulnerable. Benjamin wondered if that was a good sign or not.

Had Rebecca spent all her murderous energy scrubbing and cleaning, he also wondered, *or was she still fuming?*

The old man glanced at the boys before pulling a letter from his vest pocket and tossing it on the table. The seal was broken. Benjamin glanced up as he picked it up. The Lieutenant nodded and poured a mug of cider. Denny sidled up to Benjamin as he opened the letter to read.

Benjamin glanced at the signature and saw that the letter was from a man named Branwen.

"Who's Branwen?" Denny asked.

"Secretary Branwen is the king's secretary and master of spies." The Lieutenant waved them on as he guzzled his cider.

The letter was addressed to Benjamin, since he had written the letter to the king to inform him of the Lieutenant's rescue. Branwen begged him to take no action against Shreb or Mouthrot. Any action of the king's men against the archvillain would destabilize the treaty forged between King Zavier and Val the Foul. The king commanded Benjamin to bring the princess to the castle immediately, using extreme caution.

"We're supposed to bring the princess to the castle?" Denny's head jerked up. "You know where the princess is?"

"What?" Benjamin examined Denny's confused expression and glanced at the Lieutenant, who shrugged. "You didn't tell him?"

Denny glared at the old man, affronted at being left out of the Lieutenant's complete confidence. The old man set his mug down and settled into a chair that creaked as he leaned back, weaving his fingers behind his head, his elbows splayed like wings. He rubbed the tie to his scuffed eye patch. "I didn't tell anyone." The one-eyed man looked at Denny earnestly. "It is obviously sensitive information."

Denny nodded at this but still frowned at his shoes. "How does Benjamin know?"

"Rebecca told me." Benjamin gazed at the master of spies' signature and seal. *He just ordered me to the castle.* Benjamin swallowed the acid burning up his throat. He then pulled out his book to write the name down.

The Lieutenant grimaced as he scooped up two more mugs, filled them, and handed them to the boys. Benjamin thanked him and gulped the cider down, desperate to erase the sour taste in his mouth. Denny stared into his mug sternly. Sorting through the information, he was unwilling to come up with a conclusion. Denny had known Rebecca for many years and had obviously become fond of her. Denny was ambitious enough to marry up and had probably assumed that Rebecca was of lower nobility. With his connection to the Lieutenant and a few grand deeds done in the king's name, he could be a potential suitor for the lovely Rebecca. A princess would be, sadly, out of Denny's reach forever. So maybe those hopes blunted his ability to connect the dots here.

"Rebecca knows?"

Benjamin folded the letter, stepping away from Denny, and handed the letter back to the Lieutenant. The Lieutenant accepted the letter from Benjamin but kept his eyes locked on Denny. *Was he waiting for Denny to sort through things on his own?* Benjamin wondered. *Good luck with that.*

Benjamin sighed. "Denny, Rebecca is the princess." He kept his voice gentle, but the force of his words still physically jarred Denny. Benjamin glanced at the Lieutenant, who clenched his jaws. Did the Lieutenant know about Denny's feelings for Rebecca?

Denny's bright blue eyes flashed between Benjamin and the Lieutenant. He turned away for a moment to rake his fingers through his hair. The door opened. Odie frowned down at his older brother. He nodded in confirmation of what Denny had heard. Odie must have been listening outside.

The Lieutenant tugged on his eye patch as he chewed on the inside of his mouth. He handed the letter back to Benjamin and gestured toward Rebecca's door, not taking his eyes off the brothers.

"What? Are you kidding?" Benjamin pulled his dusty cap off. "I brought her back here. She's probably lying in wait with a knife. Send one of them in."

The Lieutenant dismissed him and leaned over the table, pressing his fists into the map. Odie eyed the letter in Benjamin's hand and glanced at Rebecca's door, offering a silent good luck.

Benjamin knocked on the door. Surely, Rebecca had heard some of that discussion. How strange that the Lieutenant gave him this job. As her guardian, it should be *his* job.

He knocked again. Silence.

"Rebecca?" Benjamin knocked again and looked over at Odie. "Are you sure she's still in here?"

He nodded over Denny's bent head.

"You bolted the windows from the outside?"

Odie nodded again. He looked relieved not to be Benjamin.

"Rebecca? I'm coming in. We need to talk. Do not hide behind the door and attack me."

"Fine."

Benjamin shoved the door open and waited for it to hit the wall before he entered. His caution was unneeded. Rebecca sat on the bed, arms folded, staring at him. He checked the inside of the door for booby traps. Nothing. Rebecca rolled her eyes. He could see wood over the outsides of the windows. There was a candle on the table between two beds. He closed the door gently, keeping his eyes on Rebecca. She returned his gaze with a hard determination.

He plodded forward. This was another strange predicament to find himself in. He scratched the back of his head, hoping to stir some thoughts. Benjamin imagined Rebecca had been trained in all sorts of ways to kill a person.

"The Lieutenant taught you how to fight, didn't he?"

Rebecca nodded, curious where this was going.

"Good. Do you have a weapon on you?"

"No, of course not." Rebecca twisted her face into a scowl, affronted.

Benjamin stared at her for a long moment. He didn't believe her for a second. The Lieutenant was extremely paranoid about Rebecca—surely some of that would have rubbed off on her over the years. He raised an eyebrow in disbelief.

She smirked. "One."

"Does the Lieutenant know about it?"

"Denny didn't find it when the Lieutenant had him search me."

Benjamin closed his eyes for a moment to avoid laughing. He could imagine Denny's conflicting emotions on that assignment. So the Lieutenant *was* clueless about Denny's feelings for Rebecca. Benjamin traced the hard edge of the knife hidden under his sleeve.

"We'll need to get you a few more. You'll want to have at least one people can see, so they won't expect one to be hidden."

She nodded at this.

Benjamin pulled the letter out of his sleeve. Rebecca sobered at the sight of it. He offered her the letter to read. She shook her head as her braids scraped across her chest.

"So I'm going to the castle?"

"Yes."

She nodded, blinking quickly.

"I've been ordered to take you to the king with extreme caution." Whether that meant to use caution *with* or *against* Rebecca, he wasn't sure. Benjamin examined the shadows on the floor from the boarded windows. He allowed the awkward moment to pass before he knelt in front of her. It reminded him of something his mother would have done. He gently grabbed Rebecca's arms so that she looked at him. He used the same soft, determined tone his mother always used.

"You *are* a fighter, Rebecca, and *you are* intelligent."

Rebecca looked startled by his words. It was not what she had expected. It wasn't what Benjamin expected either. This was a real moment, a moment that counted. A few days ago, Benjamin swore to avoid her at any cost, and now he was persuading her to follow him. It felt strange, but he pushed on. "If you want to fight, fight the enemy, not the people who have sworn their lives to you." Benjamin paused. He was lashing himself to the princess by the very words he spoke. "If we are attacked, stay low, but keep your eyes open. You're going to have to look for an opportunity to run or hide. Fight only when there is no other choice."

Benjamin warily removed his hands from Rebecca and backed away. It occurred to him that she might not like him in her space. He swallowed but held her gaze.

Rebecca stared back wide-eyed for a full minute, taking in what he had said. She jutted her chin to the ceiling and then stood as though a sword had sprouted up through her spine. She turned toward the door but hesitated a moment to glance back at him, curiosity written across her features. "Why are you doing this?"

"While you're not my favorite person, I don't want to see you dead." Benjamin felt the truth of his words. He meant it. Weird. He held Rebecca's gaze for a long moment.

"No, why are you doing all of this?" She narrowed her eyes, not in suspicion, but in interest.

Benjamin had no idea how to answer that. He wasn't sure. The floor had been pulled out from underneath him the moment he walked away from his dream interview. He'd just been trying to keep from sinking into irrelevance. He didn't want to fail. He needed his name to be great, greater than his father's. Maybe it didn't matter how he did it, even if it meant working with the wrong side.

"Future employment opportunities?" he quipped.

She shook her head. A heavy rock dropped into Benjamin's stomach. He missed an opportunity she had given him. She wanted something deeper.

He fumbled at his belt, releasing a long dagger from his hip, and handed it to her. Rebecca avoided his eyes as she belted it around her waist. He opened the door for her. She walked like a queen into the waiting room.

"Lieutenant, when do we leave?" the princess asked.

Benjamin was gratified that he was not the only one surprised by her transformation. Denny and Odie gaped from their corner. The Lieutenant's single eye twinkled as he stood at attention.

The Lieutenant bowed but looked past Rebecca to Benjamin. Denny bowed sadly. This moment changed everything. As a princess, Rebecca was now forever out of Denny's reach. Odie bowed and then patted his brother's shoulder in sympathy. Once Rebecca walked out of this shack, she was no longer just Rebecca. She was a princess, and no one here could forget it.

"Almost immediately, Your Highness." The Lieutenant rolled up the map. Denny jumped at the title. "Boys, pack up the necessities."

Odie grimaced out the window at the horse.

"We'll bring her with us. She can carry a few things and walk." The Lieutenant reached up and thumped Odie on the back. "We won't wear her out. No worries."

Odie smiled at this and dove into the pantry to fetch several large packs and a box of foodstuffs. Denny stumbled to his bedroom, and Odie tossed him a pack to fill. The Lieutenant pulled up some floorboards to reveal several swords and extra knives. Rebecca gathered all the waterskins she could find and went to fill them up at the well.

Benjamin's bag was already packed, for the most part. He topped it off with more food and the cloak he'd worn when he rescued the Lieutenant. He sat down and watched the group work silently together, communicating with almost with no words. They were all cogs that fit together to accomplish the same task. It was strange watching it. He was the odd man out in this team.

TWENTY ONE

*R*ebecca spent a little too much time trying to untangle all the waterskins. The tension in her was near exploding. Fighting against the temptation to throw everything down the well, she chose instead to close her eyes for a moment. Hot, dusty air pressed against her. She wiped the back of her neck just as one drop of sweat rolled down her back. The sun was climbing high into its noon position. She pulled the lid off the well and lowered the bucket into the dark chasm.

The rhythm of the rope and pulley tugged on her thoughts. Concerns of facing an uncle she barely remembered rose with the bucket. A knot tightened in her chest. She had met him, but that had been over ten years ago, before she'd moved from the Lieutenant's eastern estate.

King Aldo had come for her seventh birthday and had given her a locket with her parents' initials inside. She wore it every day. The Lieutenant had wanted to lock it safely away in his office, but she had refused to hand it over. The Lieutenant had relented, at her nurse's persuasion.

"Rebecca had so few comforts," the nurse had reminded him.

He had stared into Rebecca's eyes, sorting through all the risks and benefits. She knew the moment she had won; she had seen it in his eyes, like a flame smothered out. It rarely happened, so she remembered the victory as one of the two greatest gifts from her two uncles.

She drowned the waterskins in the bucket, letting the tepid water rush into the skins. The horse nickered behind her. Its ears were pressed back as it tugged uneasily on its rope. Wisps of dust danced around the horse's feet as it stomped. Rina bleated and walked around the cart. Rebecca scanned the area around the barn but saw nothing. Maybe a snake had slithered past. She went over to soothe the skittish horse, but it flung its head. Rebecca tugged its bridle firmly, but the horse screamed and reared in alarm.

Rebecca dropped her hand to her dagger and spun around, slicing through the air, like she'd practiced for years—except now there was a real man towering over her. She felt the moment the dagger tore through his flesh. He dropped his knife and grabbed his stomach as he stumbled back, red blossoming across his dingy shirt. His dark eyes widened, obviously shocked to be the one bleeding. Her throat burned as her scream changed from savage attack call to a shocked cry. The Lieutenant burst outside, followed closely by Odie, both carrying tarnished swords. The bleeding man ran, knowing that was no match for two expert swordsmen.

Denny wrapped his arms around her, repeatedly promising that she was okay as he ran his trembling fingers across her braids. Benjamin grabbed her bloody knife and wiped the blade clean as he surveyed the area. He ran to the brush that fringed the farm and sliced through branches and prickles. With another knife from his sleeve, Benjamin attacked potential hiding places. Of course, only *he* thought to check for additional assassins. Rebecca scanned the area around them as well but saw nothing.

The thrumming in Rebecca's ears died down as Benjamin's stance relaxed. He shook his head at her. All clear. She allowed herself to soften against Denny's tense frame. His warmth pressed into her cold body, releasing her weariness. It felt nice to be held. She buried her face into Denny's shoulder. Her hand remembered the sensation of the blade against the man's body, and she shuddered. Denny whispered softly in her ear, his lips brushing against her hair. She had spilled a man's blood today, and while she had panicked, her actions saved her life. The memory of Benjamin's words—"You are a fighter, Rebecca, and you are intelligent"—filled her. She lifted her head. Benjamin raised his eyebrows and then nodded. *Good job.*

She smiled up at Denny, but he was unable to return it. His arms shook as he helped her back to the well to sit down. They leaned against each other while Benjamin guarded. He flicked a glance at her and Denny from time to time. Denny had slid his hand into hers and set it in his lap, cradling her hand between both of his. Benjamin raised his eyebrows at this and decided to join the Lieutenant and Odie.

Denny was absentmindedly tracing the tendons in Rebecca's wrist. She looked up to see the Lieutenant's face, dark with rage, above her. Odie followed, tapping the flat side of his sword against his shoulder as he studied the dirt. Denny stood up to meet the Lieutenant. Benjamin arrived last, casting weary glances behind him.

"Fill up those waterskins, and let's get out of here before anyone comes looking for that failed assassin." The Lieutenant clenched his jaw as he cleaned his bloody sword on a tattered rag that lay in the back of the cart. "Odie, pack the horse."

Rebecca glanced down at her empty hands in her lap to make sure they were still there. The Lieutenant scrutinized Rebecca, making sure she was alive and well. She wondered if he was thinking of his sister.

"I'm fine." Rebecca stood up, tilting her head back. "Just a little shaky."

The Lieutenant strode forward and pulled her into his arms. He smelled of hot leather and steel. "I don't know what I would have done if something happened to you." He rested his chin on top of her head. She felt the locket press into her chest as he hugged her tightly. "I don't have much family left."

Your only family. Rebecca closed her eyes and squeezed her guardian back. These moments were rare.

TWENTY TWO

They were on the road within minutes. As she glanced at her travel companions, Rebecca gripped the straps of her pack to prevent her fingers from shaking. They all seemed to take turns watching behind them or watching her. Odie followed behind with an enormous pack, while the horse carried a few bedrolls and waterskins. Rina trotted behind. The Lieutenant led them across country toward the main road. Rebecca was placed tightly between the Lieutenant and Denny, with Benjamin filling the gap between Denny and Odie.

Benjamin continually scanned the horizon, scowling. He probably wasn't happy about heading to the castle, either. At least one other person shared Rebecca's reticence on this journey. Denny would occasionally rest a hand on her pack, as if he needed to reassure himself that she was still safe.

"I'm fine." Rebecca smiled at him and then glanced at Benjamin. He was kicking a shrub, his eyes never leaving the area between them and the road. Denny scowled and stepped back.

What did Denny have against Benjamin, she wondered, *besides the fact that he was really annoying?*

She turned back to face the Lieutenant. He scanned ahead for potential danger as well. The knot of his eye patch stared at her. The shrubs and dead grass pulled at her skirt as they walked toward the Sunrise Mountains, which they would have to pass to get to the castle perched on the other side. She ran her fingers over the dipping heads of the yellow grass. Grasshoppers chirped around her. On the other side, in the east, the mountains were named the Sunset Mountains and the world was green. Trees and rocks sprouted from the ground. Green fields rolled out, full of crops and sheep—at least where the Lieutenant's estate was, if she remembered correctly.

The Lieutenant turned and lifted his eyebrows as if to ask if she was okay. She smiled and nodded back, shoving aside the image of the assassin's dark eyes bulging in surprise. She gripped at the hilt of the knife Benjamin had returned to her. *You've baptized it. It's yours now.* He'd barely glanced at her as he handed it back.

The Lieutenant turned his head at the sound of hoofbeats, and Denny pulled Rebecca to the ground. Only Odie with his horse and goat were left standing. A dust cloud marked the road's location, but it wasn't close enough to see the rider.

The Lieutenant pressed his finger unnecessarily against his lips. She had no desire to make a noise, even with Denny painfully squeezing her arms. She wiggled them a little, and Denny eased his grip. They all watched the dust cloud as it faded into the distance. They listened to the silence on the road for about ten seconds before the Lieutenant gestured them to move quickly. They dropped their single-file formation and clumped together around her. Benjamin breathed heavily on the other side of Rebecca. She glanced up at his overheated cheeks. He struggled but stayed even with her, and just like Denny, he tried to shield her from view.

Rebecca spotted a billowing cloud of dust building on the road. Her gasp alerted Odie, who in two strides scooped up Rina and Rebecca and climbed onto the back of the horse. Rebecca found her arms full of protesting goat as Odie slid behind her and dug his heels into the horse's flank. They rushed so fast past the Lieutenant and the road that Rebecca could barely breathe. She was thankful she hadn't dropped Rina; she didn't want to know how Odie would handle losing his best friend. She squeezed the flailing goat to her chest and closed her eyes just as they hit an overgrown path. Odie pressed her head down.

The horse slowed, and she opened her eyes to see a worn-down hovel. A broken shutter dangled from the front window. A gate lay broken beside a tangled fence. An empty woodshed leaned sharply to one side. Odie slipped off and reached for Rina, who lectured Odie after he set her on the ground. Rebecca swung over the saddle and slid to the ground. Her knees buckled, and Odie reached out to catch her. His ears burned red as he caught her and set her back on her feet. He stepped back and averted his gaze to the front door.

This was a safe house she'd never actually seen. The Lieutenant would point out its location regularly as they passed it, but he had always refused to go anywhere near it. He wanted to keep it safe.

Hopefully it's livable, she thought. *Oh, well. It'll just be for a day or two.*

Odie fumbled around the doorframe until he found an oversized key and unlocked the front door.

It was dusty but neatly arranged. A few dishes were on the counter, as if someone had just left with all the intentions of coming back soon. Odie left, more comfortable with the horse outside than alone with Rebecca in the house. She toured the house in a single lap. It was one room, with the kitchen in the front and two beds tucked against the back wall, the blankets pulled tight and flat. A small window hung between the two beds, covered by a dark, moth-eaten curtain.

She heard heavy running, and the horse whinnied outside. The Lieutenant collapsed against the doorframe, panting. Her guardian stepped inside and closed the door. He closed his eyes and heaved a sigh. "There's something I need to tell you."

Rebecca pulled open a stiff curtain to let light into the room. The Lieutenant paced while wringing his hands. She sat down to prepare for the bad news.

TWENTY THREE

The boys pressed themselves flat against the rough ground and stared at each other as the storm of hooves passed by on the road. The Lieutenant had chased after Rebecca and Odie before the riders appeared on the road, stranding them on this side alone.

As the rumble faded down the road, Benjamin lifted his head, only the trailing dust visible. He laid his head down and began to breathe again. Denny rolled over onto his back, resting next to his heavy pack, and forced a short laugh.

"Any chance we're overreacting?" Denny flung an arm over his eyes and peeked out at Benjamin.

Benjamin raised his head, shook it, and then let his head fall back down.

"I didn't think so." He dropped his arm back to his side and stared up at the cloudless sky for a moment before suggesting they catch up.

"You know where they went?" Benjamin asked, pushing himself up halfway. Denny pulled him up the rest of the way and tugged his huge pack back on.

"That way, I think." Denny pointed past the bushes the Lieutenant had disappeared into. He looked antsy to catch up. "There's a place out here that the Lieutenant pointed out to me a few times. That's got to be it."

Denny pulled Benjamin across the road, forcing him to run faster than he wanted. Denny kept assuring him that they were close, but Benjamin wasn't sure he believed him. Just a little ways up the road, he recalled, was where he had met the Lieutenant. There was nothing else in the area for leagues.

As they stumbled through tangles, Benjamin paused to scan the path. *This looked very familiar.* He shoved his pack into Denny's arms and sauntered off alone. Barbs pulled on his jacket and tore at his hands and face. He punched through to a clearing. A broken shutter hung loose from a grimy window. Rina was tied up to a broken gate in front of his door. Shock slapped him hard; all he could feel was silence, and it stung.

Denny's lips moved, as if he were speaking. Silence wrapped around Benjamin tighter, suffocating him. He heard nothing as he ran, the ground swaying under him. His cheeks burned as he lurched for the door, ready to demand explanations. There would be no wiggling out this time.

But as he opened the door, he merely slumped to the wall, his mouth gaping open like a fish. Rebecca sat at *his* table talking to the Lieutenant. The confusion on her face must have matched his.

She stood up. His knife was belted around her hip. A scrape grazed her cheek. He blinked. The Lieutenant faced Rebecca, his back rigid.

"Look at me!" Benjamin closed his mind against the memories of this place, his sanctuary. The place he used to share with his mother. "You know where I live? How do you know where I live?"

He had nowhere else to go now. The Lieutenant turned stiffly. His eye met Benjamin's angry gaze. There was something written in the Lieutenant's expression that Benjamin couldn't read. His legs collapsed, and the room dimmed as his head hit the floor.

TWENTY FOUR

"I think I would like to hear some of these explanations myself," Rebecca said, tapping her foot.

"When you live with deadly secrets, they become your lifeline. Holding on to them is what keeps you alive," the Lieutenant said, shaking his head. "It's not an easy thing to just let go."

Benjamin lay on the hard floor, blinking. All was dark and he couldn't move. He felt as if he'd been wrung out. All that exertion. Running, running, running—that's all he could remember. Where had he been running to? *Wait! I ran home!* The very hideout he grew up in, his home. The one he sat alone in during every school break, thinking about how happy his mother would be to see him in the Villains' Academy. It was her dying wish.

He came to his body again and bolted upward. Everything in his vision went purple and black. He fell back and would have collided with the floor again, but a large, warm hand caught his head and laid him down. "Shh."

Odie knelt over him, his eyebrows squishing together over his brown eyes. Denny stood behind him, flexing his jaws. Benjamin took an internal inventory. Had he been seriously hurt? He had some scrapes that burned. He cautiously moved his legs and arms, and then he slowly sat up with Odie's help. His head swam a little, but it soon cleared. The Lieutenant sat on his mother's bed, scrubbing his face with his dirty hands.

Benjamin didn't have the strength for shouting, so he took a calming breath of restraint and looked the Lieutenant in the eye. The old man tugged at his eye patch and glanced away.

"I was wondering how *everyone* knows where *my secret* hideout is? Pretty sure no one else has ever been here but me and my mother."

Odie helped him stand, with a hand on Benjamin's back for support. The whole room waited for the Lieutenant's answer, but he merely stared silently at Benjamin, pressing his lips together until they turned white. He stared long enough to make Benjamin squirm. Rebecca threw her hands into the air and then focused a cross look at the side of the Lieutenant's head. "And?"

The Lieutenant unlocked his gaze with Benjamin and looked almost nauseous as he met Rebecca's eyes.

"And—" His voice caught in his throat. "It was mine first. I gave it to your mother."

"You knew my mother?"

"Ursula? Yes, I knew her."

A catch in the old man's voice ripped at a scar deep in Benjamin's chest. He blinked before tears could pool in his eyes.

"She's dead."

"Yes, I heard."

The old man closed his eye and brushed his silver-laced hair from his face, pain rippling across it. He must have been thinking about

Benjamin's mother. Benjamin had many memories of his mother that made him look like that too.

She had been so focused on making him into the image of his father, it had left little room for much else in their relationship. As he got older, there was less and less room for motherly affection. He wondered if she had always been that way.

"I don't remember you. She never let people come here."

"No, she didn't want to see me anymore."

"Oh." Benjamin's voice sounded small and far away. He stepped back into Odie, who steadied him.

"I assumed Ursula had abandoned it until I saw you on the road."

The Lieutenant peered cautiously at him, perhaps gauging how much he actually had to tell. So there was more? Did Benjamin really want to hear all of it? Panic welled up in him. He swallowed it whole. It scratched and scraped all the way down.

"Have I seen you before?"

The Lieutenant's face tightened.

"You were at my graduation, weren't you?" A light bloomed in Benjamin's head.

"Yes."

He saw the grisly gray hair (a wig?) under a heavy hood, the sparkle in the shadows of the hood where his patch would have been.

"What is going on, Lieutenant?" Denny burst out. Emotion ripped through his voice, his hair pressed flat against his head with sweat and nervous hands.

Did Denny already know? Did everyone see but him?

"I was just surveying the graduation to see if Shreb had any intentions of recruiting. More work for the king."

Denny breathed heavily. He unclenched his fists and rubbed them on his pant legs. He glowered at his brother, who still held Benjamin up.

"I recognized your name on the program. But when I saw you, I knew who you were. You have her dark hair and fine features."

Denny began pacing the room. Odie's grip tightened on Benjamin's shoulders. This man had been like their father. Did the truth coming forward affect them all?

The tension pressed into Benjamin's chest, threatening to crush it. The old man licked his lips and looked away. He studied the shadow of the broken shutter against the filthy window. Benjamin's mind shut down. The room was stale. When had he last opened a window? Years. He couldn't breathe in this tomb. This place where his mother had built a relic to a past she had lost. It was sacrilege, wasn't it? They had desecrated a holy site devoted to Benjamin's father, Black-Eyed Barnaby.

"Did you know my f—" but the words clung in his throat. He didn't want to know about his father. He wiped his sweaty palms on his sleeves. "How...how did you know my mother?"

"We met not long after I entered the king's service. My first friend in my new life." He looked down at his boots caked with dust. "She helped me find a job with the archvillain at the time."

The words hit Benjamin like cold water thrown in his face. "You worked for Shreb, the first one?"

Benjamin could feel the information drip down him and puddle around his toes. He must have known his father as well. What was this man afraid to say? The history books were so vague about what happened to Black-Eyed Barnaby, but his mother was certain he was dead. She saw it happen, she said, but not how.

The Lieutenant met his gaze and nodded.

"My father worked for him, too."

"Black-Eyed Barnaby."

Benjamin dumbly nodded in response. There was a terrible intake of collective breath around him as the final piece slipped into place for Rebecca, Denny, and Odie. Benjamin scanned the room, but all eyes were turned to the Lieutenant. Benjamin's heart beat against his chest. He rubbed his cold fingers together.

"Y-" Benjamin choked, his mouth too dry for speech. Hot tears stung his eyes. "My mother used to tell me stories about him. He didn't sound like a real person." Tears scalded his cheeks. He looked down at his hands. His fingernails were rimmed in dirt. He flipped a hangnail on his thumb back and forth.

The old man peeked up at him and then closed his eyes. He took a deep breath and spoke, a quiver in his voice. "That's probably because he wasn't. Not really."

"I don't understand." Benjamin wedged his eyebrows together. "All the stories? You said you worked with him?"

"The history books are right, mostly." The old man shrugged as he scrubbed the back of his neck. "It's just that he didn't...he wasn't...he was one of my lies."

The Lieutenant's one pale-brown eye watched Benjamin closely. He bit the inside of his mouth for a moment and then rubbed his hands together.

"The name I worked under was Barnabus Black. I'm not sure who came up with that other name."

A tear fell from the Lieutenant's face as he lowered his eye. Benjamin heard it hit the floor. The words rolled over him and settled in the cold puddle of dread at his feet. He didn't understand. Benjamin could not speak, could not breathe, could not move. There was no one in the room with him. He stood alone in his empty house. Helpless. Then the words trickled into his mind, drowning him.

"When the first Shreb died, my mission ended. I had to return to the king. I could finally tell your mother the truth. I thought Ursula would understand. *Somehow* she would understand. I thought she loved *me*." The old man's breath trembled in his chest. He clenched his hands together to steady them, unable to meet Benjamin's horrified gaze. "She wouldn't forgive me. I begged. I told her I would wait for her. I would give her time. Anything, *anything* she wanted. I had estates and wealth." He closed his eyes against the memory. "*Traitor.* That was her answer. I never saw her again."

Benjamin collapsed into a heap. Odie sank with him, his thick arms wrapped around him. Tears puddled on Odie's large hands. Benjamin reached up and touched his cheeks. They were wet. He turned. Odie's face was smeared with tears as well.

This man, who was father to all, did not exist. Benjamin did not have a father after all. Lies, the father of lies. Lies twisted into shapes by his mother. Hot rage bubbled up in his chest and formed a hard fist. He felt it punch out toward the man who sat on his mother's bed.

"No! No!" Benjamin fought to stand, shaking his head violently. Odie's arms tightened around his chest. "It's all just lies! It doesn't make sense!"

The Lieutenant pulled his eye patch down, letting it slide around his neck like a noose. He blinked in the light and looked up. A dark, dark eye—almost black—looked back at him. The ghost of Black-Eyed Barnaby locked eyes with Benjamin.

"You are my son," the Lieutenant breathed more than spoke.

Benjamin Black closed his eyes and slumped into Odie's large frame and felt Odie's warmth against his own cold, dead body. Benjamin had to be dead. He had to be dead. Surely *one* of them was dead. In this world one of them was dead.

✝ ✝ ✝

Benjamin sat in the corner, the walls holding him upright. He clutched a warm cup of something in his dead fingers. Rebecca insisted he sip it while she rambled on about something or other. She wrapped a blanket around him.

The brothers sat on his mother's empty cot and watched Benjamin through sidelong glances as they pretended to admire the sparse furniture. The Lieutenant paced around the room, looking at things, remembering.

Awkwardness had bonded with the dust in the room, making it difficult to breathe. Odie opened a few windows. Unfortunately, there was no breeze. Finally, it was too much, and the Lieutenant excused himself to find more water.

Denny stood up and strode around the cot and, in a stroke of courage, attempted conversation. He asked Odie about the horse. Odie just looked at him blankly and shook his head.

"The Lieutenant always pointed this place out to me when we were in the area. We never got close. I think this was...*is*...a painful place for him."

She wrung a kitchen rag in her hands. "I never knew, I swear, Benjamin. He rarely speaks about his past unless you ask him direct questions. I never would have known to ask." She wiped the table with the rag and collapsed into a chair. She shook her head, bewildered.

Knowing they had never actually set foot here before comforted Benjamin somehow. Why, he couldn't say, but it was something.

Benjamin nodded at Rebecca and realized that wasn't enough. "You've done well today."

Her cheeks flushed "Yes, thank you for the knife and...for believing in me," she said as she leaned in closer.

Denny jostled a chair up against the table. He probably wanted to forget about the whole thing.

Benjamin looked at each of them. "Did you know about me?"

Rebecca looked at Denny. He stared at the chair he gripped with white knuckles, his lips pressed tightly into a frown. Rebecca turned to meet Benjamin's eyes.

"I knew that the Lieutenant thought he *might* have a child, but he didn't know for sure. Last I knew, he had given up the idea."

Rebecca peered back at Denny, who confirmed her words with a single nod. Odie stroked the blankets of the bed until they were smooth, trying to blend into the background.

"We didn't put it together until he told his story. Please believe us when we say that we didn't know anything about you before we met." Rebecca reached over and adjusted Benjamin's blanket. "I don't think he meant to tell you so abruptly. If the situation had been different—"

Benjamin flipped away her response. He couldn't listen to more. Things were not different. He wanted to ask this man where he'd been all his life, but he knew. He was taking care of the king, Rebecca, Denny, and his brothers. Isn't this the sort of information that should make everything better?

Well, it didn't.

He felt as if the Lieutenant had ripped all the scabs off his secret wounds. This new truth was the rot that fed the infection in his heart. He felt like he was dying from internal injuries.

"All of us here have lost our parents," Denny said. "My brothers and I—"

"But I thought my father was safely lost!" Benjamin blinked through his angry haze. "Who's the liar? My mother? My fa—I mean, the Lieutenant? The very books I studied in school? My mother never wanted to let people know who my father was. Was this why? All the lies that made up her life, she passed on to me."

Denny sat down, and the room went quiet. Everyone became very concerned about the state of his or her boots. Odie scooted closer to the wall, hoping to disappear into a shadow. Denny set a hand on his brother's back in a comforting gesture. The silence stretched on.

The Lieutenant came back a few minutes later. He looked miserable. He didn't press Benjamin in any way, but he didn't seem to know where to sit or where to look. Finally he began to look through cupboards and packs to make dinner.

Benjamin stood up, letting his blanket fall to the floor. He stepped out into the fading light of another day's end. He couldn't think of how to get out of this. He had nowhere else to go. All his troubles had lodged themselves into his place of sanctuary.

A spike of gut-wrenching ice—akin to blind fear—nearly brought him to his knees. He wanted to run until the ice bled from his soul. While his panic was strong, his physical body was exhausted. He settled for roaming outside the little hovel that had been his hideout his whole life. Thistles with expired blooms clustered in the yellow grass as he felt the pokey heads of weeds burrow into his socks. He didn't care. He just had to keep moving. He stumbled over a camouflaged rock and was brought to his knees in front of a broken tree that had collapsed on itself and died. Before it had lost all of its leaves, he had sheltered underneath it when his mother had pushed him too far. She never found him there. He could just make out her third-hand boots and the torn hem of her skirts from inside. He'd hold his breath until she stomped back inside. He waited until he was ready to face her. It was too small for him to hide in now, so he sat on the rock instead.

A plate of food appeared just under his nose. The Lieutenant set it down between his feet, and then gazed into the collapsed tree and sat down. Benjamin stiffened. The man said nothing for a long time. Silently, he gave Benjamin the time he needed to get used to his presence.

"When I realized who you were, at the graduation, I was in shock." The man's voice was surprisingly soft. "I didn't know what to do. I had before me an answer that I had been seeking for over fifteen years. I couldn't just leave that alone."

The Lieutenant rubbed at his newly exposed eye. A painful knot formed in Benjamin's throat. He furrowed his brows together to keep the tears back. He did not want to cry in front of his father.

"I should have told you from the beginning, but I didn't want to drive you away. I wanted to give you time." He rubbed his hands slowly back and forth. "You are free to do whatever you want, but you are welcome to work with me. I see potential for greatness in you. I'd like to be a part of that, as your father, or in any way that you will let me."

Benjamin looked up, dazed. He could see the Lieutenant was earnest, but Benjamin couldn't pry his mouth open to say anything. He stole glances at the Lieutenant, not strong enough to face him straight on yet.

The Lieutenant stood up and dusted off his pants. He turned and demanded eye contact, his one black eye sucking Benjamin's attention.

"I'm sorry," he said. He waited for Benjamin's response.

Benjamin nodded quickly and wiped his sleeve under his nose. He'd never remembered anyone apologizing to him before. He wasn't sure what to say to that, so he kept nodding as he chewed on the Lieutenant's words.

The Lieutenant patted Benjamin on the shoulder. Benjamin met his father's gaze for a second before he returned inside. Benjamin pulled out his little book and let it fall to the ground next to his plate. Two blank pages looked up at him.

He sat there for a long time without thinking. He should have said something, but even now he couldn't think what. Too many words tangled in his mouth, down his throat, and back into his head. Hunger churned his stomach, but he could only stare at the plate of food.

The light was beginning to fade when Rebecca's feet appeared next to the plate. She knelt beside him, picked up the plate, and set it in his lap. His hand lifted the food to his mouth, and he ate. With some food in his stomach, his body relaxed. He drank from the cup she offered. The rock he sat on felt hard. When he'd finished the food, Rebecca slid her arm under his and stood. She led him inside to his mother's bed. She removed his boots and then pulled a blanket over him.

"It's been a hard day. Tomorrow will be better," she whispered.

The only thing he felt as he dozed off was the heavy beating of his heart against his breastbone.

TWENTY FIVE

Rebecca had slept miserably. She had taken the bed next to Benjamin's, and Denny had wedged himself into the narrow space between the two beds, his pale locks tangled around his head.

She was getting a little tired of his close proximity. It was a bit much to deal with first thing in the morning. She tried to figure out the best way to slink past Denny. Perhaps that was why he slept there. He was afraid she'd disappear in the night, though the Lieutenant had probably ordered him to. Their combined vigilance was grinding on her nerves.

She rubbed her right shoulder as she sat up. The soreness was a small price to pay for being alive. The wide eyes of her assassin flashed before her, and she shook him out of her head. When her breathing returned to normal, she climbed down the back of the small bed, bypassing Denny all together.

She tripped over a rug and was surprised to find the Lieutenant had slept there all night. He blinked up at her with two eyes. That black eye was unsettling. Rebecca swore it saw all things hidden, including her feelings and thoughts. She mutely apologized and gestured to her bed. *Sleep in my bed. I'll make breakfast.*

Rebecca tiptoed around him to the stove. She opened the hatch to check inside. It hadn't been used for a really long time. She saw evidence of mouse nests. She locked the hatch and thought about a cold breakfast. A warm bowl of porridge would have to wait for another day. The Lieutenant stretched as he stood up and raised his eyebrows with a question.

"Mice." She shook her head. "I guess Benjamin doesn't cook much."

The Lieutenant frowned in response, and Rebecca bit her lip. He would probably blame himself for that. It was hard to tell with her guardian. He took responsibility for too many things. Maybe guilt became like air for some people. They had to seek it out to keep living.

"It's just as well." The Lieutenant dipped some water out of the bucket to drink. He shrugged. "Our smoke might be visible from the road."

Rebecca nodded at this. Questions welled up in her chest and pressed against her tongue. She didn't trust herself to speak yet. The Lieutenant always said that she went too far with her words. How did she ask the Lieutenant if he was okay? Benjamin hadn't taken the news joyfully; it had been too huge of a shock. It must have been hard on her guardian, though he'd never let anyone know. Yesterday was the first time she'd seen him not know what to do. She thought he could swim in any depth; perhaps the weight of the lives he left behind was too much. He was the one who needed rescuing now. She wished she knew how.

She set several packs on the table and began to hunt through each for a breakfast of dried meats, apples, and hard rolls. The packs had been forgotten on the floor and were still covered in dust.

What if she'd found out that her parents had just been playing dead and showed up one day to claim her again? She'd had several daydreams where her parents miraculously showed up alive. They would hold her in their arms and cry. They would then explain how they had been captives all these years and hadn't been able to escape until now. In her dreams, it was a happy reunion with kisses and hugs. But now she wondered if that would be an accurate reaction. Somehow the pain of their loss would have to be accounted for. The sudden change of what her life had meant would be flipped on its head. The sudden shift might break everything inside her.

"Torrin," she whispered.

The Lieutenant stiffened at hearing his real name. "Benjamin just needs time." she said. *What do* you *need?*

He turned and glanced to where the boys were sleeping. She hadn't used his real name in ten years. He met her searching look. His expression was naked; it unsettled her to see that he was a fragile person like everyone else. He then he turned away and nodded. She remembered his powerful embrace yesterday. *He did get scared sometimes, but he didn't let the fear stop him from doing what needed to be done. I need to remember that,* she warned herself.

Odie opened the door, yawning. He insisted on sleeping with his goat outside. Rebecca was sure that wouldn't work at the castle. Odie nodded shyly at Rebecca and then made his way to examine the stove. He grimaced and closed the hatch, picked up a pot, and headed outside. Odie was probably the one with the most experience cooking on the road. He was easily the best cook out of the brothers as well. They would all have a good breakfast with him in charge of the food.

"We should probably discuss how you're going to get to the castle." The Lieutenant tried to adjust an eye patch that wasn't there.

"We can't just walk down the road now, I suppose." Rebecca crossed the room to look into a mirror by the wardrobe. Her face was puffy and streaked with dust, the restless night evident on her face. Stray hairs looped around her head. Her blouse was worn thin and stained with sweat. She unbound one braid and combed through it with her fingers. She braided it and attacked the other side.

The Lieutenant watched her with both eyes, but his mind was somewhere else entirely. Was he remembering Brynn, his sister and Rebecca's mother? Was her hair this yellow? Did she wear her hair in braids? He rested his hands on the table with a sigh. "I haven't done much to prepare you for court life, have I?"

Rebecca chuckled at this. "No, but you taught me how to stay alive. Isn't that better?" She sat across from him and took his hands. They were rough and warm. "You and Aldo both agreed that I needed to hide until Mouthrot's conspirators among the nobles could be found. You made the hard choice. I'll figure out the rest. Somehow."

The Lieutenant squeezed her fingers and looked out the window. *We should probably discuss how you're getting to the castle.* His words echoed back in her head and she dropped his hands. "You're not coming, are you?" Her voice shattered the morning silence. She stood and stared down at him, pressing her fists into her hips.

He shrugged and looked past her to where Benjamin and Denny bolted upright, bewildered. The Lieutenant motioned her to be quiet. She waved off the boys behind her.

"Where exactly are you going?" She scowled down at him. Her guardian's main concern had always been to keep her safely tucked away. He must be plotting something. "This trip is dangerous. I would think you'd want to see me personally to the king."

"I do," her guardian said in a low voice, hoping that would calm her down. How wrong he was!

"But?" She flicked her heated glare at Odie as he walked through the door carrying a steaming pot of porridge. He nearly retreated outside, but the Lieutenant urged Odie in as if there were nothing wrong. The Lieutenant gave her a warning look that urged her to keep stray hostility away from Odie's tender heart. She sighed and sat back down.

"Benjamin was ordered to see you to the castle," he said as he shrugged an apology. "*He* was forbidden from taking any direct action against Mouthrot or Shreb, not me."

Rebecca slapped the table so hard that her scream was more from the sting in her hand than her outrage at what her guardian intended on doing. "That's because he thinks you're in a dungeon!"

Odie set the pot down and slipped out the door. She pressed her hand into her skirt, hoping to squeeze all the pain from it. The Lieutenant tried to adjust the strap of his missing eye patch but bit his lip and scraped his hand against his stubble instead. She knew he missed his eye patch now. He couldn't hide behind it.

"What are you planning to do to Mouthrot?" She stepped closer to him until she could make out the dirt outline of his old eye patch.

"Nothing. I swear."

Rebecca guffawed.

"I'll just keep an eye on him. Plus, I can create a diversion or throw his men off your trail—if needed." He scratched the back of his head. "I can protect you better from here."

All her words locked together in her chest as if she had a dam in her heart and nothing could get through. She was going to burst. Too many thoughts, too many feelings were flowing in, and there was no way for them to get out. She didn't know how she felt about this, which only made the whole thing worse. Hadn't she wanted something just like this? A chance to be on her own? Now that she got what she wanted, it didn't feel as wonderful as she'd hoped. She felt something tear inside her. She slapped the table again and stormed out of the little house. The pressure in her chest twisted into a point that stabbed her heart.

Odie ducked against the post where Rina was tied. There was nowhere for Rebecca to go, even for a minute. She collapsed against the house. Odie scrambled back inside for his breakfast. Rebecca closed her eyes and refused to cry or scream. Instead she focused on the warmth of sun on her face. *It was going to be a hot day again.* She tugged on her braid until she felt the pain of it. The pressure in her chest ebbed enough that she could breathe again. She thought of her mother and father and wished she could ask them if this was the life they wanted for her.

TWENTY SIX

*B*enjamin and Denny couldn't pretend they were asleep once they heard the Lieutenant declare that Benjamin would take Rebecca to the castle. Benjamin had read the letter, so he knew he would be going with her. But the image of him and her alone trekking across the Thieves' Plain was unsettling. Benjamin had assumed the Lieutenant would lead them. He glanced briefly at Denny, feeling the flame from his glare. It was easy to guess that Denny would have liked that honor to be his. After the yelling stopped, the door slammed. Benjamin stood up, only to have the ground (or rather, Denny's legs) pulled out from underneath him.

"Get off!" Denny shoved Benjamin back to his cot. "Lieutenant, sir. You can't have Benjamin alone with Rebecca. That can't be safe."

The Lieutenant leaned back in his chair, his hands over both eyes. He peeked at Denny and sat up. The Lieutenant looked spent. This last couple of weeks had wrung them all near dry, but the Lieutenant was the only one to sit in a dungeon for part of it.

"You're right, Denny. Maybe you should go too." The Lieutenant studied the bowl of porridge Odie set in front of him and then peered at Denny.

Denny blinked, unsure if he'd won or lost the argument. "You want us to leave you alone?"

"I've got Odie and a horse." The Lieutenant's eyes strayed to Benjamin as he stumbled to the table. "That will be enough for what I need to do."

Odie set bowls down for everyone including Rebecca, who was still cooling off outside. Benjamin nodded his thanks to Odie, who shrugged and dug into his bowl.

"I envy you," Benjamin said, getting a smile from the Lieutenant as well as Odie. Denny scowled at him and stabbed his breakfast with his spoon. The room quieted as they ate their breakfast. Rebecca marched back in with an abundance of determination, more than what was needed to eat breakfast. Benjamin kept an eye on her; he had a feeling his very life might be in danger.

She pressed her faded skirt flat against her lap as she sat. She looked across the table at the Lieutenant, who stopped midbite to raise his eyebrows. *Yes?* She nodded and began to eat in a formal manner that made everyone at the table squirm in his seat. Odie refilled bowls. Rebecca plastered a smile on her face and ate.

The Lieutenant finished his breakfast and waved off Odie's offer of thirds. He rubbed the back of his head, hesitating as he looked at everyone at the table.

"Odie, you're going to stay here with me. You can run messages for me and keep your eyes open."

The giant brother lifted his head and nodded. He looked relieved. Benjamin guessed Odie preferred to work alone (or at least away from Rebecca). *But don't we all?* Benjamin thought.

"Denny will make sure Benjamin and Rebecca get to the castle safely." The Lieutenant paused to emphasize the importance of Denny's part.

Benjamin shoved his bowl back, folded his arms, and tried to look at the Lieutenant, but settled for the old man's hands instead, which were tracing the edge of the table. The Lieutenant didn't speak. Benjamin glanced up, only to be met by his father's uneven gaze. His black eye sucked Benjamin in. *The man really needs to put his eye patch back on, Benjamin thought, unsettled by the scrutiny.*

"I'll take Rebecca to the castle, if that is what you want." He shrugged and tugged on a hangnail.

"It's going to need to be more than just taking Rebecca to the castle, I think."

Benjamin sagged into his chair and peered into his father's black eye. What more could the Lieutenant expect from him? Black-Eyed Barnaby's death had been his guiding star. In the world of villainy, a dead father was far more desirable than a living one. He didn't know what to do with a living father. He'd never dreamed his father was alive, ever. And yet, here he was, sitting with his father, a spy for the king and the guardian to the heir to the throne of Lam, and plotting against the archvillain he'd dreamt of serving. No one could dream this.

The Lieutenant sighed. "If you were king, what would you do about Mouthrot?"

Benjamin raised his eyebrows. "I would have already sent troops in and razed the whole fortress. Left nothing standing."

Denny rolled his eyes with a groan. He'd already explained why that was a bad idea. Any direct action by the king would shatter the treaty King Aldo's father had made. The Lieutenant ignored Denny's objections.

"Why?" the Lieutenant asked.

"Because a man who killed my brother and sent an assassin against my sole heir is not a risk that should be tolerated." Benjamin shrugged. "If word got out how successful Mouthrot was at nearly destroying the royal family, the risk to Lam would be more than breaking a treaty. The people would lose faith in King Aldo's sovereignty."

The old man grinned back, lifting his chin high. He didn't look quite as old when he smiled like that. Benjamin focused on a glob of porridge on the table.

"You can't let an enemy like that live," Benjamin said. "Everyone in the Thieves' Plain knows that."

Rebecca looked up, wide-eyed, seeing the truth of Benjamin's words. Denny rubbed his chin, uncomfortable with the change of wisdom. Benjamin smirked. It hit him: *this was why the Lieutenant needed him—a native who could explain the Thieves' Plain to gentry.*

"That is exactly what the king needs to hear." The old man continued to smile, his dark eye sparkling. "The Thieves' Plain is a foreign place. His counselors have never understood its differences or its similarities. There are rules older and deeper than any treaty. You are a native of this land, Benjamin. You will not be blinded by Lam's fears and misunderstandings."

Benjamin laughed at this. He stood up and strode around the table. Rebecca watched him intently while Denny watched Rebecca. Benjamin liked the idea that the king needed a true villain to lead him and Lam to safety. It tickled him deeply. This was an opportunity he wouldn't dream of passing up.

Odie cleared the bowls to make room for the map the Lieutenant pulled from his pack. Benjamin focused on the Lam side of the map. He'd never dreamt of crossing the divide marked by the Sunrise Mountains in the north and Waldren's Wood in the south. Both cursed places held the last remnants of magic in the world. Goose bumps tingled down his arms. *Oh Great Wolves! Maybe this is what I was really meant to do!*

He met the black eye of the Lieutenant's gaze and didn't flinch. *This was just a man who needed his skills,* he realized. That was something Benjamin could work with.

The Lieutenant turned his mismatched eyes to Rebecca and cleared his throat. "We need to talk about disguises."

TWENTY SEVEN

The road was hot and Benjamin's stomach was empty. He glanced at Denny, who also looked miserable, but neither dared complain. Rebecca was in a mood to drive them all into the ground. She rubbed at the frayed edges of her recently cropped hair and marched unhampered by a skirt.

The Lieutenant had declared that hats could fall off, so he pulled out the scissors and cut her braids off. Brave man! Rebecca stared straight ahead, not saying a word. Even now, she remained silent, but Benjamin could see the tension screaming through her body. It drove her faster than their apprehension did.

Benjamin's feet were killing him, and he was sure he was about to collapse. He looked at Denny, who nodded. Agreed, they would be allies in this. Denny pulled out his waterskin just as Benjamin called Rebecca's new name. *"Bernie!"*

She halted as her new name struck her and turned. Her face was red and streaked with sweat and dirt, but she nodded in agreement, her fatigue finally catching up to her.

Denny sighed in relief. "I see a tree over there. We can get out of the sun for a while."

Rebecca followed stiffly, but softened as she settled under the tree to drink and eat alongside them.

Oh, the relief! Benjamin was tempted to take his boots off, but was pretty sure he'd never get them back on again. Instead, he put his feet up on a rock and chewed on his apple. Rebecca drank slowly and chewed thoughtfully on some dried meat. Denny offered his own apple to her and she waved it off absently.

"I haven't seen my uncle in a very long time," she said. She tapped her hat against her waterskin, a sign of nerves Benjamin had not anticipated. Her hair was plastered down in the front and stood up in the back.

Denny scanned the horizon as he drank.

Benjamin reassured her between bites. "Once he hears about your near-death experience, the daughter of his beloved brother, you'll have him wrapped around your finger. If nothing else, tears are very helpful."

"Tears? I can't let anyone at court, especially his advisors, think I'm some fragile flower. My life depends on how I present myself at court. I may not want the throne, but I certainly do not want to spend the rest of my days a prisoner in the castle—or dead."

"Ah, I see." Benjamin perked up at the idea of the intrigue in court life. "You're right, of course. Though, many women have used tears as a shield to hide their more dangerous weapons." He wiped the apple juice from his chin.

"Didn't I hear that your uncle might marry again?" Denny asked. "That there was a duchess or some young noblewoman he was interested in?"

Rebecca nodded. "It's one of the reasons the Lieutenant tried to persuade the king to let me receive my education elsewhere. The

Lieutenant volunteered his estate in the east country, since a new queen might see me as a threat," she said with a shrug.

"Just tell her you don't want the throne," Denny said, glancing back at Rebecca.

"That might make her more suspicious." Benjamin scowled. "You would have to show her you're not a threat by becoming either her strongest supporter…or the most useless."

Rebecca frowned, rubbing her hands through her short hair.

"Mention within earshot of her spies how dull court life is and how you long for the country life." He inspected his apple core for a good place to bite. "Act dispassionately about the whole thing, but remain loyal to Aldo. Keep your head down."

Rebecca chewed for several minutes on her lunch as she thought about what Benjamin had said. Facing a near-murder had a positive effect on her, Benjamin decided. The fact that she was listening to him right now without biting his head off was a good sign. Denny bit into his apple and squeezed his brows together. Benjamin closed his eyes. He focused his attention on the weak breeze against his sweaty skin. The thrumming of distant horse hooves caused him to bolt upright. His travel companions looked around in alarm.

"Just lay down." Benjamin tipped his hat over his face and rested his head on his pack. "They may pass by if we don't give them anything to inspect."

Rebecca and Denny relaxed stiffly.

"Remember, *Bernie*," Benjamin said, out the side of his mouth. "We're on our way to our cousin's place. Sick family. Et cetera."

They felt the hooves strike the ground next to them as dust billowed over them. One horse passed by, but the second one stopped abruptly. Dust fell on them like rain.

"Hey!"

Benjamin pushed up his hat with one lazy finger. Pretending fatigue was easy. He hoped his pounding heart wasn't visible through his shirt.

"What are you doing so far off the road?" said a gruff voice. A tall man leaned forward in his saddle, the dust on his face cracked by the deep lines in his face.

The first horse trotted back over.

"The dusty road?" Benjamin coughed and fanned the dust away from his face. His gut twisted as he recognized the man from the Lieutenant's hideout. He forced his body to relax, focusing on how tired he was. He didn't look at Rebecca.

"Hmm."

"We thought we'd save ourselves some miles and cut across country."

"Just the three of you, then?" A stout thug joined them.

"Yep," Benjamin said, lowering his cap but keeping an eye on the men. *These men were idiots,* he reminded himself. If Rebecca didn't panic, they'd get out of this fine. "Don't worry; we're just passing through."

"Fine. See that you do," said the tall man.

"What's his problem?" The stout man pointed at Rebecca as she scrutinized the man's face, as if she was trying to place him.

Benjamin lifted his cap and peeked at Rebecca and scoffed, "Bernie's first time from home."

"Never seen two real-life baddies before, eh?" The stout man puffed his chest out in pride.

"Yeah, something like that." Benjamin turned his nervousness into annoyance. "Well, if we can't get peace and quiet around here, we might as well head out."

Denny and Rebecca sat up and rubbed their eyes. The tall one watched them for a moment, sneered, and waited for them to leave.

They pulled their bags on and looked around. *How to get around these marauders?* Benjamin decided the direct route was best.

"Dodger is this way, yeah?" He pointed past the men, who nodded. That was agreeable to them. A cloud of dust enveloped them.

"Stick to the roads around here if you don't want trouble!"

The men gestured in the direction of the main road and kicked their horses into motion. Benjamin coughed and waved the dust away.

"Do you think they have a point?" asked Rebecca, watching the men disappear. "Would we look less suspicious on the main road?"

"You're lucky you didn't get smacked talking to them that way," Denny said, shaking his head.

"I'm one of them. That's how we talk to each other," Benjamin glared back at Denny. "Less suspicious than *please* and *thank you.*"

Rebecca tugged her cap down. "Let's keep walking before they come back. I believe the road is this way."

"Okay," Benjamin said. "If we cut more this way, we'll join the road closer to the Gray Gander. We'll blend in better there."

"And if we run into these guys again?" Denny said.

"We'll tell them we got turned around."

Denny rolled his eyes.

Life is harder with people who can speak for themselves, Benjamin thought smugly.

TWENTY EIGHT

The Gray Gander was more of an information stop than an inn. Any traveler would be better off sleeping under the stars than in the bat-infested rooms of the Gray Gander Inn. Benjamin had passed by there a few times on field trips from school to observe highwaymen and scoundrels.

"In and out. Surly and quiet. That's your type, remember?" Benjamin turned to Rebecca and Denny, who rolled their eyes and looked annoyed. "Right?"

"We *can't* answer, remember?" Rebecca said. "We're surly and silent."

Denny barked at the comment and inspected the Gray Gander.

"Excellent." Benjamin blushed. "Last time I was here, it was full of pickpockets, so watch your purses."

"That won't be an issue, since none of us has any money," Denny squeezed his eyebrows together. "So why are we going in there, then?"

"Well, to hear the news, mainly. See how the road is up ahead. Anywhere we should avoid?"

"Won't we look out of place not eating?" Denny asked.

"Eat? Here?" Benjamin laughed. "No, I wouldn't eat here unless I was near starvation, and then I'd still think about it. Blah. I'm not sure anyone actually eats here."

"Well, what do people do here?" Rebecca added.

"What most scoundrels and robbers do: drink until they rot a hole in their guts or can't walk straight. Sometimes, they also exchange information and stories."

The inside was surprisingly bare for an inn on a busy road. They found the sturdiest table, and the man behind the bar raised his head to look at them. Benjamin raised three fingers. The man nodded back.

"What are you doing?" Denny whispered. "We don't have any money."

"Speak for yourself." Benjamin patted a vest pocket.

"I'm not sure dousing ourselves in alcohol will help us," Rebecca said under her breath.

Benjamin leaned in. "This stuff is more like dirty water than alcohol. We'll be fine. Think of it more as a prop."

The man from behind the bar dropped three glasses of brownish liquid on the table. He scooped up the coins Benjamin left on the table.

"Innkeeper? Where are all the thugs?"

"Hmm," he sniffed through his heavy mustache. "The roads have been nearly empty the last two days. Men on horseback are blocking all roads in and out of Lam. Haven't you seen them?"

Denny and Rebecca nodded.

"Hurried you along then? If this is how Shreb *Junior* plans to run Thieves' Plain, he won't last long." The innkeeper returned to his bar and grimy rag.

"Hmmm." Benjamin scanned the room. "Any talkers?"

Rebecca fiddled with her glass and avoided eye contact. Denny picked at the table's chipped paint. He rolled his eyes.

Rebecca leaned forward and muttered, "What about that one? The one with the crunched hat?"

"The downtrodden one?" Benjamin asked.

"I know some people like to talk when they're sad. A sympathetic ear?" She pushed her untouched glass over. "He could use a drink."

In a show of chivalry, Denny offered her his drink. She waved him off and cupped her hands around an imaginary glass.

"Good luck," Denny said as he brought the drink to his mouth, but then thought better of it. He looked sullen. Benjamin scooped up the glasses and strolled to the sour man.

"You look like a man who could use another drink."

The man's deep lines smoothed for a moment and then returned to a grimace. "What are you selling? Trouble? No thanks!" He held up a large, calloused hand.

"Can't a villain offer to buy information with a drink without being accused of greater mischief?" Benjamin said cheerily. He added a wink for good measure.

"Hmm." The hand came down, and Benjamin set the glass beside him.

"You're the second man to accuse me of looking for trouble just for carrying on business."

"Oh? You ran into the Troublemaker Police too, then?"

Benjamin barked a sarcastic laugh and pretended to drink.

"Those knaves on horseback broke my cart," the man said. "I was carrying cabbages to Shreb's fortress. They trampled them into mush, saying no one wants cabbage!" The sour man threw back the glass that Benjamin gave him. "They were my best cabbages! I would have made a great profit across the border!"

"Why didn't you take them across the border? Shreb closer?"

"No, sir, he is not, but those same rascals won't let anyone cross the borders. That's why I went to Shreb's. A small profit is better than nothing, and that's what I have now. If I'd have stayed home, I would at least have cabbages to eat!"

The man looked so crestfallen, Benjamin slid his glass into the sour man's large hand. The cabbage farmer slung that one back too and nodded in thanks. Benjamin nodded back and left the man to his sorrow.

After a few casual questions, the innkeeper gave Benjamin a better idea where the trouble lay. Many of the regular peddlers who passed through on their travels had not been by in the last two days. The few that had gotten through without rough encounters were trappers and miners from the north.

The innkeeper stopped rubbing his bar and just stared at his empty inn. He didn't blink as they left.

"That was grim," Benjamin said as they walked from the Gray Gander.

"Grim?" Denny said. "A few more minutes in there and we'd all be slitting our throats."

"I don't understand," Rebecca said, following a step behind. "How does this system work for the peasants who live here? How can they support Shreb or any other tyrant when they are at the mercy of their capricious moods?"

"Not much different from a king, is it?" Benjamin whispered, signaling them to lower their voices.

"Only a bad one. King Aldo does take his subjects' interest into consideration. A king is responsible for the safety and well-being of the people, and in return, they support him and obey him. If they don't receive protection or are able to feed and clothe themselves, why would they continue to support and obey their king?"

"*Bernie*, let's make sure we're not being followed before we start talking *politics*. You never know what kind of trouble that could cause."

The sun was setting and shadows were growing long over the road. Benjamin led them down the road far enough to be out of sight of the Gray Gander and then into the tall grass. They wandered far enough away so that they wouldn't be overheard or visible from the road.

Benjamin motioned to stop. He circled around them, checking for eavesdroppers, and then returned and sat down. Denny lay down, not hiding his impatience with Benjamin.

"You can't imagine how many villains benefit from a hidden scoundrel in the right place," Benjamin shrugged. "Eavesdropping is one of the most popular classes at the Villains' Academy. There are people who make a living by sitting behind bushes and rocks all day."

Rebecca knelt down and tugged at her backpack. Denny bounced up to help her, but she held out her hand to stop him. "So what now? I'm guessing that the innkeeper had no better news than the cabbage farmer. We can't go back, and we can't wait for these marauders to give up either."

"Then I suggest we go forward."

Denny peered at Benjamin, raking his fingers through his hair. "That would put us in the path of the outlaws we're trying to avoid."

"I meant forward as in north."

"North?" Both Rebecca and Denny's heads jerked up.

"Well, the castle is north of here, sort of." Benjamin pulled out the map and smoothed it out between them. "We're here. Our destination is there. We go north first and then east."

"What about all these mountains?" Rebecca pointed out in the failing light.

"Yes, what about those?" Denny asked, chalking another mark against Benjamin in his head. "All the roads are being watched."

"And the spaces in between." Rebecca pointed vaguely.

"Only those that run between Shreb's and the border. But not the ones that run north." Benjamin smiled victoriously. No one returned that smile. "The innkeeper said the only steady business he was getting was from the miners and trappers in the mountains."

"You can't be serious," Denny exploded and then lowered his voice. "You can't be serious. You want to take Re—um, Bernie through the Sunrise Mountains? Through an area that is haunted by Great Wolves?"

"Only rumored to be haunted, but yes."

Denny sat up and blinked, speechless.

Rebecca wrung her cap. "Have you ever been through the mountains?"

"Well, it's just land that goes up and then back down again."

"Oh, never mind about the bears, giant wolves, and the *cold*."

"The Great Wolves are just myths. Plus, it's summer, not winter. It will be uncomfortable, but it won't kill us," Benjamin said, folding the map in half.

"Not to mention it will take longer," Denny grumbled.

"Longer than being caught by Mouthrot's men?" Benjamin said. "Listen, there is a pass through the Sunrise Mountains that is almost directly in line with Ulmer Castle. It will be a harder path but shorter than having to go all the way around, especially dodging marauders on horseback."

"We could go south."

"But how far south, Denny? You won't go through a pass in the Sunrise Mountains, but you *will* go through Waldren's Wood? The Cursed Forest of the Damned?"

Rebecca pressed her lips in a firm line before issuing her opinion. "I have no desire to see Waldren's Wood again anytime soon." Rebecca closed her eyes against a vision in her mind. "But I know the pass you are talking about. No one takes it because it is also cursed."

"No, Tagrin got cocky and walked into a blizzard, midwinter. Sure, he was a legendary warrior who couldn't get lost, blah, blah, blah." Benjamin pointed a finger at Rebecca and Denny. "Let that be a lesson to us all. Arrogance will get you killed."

"Thank you for the history lesson, but now it will be little more than a goat trail." Rebecca folded her arms across her chest. "How will we find it?"

"There is a lower pass—" Denny reached for the map.

"That's why they put a road through it." Benjamin was getting tired of this debate. It was obvious what needed to be done. "That road will be watched."

Denny growled. He got up and marched around them, his patience wearing thin. Denny had been agitated since leaving on this trip, untypically so. Maybe Denny resented Benjamin's position of authority, since Rebecca never seemed to annoy him.

Rebecca turned to Benjamin. "We'll start in the morning."

TWENTY NINE

*B*enjamin shivered awake. The sun was still not up, but he was too uncomfortable to sleep for another moment. He peeled himself off the cold ground, taking note of all the bruises on his back and hips from the iron-hard roots he'd slept on. He blew on his icy fingers as he listened to the sound of birds chirping to each other.

Denny groaned as he sat up, gripping a crick in his neck. Rebecca rubbed her arms through the blanket that was wrapped tightly up to her chin, her nose and cheeks red from cold.

"Do you think we could light a fire tonight?" Rebecca said through chattering teeth.

Denny pulled an extra pair of socks out of his pack and handed them to Rebecca, who accepted them with a blush. She dug a small jar out of her pack and offered to rub liniment on his neck. Denny unbuttoned his shirt and pulled it down to expose his shoulder, closing his eyes at the touch of her cold fingers as she worked the pungent ointment into his stiff muscles. Benjamin rolled his eyes at this and struggled to his feet.

"I hope so," Denny said, blowing on his blue fingers. "With the wildlife, we'll need one for sure."

"We'll need to reach the thicker trees, so it's not visible," Benjamin said, feeling Denny's glare more than seeing it. "I want a warm night's sleep as well, but we're only a day up. We don't want anyone going out of their way to check on a stray campfire light."

"I wore all my extra clothes last night, and it didn't help much." Rebecca pulled Denny's shirt back up and slid her jar back into her pack. "We could make a lean-to with more trees as well. It would definitely keep us warmer. Thank goodness it's summer."

"And in a few hours, we'll be sweating again." Denny helped Rebecca slide the gloves over her hands, a daffy grin on his face. "How can it be so hot during the day and still get that cold at night?"

Benjamin bit into a hard roll and wandered up the path, pulling out his book to make an entry:

Never flirt in front of others. You say and do stupid things. It's annoying to others.

By lunchtime, the hikers had shed their blankets and cloaks, and Rebecca had surrendered Denny's extra socks. They drank heavily from the waterskins that now hung uncomfortably light at their waists. They hoped the map was correct about the location of the next stream, but by the time the sun dipped behind their backs, they still hadn't found the elusive stream. They found a sheltered spot among some tall pines, with a wall of rock at their backs and started gathering firewood for warmth and protection against night predators. Rebecca weaved pine boughs into a shelter by the rock wall that still gave off heat from a day's worth of sun. Benjamin yearned for sleep already.

The boys stumbled through shady pines, picking up branches and sticks. By the time Benjamin's arms were half full, he found himself peering at an enormous set of paw prints that dwarfed his hand. Denny leaned silently over his shoulder to see what Benjamin had found.

"No point in mentioning it to Rebecca," Denny said, checking over his shoulder as he continued to pick up more wood.

Benjamin swallowed dryly but picked up his pace. Soon the ground became muddy, and he waved Denny over to the spring he'd found.

The boys filled their waterskins and pounded a few taller branches into the ground as markers. They'd want to refill their waterskins in the morning.

Rebecca was examining the finished shelter when they returned. Denny handed her a waterskin.

"You found a stream!" Rebecca said, gulping down the water. "Did you see any animal tracks?"

"Oh yes, plenty," Benjamin said as he dumped his firewood.

Denny glared at him.

"Um, I think we'll need a few more armfuls of wood." Benjamin ducked his head and strode in a new direction.

"Denny, you're best at fires," Rebecca said, pulling a pine needle from her hair. "I'll help Benjamin gather firewood."

Denny nodded stiffly.

"I hope we don't have too many days of this left," Rebecca said, wiping her face on the sleeve of her jacket. "I don't want the Lieutenant to start assuming the worst." Her shoulders sagged.

Benjamin kicked at a shattered stump and picked up the broken pieces.

"I know you don't think much of him, but that's because you don't know him. He does really care for all of us, including you." Rebecca straightened to rest her back. "I would give anything to have my parents back. Maybe you're not ready to see it yet, but you're lucky. Give the Lieutenant time."

A knot tightened in Benjamin's chest, as he thought about the shifting realities of his past and present. He had no idea what the future held, and it scared him. After a long silence, they turned back. Rebecca wrapped her cloak around her bundle and threw it onto her back. Benjamin frowned, wishing he'd thought of that.

A crackling ripped through the forest behind them. They froze and peered over their shoulders. Hair rose up on the back of Benjamin's neck as rabbits and deer scrambled out of the trees past them. Ice filled Benjamin's stomach as his caught sight of a bear-sized shadow, skulking toward them. Two eyes of moonlight peered out from the deepening gloom. Distant howls rang through the trees, and Benjamin spun around searching for more glowing eyes but found none. Then the hulking shadow was gone.

Rebecca's eyes bulged in her pale face. Denny erupted into the clearing holding a ready slingshot. Benjamin's knees swayed under him, and he dropped his load.

"Back to the fire!" Denny said, scanning the woods looking for signs of wolves.

Benjamin scraped his kindling off the damp ground and stumbled downhill after Rebecca and Denny, panting. *It was just a wolf, right?* Gooseflesh rippled down his arms.

Benjamin and Rebecca dropped their kindling on the pile and collapsed. Denny studied them as they stared at the fire for a moment before asking what happened.

"I'm not sure," Rebecca said, glancing at Benjamin and rubbing her arm. "We saw something big in the shadows, but—"

He shrugged, unwilling to speculate. He pulled out his waterskin. He wasn't sure if he had much of an appetite at the moment. His fingers shook as he fumbled with the stopper.

Denny fetched Rebecca's bag so that she could eat something and then gathered more stones for his slingshot. He demonstrated to both of them how to use it. A few loud cracks sounded as two rocks chipped the trunk of a tree not far off. He looked at Rebecca, who looked dazed, and then back to Benjamin for some kind of response.

Benjamin strode over and took the slingshot. A few of his shots nearly hit the tree he aimed at. Satisfied, he handed the slingshot back to Denny. Whatever they'd seen in the shadows was much wider than a tree.

THIRTY

Rebecca listened to Benjamin crawl into the shelter as she stared into the fire. She tried to remember everything she'd heard about the Great Wolves. Not much. Their names were just used in oaths anymore. No one spoke of them. No one believed in them, not even the Lieutenant, and he believed a lot of things others did not. An image of the pale, glowing eyes that she'd seen with Benjamin flashed into her mind. She shivered and closed her eyes, gripping her blanket tighter.

Denny stacked the wood onto the fire, his movements throwing shadows into the night. That was when the howls started. Each one ricocheted around them. She jumped and pressed her hand to her chest, her heart hammering to get out. Denny scanned the dark and gripped his slingshot with white knuckles. Finally he relaxed and pulled his extra socks out. He held them out so she could slip her hands inside, one at a time. He squeezed her fingers and then sat next to her, his leg resting against hers. The touch was comforting, and she made no effort to move away.

Denny stared into the fire, listening to the haunting chorus around them. She reached for an absent braid. They only had crickets on the Thieves' Plain.

"I heard once that Aldo had a treaty with the Great Wolves," Denny said, watching her from the corner of his eye as he buttoned his jacket. The frayed edges of his sleeves stood out against the firelight.

"I think it was his grandfather or great-grandfather." Again she reached for a braid that wasn't there, shaking her head. She let her hand fall into the blanket across her lap. "Aldo said that was why the wolf was our family crest. They helped clear Ulmer's path to the crown. That's all I know."

She pulled her knees into her chin as she watched the flames. "It's hard to believe the Great Wolves are just a story to strengthen a claim to the throne, when you're surrounded by howling mountain wolves."

Denny's gaze dropped when she looked up. He rubbed his hands on his pant legs and swallowed. A bubble of fireflies erupted in her chest, and her mouth was dry. She glanced at her waterskin but found her arms were unable to move.

The wolves stopped for air just then, leaving only the chirps of crickets around them. The night felt naked without the howling.

"Everything will be different when you get to the castle," Denny said, turning his face to hers. The fire lit his blond waves, creating a halo around his head.

She looked down at her hands. Of course things would be different, but she'd still need friends. She needed people she trusted. They were more precious than jewels or crowns in the royal world.

She looked up to tell him that, but then Denny's lips were on hers like a butterfly's wings. There and gone. Warmth spread through her face and into her chest. She pulled back, unable to breathe. His eyes reflected the fire back to her, full of the yearning that ached in her own heart. She felt herself leaning forward to meet his lips again. He smelled of tree sap and campfire, but there was *something* inviting underneath it. He brushed his thumb across her cheek and bent to take her kiss.

She could feel his breath against her lips just as her fingers brushed across the heavy locket. The warmth in her chest clenched into ice-cold panic, as she pulled her heart back into her chest. There was no future in this. He was her friend, and she couldn't do that to him. She was already married to whomever the king picked. She scooted back. He froze, his fingers marking the spot where her face had just been. Her arms and legs shook. He sat back, allowing the firelight to expose his pained expression. She closed her eyes as lists of potential suitors floated in her vision. Her chest ached as her heart clawed itself into a place of safety. She dropped Denny's blanket and crawled into the shelter with Benjamin. He snored, deep in his dreams, as she cowered against the wall of the shelter and shivered.

THIRTY ONE

*J*ust as the howls began to fade, Rebecca stumbled out into the twilight. She breathed in the sharp air and slapped her arms. A bird dared to call to its friends. She nodded at Benjamin, who clung white-knuckled to Denny's slingshot. She dropped her blanket next to him and ventured down the path to pull a large branch into the fire. Benjamin surrendered his weapon and crawled into the shelter, already asleep.

She dropped the splintered weapon on the pile of rocks and settled into the faintly warm spot that Benjamin had abandoned. She lifted her face to the sky, watching for the famous sunrises these mountains were named for. She could feel the warmth of the fire on her throat, but the fire couldn't reach the icy burning around her heart. A tremor began in her arms and then spread to the rest of her body. She pulled her knees into her chest in a vain attempt to silence her body. It wasn't until she felt the frosty tracks of tears on her cheeks that the trembling slowed. After several minutes or hours of tears falling unchecked onto her blanket, the shivers stopped, and the ache that pressed against her sternum slid to almost nothing as the last tear fell.

The sky awoke into violent pinks and fiery oranges above her. The birds stopped chirping in reverence to the rising sun. She breathed her heartache out to the morning light, praying that she could leave it here by this campfire to haunt the mountains alongside the wolves that cried to the moon at night.

THIRTY TWO

*B*enjamin awoke to the morning sun filtering through the door, barely touching the spot where Denny had slept the night before. Benjamin wrapped up his blanket, packed his gear, and pulled out some strips of dried meat. Rebecca met him with a cup of hot water.

"It's not much, but it will help warm you." Rebecca's cheery voice didn't quite ring true.

Benjamin thanked her and glanced at Denny, who sat looking at his own cup of steaming water, his shoulders slumped.

"Rough night," Benjamin said, standing by the smoldering embers of the night's fire. He wrapped his hands around the warm cup and scooted his toes closer to the white ash that still held some heat. He remembered the extra pair of Denny's socks in his pocket and handed them over, but Denny just let the socks fall to the ground and said nothing.

Benjamin glanced at Rebecca as she hiked off with all their waterskins. He sipped his warm water that tasted of damp wood. The jerky was tougher to chew in the frosty air.

✝ ✝ ✝

Benjamin stopped to take a drink and looked back at Rebecca as she struggled up the mountain. She seemed distant and unusually quiet this morning. Well, that was to be expected, as she got closer to the castle. She was about to become a princess in fact and not just in memory.

Benjamin wiped the sweat from his eyes, in order to examine Denny, who was leaving them farther and farther behind. While Denny didn't care about Benjamin's comfort, it was unusual for him to ignore Rebecca's. She was breathing heavily as she leaned against a rock and guzzled from her waterskin. Sweat dripped from her cap. Benjamin picked up a rock to judge its weight. If he threw it hard enough, would he be able to hit Denny with it? But Benjamin's arms felt too much like jelly. *Besides,* he thought, *that'd probably only provoke Denny into a fight—one I would definitely lose.*

"Denny is going to kill us before we get there," Benjamin said, letting the rock slip from his fingers. "If he keeps up this pace, I mean."

"I think he's just ready for this to be over," she said through panting breath, squeezing her eyes closed in pain.

They didn't stop again until they reached the top of the pass. Denny was waiting for them, his blue eyes blazing in his flushed face. The trail they followed had petered out into several rambling game trails. Denny had cut through in a straight line to the top. Benjamin and Rebecca had done their best just to keep him in sight.

Rebecca collapsed against a rock and wiped her face on her sleeve, unable to catch her breath. Benjamin's fingers felt thick and clumsy as he tried to open his waterskin, but a trickle of energy returned to him as he drank. Rebecca's face was ashen and slick with sweat. Dark circles hung under her eyes.

Benjamin started to get up, but Denny waved him off and went to her aid. He got her pack off and opened her waterskin for her. He wet a rag and gently placed it on the back of her neck. She looked a little green. Benjamin closed his eyes, no longer needing to worry about her. All the while, Denny murmured gently to her. Benjamin couldn't be sure, but it sounded like an apology as Denny fanned her with her cap.

THIRTY THREE

When Rebecca's color returned and her breathing steadied, Denny pulled out the map. He spread it on a table-like rock to study it, casting glances below him. Benjamin's legs felt like raw dough, but he crossed over to check on Rebecca, who was slowly chewing an apple. She opened her eyes as he approached and nodded that she was fine. Benjamin rewet the cloth wrapped around Rebecca's neck and then joined Denny, whose face had returned to its natural color.

Together they found their location on the map and looked for a way down. No visible path existed to the castle, so they'd probably have to pick their own way through the rocks. It was a shorter distance down but much steeper.

Denny pointed out a route below them that he thought would work best. "I think once we get past that outcropping, we should be able to see some sign of the castle or at least the main road below," he said. "If not, we'll know we strayed too far."

Benjamin looked over at Rebecca, who looked wilted, though most of her color had returned. She had finished her apple and was resting with her waterskin in her lap. Benjamin nodded in her direction. "Maybe you should check it out first?"

Denny nodded curtly, and Benjamin flinched. He hadn't wanted his suggestion to sound like a reprimand, but it had. Ducking his head, he slid down next to Rebecca. Denny flung his waterskin over his shoulder and strode away. Benjamin sighed and closed his eyes. There wasn't much in the way of shade up here.

"Everything okay?" Rebecca peeked out one eye.

"Just dandy. Denny went to look for the best way down. We don't want to backtrack."

Rebecca agreed weakly and then apologized for Denny.

"He's not your fault," Benjamin said. Feeling any better?"

"Fine. Just tired."

He adjusted his cap to shield the sun from his face and took inventory of the aches and pains that had welled up under his fatigue. Where did Denny get his drive so far into their journey? Benjamin shouldn't complain. They would still be climbing right now if some sort of demon hadn't taken hold of Denny this morning.

Benjamin jerked his head up at the sound of heavy tread approaching. He blinked the sleep from his head as Denny jogged toward them. He looked pleased but grimaced for a moment as he eyed Rebecca. "I found a trail below—and a patrol."

"Is the patrol coming up or going down?" Rebecca asked, standing stiffly.

Denny grabbed her pack and emptied some of her gear into his pack and handed it back. Rebecca did not complain.

"They were headed back down. Did you want to catch them?" He looked over his shoulder. "Or I could?"

Rebecca shook her head. "We'll be there soon enough. When we get there, I'll have to declare myself."

Denny snapped his head forward and set a gentle pace. They followed silently, keeping an eye on the steep drop.

How could they convince King Aldo to cross the boundary? King Zavier set that boundary in a treaty with the archvillain Val the Foul. The land west of the Sunset Mountains and Waldren's Wood would belong to the thieves. That decision changed the fabric of the country, tore it in half. But had there really been peace since the treaty? The only way that would happen was by ending the archvillain's reign.

Benjamin had slowed so much that Rebecca asked Denny to wait for him. He tried to drink away the sick feeling in his stomach.

They found the trail and followed it down to a stone hut just large enough to house a handful of men through a snowstorm. A soldier wearing the gray and blue of King Aldo stepped out and stretched. His eyes fell on them, locking him in a strange pose before Rebecca could step in front of Denny. She removed her cap, tousled her hair, and stood with more regal power than such a taxing trip should allow.

"I am Princess Reyna Brynn Rae Ulmer, daughter of Prince Evan and niece to the king." She raised her chin. "I believe King Aldo is expecting me."

At this, the guard's eyes widened, and he nearly fell over. He fumbled with the horn on his belt and then sounded three short bursts, bringing another guard from inside. This new guard's uniform was disheveled, and he had porridge on his chin. He nearly dropped his sword when he saw the three bedraggled youths standing at his doorstep.

Rebecca sighed and then reminded them it was customary to bow to a princess.

THIRTY FOUR

*R*ebecca wasn't sure if she felt relieved or enraged that her reunion with Aldo was delayed. She was dropped at the foot of some clerk while the king was in conference with his nobles.

He flicked a bored eye over her ill-fitting britches and ragged cloak. He then sneered at her dirty hair that would no longer lay flat. Yet she held herself all the more proudly. She hadn't seen her uncle in years. She doubted he would recognize her even if she were dressed as a princess.

She silenced Benjamin when he offered to explain things to the clerk, who inspected the underling smugly. The worn state of the clerk's cuffs suggested he wasn't important. His wiry fingers tugged at his cap. He motioned to her to speak. The clerk blotted his quill and then smoothed the paper. Silence filled the room. Benjamin cleared his throat, while Denny examined the ends of his cloak, both glancing at her sideways.

This is ridiculous! she raged silently. Her heart pounded in her chest. She was not about to give this *nobody* any piece of the story that had kept her alive for more years than this underling had worked in the castle. She dropped her pack loudly to the floor and pressed both fists into her hips. Both boys fidgeted nervously behind her. She glared pointedly at the dull clerk.

"If you will not let me see my uncle, the king, who requested my presence, then perhaps you might let Branwen, the master of spies, know I carry an urgent message from the Lieutenant." She folded her arms over her chest.

The clerk blinked down at her from his perch. "The Lieutenant?" he said, sneering as he set his quill down. "Fairy tales and legends will not get you an audience with my master Branwen, let alone the king. Besides, Secretary Branwen is also in conference and cannot be disturbed."

Rebecca stepped forward, squeezing her fists until her nails dug into her flesh, trying to resist the urge to climb up there and strangle this fool.

A woman's gentle voice broke the stalemate. "Perhaps I could be of assistance." It was not a question but a statement of fact.

Rebecca turned to face a gray-haired woman who stood with the authority of one used to being obeyed. The old woman raised a well-shaped eyebrow as she took stock of Rebecca with her sharp eyes. Her dark, heavy skirts rustled across the hushed room, and Rebecca examined the woman in return. There was something familiar about the way the woman pursed her lips. Rebecca noted a silver scar that poked out from her hair just above her ear.

"Let me see your hands." The woman held out two well-manicured hands.

Rebecca hesitated, aware of the roughness of her own.

"Oh, these are not the hands of a lady!" the woman said, tracing the calluses of Rebecca's hands with her fingers. "I see that the Lieutenant has been teaching you swordplay instead of needlework."

The smirk slid off the clerk's face as he went ashen.

"And you really need to stop chewing your nails. A lady is judged harshly by the state of her hands." The woman's brown eyes softened with budding tears. "Do you not remember me?" she asked, gently cupping Rebecca's dirty face. "I see that you have turned into a young woman in my absence. And I? I've turned old."

The deep lines of the woman's face shifted as she smiled, stripping away the hardness of her face. As kindness bloomed on the woman's face, warmth wrapped its arms around her heart. How did this gray-haired woman know her? Rebecca hardly knew anyone outside of the Lieutenant and Denny's brothers. Oh, and Benjamin. Could she have known her before she moved to the Thieves' Plain?

"Nurse Dally?" Rebecca burst out, clutching the woman in her arms. The old nurse smelled of soap and lavender, stirring deep memories of nursery songs and garden walks. Tears stung her eyes.

"Princess Reyna!" Nurse Dally held her at arm's length, smiling. "You smell awful! Let's find you and your friends a bath and clean clothes."

"Separate baths, I hope," Benjamin said, winking.

Rebecca closed her eyes, praying that somehow no one else had heard that. Nurse Dally merely smiled sourly at Benjamin and led them away from the bewildered clerk.

THIRTY FIVE

The bathwater was the perfect temperature and smelled of sweet violets. The old nurse scrubbed and admired her. She told happy stories of a time she had nearly forgotten. Rebecca laughed and cried. *Is this what happy felt like?* She couldn't remember. Dally combed through her hair, clucking loudly about its shortness.

"I know the danger was great, but such short hair?" Dally shook her head and puckered her lips in deep thought. "What am I going to do with it? There's nothing to work with!" She met Rebecca's eyes in the mirror and sighed. "We'll just have to start a new fashion—or bring back an old one."

Dally twisted and pinned her hair, hoping it would dry into curls. After the bath was done, she sent for Rebecca's childhood favorite: sweet buns. Rebecca devoured nearly a whole plate, along with spiced berries, soft cheeses, and cold chicken. It was a simple meal for a princess, but indulgent for the simple life Rebecca had lived for so long.

Her eyes roamed over and over the opulence of the rooms. Dally assured her that these were her parents' rooms, and now they were hers. She remembered nothing of fine linens, soft beds, decadent foods, and servants coming and going. The idea felt more like a story someone had made up than her actual birthright. A part of her knew what to do and what to expect, but most of her was in shock. *How was this ever my life?*

"Wow, you must have been really dirty!" Benjamin said, closing the door quietly. "Looks like you just got out."

A warmth rose in her voice. "It was the strategy session we had for my hair! *Or the lack of it!*"

Benjamin merely shrugged. "Hair grows back. Heads do not."

Rebecca rolled her eyes and huffed through the flash of heat on her cheeks. "What do you want?"

"Just checking in. Denny is about as pleasant as a headache right now. So, of course, I thought of you," Benjamin said with a chuckle.

"Oh, Denny." Rebecca closed her eyes, thinking of the campfire.

"Surprisingly, he's not enjoying his time in the castle."

Rebecca turned a questioning look toward him as Benjamin picked through the dishes of food on Rebecca's table. *Does he know?* She slapped his greedy hand away too late.

"I'm not sure being a profitable farmer or merchant will be enough for him now, do you?" He bit into a sweet bun. His eyes widened in enjoyment. "You and the Lieutenant ruined all those dreams for him."

Rebecca bit her thumb and nodded. Benjamin was astute, but he couldn't possibly understand how complicated her relationship with Denny was.

"What are you doing in a lady's room?" Dally gasped, entering the room carrying gowns for Rebecca in her arms. She staggered around to find an acceptable place to set them down. Meanwhile, Benjamin looked around, confused. Rebecca threw a napkin at him in disgust at having to clarify who the lady was.

Dally herded him out into the hallway, a gray strand falling from her elegant twist. Rebecca could hear her shrieking about decorum. She then hurried back into the room, appalled that Rebecca would let a young man into her rooms unattended and while only in her dressing gown. It took several minutes to assure Dally that she had not let Benjamin in. Now that Benjamin was thoroughly educated in the matter, it definitely wouldn't happen again.

They settled on a lavender dress that had to be put on in two pieces. Thankfully it was well suited for summer; its fabric was light and soft, as opposed to heavy winter dresses. Dally pulled out the pins that released unruly corkscrew curls all over her head. With a few silver combs in place, Dally tamed them. Tingles rippled across her arms when she looked in the mirror.

"I look like a girl!"

She turned and examined the flowing skirt that trailed behind her. Dally leaned over and wrapped a silver chain around her neck. A wolf ran midstride within the chain and rested just above the locket with her parents' initials.

In the sitting room, Benjamin paced back and forth in front of the guards. Denny slouched, tracing the pattern on his chair. Both boys stopped to look at her as she entered the room. Denny staggered up and then bowed. Benjamin just gawked until Dally cleared her throat a few times, and then he also tipped forward. Dally kept an icy stare on him, freezing the words that he was about to utter on his lips.

Rebecca nodded, releasing them from their bows. They both wore borrowed military suits. The cut flattered Denny's broad shoulders and athletic build. The blue and gray set off his eyes and blond waves perfectly. He looked like a soldier. *Whereas Benjamin*, she noted with a knowing smile, *just looks out of place.*

There was a commotion in the hallway outside her door. A man wearing elegant ochre robes with sandy-blond hair burst into the room. His finely groomed beard showed signs of white. He looked nearly as fit as the Lieutenant, though a deep crease marked his brow. He just stared at her, his hazel eyes burning with unnamable emotions. Would her father have looked like that?

A hunched man in black robes with startling white hair entered behind him and gestured for the guards to wait outside. With the click of the door, the king strode across the room. He embraced her, tears brimming in his eyes. Rebecca pressed her face into his warm chest, her throat pricking with unshed tears. Would her father have hugged her like this?

"Oh, Reyna, I was so near to accepting that the worst had happened to you." His eyes reddened, but tears did not fall as he gripped her hands. "How much you look like your mother! So beautiful!"

The knot in her throat kept her from speaking. She could only smile in response.

"Forgive me for not meeting you when you arrived. I was in counsel and had ordered no one to disturb us." The king's eyes were eager for news of Rebecca's adventures. "No news of your guardian?"

"He escaped." Rebecca swallowed. No need to go into all the details. "He stayed behind to watch Mouthrot and Shreb."

"But he let you come ahead alone?" Aldo's eyes flared green.

"No! I came with Benjamin, as you ordered." Rebecca placed a calming hand on his chest. The king looked past Rebecca and scrutinized the two young men standing behind her. "And Denny. They are both proven and loyal friends."

"They are mere boys!" The king tugged on his tunic as he looked to his secretary for an explanation. The crook-backed man narrowed his eyes at the boys.

Benjamin and Denny both bristled at the description. Dally laid a firm hand on Benjamin's shoulder to silence his protest. He raised his chin higher but did not speak.

"Benjamin and Denny allowed me to travel discreetly across the Thieves' Plain when all roads were closed by Mouthrot's men!" Her heart pounded in her ears, and she knotted her hands together to keep them from trembling. "Mouthrot had sent an assassin after me. I escaped unharmed, but marauders were combing the countryside looking for me."

"How did Mouthrot know anything about you?" With firm hands on her shoulders, King Aldo turned Rebecca to face him.

Breathless and dizzy, Rebecca glanced toward Benjamin, whose eyes were focused elsewhere. She took a step toward Aldo. "I've also come here to let you know that this danger is aimed at you as well. Mouthrot wants the throne."

The king furrowed his brow at her, deepening the line that was already there. He was unimpressed with her clumsy dodge of his question, but she refused to admit defeat. She was safe now, and that was all he was going to know. He smoothed his beard with his long fingers and glanced toward his secretary.

"Yes, well, there is always danger aimed at the king." He tried to peer into Rebecca's silence for answers. He looked far away for a moment before he returned his attention to Rebecca. "Please don't think that I do not take your warning seriously. Mouthrot should always be taken seriously, even when he's supposed to be dead, apparently."

Aldo turned an eye to the black-robed man, running a finger down his beard. "There's little I can do. I cannot simply march into the

Thieves' Plain without upsetting the fragile balance of my kingdom. Lam is teetering more than usual at the moment."

King Aldo turned to the young men, while pulling Rebecca gently to his side.

"Forgive my alarm. I've had great anxiety about the princess's safety. She is the only family I have left and is ultimately my responsibility. I took a great risk allowing her to dwell so far away from me. Thank you, Benjamin and Denny, for bringing the princess safely here."

She let out a breath as she watched them bow in return. Benjamin tapped his chin in thought, however. Heavy bands squeezed around her chest.

"Your Majesty." Benjamin bowed again. "It is an honor to meet my father's greatest supporter."

Rebecca bit her lip and forced a smile as she glared a warning. But Benjamin kept his eyes focused solely on the king, ignoring her silent pleas to shut his mouth.

"Your father?" The king glanced at his secretary.

"The man we all so affectionately call the Lieutenant," Benjamin said.

The king's face went slack, and his hunched secretary swooped to his elbow. After a brief whispered conversation, he addressed Benjamin in a low voice. "So Torrin has a son after all. He must be greatly relieved to have found you. Welcome. We must strongly urge you to not speak any of his names here in the castle." His eyebrows knitted together. "Unfortunately, secrecy is sometimes needed for the security and stability of the kingdom."

"A kingdom held loosely together with butcher's string. It is the unstable relationship between Lam's two halves that is the greatest threat to the kingdom's security and stability." Benjamin lifted his chin, pressing his shoulders back. "Forgive me for speaking plainly. This may be my only audience with you, and this must be said."

The secretary stepped from the king's shadow to scold Benjamin, but the king raised his hand.

"While the kingdom of Lam claims the Thieves' Plain, no one there recognizes its authority over them, since Lam is silent through all of their suffering." Benjamin leaned forward onto his toes and held the king's gaze. "All revolves around whatever tyrants sit highest on their self-made thrones. The peasants suffer under the whims of archvillains at war—villains, I might add, your father exiled to the plain in a desperate attempt to save his crown from the noblemen who plotted tirelessly against him. King Zavier hoped they would destroy each other, which they did. But now, the few left over can focus their attention back to the king's throne.

Benjamin took a breath. "And while many may laugh at Shreb, I assure you his goals are just as ambitious as Mouthrot's. There will be all-out war in this country. It is time to end the cease fire and purge the infection before it kills us all."

Rebecca felt King Aldo's arm stiffen against her shoulders throughout Benjamin's speech. Her own hands were clenched into fists at her side, dreading every word he said, but even more afraid of his silence. Something horrible would happen once he was finished.

The king's arm fell from Rebecca's shoulder as he stepped a mere breath away from Benjamin. Aldo was a good head taller than the young man, but Benjamin met the king's gaze without flinching.

"I am not a thief, and I will hold to the letter of the law!" Aldo stepped back to examine Benjamin. "Where did your father find you? Where did you learn such a complete lack of respect when standing before your king and lord?"

"I graduated with honors from the Villains' Academy, Your Majesty." Benjamin bowed with extra flourish.

THIRTY SIX

It was a surprisingly quick trip to the dungeons. The cells simply weren't deep enough to be cold and damp. When he got out of here, he would have to suggest improvements.

Benjamin sighed and pulled out his notebook to sketch a map of the dungeons for later reference. If working for the king only got people ignored and overlooked, it was surprising that everyone hadn't turn to villainy. At least people listened as you demanded their purses and personal property at knifepoint. Benjamin sat on the cot, but Denny shoved him off.

"You just couldn't keep your mouth shut?" Denny growled. "If we swing for this, I'll kill you."

"Relax. Look how clean these cells are. We'll be fine." Benjamin rubbed his arm. It still stung. "At the worst, he'll toss us out, and we'll head back to the Lieutenant. Then we can really get things done."

Denny groaned and flopped down on the cot. "I'm sure ending up in the king's dungeons is just another rung on the ladder for you. But for me...oh, just shut up!" Denny turned sharply to the wall.

"No, ending up in a dungeon is typically a bad thing, unless you escape. A great escape story can open doors! But in our case, it would only make things worse for us." Benjamin flipped to a blank page.

"Do you think?" Denny's voice was muffled in the sleeve of his shirt.

"Which is too bad because I think I could get out of here."

"Shut up!"

"I wonder how many different ways I could escape. It's always a good idea to have a backup plan."

Denny spun around and stared at Benjamin, livid. "Yes, please escape so I can have silence!"

Benjamin sat down and leaned against the bars, tucking his book away to examine Denny, who was bent over with his hair gripped in his fists. "Why don't we talk about why you're really upset?" He casually inspected his nails.

"You mean I'm not really upset about being thrown into the dungeons because of your mouth?" Denny glared up at him.

"You weren't in a dungeon as we climbed over the mountain. Or were you?" Benjamin laced his fingers together and set them in his lap.

Denny's eyes went cold. "Shut! Up!" He jumped up and paced, clenching and unclenching his fists.

Benjamin swallowed. Hopefully, things wouldn't come to blows. Denny definitely had the advantage there.

Well, they were going to be here for a while. Benjamin could wait for the vein in the older boy's neck to stop bulging. He leaned back and closed his eyes. Were all good guys in denial of their base desires? Admit them and move on. Before any good villain could do anything, he had to acknowledge his desires, come up with a plan, and then work the plan.

As he waited, Benjamin examined the bars, the hinges, and the lock. He cataloged their resources, which included their clothes, the cot, a blanket—and the key in his pocket. The guards were so quick to throw him in the dungeons that no one thought to check his pockets. *Big mistake.* He probably wouldn't need it, since Rebecca would get them released eventually. While Benjamin definitely drove her crazy, she liked Denny. So he worked out several plans.

Breakfast was a simple fare of cabbage soup and bread. If word got out how nice it was down here, people from the Thieves' Plain would line up to offend the king.

Denny chewed silently, staring at the bars.

"Denny, what's bothering you?" Benjamin sighed. He was bored of mapping out escape plans.

"I'm not talking about it with you!" Denny scowled.

"I'll just say it then." Benjamin took a breath and waited. "Fine. Your future plans hit an unexpected wall. As the heir apparent, Rebecca is out of your reach."

Denny's back went rigid. Benjamin smiled and tried to look sympathetic.

"I can't stand seeing you so glum. Aldo looks to be in good health and not so old. He could marry again. There have been rumors. Any offspring would naturally bump Rebecca out of the running. And so what if Rebecca becomes queen? She makes the rules, right?"

Denny turned to him. His face twisted in an attempt to lock his emotions out of sight.

"You're going to sit there and act like you—the *great* Benjamin—don't care? That you don't care for *Rebecca*...or for the Lieutenant? You've just walked into this perfect situation. The long-lost son found just in time to fit into a role complete with future bride, titles, and land, with a father who has wanted only one thing for many years?

That would be you, by the way." His voice shook. He looked down at the stone floor. "And you're just going to walk away from it all, aren't you? All those things that you don't want but I do."

Jealous? Of Benjamin? "I'm not interested in Rebecca. Plus, she's connected to the crown." Benjamin threw his hands up in the air. "Besides, she has no interest in me."

"Are you so sure about that?"

"Yes! We've come to a mutual respect for our dislike of each other. Trust me. She's all yours."

"That's not what I see."

"Well, *you're* crazy!"

Benjamin kicked all the straw across the floor into a pile and sat down on it. He clenched his fists until his fingernails dug into his flesh. His jaws ground into a locked position. What did Denny know about his life and what options he should or should not embrace? How did everything get so messed up in such a short time?

The next time I see a one-eyed old man, Benjamin admitted grimly, *I'm running the other way.*

THIRTY SEVEN

After what seemed like hours, the guard showed up with the king's black-robed secretary, who was introduced as Secretary Branwen. To cover his excitement, Benjamin lowered his head meekly. He tried to look bored.

Denny stood up. The secretary paused to examine them. The guard brought in another lantern. The man's robes rustled across the floor as he circled around the young men. Benjamin stood so that the man could see him better. With his hunch, Branwen was at eye level with Benjamin. The secretary stood so close to Benjamin as he examined him that he could feel Branwen's heavy robes rub across his boots. Benjamin met the man's stare and saw acute intelligence, with a touch of amusement, in his eyes.

"A few brash words from a presumptuous young man can usually be tamed by a simple look from the king." The man stepped back, tapped his chin, and looked at both boys. He turned to the guard. "You may leave; I think I'll be safe with these young men."

The guard nodded and hung the lantern before he left, leaving the door open.

"But you, Benjamin Black, caused the king to shudder. That is why you and your friend are now in the dungeons. However, I believe that was your intent."

"Unbelievable," Denny mumbled.

"I heard you had lovely dungeons. These may be the nicest ones in the kingdom."

"Ah, but these *are* the nice ones." The bent man smiled wickedly. "The not-nice ones are much damper, darker, and much *less* comfortable."

"I have nothing to do with him," Denny interjected. "I'm just here to see Re—the princess safely to the castle."

The secretary raised a white eyebrow. "And why are you here, Benjamin? If he came to get the princess here, what are you here to do?"

Benjamin examined the hump. It looked real enough. "It's time to move forward. The Thieves' Plain served its purpose, and now both sides are ready for this truce to be over."

"War and chaos, then?"

"This truce is a war between two sides that refuse to look at each other. That doesn't mean there isn't pain and suffering. We just refuse to see it." He took a breath to help him say what he did not want to. "Only when men like Mouthrot *and* Shreb are brought under the law will we have peace and prosperity. The king's father made the truce, because it was the only way to save the kingdom. Now the only way to save Lam is to break that truce. Mouthrot broke the truce when he killed Rebecca's parents ten years ago and committed an act of war in trying to kill Rebecca."

"This from Benjamin Black, son of Black-Eyed Barnaby, head of his class at the Villains' Academy and applicant to the Mighty Shreb?

The boy who wanted to be the best villain's assistant that the plain has ever seen? Better than your own father?"

Cold sweat prickled at Benjamin's scalp. The Master of Spies network was more thorough than he'd imagined. The secretary continued to circle Benjamin, only his white hair visible as he lurched into the shadows between the two lanterns. He wanted something from Benjamin, something specific. Perhaps his soul? Would he let him have it?

"My father doesn't really exist, does he? Fiction from start to finish," Benjamin said, refusing to turn and face Branwen, who stood behind him.

"No, no, he wasn't. You have a father, but who is he? Black-Eyed Barnaby? Or Torrin, Duke of Gehnry?"

Duke? "It doesn't matter. Neither man exists." Heat threatened to burn out Benjamin's heart. He squeezed his hands behind his back. "The only man I've seen is the Lieutenant, and he's nothing but a ghost trapped in purgatory compliments of his king. He is no one."

"But it does matter." The hump bobbed up and down as the secretary circled to face him. "Black-Eyed Barnaby, the famed villain's assistant, or Torrin, the Duke of Gehnry?"

Heat rose to Benjamin's face. The secretary's pale eyes waited eagerly to pounce on Benjamin's answer. An answer he didn't have.

"Villain's assistant or duke?" The secretary's voice skewered him, his eyes widened in earnest. "Who do you chose as your father? Villain's assistant or duke?"

Ice ran under Benjamin's skin. His arms grew stiff and he shivered, though the cell was not cold. He clenched his fists together to keep them from shaking.

"It's a simple question, Benjamin. Villain's assistant or duke? What are you going to be? You could go either way; both doors stand open before you. Which will you choose?"

"I don't know!" Benjamin wrapped his arms around himself to try to still the shivers that rolled down his body.

The secretary's pale eyes flashed in response. Silence filled the cell. Denny shuffled his feet.

"That's not good enough." Branwen turned to Denny and waved him to the door. "You, young man, may go. The princess is waiting for you."

The cell was left dark and empty except for Benjamin, whose shivers had turned violent. He rubbed his arms and lurched around the cell.

What just happened?

They all had asked so much from him already. Why did they need this as well? To choose? No, he could not choose.

THIRTY EIGHT

*R*ebecca paced, twisting the ends of her silk sleeves. Dally watched the princess as she fitted a jeweled veil to a cap. Dally had been weaving scarves and reworking old hats all morning. Occasionally, Dally would order her to stop wearing a hole in the floor and try out her creations. When her fidgeting grew unbearable for both of them, she would release her.

"You've done all that you can," Dally said. "They'll get out. Secretary Branwen will probably let them sweat first, but he'll let them out. You're making yourself sick for nothing."

Rebecca collapsed in a soft chair and closed her eyes as she rubbed the knot in her chest. Dally was right, but it was taking too long. Mouthrot could be burning the entire Thieves' Plain or marching on Ulmer Castle right now! The Lieutenant and Odie could be captured or worse. And she was left simply trying on hats and gowns.

How could the king be *so slow*? He wanted her here to be safe, but that was not how she felt. She was locked in her rooms, her very presence a secret from conspiring noblemen. Everyone was fixated on the ascension and nothing else. Benjamin had no idea how broken this kingdom really was.

On top of everything else, Jalene, the king's future wife, was in the castle. They had been secretly courting for the last year, and their engagement would soon be announced. Jalene was young, healthy, and came from great breeding stock. King Aldo needed heirs, with the emphasis on more than one. Rebecca was the backup plan if an heir wasn't produced from their union.

The most preferred plan would have been for Queen Lorrina and her son to survive childbirth twenty years ago. Aldo had been devastated by her death and had even dismissed one counselor for suggesting possible brides. But when half of one's nobles plotted to steal one's throne and the other half connived to get themselves named as the heir apparent, even the most reluctant king could be forced to take action. Rebecca cheered for Jalene and her rumored fruitfulness. The more babies between her and the crown, the better. She would gladly be the old supportive aunt from behind the scenes. She might go back to her father's castle and rebuild it in honor of the king and all his heirs: a castle built to defend and protect the crown, safely ensconced in the Sunset Mountains.

A guard ushered Branwen in, his black robes swaying through the door. He dipped his white feathery head in a bow, and Denny emerged behind him. He looked relieved to be above ground. Rebecca exhaled in relief. She looked past Denny, but the guard had closed the door. Denny scowled and shook his head, dislodging a piece of straw from his golden waves.

What had Benjamin done now?

"As you can see, young Master Black is not with us." The secretary raised a hand to silence her questions. "The stew needs some more time. I turned up the heat a little. I have full confidence that he will come to a decision."

"Great! He'll do the opposite just to prove he can." Rebecca stood and began pacing the room, her long skirts tugging against her. "He'll be in there forever! I need Benjamin out here," Rebecca said as she rubbed her temples. Denny glowered at the rug. She strode over and squeezed his hand. "We *all* need him. He may rub us the wrong way, but he gets things done."

Denny glanced up. "All the same, I hope you don't mind if I enjoy taking a break from him. Benjamin's getting off easy being down there alone. We need to find another Benjamin to lock in there with him. That kind of torture would motivate anyone, even Benjamin."

"Don't worry, Princess," Branwen said. The use of her title caused Rebecca to jump. "I don't care what decision he makes, just that he makes one."

"Decision? What is it he must decide?"

"Who he is. Is he a raggedy scoundrel from the Thieves' Plain, or is he a member of the nobility?"

"He's only known that the Lieutenant is his father for less than a week, and you want him to make that decision right *now*?"

"Your Highness, Benjamin has based his whole life on surpassing his father's achievements, so my sources tell me. But which father? The villain's assistant who stabilized the Thieves' Plain through the reign of Shreb the First? Or the duke who dedicated his life to protecting king and country? It is a vital question." Branwen clasped his hands at the base of his hump. "I like to know who and what I have in my arsenal when I'm about to go to war."

"You'll support the Lieutenant's plan?"

"Was this the Lieutenant's plan? I thought perhaps it was Benjamin's." Branwen arched his white brows.

"Benjamin has made it his own," Denny said, sighing thankfully as Dally handed him a cup of tea and a sweet bun. "That's why the

Lieutenant sent him in the first place, isn't it? He was so certain Benjamin could convince the king to take action."

Branwen circled like a vulture around the space that Rebecca was not using. The secretary paused and turned to her.

"He's working with us now, because he found himself on the wrong side of events. I want him long term. As you say, Your Highness, we *all* need him. If he's anything like his father (or his mother, for that matter), he will be a great man. I'd like him on our side of the line."

Branwen accepted a cup of tea from Dally, drank it quickly, and returned the cup. He bowed his head slightly to the ladies and left the room.

Dally gave Rebecca another sweet bun. "I think we'll need another cup tomorrow for tea. Secretary Branwen may be a dreary man, but he gets things done. You'll see." She smiled and went to order lunch.

Denny beamed as he grabbed another sweet bun.

"Well, you know what we have to do, don't you?" Rebecca said, after sipping her tea.

Denny raised his eyebrows as he bit into his bun, icing sticking to his lips. His tongue darted out to remove the crumbs, and Rebecca looked away, her cheeks burning. She'd been watching too closely.

"We've got to get Benjamin to think about something other than his father. He's got to see the big picture."

Denny washed his bun down with his milky tea.

Rebecca sipped her own tea, its warmth bringing her thoughts back to the present. There were many dangers, known and unknown, in her life. It shouldn't be hard to find something to dangle in front of Benjamin. The king had limited her movements around the castle for her own safety. How was she supposed to learn anything trapped in here? The castle held a web of possible allies and enemies. Benjamin could be gathering information and coming up with a plan.

She finished her tea in one long swig, to the horror of Dally, who had just returned from the kitchen. Rebecca set her cup on the tray, slipped one bun into her sleeve, and walked out the door.

"Where are you going? Don't forget your guard," Dally called after her. She then turned to Denny for an answer.

He swallowed forcefully before speaking. "I think that she went to dangle a carrot." He stood up and took the lunch tray from her. "Thank you."

THIRTY NINE

Rebecca followed her guard through a dark maze to get to Benjamin's cell. He sat in a shadowy corner. Rebecca couldn't see his face. Was he sullen or secretly plotting? She asked the guard for privacy, and he stepped back an appropriate distance.

She pressed against the bars and hissed Benjamin's name. When he did not look up, she held out the bun that she had hidden in her sleeve. Hopefully it wouldn't leave a stain: Dally was already worried about her lack of wardrobe options. He looked up and crept toward her without speaking. He palmed the bun, sliding it into his own sleeve.

"I'm sorry you're stuck down here. If it helps, the king has asked that I keep to my rooms," Rebecca said with a sigh, trying to only let a little of her real annoyance show. "I have guards posted outside my door and no idea what is going on."

"Why do you need to be kept safe in the castle?" Benjamin stepped back from the bars, one of his brows arching upward. "I thought we were ordered to bring you here to keep you safe."

"I don't know, but I'm sure it's fine. He might not want my presence known until the right moment." Rebecca tried to sound light. "You do have to think about that sort of thing when you're the king. He does have to gain the support of his nobility to be able to secure his crown, and so on. Just another hiccup."

She looked around. "I hope the king makes a decision soon about Mouthrot. We've left the Lieutenant alone too long."

Benjamin nodded. "He knew it would take a lot of time and effort to convince the king."

"But he didn't know that we would have to go over a mountain." She let her worry for the Lieutenant show. "What if—"

"There's no point in worrying about what we don't know," Benjamin said, rubbing the back of his head. "The Lieutenant will have figured this all out. He's been around for a while."

"You're right. I guess I'm just nervous about Jalene." She smiled, looking embarrassed. "Dally and I are trying to decide if I should invite her to tea."

"Jalene?" Benjamin stepped closer, gripping the bars.

"Oh." Rebecca looked over her shoulder before lowering her voice. "She's the one Aldo is thinking of marrying. I think he wants us to be friends."

"Well, of course *he* does. It would be nice if wolves played nice with lambs as well." Benjamin twisted his hands around the bars, a frown tugging at the corners of his mouth.

"Honestly, Benjamin, I think you're getting extra paranoid being in this cell all alone." She smiled, amused, and tapped his arm. "I've heard very nice things about her."

"I suppose you heard these things from the king?"

"Maybe, but that doesn't mean they aren't true." She patted his hand and turned away from the bars.

"You know that Denny thinks—"

Rebecca gripped her locket. She didn't want Benjamin to finish. "Yes, I do. I think I've got him set straight on that." She smiled. Actually, she had no idea what Denny thought, and she wasn't sure she wanted to know. "Don't worry about me, Benjamin. I'm sure I'll be fine."

She followed her guard away from Benjamin, and he gnawed on his bun, staring blankly at the floor. The dark passage thankfully cooled her burning cheeks. She smiled to herself as she climbed the stairs. She would tell Dally to order an extra breakfast for tomorrow.

FORTY

B ranwen walked like an injured bird, straining for each step. And yet, he had fetched Benjamin personally from the dungeons. Benjamin was shocked. What drove this man through so much physical difficulty? *It must burn to know he cannot fly. And yet he shuffles along awkwardly, because that is what he must do.* Why was he so devoted to King Aldo?

Once inside the antechamber, Branwen dismissed their escort with a flap of his arm. He instructed the guards at the door to announce them. When they were alone, the secretary gathered his black robes around him like wings.

"See if you can be respectful *and* truthful." He turned a granite-colored eye to Benjamin. "Aldo cannot stand falseness. He sees too much of it. Speak in a courteous tone. It will help your truth strike home. People often underestimate the power of civility."

Branwen turned abruptly as the doors opened into the king's chamber. He led Benjamin in and bowed deferentially, though it was a strain for his twisted frame. Aldo sat upon a stone throne upon which a Great Wolf had been carved. It peered menacingly over his head. Perhaps the king was doing Branwen a favor in seeing Benjamin again. *Interesting.* The old secretary stepped aside, allowing Benjamin to step forward and bow again. Aldo motioned for him to speak.

"Your Majesty, I ask forgiveness for the brashness of my words before, but—"

"Let me stop you there, before you hang yourself. A word of advice, young man: never make a wager with Branwen. He always wins." Aldo smiled good-naturedly at his secretary. "I was willing to put good money down that you would rot in my most comfortable cell for eternity before admitting any error on your part. Even now, I see pride in your eyes as you stand before your king and lord."

Benjamin bowed slightly, smiling. "It is a fault I possess, or so I've been told. I always thought of it as confidence. It's a fine line, is it not?"

The king smiled and glanced over at his secretary and then walked up to Benjamin. Their eyes locked, and Benjamin was sure that King Aldo could see every misdeed he had ever committed. Benjamin tugged at his collar and lowered his eyes, belatedly remembering that this was the correct response.

"It was not your *rudeness* alone that landed you and your friend in my dungeons." Benjamin looked up. The king frowned down at him. "To have a student of the Villains' Academy here in my court is not something to take lightly. Granted, you are your father's son, but I cannot easily overlook where your entire upbringing has been." With that, the king retreated to his throne.

"To anyone so educated, *I* am a villain and the enemy. Allowing you here in my presence is allowing a potential assassin an easy opportunity. The princess has spoken on your behalf, and Branwen has done his own investigating. You recently discovered who your father is; I wonder if you know who your mother is as well?"

"I know she was a bitter woman who could not resolve herself to who my father really was. It drove her to an early death."

A look passed between Aldo and Branwen. Both faces remained as blank as slate.

"Your Majesty, forgive me, but I have no desire to discuss my family history. My mother's life is behind me, and she is gone." Benjamin swallowed, trying to gather his thoughts. *What did my mother have to do with this?* "I came here to ask you to destroy the world I was raised in. There are two archvillains on the horizon, and both wish to wear your crown. The truce has not bound them. In fact, one attempted to kill the crown's only living heir. If you will not heal this country, they will gladly bleed it dry.

"When it is known that Mouthrot murdered Prince Evan and his wife, Brynn, and made an attempt on the princess's life, the people of the Thieves' Plain will expect you to act boldly. Mouthrot is still connected to Shreb. Waiting will allow him time to disassociate himself, and then it will get messy."

"It is not so easy," the king said, his brow creasing. He ran a finger over his auburn beard.

Benjamin bit the inside of his lip as he considered his response. The secretary shook his head ever so slightly.

Aldo looked past him, probably deciding how seriously he should take a sixteen-year-old boy. *Well, in the king's defense, most boys my age* are *idiots, Benjamin thought smugly. Look at Denny.* The monarch finally nodded. "I agree, but how? I'd rather not send in a full force." The king pressed his lips together for a moment and then glanced at Branwen. "I want to see some different options, Secretary. Something subtle."

Branwen's lips pulled back into a smile revealing small, sharp teeth. He bobbed his head in a bow. Goose bumps ran down Benjamin's arms. He hoped never to see that smile again.

"Whatever I may do to aid Your Majesty in this," Benjamin said, bowing more deeply than needed.

"I'll leave that to Branwen."

And with that, Aldo dismissed him.

Two guards escorted Benjamin to the princess. His chest tightened as he walked the long hallways. It was the right decision, and he had meant it. He would help the king. Why couldn't he breathe? *Great Wolves! How did I get here? I just agreed to tear down the Thieves' Plain.* Benjamin staggered. Feeling lightheaded, he paused to take a few deep breaths outside Rebecca's door.

The guards looked straight ahead but seemed keenly aware of his position. *Of course they're keeping a close eye on me.* He straightened up, walked through the door, and his guards left. Rebecca already had her own guard outside her door.

Denny was eating happily at a table, and Benjamin felt an urge to punch his well-groomed face. He simply looked too happy. Denny nodded as he continued eating. Benjamin spied an empty plate. Rebecca wore a light summer gown of teal that flowed like water around her. She paced in the far corner, wringing her hands. She looked up and smiled as if all were well.

Dally nodded and pulled out a chair for Benjamin. While he certainly had not been starved in the dungeon the last two days, the cuisine hadn't satisfied him. He had just climbed a mountain, after all! He clenched the padding of the seat as he sat down. His movements felt stiff and artificial as he picked up his napkin and laid it in his lap.

The sight of herbed chicken, fragrant root vegetables, bread, and sweet honeyed pears softened him. Benjamin planned on enjoying this meal thoroughly. Rebecca also sat at the table. Denny was already up and helping her with her chair. Benjamin grabbed a berry and popped it into his mouth. The sweet burst silenced his raging thoughts.

Rebecca motioned for them all to eat. Dally filled their glasses with something that smelled sweet.

"Normally, you'd wait for the princess to sit and eat before you start, but this is a special circumstance," Dally said, eying Denny.

Rebecca sighed. "Thank you, Dally. It's good for all of us to keep that in mind. But when it's just us, I'd rather they carry on as normal. It's nice to have something familiar."

"Well, we could have Dally sit down, and you could serve us instead." Benjamin winked at Dally, who quickly knocked his head with a surprisingly firm knuckle.

"I don't even like to think about that." Dally sat down to eat, clearly demonstrating the correct way to eat in polite company.

Benjamin made the appropriate adjustments and continued to eat quickly.

Rebecca sat down and laughed. She stuck her tongue out so only Benjamin could see.

"Isn't this cozy?" Benjamin said with feigned gaiety. "What have you all been doing while I was downstairs?"

Rebecca rolled her eyes at Benjamin in disgust. She deliberately put chicken in her mouth and chewed thoroughly. Her gray eyes glinted wickedly at him. *And Denny thinks I have amorous feelings for Benjamin? Bah.*

"Picking fabric for dresses, as well as feathers, bows, and flowers for hats," Denny said. "Trust me; you had it easy, except for the food. Oh, never mind; the food made it all worth it."

"You've just been eating since you got out, haven't you?"

Denny just wagged his eyebrows as he chewed. Benjamin wanted to weep as he ate. The robust flavors entwined in every bite he took. It was unbelievable how a mere bite or two lifted his mood so completely. As he raised his glass, Benjamin noticed Dally watching Rebecca push her food around her plate. The juice sang on his tongue. He forced himself not to drink it in one swallow.

Rebecca sipped from her own glass and met Benjamin's gaze questioningly. He immediately focused on his meal and the ecstasy of truly fine food. Every new flavor seemed to complement the previous. He was sure that in his darkest hour, he would merely have to close his eyes and remember this meal to find happiness again.

FORTY ONE

*F*eatherbeds are divine! Benjamin almost gasped out loud. He
didn't want Denny to suspect that he hadn't enjoyed his stay
in the dungeons. They were assigned the same room, which was big
enough for ten beds, instead of just the two. Two chairs and a sofa
sat by a fireplace. It was nowhere near as grand as Rebecca's room
(and rightfully so), but it was still luxurious.

Denny's bed was at least two arm lengths away, providing an
acceptable safety buffer. His antagonistic ally already breathed deeply
on his bed. Considering the amount of heavy foods he ate all evening,
it wasn't surprising. Benjamin had also eaten at a healthy pace. He felt
his dinner heavy in his belly. Dally had ordered extra dessert for the
boys with only the slightest shaking of her head. She was a dear
woman! He made a note to stay on her good side.

Besides gloating over the luxuries that Benjamin missed for two
days, Denny stayed clear of him. While he appeared less hostile,
Benjamin wondered if his wounded feelings were still on the mend.

Denny watched Rebecca closely whenever she and Benjamin talked. Hopefully he was seeing their interactions with more objective eyes.

Denny was not a bad guy. Benjamin trusted him to act in a predictable manner. He would hate to lose that. But if Denny continued being resentful of him, he could sabotage things, whether purposely or not. If Benjamin couldn't convince him of their disinterest in one another, he needed to point out Rebecca's feelings for Denny. *Whatever they were.* Benjamin had never thought about it before, but Rebecca had to have some. The two had worked together for several years. They had history.

Denny sat up, pummeled his pillow into a better shape, and lay down again, rolling away from Benjamin.

"Denny, how long have you worked with the Lieutenant?" *And Rebecca?*

"Hmmm?" Denny sounded annoyed.

"How long have you been with the Lieutenant?"

"I don't know, a few years. Three, I think."

"Well, how did he suck *you* in?"

Denny propped himself up with his elbow, combing his hair back with his fingers. "Why do you care?"

"I just realized I don't really know that much about you or your brothers. Everyone seems to know more about me than I do about everyone else." .

Denny narrowed his eyes, rolled over onto his back, and exhaled loudly.

"The Lieutenant worked with my father once, years before, when he was Black-Eyed Barnaby. When the Lieutenant returned with Rebecca, Dad agreed to help him. Mother had just died a year earlier, and the Lieutenant brought a spark to our lives. Then Dad got sick, and we were left on our own.

"The Lieutenant got us established so we could take care of ourselves. He pointed out what we already could do and how to use those skills to support ourselves."

"And how you could help him?" Benjamin looked at Denny.

"Well, yes," Denny said. He rolled over and looked at Benjamin, his blue eyes burning, "but that's not why he did it. He occasionally asked us for small things, and that was all. I volunteered to help him because I wanted more. I saw an opportunity. I was the head of the house with mouths to feed. You've never met Baldo. He could do anything if he was in the right place. He's such a runty thing. He needs his brains to earn a living."

"So the door to all of that was through the Lieutenant? An opportunity for your brother?"

"Well, and for me; I'll admit it," Denny sighed. "What would happen when the Lieutenant packed up and went back to the king? He'd become like a father to us. After Mom died, Dad provided for us, but he was just a shadow."

"There aren't many people like the Lieutenant on the plain, not that I've ever met...or Rebecca."

Silence settled around Benjamin as he took in Denny's words. He pictured the brothers' need for humanness amid emptiness. It was a scene he could picture easily enough. What was hard for him to imagine was what it would be like to have that void filled. Benjamin's mother was attentive more to her schemes for him than actually to him. It was like living with a harness whose sole purpose was to drive him down a narrow path. She had very little interest in how he felt about things or what he wanted to do with his life. If he resisted, she would go to war with him, and war in his face every day was exhausting.

"Benjamin?"

"Yes?"

"I don't know how you feel about the Lieutenant. Maybe you don't want him as a father, but I think he's a good person to have in your life. I...I think he would do anything for you."

"Why do you say that?" Benjamin stared blankly at the shadows on the ceiling.

"Because he was looking for you. Because all the stuff he's done for me and Odie and Baldo and Rebecca, he really wanted to do for you. He always wondered if he had a child, but he didn't know for sure." Denny cleared his throat. "It bothered him, not knowing."

Benjamin couldn't say anything; a deep ache stole his breath for a moment. Every scrap of information that he gleaned about the Lieutenant clashed against the image of Black-Eyed Barnaby that his mother described to him every day until she died. It was mental whiplash. The Lieutenant was a good man; Black-Eyed Barnaby was a villain. How could his father, the Duke of Gehnry, be both people? *They were so different.* Benjamin studied the shadowed corners of his room and waited for sleep.

FORTY TWO

*B*enjamin woke early and dressed quietly. He stepped out onto a small balcony and looked up at the mountain they had been on just a few days earlier. *I climbed that mountain!* From here, he could see how large a task that had been. He examined the castle and saw a few guards standing on parapets, watching the morning sun. Tightness built in his chest; he needed to close the deal. They had left the Lieutenant dangling. Mouthrot would realize Rebecca wasn't on the plain soon. It was possible that Mouthrot would know *everything* that was going on in the castle.

Benjamin ran to the door, leaving Denny sleeping under twisted blankets. Two guards played cards outside the door. *Glad to know I'm not a prisoner anymore. Oh, the irony!* The guards dropped cards and coins to stand at attention.

"Branwen? This way, yes?"

He pointed down the hall and marched off, not waiting for permission. There was a moment of uncertainty before a single set of steps caught up with him. The guard nodded to Benjamin and silently led him to Branwen. There must be some edict that forbids the guards from talking. *Wonderful, if it's true!* He could work with that.

Branwen perched on a tall stool, curled over a slanted desk, not unlike the clerks who were reading over yellowed sheets of parchment and scrolls. Each held a quill in his hand. Nothing denoted his rank other than his age and the quality of his dark robes that brushed against the stool as he wrote furiously. One of the bleary-eyed clerks tilted his head up and stared blankly at Benjamin for a full twelve seconds before any acknowledgment sparked behind his eyes. He looked at his master, who noticed nothing outside of his world of paper. The clerk slid from his stool and sidled next to Benjamin. He queried Benjamin in a whisper. "Yes?"

"I'd like to speak to Branwen," Benjamin said in a low tone that was still loud enough to upset the room.

The clerks all turned to Branwen with a look of panic, but Branwen merely waved them off.

"He needs to finish his thought," the clerk pleaded with bloodshot eyes. "Wait here. *Please.*"

Branwen was a master to be feared then. The clerk rubbed his stiff, ink-stained hands and climbed back on his stool. He blinked a few times and bent back to his work.

Benjamin let his eyes roam over stacks of papers and overlarge rolls that must have been maps. His fingers hungered to unroll a few to discover what lay inside, but he tucked them behind his back and waited.

Branwen looked up and shook his head slightly. "And what do you want, exactly?" He harrumphed as he leaned back, relieving his curvature by half. His arms braced against the desk for support.

What do I want? Benjamin could only respond with silence as Branwen stared at him.

Branwen glimpsed at his scribbling clerks. "You all look terrible. Go to bed." A few clerks cracked smiles, but out of relief or humor? It was hard to tell. "This way, young man."

Branwen dismounted and tottered with a more exaggerated limp than usual. He led Benjamin into a dim room lit only by the early-morning light that poured through two very small windows. A small pallet for sleeping was tucked in a corner. Branwen lit a lantern, illuminating a wall of pigeonholes filled with scrolls, each securely locked behind metal meshing. Several boxes with locks on them were stacked neatly in a dim corner.

"Guard, tell Sir Wendell that I'm finished with these boxes. They may be returned to the vaults. They will need to be escorted, and they are heavy."

The guard nodded at the dismissal and left without comment. Branwen sat behind a solemn desk with a high-backed chair. He jabbed at a lumpy pillow that was meant to support his twisted frame.

"You must have Aldo's complete trust," Benjamin said.

"As much as he trusts anyone." He pinched the bridge of his nose and looked directly at him. "I gather information that has helped him keep his crown. Every ounce of trust I have, I've earned through sleepless nights and other men's lives."

"Is that the path to the king's ear? The lives of other men?"

"No, not exactly. You see, first, you must give up your life. His interests are now mine. The princess will need that too. I don't have another life to give."

"Rebecca?" Benjamin scoffed. "She could kill a full-grown mountain bear with a single glare. Besides, she doesn't want to be queen."

"Then what does she want to be? Alive?" Branwen picked up a stack of papers and locked them in a drawer. "To the king, she is an insurance policy. To *many* others, she is a roadblock."

"Don't say that in front of Rebecca, or you'll make her blush." Benjamin sat down in a hard wooden chair meant to keep conversations short. "I know she needs help. She's made for the demands of royalty, though, more than she knows. I could help her, but—"

"What's in it for you?" The secretary lifted his eyebrows, causing his gray skin to crackle.

Benjamin shrugged, ignoring how the chair pinched the back of his thighs. "I was thinking more that Rebecca's biggest weakness lies in her ignorance at court and who the players are. I cannot provide her with that information." The edge of the chair dug into the back of Benjamin's legs. "What I *can* do is go back to the Lieutenant and take down the king's rivals."

"A few of his rivals. What do you think the princess has been doing while you were 'making a point' in the dungeons? She has been frantic about her friends. She is all but ready to lead an army to Shreb's fortress."

"That will never happen."

"Agreed. The king believes she will be safer here."

"Will she?"

"With some education and protective measures, yes."

"So the real trick is making sure she'll *want* to stay here. She tried to bolt once before. She's been told what to do all her life, and she's getting pretty tired of it."

"A willful royal? How novel." Branwen squeezed the bridge of his nose. "I've been around for a while now."

"Send me! I'm pretty unemployable on the plain by now. If I can't work for those villains, I might as well take them down."

"To make room for yourself?"

Benjamin stood up, his legs tingling. He walked around the chair to gain his feeling back. A thought pierced him like an icicle. "You're not thinking of putting me in as archvillain, are you? That's the last thing *anyone*—including me—wants!"

"No, but that's good to know. We can't very well disregard your entire upbringing in our plans, can we? Do you think that your mother wanted you to stop at villain's assistant? Really?"

Benjamin rubbed his hands on his legs. Conversations never went the way they were supposed to when he talked to Branwen.

"I don't know what my mother wanted. It doesn't matter now. She's dead!"

There was a knock at the door. Branwen raised a finger and allowed a retinue of guards in to remove the boxes. Benjamin watched in frozen frustration. The secretary ordered Benjamin's guard to take him back to his room. "I believe the princess is expecting you for breakfast."

Back in his rooms, Benjamin was surprised to find Denny up and fully groomed in fresh clothes. Denny raised his eyebrows and declared he didn't want to know. He pointed out Benjamin's pile of clean clothes and a basin of fresh water.

Benjamin washed in their dressing room. It allowed him a private moment to fume at the sudden realization of how much freedom he had lost since joining this roadshow. Benjamin knew what needed to be done, and all these people, walls, and rules were getting in his way. If it wasn't for the example of the neighboring country of Snood, he would lean toward no government at all, but he wasn't really interested in goatherding and growing rocks.

Benjamin stepped out into the room, freshly combed and scrubbed. Denny was hunched over a map. "How would you sneak an army into the Thieves' Plain?" Denny asked no one. "I don't think it can be done."

"One soldier at a time, I guess." Benjamin shrugged.

Denny laughed as he opened their door. "If we wanted to attack in ten years."

"At least ten years," Benjamin said, stumbling out the door after Denny.

FORTY THREE

*B*enjamin took a comfortable seat next to Dally and finished his eggs and sausage quietly. He nodded and agreed with everyone's comments. It was lovely to fill his belly and to know that the food would not run out. Dally had ordered extra sausages and eggs for the two boys, and they both showed their appreciation by eating them quickly. As Dally cleared the dishes, Benjamin noticed that Rebecca had covered her unfinished breakfast with her napkin.

"If only we could stroll around the grounds. I'm sure that would take the edge off," Dally said, glancing out the window. "It's a beautiful day, and the gardens are lovely."

"Why do I have to be hiding again?" Rebecca crossed the room and pressed her forehead to the leaded glass window.

Dally called for a guard to remove the trays. "Aldo is a little paranoid about your safety." She turned to face Rebecca with a sigh. "Can you blame him? Rebellious nobles in his ranks and Mouthrot on the plain?"

"Not to mention Mouthrot probably has spies in the castle," Benjamin said, pushing his chair back.

Rebecca glared at Benjamin, pressing a fist into her hip. She tightened her lips into a grim expression of determination. Denny gave Benjamin a look of concern, and he nodded.

"Perhaps King Aldo would let me go back," Denny said, keeping his voice light. "You know, just to check in with the Lieutenant. I think we'd all feel much better just knowing."

"Aldo has already outfitted a group to do that." Rebecca dropped her hands to her sides and wandered to the back of the couch to trace the floral pattern. "And none of us are in it."

Denny slunk into a chair.

"So it's been finalized?" Benjamin asked.

"For the most part. I know it was foolish, but part of me was really hoping to go." Rebecca slammed her fist into the couch. "That's where I belong. If I were a prince, I would lead the attack. It would be part of my training."

Denny glowered at Rebecca's words.

"My world was already too small." Rebecca traced the edge of the couch with her finger as she circled around it. "Now it feels as if it's shrinking to the size of a single room. My life hangs in the balance with the fate of Lam." She collapsed into cushions.

To put your life at the mercy of something larger than oneself? Benjamin thought of Branwen painfully scurrying around the shadows of the castle, not for a king, but for the good of the kingdom. It was a distinction he had not considered before, but an important one. *Is personal pain sometimes worth the fate of something bigger?*

Dally sat on the other side of Rebecca with a basket of white handkerchiefs. She patted her leg affectionately and began the process of embroidering Rebecca's initials into an intricate coiling pattern.

Rebecca tilted her head back and stared at the ceiling. Dally took this as a cue to dive into some court gossip that no one was really interested in, but it gave everyone a good excuse not to talk. Benjamin felt the outline of a terrific *something*, maybe even a plan, standing in the shadows of his mind. He needed time to coax it into something solid.

Benjamin demanded to go for a walk, telling his guards that he needed to escape female gossip. The guards, normally unresponsive, had to fight off sympathetic smirks. They nodded and escorted him through the castle's dark, forgotten corners. He toured rooms full of cast-off furniture and smiled as he wandered freely.

The guards didn't say anything, but they seemed to be enjoying the change of scenery. How boring it must be to park outside a lost princess's door and not even be allowed to complain to anyone.

He found himself standing in a large room full of heavy banquet tables built to withstand anything. He marveled at their solid construction. *Oak maybe?* He could imagine ancient jousting tournaments on them, they were so large and solid.

His fingers just brushed against his notebook when a voice interrupted his reverie. "And what are you up to, I wonder?"

The guards snapped to attention, growing in height as they saluted the bent figure in the doorway.

"Trust issues?" Benjamin spoke over his shoulder.

"Are we talking about me or you?" With that, the secretary dismissed the guards.

Benjamin watched the soldiers leave and said, "I've been thinking about how you would get an army onto the Thieves' Plain without anyone knowing."

"It can't be done."

"Really?" Benjamin turned to face Branwen. "Because I thought there already was one there."

Branwen nearly stood up straight at that, his physical reaction limited by the curvature of his spine.

"A system of spies and soldiers have been in place from the moment the truce was established," Benjamin said, glancing at Branwen's smug expression to confirm his guess. "Of course there are, because Aldo and his father were rightly paranoid, as any good king should be. The army of spies might be old and forgotten, but they're still there. Aldo just needs to give the order."

"Timing, remember?" Branwen said, the dark circles under his eyes deepening.

"I'll set it in motion myself. Heck, I'll take Denny along for good measure to keep me on the straight-and-narrow path to the Lieutenant's door. Isn't that what you've been waiting for?"

The old crow lifted his head and cawed. "Come with me, Master Benjamin."

FORTY FOUR

The morning was gray with a touch of chill. Denny slapped his arms but was obviously excited to get out of the castle. Benjamin handed him a tattered wool cloak that he had just stomped dirt into. He'd stopped just short of rubbing it into a pile of fresh horse dung. Denny rolled his eyes but put it on.

"Better dirty and smelly than skewered on a roasting stick," Benjamin said as he repeated the process for himself.

Two of the soldiers who would be accompanying them shrugged, and then they rubbed dirt and straw on their boots and clothes as well.

"That's right; we want a real lived-in look." He winked at Denny, who shook his head.

He scanned the stone courtyard. It was empty apart from their party. The boys hoped to keep their departure from Rebecca. They had retired to bed early, citing boredom and too much dinner—believable excuses for teenage boys forced to listen to Dally discussing hair strategies. Unable to escape her own rooms, Rebecca glared at them as they left. They would be gone before she woke and hopefully be gone long enough for her anger to be spent on other people.

A few soldiers were already on their horses. A small soldier in the back had pulled his hood up, shading his face. Benjamin stood next to Denny and gestured behind him with his head. Denny swore quietly under his breath.

Sir Wendell, the captain of the guard, approached in answer to their signal. He was a stout man with a curled moustache. He was here as a formality only, but Benjamin was thankful to have an extra man now.

"Do you have everything you need?" Wendell asked.

"Yes, *and more.*"

Wendell followed Benjamin's eyes. He paled and bit his lip. He signaled two men to follow him.

"Hell hath no fury—" Benjamin muttered at Denny, who slunk into a shadow.

Wendell approached the hooded rider and bowed. The men took hold of the reins, causing Rebecca to swear. The men blushed. She lifted her head to stare down every single man in the company. Her glare took on a murderous glint when it hit Benjamin. White with rage, Rebecca ground her teeth in frustration. He bowed slightly in return and turned to Denny, who cowered behind his own hood.

Sir Wendell reached out a hand to guide the princess along, but she flung it away. "*I can* walk by myself," she growled, shoving through several gaping soldiers. Sir Wendell escorted her to her rooms at a cautious distance.

"We're probably better off getting killed in the line of duty than returning alive and well," Denny said, fidgeting with his cloak.

"You're probably right."

They climbed on their horses and trickled through the heavy gates and onto the main road.

She might forgive us if we were either severely wounded or dead, Benjamin mused. *Maybe after a few months of solitary confinement in her dungeons, she might come around,* he added with a smirk. Benjamin would solve that problem when he got there and probably with a lot of batting of lashes from Denny.

+ + +

Denny took to horseback riding as if he'd done nothing else his whole life. Benjamin struggled. He loathed every moment of it. His backside would never be the same again. Yet he needed to learn to ride to survive and to work with the king's men. *By the Great Wolves! Why didn't they teach this sort of thing at the academy?* Horseback riding should have been part of the curriculum. But then, no one could afford horses.

When they stopped to rest, one of the soldiers adjusted Benjamin's stirrups, while another demonstrated how to use his legs to reduce the jarring. His back muscles pulled tightly from his shoulders to his legs. His butt hurt. There had to be a more efficient way to travel than by horse. Benjamin thanked the soldiers and then collapsed under a tall pine tree. He felt like he was still on his horse. The ride never ended.

The plant life along the wide main road was green. He could feel a slight dampness in the air. Tall trees stood next to the road, flush with green needles. Benjamin missed the drag of dust in his throat as he breathed the moist air. Was it possible to get too much air at one time? He dug the heel of his boot into the moist earth.

Denny examined a flowering weed as he led his horse to a green spot to eat. "It really is a different world here, isn't it?" he said, shaking his head.

Benjamin nodded.

When they started again, Benjamin stole glances at Lam as he rode. It looked as if the Sunset Mountains had shed giant rocks all around them and trees had sprouted out of them. As they traveled south on the road, the mountains were always visible above them to the west. They passed farms as the sun filled in colors around them. The day warmed, drying the morning dampness. Benjamin's horse rippled like silk under the sun.

To accommodate Benjamin, they stopped more often than the soldiers wanted. Normally that would bother him, but he felt as if his backside had been molded to the saddle. He was sure blisters had formed on his inner thighs from the heat that burned there.

Waldren's Wood was now in view, its dark trees staring up from below. A river poured down the mountainside and plunged into the cursed forest. They let the horses drink; the animals did so skittishly. Dark shadows reached out from the black-needled trees. Every noise sent a jump through the men and horses alike.

They slept in the ruins of Prince Evan's castle on the edge of the forest. Benjamin tried to imagine Rebecca toddling around there, but he couldn't. There were plenty of solid walls in many places, and the damage was mostly on one side, but it was empty. Provisions were locked in an old cellar. The men built a fire in the old kitchen hearth. They told stories of the sad ruins as they ate dinner. There were plenty of tales of weeping ghosts and phantom smoke. Benjamin just rolled his eyes and discovered Denny missing. He slipped away and found Denny standing in the great entry at the bottom of the stairs, his head tilted upward, hunting for the ceiling in the darkness.

"Looking for ghosts?" Benjamin asked.

Denny turned and shook his head. The empty room still stank of smoke.

"I'm trying to imagine Rebecca here, a whole castle of people devoting their lives to her, only to be turned out into a hovel on the Thieves' Plain, where she cooked and cleaned *for us*. We're so far beneath her; we should be like ants to her."

Benjamin had never thought much about Rebecca's past, other than how it complicated his life. (But then that was how he thought of most people, really.)

"You're still her friend," Benjamin said, shrugging.

"For how long?" Denny scrubbed the back of his neck. "Things have changed."

"You've earned her trust. That hasn't changed. She will always need that."

Denny gazed around the empty room. "I would do anything for her."

"Never give her reason to doubt that, and you will always have a place in her life."

"I wanted more."

"I know," Benjamin said. "Friendship is more. She needs that. You need that."

Denny nodded and then locked eyes with Benjamin. "You don't need friends, though, do you?"

Denny's words echoed in Benjamin's footsteps as he walked away.

FORTY FIVE

Rebecca huffed and glared at a pink flower woven into the pattern of the rug by her feet while Dally lectured in the background. Thankfully, Branwen decided against telling Aldo about her attempt to ride into battle. He simply stated that while her actions were noble, they lacked foresight, and something else about the "big picture."

She ground her teeth as they accused her of losing control and acting childish. They had *no idea* how much self-control she was using right now. She felt like screaming until there was nothing left of her but a scream. They hadn't even begun to see her lose it yet. Fuming on the couch was a huge display of self-control. The only ones who could appreciate that were galloping away to battle. Dally had paced, spouting words of rebuke mixed with sympathetic shoulder pats.

"Do you really think I'm just going to sit here in this room and drink tea for the rest of my life?" Rebecca glared straight into Branwen's eyes of polished granite.

"No, not a future queen." The secretary's face softened at her words. "This seclusion is just temporary."

"*Possible* future queen," she said. "I'm just an understudy. What about Lady Jalene?"

Branwen sat in a chair opposite her, tucking his hands into the sleeves of his robes and sighed.

"Not all the nobles are happy about the king taking another bride. There are those who had their own offerings rejected and those who want *no* queen next to the king at all—unless they are king themselves."

"Besides Mouthrot?" Rebecca slumped.

"Your uncle has been playing chess with many of his nobles. They will not act directly against him, but they wouldn't bat an eye at removing you, Lady Jalene, or any child she may have. Her enemies are your enemies. It might be good for her and her supporters to know that."

Rebecca leaned forward and picked up a roll from the plate that Dally set prominently in front of her. Rebecca chewed slowly, aware that both adults were watching her closely.

"Perhaps we should arrange a less formal meeting?" She scanned the room. "Have the maids finished their rounds?"

"No." Dally scowled in concern. "You aren't planning on making a run for it, are you?"

"Not the niece of the king. No, I don't think so." Branwen gathered his black robes around him. "*She* can't go anywhere."

"I need to know this castle. I need to know who people are. I'll never do that in here," Rebecca said with a sly grin. "If there's one thing I know how to do, it's to act like an overlooked servant girl."

Branwen raised an eyebrow.

"Don't worry, I can drop the attitude for a while."

He rubbed his chin for quite a while at that, his sharp eyes studying her face.

FORTY SIX

*I*t felt good to be in a simple skirt again: she literally felt lighter. Rebecca was in her element. Her maid's dress was nothing fancy but was certainly finer and cleaner than what she wore around the Thieves' Plain. She wrapped a scarf tightly around her head. Dally pinned it in place for good measure and then handed her a basket filled with laundry.

"Well, now that we've hit upon this idea, I don't know why I didn't think of this before. It would have been less conspicuous than having me or the guards carting things to and from your room." Dally paused and cast a sideways glance before adding, "I mean you posing as a serving girl, not you doing your own laundry."

Rebecca laughed as they passed the guards. Dropping her laundry off for someone else to do was moving up in the world for her. The guards stood straighter as the women walked by, nothing more than what Dally would normally get. By herself, a simple servant girl would barely get a nod.

She adjusted the basket against her hip as they passed another set of guards, who followed her with their eyes in a stiff, uneasy manner.

"I hope this doesn't open the door for them to slack off."

"Of course not. They need to project the attitude that someone is still in your rooms and not running around the castle, vulnerable," Dally whispered.

They dropped the laundry off first. Dally introduced Rebecca as Sara to Brigit, the head laundress, a red-faced, well-muscled woman. "Finally got someone to help you out? Here, I'll take that."

Dally nodded in response. "Brigit."

Brigit clenched the basket with rough, chapped hands. "You'll pick it up here." She pointed to a shelf with a thick finger.

"Thank you," Rebecca said. She curtsied and avoided eye contact, exaggerating her nervousness.

Dally smiled at Brigit and then continued the tour. They passed all sorts of servants. Some wore nothing more than simple peasant attire with an apron or vest to mark their employment, while others wore Aldo's colors in various cuts and designs that marked them as guards, soldiers, or high-ranking servants.

Those who worked directly with the gentry had their own servants who followed them in little packs and looked finely dressed. Efficient clicking of heels on the floors and stairs surrounded Rebecca. There was so much to be done and transported through these back hallways; it amazed her. Servants could more easily get to one end of the castle by using these back halls than the main halls.

"Stay close to me, dear. It gets a little rowdy in the kitchens. They'll plow right over you if you get in their way." Dally paused in the entry and guided Rebecca to a safe corner. "Let me introduce you to Molly. That's her, the one with bright-red hair. She does odd jobs for me."

Molly set down the pot she was carrying when Dally summoned her. She wiped her hands on her apron and bobbed a short curtsy to Dally. A loose strand of copper hair fell from her crisp, white cap.

"Molly, this is my new girl, Sara. She's never been to the castle before and will be running errands for me."

"Of course, she'll get lost at least five times a day and at least two of them in the kitchen." Molly winked. "On my first day, I went to the pantry and ended up lost in the laundry."

Rebecca grinned back. She loved the feeling of being taken under this girl's wing. Molly glanced around the kitchen, looking for something. "My brother is always a safe bet too and easy to find. His hair is every bit as red as mine, and he's very tall. Sticks out like a sore thumb. He started out in the kitchens but has moved up to a footman, so he knows more of the castle than I do. His name's Robert."

Molly nodded at Dally before returning to her pot. "Oh, watch out for Martha; she's head of the kitchen and has a frightful temper. She makes everyone cry at least once a week. So don't worry if she sets you to tears too." The maid's eyes twinkled as she carried her pot to a plump woman with deep grimace lines folded into her face.

"That Martha?" Rebecca whispered.

"Yes, but she can be very sweet *if* you stay on her good side," Dally said.

"That's where I plan to stay."

They wandered through the kitchens as Dally introduced Sara to everyone and pointed out where she should go to ask for meals, where to pick them up, and who to give meal orders to.

Most of the staff barely glanced in Rebecca's direction; they were all busy cleaning, cooking, or yelling. Some stopped and chatted briefly with Dally though. She seemed to be on good terms with everyone, and they all seemed eager to help her.

Their last stop was in the bakery, where loaves of bread were being hauled in and out of the ovens. In the back, Rebecca could see cakes and sweet rolls being made.

A short round man with a couple of days' worth of stubble greeted them. He was the head baker. "It looks like you've finally gotten a little helper."

Little? Rebecca smiled demurely. *I'm seventeen, not five, you fool!*

Dally introduced her to the baker.

"I know that it is tempting, but I must warn you we don't allow pinching of cakes and sweets. Sometimes we allow samples when we are testing a recipe. We dump damaged goods over there in that basket. Otherwise, everything is off limits, except what is served with your meals."

Rebecca nodded in awe as she watched men and women shaping dough and decorating sweet things.

"I, however, can eat and sample everything," he said, slapping his belly and laughing. "Dally can get whatever she wants as well. Come to me—my name's Henry, by the way—and I'll arrange it." He grabbed a small powdered cake off one of the trays and offered it to Dally, who chuckled but waved it off.

"It's your lucky day," he said as he broke the small cake in half. He popped one piece into his mouth while handing the other half to Rebecca. Dark fruit filling oozed out of the center. "What do you think?"

She took a bite, and her mouth was filled with spiced apricots and light fluffy cake.

"Good, eh?"

Rebecca nodded, unable to answer as she finished her luscious cake.

"That is the king's favorite at the moment. Don't let anyone know I let you have any." The baker winked. "Welcome to Ulmer Castle."

Rebecca nodded in appreciation.

As they walked off, Dally said, "Henry is very strict with his goods unless you're a pretty young girl. He's a terrible flirt."

"Is that why he lets you have whatever you want?"

Dally blushed but said nothing.

They entered the main dining hall. *How did she not remember this?* She felt herself gaping and was thankful everyone would just think she was a young country girl. She couldn't let herself do this if she were the princess. The room was huge and set up with long tables in the shape of a square. Chairs covered in Aldo's coat of arms—a golden wolf's head—were being stacked in a corner, where they were given a final inspection by a thin man whose dark, sparse hair was pulled back sleekly into a tail away from his bushy eyebrows.

Rebecca watched as various footmen moved at the wave of his hand. Heads nodded in deference to his instructions with no conversation. Perhaps no words were needed. Or perhaps they were all too afraid to speak in front of the head butler, who looked all business and no pleasure. A line of footmen stepped out of the way with a slight bow, letting the women pass.

A blond boy with striking green eyes nudged the tall, fiery-haired boy next to him, who could only have been Molly's brother. Robert shook his head while the other young man winked at her. Dally sniffed at them as they passed.

"Watch out for the blond one. I hear he can be quite the charmer *when he wants*." Dally sent a warning glare that melted the grin off his face. She leaned in so that only Rebecca could hear her next remark. "Remember that if the king were to find that any young man in his employ laid a hand on you, even in innocent flirtation, he would be lucky to only lose his job."

Rebecca swallowed and eyed the boy with prim outrage. Hopefully, that would discourage him. Robert grabbed the boy's elbow and directed him toward the dining room.

Dally led her through hallways and courtyards, pointing out servant entrances behind tapestries. She relished her brief exposure outside as sunlight fell into the courtyard they passed through. She closed her eyes, leaned her head back, and smiled as a mild breeze cooled her face. It was easy to forget about the onset of autumn, locked away in the castle.

They walked past the clerks' offices where Branwen and other officials worked. Other than a curt nod, no one thought anything of Dally wandering through offices and pointing things out to a servant. She got the feeling that Dally had worked in all aspects of castle life at one point or another. All treated her respectfully, and she seemed to know everyone, with quite a few as more than casual acquaintances.

"How do you know all these people?" Rebecca asked, once they were off by themselves again.

"When you're the royal governess temporarily without a princess, they find useful things for you to do, so that when she comes back, you'll continue to be useful to her." She winked.

"They?"

"Branwen and the king."

"Really? You work directly with my—the king?"

Dally cast Rebecca a cautionary look but nodded. She cleared the corner to see if anyone was within earshot. She leaned in very close. "It helps to have been the one who got the princess out of the castle alive. That earns you a lot of trust," Dally said with watery eyes.

Rebecca nodded and closed her eyes briefly in an attempt to block out her few splintered memories of that night. She had been around two years old. Many of her memories of the fire and the death of her parents, she was sure she constructed from what the Lieutenant had told her about that night. He answered every question but volunteered very little.

She was too young to really have her own memories, but she swore she felt the flames and choked on smoke as she ran through a dark forest. This was ridiculous, since Dally would have carried her in her arms through the escape tunnels that led to the forest. When Rebecca opened her eyes, Dally puckered her lips tightly. The aging nurse met her eyes as if reading the questions written there.

"We haven't talked about that night." Dally glanced over her shoulder. "You weren't old enough to know what was going on. Do you remember anything?"

"Just smoke, fire, and screaming," Rebecca said.

Dally pressed her graying hair to the side of her head. "Yes, there was all of that." The old nurse closed her eyes and drew Rebecca closer to the wall. "There had been strange things going on all week, people and things missing or in the wrong place. When I heard the yelling and running, I panicked. I grabbed you and ran straight to the hidden passage in your parents' rooms."

Dally touched a silver scar by her temple and checked around the corner again. "I followed it out into that nightmare forest. I think we only survived because those black trees took pity on us. They understand the need to run from fire. I've never been so scared. It was the Lieutenant who found us the next day. He saw the fire and rode straight into Waldren's Wood, without the slightest thought for his safety, hoping to find his friend and sister but finding only us. He had been spying so long for the king, he didn't even know that you'd been born. You were all the family he and the king had left." Dally leaned in to whisper in her ear. "Doubly precious."

They heard footsteps. Dally straightened into her formal posture and motioned for Rebecca to follow. Sir Wendell nodded as he passed, his mustache rippling. *Did he recognize her?* Two high-ranking officers followed him without a glance their way.

Dally gave her a brief tour of the main wing upstairs. They passed women and men carrying buckets of water and baskets of crisply folded bed linens. Young girls just slightly older than Rebecca passed by in groups of twos, giggling.

"We'll walk by Lady Jalene's rooms next. They adjoin her aunt and uncle's rooms."

They rounded a corner to a quieter hallway. A formal guard was stationed halfway down the hallway from the lady's rooms. He stood at attention as they approached. Dally nodded and then knocked on the lady's door. A maid answered the door and smiled as she recognized Dally.

"I just wanted to check in with Lady Jalene and the duchess regarding the banquet."

The maid nodded and opened the door, announcing them.

A woman with brilliant gray hair set down her teacup as they entered. The duchess aimed a polished smile at Dally that complemented the elaborate display of jewels around her neck. She patted one of the two greyhounds that lay at her feet. "Dally, I just asked my girl about you. What delightful timing!"

Jalene stood up from a small desk where she had just sealed a letter and tucked a black curl behind her ear with a long finger as she handed the letter to her maid. Jalene's dark eyes flicked warmly to Dally and Rebecca in welcome.

"Pauline, can you have this sent out for me, please?"

Pauline took the letter with a curtsy and left the room.

"How were the last samples I sent you?" Dally asked.

"Brilliant!" the duchess beamed. "The gold thread around the edges of the napkins came out perfectly!"

"Thank you for letting us help," Jalene said with a smile. "It's been so nice to have something constructive to do."

She settled next to her aunt, in many ways a darker and younger version of the duchess. Jalene glanced politely at Rebecca; the aunt ignored Rebecca's existence. That alone told her more about Jalene and her aunt than anyone could have.

"Well, seeing as how you'll be needing to run a whole castle soon, my dear—"

Her aunt smiled sharply and patted her niece's hand triumphantly. She paused to give her niece an inquiring look as she sensed her unease. Dally smiled affably and then gestured to Rebecca.

Rebecca took a deep breath and stepped forward. The bold motion caught the duchess's attention. She looked with full scrutiny at the bold servant girl.

"Duchess, Lady," Dally said, "may I introduce you to the king's niece, the princess Reyna Brynn Rae Ulmer."

Rebecca curtsied slightly more than necessary, in a conciliatory gesture.

"I apologize for the deception, Duchess. I felt that we needed to meet in order to speak plainly about our situations."

The duchess's back went rigid, and her face froze into a glassy smile as she took in this new development. After a few awkward moments, the duchess stood and bowed deeply, her niece complying with her.

"Please, Duchess, Lady, sit. It will soon be I that will be doing the bowing and pleasing before you."

The duchess looked up, her pale face nearly matching her gray hair. She flicked her eyes toward the rooms next door where her husband must have been.

"It has been brought to my attention that there are individuals who may not fully support the king's intentions to marry," Rebecca said. "I want to openly support his marriage to the Lady Jalene."

The duchess narrowed her eyes, and her smile tightened.

Rebecca sat and gestured for all to join her.

"After spending years in hiding and carrying the burden of being the one heir of the kingdom, I am more than willing to share that burden with someone else. In short, I'd like to put as many people between the throne and me as I can. I would love nothing better than to support the claim the lady's offspring would have to the crown of Lam."

"Why?" The duchess shed her mask of civility, revealing blatant skepticism. "Doing so would be handing over your power. What will that leave you to bargain with?"

Rebecca took this in and set it on a shelf to think over later but proceeded on. "Because they will be my uncle, the king's, children as well. One thing that has been instilled in me from a young age is this kingdom's need to heal. Lam needs a stable crown, not more wars and double-crossings. The people prefer a straight line that is transparent and clear. An heir that could not be contested—that is what King Aldo wants. Therefore, Duchess, that is unquestionably what I want."

The noblewoman pondered this silently. Jalene glanced gingerly at her aunt.

"I would prefer an alliance over yet another rivalry," Jalene said. Her dark eyes pleaded with her aunt. "My uncle, the duke, only yesterday was guessing at those who may wish me harm and the plots set against me *and* my family."

The duchess frowned slightly at this and gently touched Jalene's arm.

Rebecca smiled but kept her voice even. "We share many of the same enemies. We both represent a new future. We would both live better and longer working together rather than against one another. The worst thing that could happen is for us both to lose."

The duchess stared into the distance as she fingered the bloody rubies at her throat. They all watched her as she pulled apart the secret plans she had held on to for many years and weighed them one by one. Finally, the duchess nodded as all the pieces were accounted for. "I think that such an agreement can be reached, at least for now. We are concerned about the banquet. We have heard whispers of how easy it would be to let a little poison slip into the right goblet." The duchess shook her head, causing her silver-streaked curls to swing at her temples. "Honestly, we are not sure who the intended target would be—Jalene or the princess. Though, no one is entirely convinced that there *is* a princess. So Your Highness is protected that way." The duchess of Alain smiled like a cat who knew her advantage.

"I appreciate that fact dearly." Rebecca met the duchess's eyes, not blinking. She knew that she still held the highest card, her uncle. "I'm sure the king does as well. I'm sure that he will reward you for all that you have done for his sake."

FORTY SEVEN

*B*enjamin shivered awake. He tugged his blanket over his shoulder, the rough wool scratching his chin. The world was covered in weak light that was still devoid of the sun's warmth. They stood at the cusp of the autumn months. The soldiers quietly rolled up their blankets while Benjamin stood with help from Keston, the captain of their expedition.

Benjamin's muscles had clenched up during the night and now protested with every movement. He had no idea how he was going to survive another day on the back of a horse. Denny strolled to his horse with his roll under his arm. Benjamin clenched a biscuit between his teeth as Keston shoved him on his horse. Soon the sound of horse hooves set the rhythm to Benjamin's thoughts. *Please don't fall off. Please don't fall off. Please don't fall off.*

The group of clandestine soldiers paused not far from the gateway—just two crumbling piles of stones—that marked the division of the kingdom. Mouthrot must have known the princess was at the castle, because the road was no longer guarded. The men divided into twos and waited fifteen minutes between departures. Each rider securely stored his maps and orders in his head. They raced toward their different destinations with nothing that would betray their mission.

The roads were uncomfortably silent for most of the day. The sparseness of the Thieves' Plain was shocking after so much forest. Benjamin and Denny pulled off the road and hid behind a tangle of bushes, not far from the Gray Gander. As a group of marauders rode by, their eyes firmly pressed to the road ahead, the boys held their breath. The rider all carried rapiers. The boys sunk against their horses and exchanged looks of relief before climbing back on their horses.

Benjamin and Denny arrived at the hideout late afternoon. They led their horses through the brambles that surrounded Benjamin's old hideout. Odie stepped out of the bushes with Rina at his heels. A grin spread across his face, exposing large, rocklike teeth. He hugged Denny, lifting him several inches off the ground. Denny slapped him on the back and let his brother take the horses.

Benjamin paused in front of his door. *So much had changed.* The memory of the unfinished business with the Lieutenant held him at the door, twisting into a knot deep in his chest. Denny sighed and then pressed Benjamin inside.

The Lieutenant peered up from the map he was studying and nearly dropped his chipped mug, one of Ursula Black's. Benjamin cleared his throat, unsure how to start.

"Well, it's good to see you're still alive," Benjamin said. "We're going to need you."

Denny slapped Benjamin on the back, shaking his head. "Translation: 'We have a plan. We think you'll like it.'"

The Lieutenant set his mug down, crossed the room, wrapped an arm around each boy, and squeezed. Benjamin's head knocked into Denny's. The Lieutenant stepped back and smiled at both of them, his hands resting on their shoulders. Benjamin squirmed a little, uncomfortable with the unfamiliar gesture. He slipped quietly off to check the contents of a pot on the stove. The Lieutenant bit his lip and gave Denny an extra squeeze. Benjamin spooned up the gruel to allow the awkward moment to pass.

"The king is sending an army?" The Lieutenant fiddled with the buttons on his shirt, watching his son warily.

"Not exactly." Denny slapped the Lieutenant's back and went to accept the bowl of gruel from Benjamin.

"There's already an army here," Benjamin said, setting the warm bowl down to hunt up a clean spoon.

The Lieutenant tugged at his missing eye patch and glanced back at Denny for an explanation.

Benjamin coughed. He clenched his spoon and forced himself to look at the Lieutenant's brown and black eyes. "Branwen's been running men all over the Thieves' Plain for years. That man has serious trust issues."

"Dirty old crow!" The Lieutenant laughed.

"Don't I know it!" Benjamin raised the pitcher of milk in agreement.

"So how are we going to gather so many strays and make them useful?" The Lieutenant's eyes lit up at the possibilities, the wheels visibly turning in his head. He cleared the maps.

Benjamin swallowed his bite forcefully. "It's already begun."

Denny stirred his gruel. "We've sent men to gather the network."

"We need to be ready in three days," Benjamin said through a mouthful of food.

"Three days?" The Lieutenant's mismatched eyes widened.

"We want to attack before Mouthrot has time to hear from his castle spies." Benjamin shoveled more gruel into his mouth.

"We'll use Baldo for our eyes and ears," Denny said as he reached for the pitcher.

"I know another." The Lieutenant scratched his chin. "Helda works in the laundry. In her prime, she could fight as well as any man."

"Two is always better than one." Benjamin filled his empty bowl with milk. "Then we need to find a way to lower morale, lure the men out, or render them useless."

"More bad food?" The Lieutenant pulled the empty pot off the stove. "Rumors of easy money?"

Benjamin smiled. If there was one thing that would cause anyone on the Thieves' Plain to pick up and move, it was the promise of easy money, no matter how improbable. He tipped his bowl back and drank. "That was Rina's milk, wasn't it?"

Benjamin waited to see if his body would revolt against it. He shrugged and finished the goat milk unharmed.

† † †

The brothers went to the fortress to say good-bye to Baldo and tell him about the new gold mines in the mountains, assuring all who overheard that there were many employment opportunities available. They'd come back in a few months with buckets of gold.

One day later, men bled from all the cracks of Shreb's fortress. Not that any of them would dream of working in the mines. No, there was money to be made from the mule trains that carried supplies and gold. Pockets to pick. What else were young, underemployed men from the Thieves' Plain supposed to do?

Benjamin sat with Denny, watching Shreb's men slip out among the farmers. Benjamin scratched a few more tally marks into his notebook as he noted a few more poorly disguised guards walking away from the fortress.

"Baldo nearly split a gut when I told him." Denny rested the spyglass on his knee, smiling as he remembered. "He thought that story was brilliant."

"Well, it's nice to know someone around here can appreciate a brilliant plan."

"And from Baldo. He's only twelve but as smart and clever as they come."

"Hmm."

Benjamin grabbed the spyglass and counted the guards. Many of them stopped to gaze at the mountains in the distance. No one stopped the men from fleeing the fortress.

"You know, I think you and Baldo would really get along. Maybe when this is all over, he could be your man when you're a duke or lord or whatever."

"I'm sure that the Lieutenant could find something for him to do." Benjamin examined the spyglass's finish.

He still wasn't sure what he was going to do when this scheme was over. Benjamin couldn't imagine living in the same four walls with the Lieutenant when the old man finally retired to his quiet estate. He couldn't imagine the Lieutenant not taking his band of young men with him. Denny and his brothers would always be underfoot.

Perhaps traveling was in Benjamin's future. A few gold coins in his pocket and he could go anywhere and do anything. Anything *he* wanted. It would be bliss.

A bird screeched behind them, and Denny turned around and waved Odie over, but he just shook his head and motioned back to the road.

"Guess he's got something to tell us," Denny said, standing up.

"You know Odie; he's always a wealth of information," Benjamin said.

Denny punched Benjamin good-naturedly in the shoulder as he shoved his book into a pocket. It still hurt. Benjamin rubbed his arm as they walked. Odie led one of the horses, which was packed with supplies from the brothers' place.

"Looks like the place was clean," Denny said, poking under the blankets and bags.

Benjamin watched the brothers carefully, unsure how they communicated. Odie never talked, though Benjamin was sure he was capable. Maybe he was just used to Denny talking for him. "Great! So we can use it as a second staging area?" Benjamin asked, fixing his eye on Odie, waiting for a response. Odie simply nodded.

Denny readjusted the coverings on the horse and placed a hand up on Odie's shoulder that was level with Denny's ear.

"Well done."

Watching Denny reassure and care for his giant-sized brother was bizarre, to say the least. A mute giant. Odie set a plate-sized hand on Denny's head and rubbed, a smile transforming his still face.

It struck Benjamin how sad the brothers were. Odie was the worst. Were they still mourning their parents? Benjamin had lost both parents and then found one of them again. He wasn't a smiling, rosy-cheeked, sixteen-year-old boy, but then, who was? Of course, he'd grown up around what many would consider juvenile delinquents— or at least youth who aspired to be delinquents someday. Perhaps Benjamin was not in a good place to determine such things. But that was only the second smile he'd seen on Odie's face.

Odie shook his head as he listened while Denny described all he'd seen on his journey to the castle and back.

Back at Benjamin's house, Odie handed the Lieutenant a few squares of thick leather with an eye-shaped symbol stamped in the center. The Lieutenant smiled back and clapped Odie on the shoulder.

"Thank you, Odie!" He looked up into the boy's face. "You've done very well!" He held up the stamped leather.

"What's that?" Benjamin asked.

"I had Odie collect a few favors people owed me."

"Ha! More than half the Thieves' Plain owes you something, whether they know it or not." Denny pulled a ham from one of the sacks Odie had brought in.

"I hope they are paying with more than just ham," Benjamin said. His mouth watering as he reached across the table.

The Lieutenant chuckled and sliced a few pieces off for Benjamin. The ham nearly rolled onto the floor when the tabletop tipped under Benjamin's weight. The Lieutenant caught the ham before it soiled the entire map that had been left on the table. Benjamin had forgotten the top was still loose; his mother had never bothered to fix it.

"Thanks." Benjamin made a point of smiling at the Lieutenant, who smiled back.

"You can thank Odie for that!" Denny said through his mouthful of ham. "Odie made it. He's really good with curing and smoking. He started helping Mom with the food when she got sick."

"Really?" Benjamin bit into the ham and mumbled, "Fantastic job, Odie!"

Odie blushed in pride and then rushed back outside to the horse. When he returned, he set a jug in front of the Lieutenant, who pulled out the stopper and sniffed the contents. A smile spread across his face. He poured a glass of what looked a lot like mud and swallowed it with a look of determination.

"What is that?" Denny asked. "I thought that was spirits."

"No. That would be nice, but this is much, *much* better." The Lieutenant's face twisted. "It's a tonic that speeds up healing, or at least makes you feel better: one of Helda's specialties."

Denny and Benjamin exchanged skeptical looks but didn't press any further.

Benjamin rolled out the map of Shreb's fortress to query the brother's about the fortress. Denny marked Mouthrot's movements while Odie pointed out where Helda could be found. According to Baldo, Shreb spent most of his time in his rooms. They went over the plan before pulling out a map of the Thieves' Plain.

"Two riders went north toward the Villains' Academy. They were going to split here," Benjamin said, setting his finger down where the northern road divided, "and gather men as they went. They're supposed to meet at the Brick. It's just north of here."

Benjamin looked at the Lieutenant, who nodded as he followed Benjamin's finger across the map, looking pleased. "Another two riders went south down the main road toward Thistle Rock. They're to meet at Denny's."

"Odie said Laford and Weston were already there with their men. We'll head over there and fill people in," Denny said.

Benjamin looked at Odie, who nodded silently as he stared at the map. *So he* can *speak!* Odie drew a line with his finger that ran between Shreb's fortress and their house.

"Oh, yes," Denny added. "There's a patrol that circles the area around the fortress. They never get as far as our place, though. So men approaching from the south should be fine. The patrols might disappear completely as more men desert."

"That sounds good." The Lieutenant rested his black eye on Denny. "You know the location and time they need to be in position? We'll light a fire if we cancel."

Denny nodded, and the brothers headed out on foot.

Later, Keston arrived to update Benjamin and the Lieutenant. Benjamin marked the location of men and numbers on the map, while the captain helped himself to ham and potatoes. The lieutenant poured the limp man some apple cider.

Keston spoke between greedy bites. "Between Denny's place and the Brick, we have just about one hundred men. Not everyone is accounted for yet, but they know to go straight to Shreb's." Keston drank deeply. "With most of those good-for-nothings behind Shreb's wall slinking away, they'll fold like a poorly staked tent."

The Lieutenant walked over to the map and ran his fingers over the markings. He nodded in appreciation and then examined the captain. "You look tired. Have you gotten any rest?"

Before Keston could protest, the Lieutenant pointed the soldier to Benjamin's cot. Benjamin sighed.

Great; another night sleeping on the ground.

Benjamin traced a path on the map between the different camps and Shreb's fortress—the very fortress he had wanted to defend and work in not so long ago. *How did I get here?* He'd spoken with King Aldo face to face, crossed a mountain, and planned an attack on Shreb's fortress with Lam's master of spies. He discovered his father was alive. He'd survived a princess. This was the opposite of every plan Benjamin had ever made for himself. Could he be happy with this? Would he be able to live with this choice? He felt weary and cast his eyes to his mother's bed, the one the Lieutenant had claimed as his own.

"I have always known this moment was inevitable, but still, it doesn't feel quite real." The Lieutenant stepped beside Benjamin and patted his shoulder briefly. Benjamin did not flinch. "A part of me is going to miss all of this. After we enter that fortress, everything will be undone."

"What are you going to do then?"

"What I intended to do years ago. Go home to Gehnry, my estate in the east." He walked around the map and followed the notes and marks. "You are welcome there." The Lieutenant gave Benjamin a sideways glance. "By all rights, it will be yours after I'm gone. I'd understand if you didn't…what I mean is, you're welcome there whenever and for however long you wish."

Benjamin nodded, even though the Lieutenant was focused on the map. His stomach twisted. He didn't know how to answer. Benjamin picked up the empty plates. "Thanks."

"I would happily welcome Denny and his brothers at Gehnry as family or help them start somewhere. I think I owe them that much. Do you think they would accept that?"

Benjamin set the dishes in the sink. "Denny would, I think, as long as Baldo was taken care of. Who knows what Odie wants?"

The Lieutenant flexed his jaws and nodded, trying not to look directly at him. "What about you?"

What would he do at an estate? Go hunting? If nothing else, he could sleep and eat enough food to make boredom worth it until he figured out a plan.

He had hardly spent more than a few days at a time with his father. He still didn't really even believe he had a father. Did he owe the Lieutenant that much? Did he owe him *anything*? He'd been alone for so long. It was strange to think he could belong to someone. *But,* he reminded himself, *Branwen has practically offered me a job working with him—and Rebecca.*

He was concerned for Rebecca, even if she was planning a slow death for him right now. A dangerous machine of ambition surrounded her. Many noblemen and one fiancée to the king may wish a terrible accident upon her. It was a knotted mess. Once you started untying, you could never stop. Benjamin wasn't sure whether he wanted to be sucked in or not.

"I don't know. Honestly, my head is still spinning." Benjamin flicked a glance to the Lieutenant and shrugged. "Branwen hinted at employment opportunities. Maybe when the dust settles—" It was the only fair answer he could give. *I'm not entirely sure that's up to me.*

The Lieutenant nodded. "I think—" he paused. "I think coming to Gehnry might answer some questions for you. Fill in a few of the missing pieces to your story."

Benjamin met the Lieutenant's one light eye and one dark eye for a moment. The truth of that statement pricked his heart. He blinked at the map and then nodded. Benjamin's voice was not available to comment.

"Go to sleep. We're all going to need to be awake and operating at our fullest tomorrow."

Benjamin piled several cloaks on the floor and lay under the kitchen table, leaving the spare cot for the old man. He watched the Lieutenant's feet as he made nighttime preparations. Benjamin rolled onto his back. He looked up at the underside of the rickety table where he had eaten all his meals with his mother and saw something he'd not seen before: curly letters. The writing was upside down and impossible to read in the shadows. The room went dark, and the words were gone.

Ah well, he thought. *Morning will come soon enough.* He rolled over and slept.

FORTY EIGHT

The guards camped outside Rebecca's hallway stood at attention as she walked by, relief evident on their faces. One stood forward in a silent offer to carry the basket, but Rebecca discreetly waved him off.

She hiked her laundry basket up her hip. The hallway was much longer than she remembered. Sir Wendell, the captain of the guard, stood in front of two sentinels placed outside her door and directed one of the guards to take the basket.

He then followed her into her rooms. "I think I can now officially breathe easier," Sir Wendell said through locked jaws.

He glared at the teacup Dally offered him. She returned it to the tray untouched.

Rebecca explained how she needed access to the castle for her own safety and sanity. She checked her rekindled wrath as she remembered his order to remove her from her horse this morning. He stared hard at both of the women, biting the inside of his mouth.

His eyes blazed hotly. Closing them to speak, he nodded in acceptance. "I do not want to find out these things as I stroll through the castle reviewing all our security plans with my lieutenants." He opened his eyes that had cooled beneath his lids. "I don't need to know every detail, but it might be good to know a few things you and Secretary Branwen are up to."

He pinched the bridge of his nose and sighed. Dally stepped forward in reconciliation.

"You are right." Rebecca waved her nurse back. "This plan was hastily put together this morning."

He nodded at this. No doubt he thought this was a direct retaliation for this morning's events.

"You and your men have a great responsibility to keep me safe, but I'm about to be released into a world completely unknown to me. I need to know what I'm getting into. And I need to know the castle. Being locked away is not helping me," she said, holding her ground. "Every king or queen has a bodyguard, but they also are armed with knowledge, experience, and a knife or two of their own."

Sir Wendell raised his eyebrows at this. "You remind me of your grandmother, the queen mother, rest her soul. She used to do exactly what she wanted, regardless of any advice." He smoothed his mustache as he sized her up. "Do you have a knife with you right now?"

She nodded.

"Do you know how to use it?" he asked.

"I kept myself from being killed with it."

"Can I see it?"

Rebecca's cheeks burned as she thought of how to remove it discreetly from under her clothes.

Sir Wendell turned his back. "I hope you're not so modest when it counts."

Rebecca lifted her skirt and pulled out the knife that Benjamin had given her as a going-away gift.

Sir Wendell examined the blade. "This is good for close combat but little help if you are outnumbered."

"The Lieutenant trained me how to defend myself."

"Of course he did. Probably against peasants on the plain." Sir Wendell fingered his moustache. "Here I worry more about assassins. I would feel better if I could continue your training. I'll also add a few more guards around the castle. That way if the king ever finds out that you're wandering the castle, we may be allowed to keep our heads." He rested his hands behind his back. "If anyone finds out who you are, it's over. Someone sneezes too close to you, you *run*. Find a guard and return to your rooms."

She bobbed her head obediently and swallowed. *What's the point of being a princess,* she thought bitterly, *if everyone still orders me around?*

Sir Wendell nodded and left the room. Rebecca sat down, feeling a touch sick.

Dally looked at her and smiled. "I think that went very well!"

FORTY NINE

*B*enjamin's shadow stretched in front of him as he walked along the road with the other fake merchants and farmers toward Shreb's fortress. He felt as if he was walking through mud, though the road was as dry as powder. Every step felt heavier than the one before. He scanned the merging groups for Denny or Odie. Rina walked beside him. She refused to be left behind and had chewed through the rope the Lieutenant had used to secure her. He felt a pang of nerves in his chest, like bat wings flapping wildly.

Odie was the shyest person Benjamin had ever met, but he was strong. He also had a tender heart. Perhaps that was why Rina followed him so closely. That was her job. Benjamin peeked at the Lieutenant ahead of him. He wore a patched blanket as a cloak and his scuffed eye patch again, the strap pressing into the permanent dip in his hair.

His father glanced back at Benjamin and gestured with his chin ahead of them. He must have seen Denny or at least Odie. Benjamin weaved through the parade of spies and allies until he caught up to the old man. The Lieutenant was checking the sword that was hidden under his cloak as Benjamin touched the long knife he wore under his own.

A group, led by a man in a crumpled hat, filtered into their group. He nodded to the Lieutenant with a knowing smile. "Well, if it isn't the one-eyed dragon back from nowhere." The man lit his pipe and then tossed a square of leather to the Lieutenant. An eye was stamped into the center. "I'd heard a breath of a rumor, of course, but everyone was so tight-lipped about it—which is saying a lot for a network of spies."

The Lieutenant smiled, leaving visible crinkle marks in the film of dust around his eyes. He adjusted the strap of his eye patch but said nothing.

"So of course that meant you were tucked away, doing something serious for the king." The man pulled his pipe to the corner of his mouth. "This should be interesting, if nothing else."

"And that's why you came?" the Lieutenant asked, sounding doubtful.

"Well, there is so little unknown to a spy."

"Except to find out if any of those secrets are true." The Lieutenant faced the man. "Pete, this is Benjamin. Benjamin. Pete."

Pete pushed back his crumpled hat and focused intently on Benjamin. His eyes lit up and then flickered back to the Lieutenant. "Nice to meet you, Ben-ja-min."

Pete emphasized every syllable in Benjamin's name, sending a shiver down his spine. This man knew something about him.

This guy knows something the Lieutenant doesn't know, Benjamin thought as a chill ran down his spine. *Something dangerous.*

Pete nodded and blended back into the crowd.

Once he had gone, Benjamin spoke. "That guy," he said, "gives me the creeps."

The Lieutenant chuckled. "Okay. Anyone else?" he said, lifting his eyebrows.

"Well…" He looked around him. "I wouldn't let my guard down around any of these guys, really. They *are* spies, after all."

The old man nodded approvingly as Rina butted Benjamin's knee. "Do you see Odie or Denny ahead?"

"Yep. Just follow Rina. She could find Odie anywhere."

It was strange that just knowing where Denny and Odie were eased Benjamin's mind. Things were moving, as they should. He caught a glimpse of Keston, who scanned the line from horseback. He dismounted and led his horse over to Benjamin.

"We still have two riders out, but our numbers look good." Benjamin and the Lieutenant nodded. Keston left them to check in with the groups behind them.

Soon the fortress was in view. Benjamin noted the prominent lack of guards on top of the battlements. There were two men leaning against their spears who appeared to be dozing off. One guard stood in front of the entry, ushering people in with a wave of his hand.

Inside, a frazzled man with quill and paper sat at a table, trying to note all goods that were being brought in. A spindly youth stood next to him with loose pants cinched around his waist. His hair was the same color as the dust that coated the traveling cloaks of the men. The boy looked bored, but his eyes lit up when he saw the Lieutenant.

"That's Baldo," the Lieutenant mumbled. "I thought he worked in the kitchen."

Benjamin glanced over his shoulder to catch another glimpse of the famous Baldo. He was surprised to see how waiflike the boy actually was. He was quite a bit smaller than Benjamin, even for a twelve-year-old. Baldo smirked at him before turning back to the kitchen.

"He must have wanted to keep his eye out for his brothers."

They found Denny. Odie was circling the courtyard, taking count of everyone. They were supposed to meet in the dining hall to buy a mug of penny ale.

The more disguised spies who filed in, the more uninterested the guards became. It was a logistical nightmare of herding bodies around and answering questions. The clerk, sitting at his table with ink and parchment, grew paler and more frazzled as men and animals swirled around him. Many asked about prices to keep up appearances. Very few had brought anything real to sell. The Lieutenant nodded at Pete and Keston. They all moved around the fortress to their areas.

The Lieutenant pulled his makeshift cloak around himself and shielded his face. Benjamin headed to the back entrance where the laundry hung. A broad-shouldered woman fidgeted with some rugs on the line. She held an oddly shaped stick to beat the rugs. She caught Benjamin's eye and then purposefully stepped behind a rug. He checked that no one was in the area and cautiously approached.

"Excuse me," he said. "I'm looking for Helda." Benjamin stepped behind the cover of the rug, but out of reach of her rug beater.

"Of course you are. Benjamin?"

"Helda?"

"Was it you who spread the rumors about the gold pouring out of the mountains?" Helda grinned, one tooth missing.

Benjamin nodded and peered around to let her know he was in a hurry.

"I put a little sleepy in the men's breakfast…the ones who are left."

Benjamin smiled thankfully back.

"Listen," she said, "do you have someone else in the fortress besides me?"

"Yes. Why?" Benjamin examined her with suspicion.

"You shouldn't tell me his name, but I must know. Is it Baldo? That runty kid? Shreb's personal servant?"

"Wait—he's Shreb's personal servant?"

"Listen. Does he know about me?"

"No, I just found out about you yesterday."

She nodded in appreciation. "Good. You can't trust that kid. Maybe he is helping you, but not without helping himself first. When Baldo first showed up here, some other boys gave him trouble, and not less than a week later, one boy had an accident. A barrel fell on him in his sleep. Another fell down the stairs and cracked his head almost *in half*."

Benjamin had nothing to say to that. A sinking feeling in his stomach swallowed all his words.

"The other boys just up and ran off after that. Pretty sure that runty kid doesn't care for competition or people giving him a hard time."

Ice spread through Benjamin's chest as he remembered Baldo watching him enter the courtyard. He had assumed he waited for his brothers. How much had Denny told Baldo about him? Something, obviously. Benjamin snapped back to his task.

"Where are Mouthrot and Shreb now?"

"Shreb is shut up in his rooms upstairs, as usual. Mouthrot has been in tirades about losing so many men. He should be reporting his daily lies to Shreb, but he threatened to wake the night watch, if there's any left. Don't let him do that."

Benjamin thanked her as he ran across the laundry. He slowed as he entered the hall. Men were bunched up, pretending to drink their penny ales. He saw Denny in a corner looking around the hall, probably for Baldo, who wasn't there. Odie walked past and raised his eyebrows questioningly. Benjamin swatted the silent question away. Nothing good would come of telling the brothers about Baldo now. He wasn't even sure there was anything to tell.

He didn't know who to talk to first. The Lieutenant was going after Mouthrot. Keston was to arrest Shreb. Benjamin surveyed the congested hall. The Lieutenant must have already gone upstairs. They were expecting Mouthrot to be there, in the opposite wing from Shreb.

Keston approached the stairs with a cluster of men. Benjamin crossed over to him before he got to the stairs and motioned to him. The captain drifted over while the others continued toward the stairs.

"One of our informants says that Mouthrot is suspicious and threatened to wake the night watch. I think the Lieutenant went up looking for him, but it's very likely Mouthrot's not there."

"That changes things, doesn't it?" Keston looked back at his men, who had gathered at the bottom of the stairs waiting for him. "Should I go support the Lieutenant or continue to Shreb?"

Odie and Denny started toward them. Benjamin and Keston moved to the center of the room to avoid drawing attention to the stairs, though there weren't any guards visible in the hall.

"We think that Mouthrot may have woken the night watch. He's suspicious."

Denny bit off an oath and fiddled with the sword under his cloak.

Wait, Benjamin thought. *How did he get a sword? Does everyone else but me have a sword?*

"The guards are the biggest threat." Benjamin gripped his long knife with a sweaty hand. "I think Keston and his men should head down there. If the guards haven't been alerted, they can head back to us for support."

"None of you are strong enough fighters to take on Shreb or Mouthrot if he's over there." Keston cast a look toward his men. "You'll need support!"

"Odie could probably handle it, but I'd rather not take that chance," Denny said, glancing up at his brother.

Odie nodded and revealed the sword under his cloak.

Seriously! Benjamin growled to himself. *Is someone handing out swords?*

Benjamin looked around, trying to look casual. He flipped through the pieces of the plan in his head. Pete shuffled their way with two mugs of ale in each hand, followed by another man who was similarly attired. They passed out the mugs.

"What's the problem?" Pete guzzled his ale.

Benjamin waved away the mug; Keston held his stiffly. Pete shrugged and finished Benjamin's. Benjamin explained about Mouthrot and the guards.

"Easy enough." Pete belched and handed the empty mugs to one of the men wandering around. "You and me up to Shreb's, and soldier boy here off to the guards. That isn't a deal-breaker."

Keston nodded, and his men trickled up the stairs, while Pete got a group singing blushworthy drinking songs. Then Pete accompanied him upstairs with a dozen men. "Another half dozen will be up when they've started the next song."

They turned right at the top of the stairs, and Benjamin tried to remember everything that Denny had said about Baldo. *"He was clever,"* he'd said. *"You'll get along."* No mention of an interest in villainy. Benjamin caught Pete eyeing him.

"So what's the horrible bit you didn't tell us down there?" Pete asked, searching for guards.

"Let's just say there may be a factor we didn't take into consideration."

Pete wiped the back of his dirty hand on his nose. "Always is."

Benjamin peered at the brothers walking stiffly ahead of him. *What if it were true?* They hadn't recovered from losing their parents yet.

Losing a brother? It couldn't be true, even if his gut screamed otherwise.

As Benjamin counted doors, he heard a door open behind them. Baldo poked his pale face into the hall, a dark smudge under one of his wide eyes. Denny motioned for him to get out. He raised a delicate hand in acknowledgment and slunk back in and closed the door.

"I hope he's smart enough to stay out of the way," Denny whispered to Odie, who nodded and cast glance to Baldo's closed door.

The group approached Shreb's door and lined up the additional six men approaching quickly behind them. Benjamin arranged for a few men to stand guard. He would be crazy not to watch his back. Pete said that he'd take Mouthrot if he was with Shreb. Denny volunteered with Odie to take Shreb.

"Benjamin," Pete said, "you just make sure that no one escapes. I've got a score to settle with Mouthrot." Pete spit on the ground and wiped his mouth on his arm.

"We need him alive!" Benjamin said, grabbing Pete's gritty sleeve. "The king *needs* him alive."

Pete's dark eyes narrowed, but he nodded in acceptance. "It doesn't mean he can't get hurt though." He winked and burst into the room.

FIFTY

Benjamin and Denny had to shove their way into the room. All the men stood in the doorway but hadn't moved any further. Finally Odie parted the men so that the three of them could gape at the scene as well.

In front of the fireplace, Mouthrot sat glaring through a gag, his hands and feet tied securely to a chair. One of his men lay on the floor, bleeding out.

Benjamin's insides turned to ice as he looked at Denny and Odie. Pete stared blankly.

Benjamin gripped the knife on his hip and barked orders to the men in the hall. "Let no one pass!" He sprinted down the hall, drawing his long knife as he neared Baldo's door. Odie and Denny were close behind him, but probably not for the same reason. He pushed through the door.

The room was empty except for a large chair, almost like a throne. Benjamin ran around the room checking behind tapestries covered in swans and horns but found nothing.

"Someone go find out if *any*one went downstairs!"

Odie made eye contact with Benjamin from behind his older brother. He did not look confused.

Denny panicked. "Where's Baldo? Did Shreb take him?" He ran to the door to issue commands.

"There has to be a door in here. A hidden staircase? A passageway? Something!" Benjamin fiddled with the arm of the chair. "There has to be a lever somewhere."

He paused midscramble to meet the still Odie's dark-brown eyes.

"You knew?" Benjamin asked. Odie closed his eyes and nodded. "Maybe we're wrong. There could be another explanation." Benjamin continued to frisk the chair.

"There won't be."

Benjamin turned, open-mouthed like a fish, as Odie's rough whisper rattled his bones. He saw it then. All of Odie's fears he never dared to utter. Hoping his silence would keep the truth unreal.

Click.

The throne tilted back. Underneath it was a spiral staircase heading straight down. Denny returned. Shouts echoed in the hallway.

"No one's come down since—" His words cut off as he caught sight of the dark hole under Shreb's throne. "We've got to get down there. Shreb took Baldo down there."

Denny shoved past Benjamin, nearly knocking him over.

"Wait!" Odie said.

Denny's only response was to set his jaw and forcefully and push his way down the dark stairs.

"I'll get a lantern!" Benjamin spun around to look.

Odie raised a lantern, filled and trimmed. "Baldo left this behind the door." He flexed his jaws.

Benjamin swallowed the knowledge that they were walking into a trap, a trap set by a cherished little brother. He raced down the stairs, nearly tripping twice. "Denny!"

"I found a lantern!" Denny called up the stairs.

Denny fumbled with an unlit lantern as he climbed the stairs. Benjamin twisted a piece of parchment to light his lantern. Before Denny could bolt, Benjamin grabbed his wrist and nearly fell face first down the stairs.

"These lanterns were *left* for us."

Denny stared furiously back at him. Odie seized Denny's other arm so Benjamin could shove past and take the lead.

The stairway twisted and twisted down. There was a landing that must have been on the main floor not far from the hall. He could hear tables being overturned. Men yelled and glass broke. Benjamin pressed on, scraping his hands as he caught himself from falling.

"He'd have gone all the way down," Benjamin said over his shoulder.

The brothers' footsteps were the only response he got. Denny's breathing sounded near panic levels. Benjamin prayed that Odie could keep Denny in check when the time came.

Benjamin was shoved into the icy stone wall, as Denny stumbled into him. His forearm and knee screamed. Limping on, he knew he had to stay ahead of Denny. Denny could not be the first one to see whatever was at the bottom of the stairs.

Denny thrashed at Odie, who held him back. Benjamin growled as his skin burned. *Please let me be wrong.* It was nothing but a feeling, really. He could be wrong about something, someday, and this could be it. Maybe they'd all have a good laugh about it after Denny punched him in the face for thinking his baby brother was the most conniving villain the kingdom of Lam had ever seen, on or off of the Thieves' Plain.

Denny's subjective claims of Baldo's brilliance and his eagerness to help them, even providing means for them, did not help. *A boy who didn't like competition wouldn't want Mouthrot around,* Benjamin thought as he reviewed the situation. *Could he be the real threat on the plain? Shreb was merely a mask he wore. No, no. Baldo could just be loyal to him. He had been working with Shreb for a while now. It was a way out for him.*

Benjamin stopped on the stairs as they ended in front of a wall. He held out an arm that Denny nearly pushed through. Odie dragged him back again.

"That's the end?" Denny cried, pushing his locks, damp with sweat, out of his eyes. "There's got to be a way through!"

Denny was wild eyed and near sobbing, his face flushed from their descent. Odie hauled his brother back a few steps to give Benjamin room. Denny collapsed against the wall, exhausted from fighting Odie the whole way. Benjamin felt around the walls and stairway, finally tugging and twisting a hook at the bottom of the stairs until it gave. The wall screeched aside, as stone grated against stone.

Odie drew a sword in one hand and a long knife in the other. He furrowed his brows at his brother, willing him to stay there. Denny rolled his head against the wall and closed his eyes, swallowing. He looked slightly green. Benjamin pulled out his long knife and waited, his grip tightening around the handle until his hand ached. Odie raised his sword, casting a shadow in front of the lantern as he bounced on his toes. Denny pressed his back against the wall, breathing heavily.

Odie bolted through the door first, his weapons ready to defend or attack. Benjamin followed closely behind, unsure if Denny followed or not. No one could get past Odie, who filled the narrow tunnel. There was one lit torch at the end of the tunnel where it turned sharply—another breadcrumb. They trudged on and on, more than the length of the fortress. Soon the smooth walls gave out to rough-cut rock. The air in the tunnels grew warmer. The floor beneath their feet was uneven, and loose rocks ground under their tread. Benjamin tripped and jammed his right hand into the wall.

"Old crow droppings!" He pressed his bloody knuckles to his mouth. He looked up to see Odie's faint outline as he turned. "I can see light around the bend."

FIFTY ONE

*O*die and Benjamin burst out into the light. Odie raised his weapons and turned right, while Benjamin turned left to secure their backs, which nearly sent him over a steep ledge. He scampered back into Odie, who stood firm as a pillar of stone. They were standing on a narrow path dug into the ravine wall behind the fortress. Benjamin turned to warn Denny, but he wasn't in the tunnel.

A man stood before Odie, wearing a gray traveling cloak over fine blue-and-red silks. His dark hair feathered away from the fine features of his face. He held a sword point under Odie's chin. The many jewels mounted on buttons, cufflinks, and rings glinted in the sun. A family could live off the jewel on his left pinky for the rest of their lives.

This had to be the "Mighty" Shreb, Benjamin surmised.

Behind him, a waif sat on a rock. He wore coarse clothing, but his grin shone with intelligent malevolence. Baldo held a small chest under his arm. He looked directly at Benjamin and winked.

Heat rose in Benjamin's cheeks. *This little twerp was no innocent!* In fact, he was the most arrogant kid Benjamin had ever met.

"You must be Benjamin," Shreb said, tilting his head to look around Odie's wide frame. "My waif here told me about you. Black-Eyed Barnaby's son, eh? Trying to overthrow me like your old man did?"

Benjamin balked at this. His father's identity was not a widely known fact. No one outside his small circle knew who his father was. Baldo wagged his eyebrows at him and grinned wider. Benjamin glared at Odie, who shook his head, denying any transference of knowledge and held his weapons at the ready. Shreb laughed as his fingers traced the brocade of his waistcoat.

"Thank you for taking my overly ambitious VA off my hands. Handing him over to old Barnaby is a much better punishment than a little poison or a knife in the back."

"His name is the Lieutenant, not Barnaby!" Odie rumbled through stiff lips.

Shreb lifted his eyebrows in surprise. "What do I care what his name is?"

He drew his sword back to strike Odie, but his blade met unyielding steel. Swords rang. Odie pressed forward. Shreb reluctantly fell back, his eyes wide. Gravel skittered down the ledge.

Benjamin glanced up at Baldo, who smirked and climbed up the rocks to a higher path. Flashing steel filled the entire path in front of Benjamin as he slid his knife back into its sheath. He'd have to climb up and over. He turned and faced the wall of rocks and reached for a handhold. Denny emerged from the tunnel, dropping his lantern.

"Denny, I need a boost!" Benjamin called.

Denny grabbed him and shoved him upward. Benjamin grabbed a hold and scrambled up the rough wall, slipping on loose rock that tumbled under him. *Please don't hit Odie! Denny would be okay, though.*

He followed a curve inward to Baldo's easier route up the hill. Baldo was running on the path above, stick arms and legs slicing through the air, the chest still tucked under his arm. The rough climb on the rock scraped more skin off Benjamin's knuckles and knees. He slipped and slammed his chin against the hard ground but quickly locked his fingers on a nub of rock.

His head buzzed with the shock of this injury and muted the screams of his lesser scrapes. There was a tang around his tongue, and he spit out blood. He pushed upward through the swell of pain. He couldn't lose Baldo now.

Benjamin rolled onto the narrow path and scrabbled after the kid, running full out to close the gap between them, focusing on the curve where the small boy disappeared.

A yell erupted from below. Benjamin hoped that was a good thing, because he knew he would be no match for anyone with a sword. He rounded the corner and slid on loose rock. He felt something whizz by his head and crash on the rock next to him. Baldo burst from his hiding place. Benjamin didn't see what Baldo had thrown, but he was pretty sure it was meant to kill him. Benjamin drew his knife, holding it in front of him, his only shield against flying daggers or bolts. He approached the next blind spot more carefully, only to see that Baldo was gaining a wider lead on him.

"This is ridiculous!" The wind swallowed Benjamin's words and blurred his vision. He wiped his eyes, feeling the sting on his knuckles. He had to find a way to get in front of Baldo. Otherwise, he'd just keep running into traps, which wouldn't end well.

Benjamin climbed up the rock to get a view. The path rippled straight ahead but then turned sharply right and wrapped behind the rock he was standing on. He clambered over the towering rock, his exhaustion making his limbs heavy and slow. Benjamin pressed through a gap, scraping a button of his shirt off. He gasped, his head swimming, as he looked down. The path was farther down on this side and more of a wall than the other side had been. He allowed himself a drink of water, slung his waterskin on his back, and then half-slid, half-climbed down, shredding the heels of his hands as he tried to slow his fall. He added them to the growing list of injured parts he'd hopefully attend to later. Benjamin's muscles burned with real heat as he worked his way down the wall. He tried to muffle his descent. Stealth was important.

He jumped down the last yard and landed shakily on his feet. He hoped that he'd still have enough energy to fight. He pressed himself into a depression in the wall and waited, panting. He soon heard footsteps on the path and held his breath, willing himself to be unseen.

Benjamin gripped his knife and readied himself to spring. He lunged too early. Baldo recoiled, screamed, and retreated. Benjamin dove, catching the boy by the legs. Baldo tripped, losing his grip on the chest. He rolled and kicked Benjamin in the stomach, knocking the air out of his lungs, allowing Baldo time to recover his precious strongbox. As soon as he had gotten two good breaths of air into him, he scrambled after the little scoundrel. Benjamin ran, clutching his stomach.

Baldo stumbled wildly ahead of him, while pain flared through Benjamin's body. He pushed the pain down and limped after Denny's precious baby brother. Benjamin rounded the turn cautiously but was surprised to come face to face with Denny.

"Where's Baldo?" Denny scowled. Sweat poured down his flushed cheeks.

"What?" Cold dread filled Benjamin's stomach. "He was—"

He pushed Denny against the wall to peer past him. There was a flash of light. Wetness coated the back of Benjamin's shirt. He waited for the searing pain to hit, as a knife clattered against the rocks, but he only felt damp.

"Are you hit?" Denny rolled around him, pressing him against the wall and then screamed.

A small throwing knife stuck out of Denny's shoulder, but his eyes were fixed on a spot down the path. "Baldo?" Denny uttered before his legs gave out, dragging Benjamin down with him.

Benjamin laid Denny on the ground. Baldo stood up, covered in dirt; a red gash ran across the sharp edge of his cheekbone. He turned and ran. Heat welled up under Benjamin's fatigue. He yanked the knife out of Denny's shoulder, but before he could shove Denny off him to follow, he grabbed Benjamin's wrist.

"No!" Denny's eyes were insistent.

But he almost killed you. Denny didn't waver. Benjamin ground his teeth but dropped the knife. He sprinted after Baldo, his head pounding with every step. "Who cares if he kills me?" Benjamin raged. "I'm expendable."

He slowed as he approached a small outcropping of rock just large enough to hide behind. Benjamin bent to scoop up a palm-sized rock as Baldo stepped out to throw another small knife. Benjamin dove forward and threw his rock, hitting Baldo's knee.

A howl erupted, and the waif crumpled into a pile of dingy clothes. Benjamin picked up another round stone and ran toward the pile, hoping to pounce before Baldo had time to draw another knife. Baldo's pale face flashed at him—and then he was gone. He rolled off the path and down the steep embankment. Benjamin peered down and watched Baldo's thin frame bump and roll through loose gravel and large spikes of rock.

Benjamin let out a breath when the boy finally landed in a puddle on a flat rock. There was no way to reach Baldo now. *But after that fall, the boy wouldn't be in any shape to go anywhere on his own.*

Denny tottered around the corner, gripping his shoulder to slow the bleeding. Benjamin reached for the waterskin on his back. It was slit and empty. He removed his scarf for a bandage for Denny's shoulder.

"Where's Baldo?"

"He's still alive. He rolled over the edge."

"What!"

Denny shoved Benjamin aside easily and dove to the edge, screaming Baldo's name. He then paused, as something on the trail caught his eye. The chest that Baldo had carried through the whole chase lay open. *Empty?*

Benjamin peered over the edge. He could see Baldo moving and heard a faint moan. "Over here."

Denny looked down ashen faced, allowing Benjamin to finally tie a bandage around his shoulder.

"Do you have a rope or something we could lower down there to bring him up?" Benjamin asked.

"Baldo!" Denny screamed.

A sick feeling rolled through Benjamin. "Odie?" he asked.

Denny reached out a hand and stopped him. "I left him with some soldiers. He was still in control."

Benjamin slumped against the rocks behind them, exhausted.

"We'll get your brother out, I promise. I just need to rest for a minute."

"Strange; there was nothing in that chest."

"Yes," Benjamin said between breaths. He opened his eyes to an accusatory stare. "Well, I didn't take it! I didn't even see it until you did! I was a little too worried about knives flying at my head to go looking for treasure." Hadn't he proved himself? "He was able to move incredibly fast while carrying it. It could have been empty the whole time."

"But why?"

"I don't know! A decoy of some sort? Or just so we could have this conversation! I don't know!"

"What?"

Benjamin froze and peered over the edge. Baldo was gone. A rope dangled from a rock.

"I know he's your brother, and I'm not supposed to—" Benjamin's voice was so cold, it startled him. "but I'm going to *kill* him."

Denny shoved Benjamin back and watched his brother limp away. "Baldo!"

There was no way to even know if their path would join the path Baldo was now escaping on, but they jogged limply back down. Further below, they heard yelling. They picked up their pace until they saw men filing out of the exit, peering below.

"Odie can't still be fighting, can he?" Benjamin turned to Denny, who was only able to shrug back before sliding down to join the men on the path below.

They found Odie resting against a wall, glistening with sweat. The Lieutenant stood in front of him with his sword drawn. Shreb stood on the edge of a steep drop-off, his small crossbow pointed at the Lieutenant's heart.

Sweat trickled down the archvillain's temples. His obsidian hair stuck to his face, and dark circles pooled under his eyes. His lips were purple; his fine clothing was slashed and bloodstained. He'd lasted a long time against Odie and the Lieutenant. A trembling hand fumbled with the ruined gold brocade.

"All these years, I dreamed of this moment, and I almost missed it," Shreb said, panting. "Where is the Heart of Darkness? I want the ring my father gave you. It should be mine!" His eyes bulged as he clutched at the crossbow. "Where is it?"

"Is that what you want? I don't have it." The Lieutenant laughed, raising his sword an inch. "I gave it to my true lord and master, King Aldo."

The Lieutenant dove before the words finished leaving his lips. Shreb's bolt went wide, as the Lieutenant rolled toward the archvillain. Once his feet were under him again, he lunged, bringing his sword down on the crossbow, sending it over the edge. The Lieutenant stepped back, pointing his sword at one of Shreb's jeweled buttons. The old spy straightened his eye patch as he watched Shreb step back and raise his hands in defeat.

Benjamin didn't like the look of this. He wiggled through the knot of men to get closer to his father and Shreb, trying to think of all of Shreb's possible avenues of escape. He had to see what lay below the drop-off. His hands ached as he drew his last knife from under his sleeve.

The Lieutenant glanced at him as he approached. "What?"

"I don't know," Benjamin said, as he staggered to the edge to look over. "Baldo's still—" He screamed.

Baldo was propped on a thin outcropping just below the edge. He held Shreb's fallen crossbow, a bolt notched tightly into its bowstring. He swung a long knife up, digging it into the ground in between Benjamin's feet. He jumped out of the way, screeching and stumbling into the Lieutenant and knocking him off balance.

Shreb jumped off the ledge and slid to the ledge below. Baldo peered up at Benjamin, aiming his single bolt at his heart. Benjamin swallowed and focused on Baldo's twiglike finger that rested on the trigger. Finally he winked and slid out of sight. Only the buried hilt of a knife into the cliff's edge marked the villain's escape route. Everyone stood stunned for a moment before soldiers erupted into yells and scampered after them. A few tried to follow them on the narrow path; but most ran down various downward paths, hoping to catch them further below, but the two were never found. Not a sign.

Benjamin suspected there were other hidden passages in the ravine. He combed over the path more closely than anyone.

Odie quietly attended to the dazed Denny, who waited for news of his little brother, not completely giving up hope of reclaiming his brother. Besides the wound on his shoulder and his aching heart, there wasn't much wrong with him, and soon Odie nudged Denny toward the fortress. They ascended the stairs behind the Lieutenant and Benjamin as they silently went to face Mouthrot. Benjamin glanced back to see tears streaking down Denny's face unchecked.

FIFTY TWO

*K*eston and Pete stood in front of Mouthrot, scowling at one another. Two guards stood on either side of Pete, whose filthy hat was crumpled more than usual. Two more guards flanked Mouthrot. He had a fresh gag in his mouth and more rope around his wrists, legs, waist, and neck.

The Lieutenant heaved a sigh as he examined the old spy's black eye.

"He started it," Pete said with little conviction as he squirmed under the Lieutenant's gaze.

"Yes, the man who had been drugged and tied up to a chair started it. Of course."

The Lieutenant signaled the guards to remove Pete from the room. He shrugged and followed his guards.

"Sir." Keston saluted the Lieutenant.

He returned the gesture stiffly and then removed Mouthrot's gag.

Mouthrot flashed a wicked smile of gold. "I see time has not been kind to you."

"And too kind to you." The Lieutenant squeezed the hilt of his sword. "Mouthrot, in the name of King Aldo of Lam, I'm arresting you for treason against the kingdom of Lam, the entire royal family, and the crown. You will be tried and, if found guilty, will be executed however your king and lord sees fit."

Mouthrot barked maliciously, "He is not *my* king! I am of the Thieves' Plain. Neither King Aldo nor his father, King Zavier, has *ever* claimed authority *here*."

"Guards, take the prisoner outside. We will transport him immediately." The Lieutenant lifted his eye patch and stared deeply into Mouthrot's eyes.

Keston and his men saluted. Shackles were brought in, and the prisoner shuffled his way through the fortress. Twenty men escorted him, with an innumerable amount of men lining the corridors and stairs. A large platoon of soldiers stood waiting with the prison cart in the main courtyard. A refined nobleman wearing Aldo's colors sat astride a horse. He saluted the Lieutenant.

Mouthrot glared at the official crest of the king on the cart. "The people of the Thieves' Plain will not stand for this! We will rise up and steal the crown for ourselves!"

Mouthrot continued to swear oaths against the king as they locked the doors behind him. The gates opened, which revealed a large group of peasants lining both sides of the road. They waved shovels, cudgels, hammers, and pitchforks angrily. The king's soldiers eyed the crowd suspiciously, preparing to push through, but the crowd cheered as they watched Mouthrot pass. Then Mouthrot's curses turned against the people he had sworn would avenge him.

No one seemed angry with the king's men for snatching Mouthrot out of the heart of the Thieves' Plain. The depressed farmer from the

Gray Gander shook his fist at the cart as it drove by, grumbling curses against him and all his kin, both living and dead. If there *was* anger, it was directed toward the villain in the cart. The group seemed grateful to have one less villain on the plain. When the cart and its escort were no longer visible, the people staggered away in small groups. They mumbled enthusiastically and shook their heads, bewildered.

Benjamin thought for a moment about mingling with the crowd to get a sense of the people's mood about the king's involvement, but he saw Pete and several other spies already starting up conversations with them. Benjamin's fatigue hit him again. He would just ask Branwen later.

Benjamin needed to get to the castle. He felt anxious about Rebecca; he'd left her too long. There was no telling what this Lady Jalene was planning to do to the young princess. He looked up at the fortress for a moment. His knee throbbed, and the other layers of pains and aches awoke to torment him. He pulled off his wet pack, dumping his torn and empty waterskin on the ground, and dug out a meager apple. It was nowhere near enough to fill his empty stomach. Neither Denny nor Odie was anywhere to be seen.

The brothers were probably inside licking their wounds still. Benjamin closed his eyes and pressed a fist into his chest and swallowed. Denny wasn't taking things well, and Benjamin didn't have a pep talk in him. Was there really anything to say? Maybe sympathetic silence was best.

Benjamin bit into an apple and trudged through the laundry area again to avoid the crowds by the main doors. Guards were interviewing Shreb's men inside. Some were being detained, but most were stripped of their weapons and let go.

In the middle of a row of drying sheets, he found the Lieutenant sitting next to Helda, sharing a drink. She picked up a familiar-looking jug and handed it to the old man.

The Lieutenant took a swig, forcing it down, and then handed it to Benjamin. "You look like you could use this."

Benjamin grimaced but took it.

Helda nodded encouragingly. "It tastes awful, but it won't kill ya. It will help you heal faster. I swear by it, and so does your Lieutenant here."

The Lieutenant looked at his empty hands and nodded.

Benjamin closed his eyes and took a swig. He could honestly say that he'd never tasted anything like it and hoped he never would again. It looked like mud and tasted worse. Overtones of rot trickled up as an aftertaste. He gasped and then gagged a little. "Any water or cider to wash this down?" he asked.

They both laughed while Benjamin focused on his breathing and keeping the contents in his stomach. Helda handed him a mug of cider. When mixed with the aftertaste of the medicine, he decided, tasted like rotten apples.

The Lieutenant patted him on the shoulder but then pulled him gently closer. "We've lost Baldo, then?"

Benjamin nodded.

"There's no chance—"

"He nearly killed me and Denny."

The Lieutenant nodded, pressing his lips together and peered up toward where the brothers probably were.

Benjamin wandered toward the main hall and took another bite of his apple and nearly chucked it. With the aftertaste, the apple now tasted bad as well. His wobbly legs insisted that he take a few more bites, so he decided that the apple was helping. Someone handed him a mug of cider, and he gingerly sipped it before pouring it down his gullet. The aftertaste was much less noticeable. He limped up the stairs. Battle was for stronger men than he.

He paused by the room with the trap door. Men climbed in and out of the hole in the floor. Baldo *was* brilliant after all. He easily had twice as much ambition as Denny and less than half the conscience. That was supposed to be Benjamin.

Would he have been tied up and delivered to the king like Mouthrot if things had been different? Benjamin should be the villain; Baldo should be working for the king. The Lieutenant had been more of a father to Baldo than to Benjamin. Was it just chance? Or had each boy been given a chance to choose something different than what life had given them?

Benjamin's chest tightened. Baldo had given up so much. He walked away from his family. He broke Denny's heart. Benjamin's own ties with the brothers, the Lieutenant, and Rebecca were tenuous at best. So many complications. Even now, he felt compelled to see Denny and Odie's pain, as if that would help. He felt a tug toward the castle, where Rebecca paced a hole in the carpets. Benjamin leaned against the doorway and closed his eyes. Why would he want this? These ties bound him to pain. *The job was finished, wasn't it?* And yet he wanted to stay. He wanted to see his friends right. He just wasn't sure if he knew how to do that, but he knew it was the right thing to do.

He straightened up and lurched down the hallway. The brothers sat on top of the table where Shreb must have eaten his meals. Odie and Denny leaned into each other. Rina, the goat, butted Odie's foot. Benjamin felt awkward, watching the brothers. The moment felt too intimate. He turned around and ran into Keston.

"We found something upstairs," Keston said in a low voice, casting a sidelong glance toward the brothers. "I think you might want to see it."

"Is this about Baldo?" Denny asked, his hair dangling over his red eyes.

Keston straightened into an official stance but staggered with his answer. "We don't know...for sure." He glanced at Benjamin for help.

Benjamin shrugged. If Keston didn't want the brothers to know, he should have been more discreet.

The brothers slid off the table and followed them up another flight of stairs to a room directly above Shreb's. The entrance was crammed full of old, dusty gear and furniture, but as they pushed further back into the room, it was spotless. Furniture was arranged into a court of sorts. Chairs sat around the room facing an opulent chair that could only have belonged to Shreb Senior. There was a wardrobe pulled open. The inside was covered with maps, notes, and lists of all kinds. Benjamin rubbed his small notebook in his pocket.

"What is this?" Denny asked.

"We were hoping that Benjamin or one of you could enlighten us."

Benjamin scanned over the lists, maps, and sketches. "It looks as if he was keeping record of everyone in the fortress, and even some people who had regular business with Shreb or Mouthrot."

"That sounds like Baldo," Denny uttered weakly. "He was always scratching away on paper somewhere. He called them his *observations*."

Benjamin flipped through the stacks of papers, many of which were clearly written in different hands. "Looks like he was intercepting people's messages." He studied a sketched map of the fortress grounds with an assortment of symbols scratched in various corners. "He knew all the secret passages in, out, and around the fortress. You'll want to pack this up and take it to Branwen. It might help locate any allies Shreb or Mouthrot had at court."

Keston blanched. "Allies in court? Surely not."

"I believe Mouthrot was a former nobleman himself and a distant relation to the king's family."

"I don't understand." Denny traced the contents of the wardrobe with his eyes. "If he had all this information, why didn't he use it against Shreb as well as Mouthrot? Why did he go through such lengths to save Shreb? Shreb is useless."

Benjamin set a stack of papers down. "He was studying both villains. He's not finished with Shreb…not yet. I can't imagine what advantage he'd have sticking with Shreb, but there must be one."

"Like what?"

"Money? Connections? Protection, perhaps?"

"But Shreb doesn't have any money. Not anymore."

Benjamin nodded to this absently. "Don't worry, he has money."

Denny kicked at a pile of yellowed paper. "Why can't you admit it? You took the money!"

The accusation felt like a physical slap. Benjamin blinked several times before he could respond. "Because I *didn't* take it! You think Baldo, *the brilliant*, who fooled us all, would allow someone to steal money from him *and* push him down a cliff? No. He wanted you to think that was what happened." Benjamin squeezed his fists, painfully tearing the fresh scabs forming on his knuckles.

"It was an insurance policy against *you*!" Denny pointed an angry finger at Benjamin.

"Right! To ensure no one will completely trust Benjamin 'the villain' who *helped* the king overthrow two archvillains. Meanwhile, poor Baldo, the villain's assistant, ensures one escapes!" Benjamin growled through clenched jaws.

Denny rushed toward Benjamin, raising his fist, but stopped just before Odie stepped in. Benjamin stumbled back into Keston, who helped him back to his feet.

Benjamin opened his mouth to yell, *I am not a villain!* But the words choked him. He clamped his mouth shut and retreated from the room, an ache blossoming in his chest.

FIFTY THREE

*E*very morning after the boys abandoned her, Rebecca rolled out of bed, pulled on her servant clothes, and dropped off the laundry. She picked up breakfast in the kitchen, where she was able to exchange gossip with Molly. It was the highlight of her day, and she thanked Branwen, Dally, and Sir Wendell every day for it. She sometimes even helped Molly with some of her tasks around the kitchen so they could chat more easily. Plus, she found Molly more forthcoming about castle news when she was in motion.

Martha, the head cook, was pleased with her eagerness to learn the inner workings of the kitchen and one day even gave her an approving nod as she handed her a tray. "You should use a cart. Then you can pick up the laundry at the same time. Save yourself a trip."

Henry would sometimes secretly slip a warm roll or cookie into her apron pocket. It felt so good to be a part of something and to have friends. Molly was certainly her favorite. Rebecca had never been around other girls before and found a hole had been filled in her heart.

Rebecca was even able to visit Jalene without her aunt hovering in the corner. She found the quiet lady a kind and intelligent woman. Jalene freely talked about her family and their drafty old manor. She clearly missed them both dearly. She also filled Rebecca in about court life, both the good and the bad. She was a fountain of information.

"Jalene, you have helped me so much, if only to keep me from going mad locked away," Rebecca confessed. "All my future efforts can never repay what I've received from you."

Jalene tilted her head. "A few stories?"

"You've obviously never lived cooped up with spies who talk only of conspiracies, knives, and food—when they talk at all."

"Well, in that case, we'd better cover the art of female warfare." Jalene laughed, her long fingers tangling in her black curls. "That information may not save your life, but it will keep you from being eaten alive!"

Rebecca endured the fitting of gowns and the twisting of her hair in the afternoons because she could silently review all the stories and events of the morning.

In the evenings, Sir Wendell would stop by for their lessons. He stared wide-eyed when she easily rolled out of his grasp the first time. He then helped refine her skills and taught her plenty of new things. He assured her that a princess was entitled to use any dirty trick she wanted, if it meant staying alive. She smirked and imagined practicing on Benjamin, and then immediately prayed *all* of her boys were safe.

Sir Wendell had his men smuggle up a training dummy so that she could practice various stabbing techniques with both knives and swords. He discouraged her from throwing her knife, even after several impressive demonstrations. "You might hit someone, but then you're without a knife," he said.

So she practiced throwing after he left.

FIFTY FOUR

*I*t was Rebecca's idea to coordinate her gown with Jalene's for the upcoming banquet. The king wanted to present Rebecca to court and announce his engagement to Lady Jalene at the same time. The future consort of the king should outshine everyone, especially the king's niece. With Dally's help, Rebecca picked a secondary color from Jalene's dress that let Rebecca blend into the background. They kept her dress simple but still not out of place for the occasion. Something no one would think about, just see and move on. If Rebecca wanted to sell the supportive role, she needed to start now.

Rebecca arranged for a few smaller knives she could strap under her sleeves easily. She knew most of the servants by sight and would notice someone out of place. Rebecca and Jalene arranged the settings at the banquet so that they would sit next to each other. Hopefully, at first glance, they would think Rebecca nothing more than a lady-in-waiting. While there was danger to both of them, Rebecca's existence was so uncertain to everyone, including the nobility, that she was sure Jalene would be more of a target than she was.

As Rebecca stood in front of a three-paneled mirror for her final fitting, she heard a scuffle outside her door. Dally set down a chest of jewels, and Rebecca reached for one of the knives up her sleeve. She was glad she had insisted on trying them on with her dress; she had wanted to see if they would be hidden and accessible. The door burst open, and a disheveled Benjamin stumbled out of two red-faced guards' grasps. They each grabbed an arm and apologized for the intrusion.

"Benjamin!" Dally barked. "You should not be allowed in a room when a lady is changing."

He rolled his eyes. "If you're talking about Rebecca, she looks dressed to me."

"You're back!" Rebecca slipped around Dally to see Benjamin for herself. He was dirty and scuffed but in one piece. Denny was not with him. She waved the guards away.

"Good news: we got Mouthrot. Bad news: Shreb is on the run."

A huge wave of relief washed over her, and Rebecca nearly hugged Benjamin, but his stench stopped her. She smoothed her expensive new dress and stepped back.

"The Lieutenant? Denny? His brothers?" Her eyes darted to the empty space behind Benjamin.

"They're fine," Benjamin said, rubbing his hair out of his face as he scanned the room for food. "Well, Denny *did* get a knife to the shoulder."

"What?"

"But he's fine. I think the shock—" Benjamin bit his lip. Rebecca held her breath. His hesitation was unnerving. He never stopped to think before he spoke.

"Just say it. What's wrong?"

"You know Baldo?"

"What happened?"

"Well, he's the one that got Denny with the knife."

"What? Denny's *little brother* stabbed him?"

Dally gasped at this.

"Well, threw it, actually. But I think he was aiming for me, if that makes you feel better." He kicked at a chair leg with his dusty boot and frowned.

"Why would that make me feel better? Why is Baldo throwing knives at anyone?" Rebecca pressed her hand against her locket.

Benjamin looked away. "Because he's a bad guy. He helped Shreb escape."

Rebecca stumbled backward. She remembered Baldo's pale face watching, always watching. He was so small. Denny was always so protective of him and gave him everything he could need. He was heartbroken when Baldo had gone to work at the fortress.

"He was *so* smart," she said, shaking her head.

Benjamin's head fell, and when he looked up again, his eyes were red-rimmed.

"Why didn't I see it? Everything was arranged around *me*," Benjamin said, collapsing in the upholstered chair. Dally grimaced. "I was Baldo's competition. *He* wanted to be the villain's assistant. He coordinated everything from the start."

"Poor Denny."

Benjamin rubbed his hair into spikes. "He's not taking it very well. I'm not sure if he knows what or who to believe. He blames me."

"What? How could Denny blame you? You've never even met Baldo before!" she said, pressing a hand to the knot in her stomach. "I know you aren't exactly friends, but Denny knows—"

"Knows what? That I'm just a thief at heart? Baldo *is* very clever. He planted seeds of doubt."

"Just small enough to wiggle down deep?"

Benjamin nodded.

She closed her eyes. This could be bad. "Where is Denny now?"

"I left him at the fortress with the Lieutenant and Odie."

Benjamin leaned forward in his chair, resting his head in his hands. Dirt and scabs covered his knuckles.

Is Denny this scuffed up as well? she wondered. She didn't dare ask. "I think Denny will be okay," Rebecca said, lifting her chin and infusing her words with confidence. "No matter what he thinks, Odie will straighten him out eventually. It's *you* I'm worried about."

Benjamin lifted his head.

"Baldo is *very* clever, but he couldn't know much about you. We barely mentioned your name." She turned to examine her sleeves in the mirror.

"But he knew I was the Lieutenant's son...or at least Shreb did."

Rebecca spun around and watched Benjamin trace the scabs on his knuckles.

He peered up, his brown eyes pained. "Odie he didn't tell him either."

She turned back to the mirror. Her own gray eyes stared widely back at her, as she listened to her heart pound in her chest. "Didn't Shreb know the Lieutenant when he worked for his father?"

"Possibly." Benjamin shrugged.

Rebecca didn't know what to think about this little twist, but it couldn't be as bad as Benjamin thought. "Not everything revolves around you."

She moved slowly through some fighting stances Sir Wendell had taught her, trying to shake off the cold that gripped her muscles. She wanted full range of motion in her dress. She looked at the deflated boy in the mirror.

"I don't know what Baldo does or does not know, but if you sit around moping because Denny doesn't trust you, or if you give up on this path you've chosen, you're the one who loses."

Benjamin stood up straight. "I will not be outdone by him!"

Rebecca smiled triumphantly. "Good! Now go take a bath. Maybe two baths. You stink!"

FIFTY FIVE

After making her morning rounds, Rebecca returned to her rooms to find a bleary-eyed Benjamin being fitted for a suit. Branwen was shuffling through papers, occasionally scribbling and crossing things out at her unused desk. He must have debriefed Benjamin this morning.

Branwen nodded absently and continued scanning his pages. "I think that should do it," he said, struggling out of his chair. He handed the pages to Dally and then turned to look Benjamin in the eye. "I want you to memorize all of these questions and comments that are *appropriate* for the banquet."

Benjamin rolled his eyes.

"And if you do sound *stupid* saying them—all the better. Consider it your cover. Can you do that?"

Benjamin sucked his lips in and agreed.

"Good. Because I'm sure I could get approval to add a mute to His Lordship's ranks."

Benjamin lifted his eyebrows.

Rebecca snorted. It was nice to know others fantasized about ways to shut Benjamin up as well. Apparently that was a natural reaction.

Benjamin scrunched up his face. "Don't worry; I'd still figure out a way to drive you all mad."

"I wouldn't doubt it for a second," Branwen muttered as he headed out the door.

"Do I even want to know where he's going?" Rebecca asked as she unwound the scarf around her head.

"No, you don't," Dally said, looking up. "Your Highness, ladies do not undress in front of—"

"Benjamin? He hardly counts. Besides, I only removed my headscarf. I didn't disrobe."

Rebecca slouched into the couch and kicked off her thin-soled maid's shoes and rubbed her feet. You would think the nobility who sit around all day would get the thin shoes, and the workers who were on their feet all day would get the better shoes.

"I'm getting my kitchen maids good shoes when I have my own castle."

Dally laughed at that. "I guess you'll have girls rotating in and out of your kitchens, depending on when they need new shoes."

"Perhaps, or maybe they'll appreciate an employer who cares about their feet and comfort."

Dally shoved the list at Benjamin and then sat next to Rebecca. She lifted Rebecca's feet into her lap and rubbed them. The old tailor removed the pinned material from Benjamin and put his things into his case.

Dally thanked him and apologized for Benjamin's sour tongue.

"Forgive me. I'm still exhausted from—" Benjamin piped in.

The old tailor waved off Benjamin midsentence. "Don't tell me. I don't want to know."

FIFTY SIX

When the day of the banquet arrived, Rebecca held up her well-manicured hand in disbelief. She had spent most of the previous day soaking different parts of her body in this or that. Jalene had even come down to participate in the facials. Dally had slathered them in what felt like thick mud but smelled like lavender.

Jalene just smiled quietly as she listened to Rebecca complain. "Trust me, as you get older you'll appreciate it. How else do you think a twenty-five-year old caught the eye of the king?"

"You're that old?" Rebecca gasped.

Dally glared intently Rebecca.

"Oh, sorry," Rebecca said, wincing.

Jalene laughed. "I'll take that as a compliment."

"I can't believe you haven't been married before. You're obviously beautiful and refined, everything a noble lord would want."

"Well, the refinement came under the firm hand of my aunt."

Rebecca thought that would be the end of the subject, but after sitting in silence for a while, Jalene continued. "I was engaged once, but he died before we could marry."

Rebecca was thankful for Dally stepping in to remove the mud from her face and changing the topic. Everyone had sad tales in their lives, it seemed.

Jalene soon left to dress in her own rooms. Rebecca wondered if Benjamin had to do anything so ridiculous to get ready for his introduction to court. He was probably stuffing himself with sweet rolls. *I hope he remembers to take a bath and comb his hair at least.* It might be nice to see him out of his depth for once. She'd like to know she wasn't the only one.

Dally hung her blue gown by the mirror and pulled out a corset, snapping Rebecca back to the present. "Okay," the reluctant princess said, groaning, "let's get this over with."

All of the air was painfully squeezed from Rebecca's lungs as Dally tightened and clasped all the machinery that went into prepping her body for a formal gown—another reason Rebecca would rather have led the attack against Shreb with Benjamin and Denny. It couldn't be more dangerous than a corset! Still, as Rebecca looked in the mirror, she had to admit she looked pretty—not quite herself, but pretty. She loved the deep blue of her gown. It didn't shine as much as Jalene's, but that was the idea. There were a few jeweled flowers around her neckline and sleeves. Dally applied another layer of powder to all her exposed flesh.

"Just a hint of sparkle, I think," Dally said, looking pleased. She placed a diamond collar around Rebecca's neck. Spikes of sapphires grazed her collarbones and chest. Two matching sapphire earrings dangled from her ears. Rebecca smiled back at the princess in the mirror.

Dally stepped back to take in all her hard work. She then turned to the mirror and smoothed her own graying hair that was twisted into a roll under beautiful curls, a much simpler arrangement than the knots and twists that Dally had spent hours perfecting in Rebecca's hair.

Dally fiddled with the diamond buttons that danced against the darkness of her own dress as she opened the door to admit Benjamin. He was wearing a trim-cut suit in a lighter shade of blue than Rebecca's dress. His dark hair was pushed back in a masculine wave, which would have looked striking if not for his expression. He obviously felt ridiculous.

"How long does it take to get dressed? Haven't you been practicing all week?"

Dally pulled on his suit jacket, straightened the diamond studs on his sleeves, and then flicked his ear.

"Start acting like a gentleman. As of tonight, you *are* one. No one need know where you grew up. This is a good time to inherit your good family name." Dally faced Benjamin with an iron expression. "This is who you are now."

Dally pulled out a silver fan from her pocket. Benjamin rolled his eyes but stood up straighter and let the irritation slide from his face.

He bowed perfectly and then offered Rebecca his arm. "Your Highness." Noticing the surprised look on the women's faces, Benjamin smirked. "We had a class for impersonating nobility."

"Of course you did," Rebecca said, taking his arm as a wave of nerves left her wobbly. She pleaded with Benjamin not to let her fall.

"Only if you promise to do the same for me," he whispered back.

They were escorted by a large group of guards, and her anonymity was now gone forever. Sir Wendell waited for them by the laundry, which was locked for the night. The hallway was ghostly quiet. He nodded at the guard's salute and then bowed to the princess.

He led the group into the kitchens, hoping to prolong the king's secret a few minutes more. Faces flashed to the princess. Servants stopped their work to watch the royal procession stride through the kitchen. Rebecca caught a glimpse of Molly's flaming hair as the maid curtsied respectfully to the princess, no recognition showing on her face. Rebecca felt a pang of sadness; she could use a smile from her friend right now. She paused and curtsied back to the kitchen staff, and Benjamin urged her on. No one seemed to recognize her. Maybe she could keep her friends a little longer.

They stepped into another hallway that led to the main hall. They waited for Jalene's group so they could enter the dining hall together.

King Aldo hoped to keep the princess's presence a secret until the moment she was announced. He claimed the secrecy was solely for her protection, but Rebecca suspected that a part of the secrecy was also about the drama. Aldo would be able to announce a wedding, the return of an heir, *and* the capture of an archvillain all at once. It would be his moment of triumph more than anything else.

Sir Wendell turned and nodded. They moved out into the hall, which was covered in candles and late-summer flowers. The chandeliers were lit, and the large fireplace was filled artistically with floral arrangements that would not be burned this night. The Lady Jalene descended the stairs, her silver gown sparkling in the candlelight. Blue jewels were sewn into the shapes of birds on her bodice and her skirt, with brilliant blue feathers woven elegantly into the twists of her dark curls.

Rebecca, now the Princess Reyna, paused with her group at the foot of the stairs. Lady Jalene curtsied cautiously, so the added weight of her gown and hair wouldn't throw her off balance. Then the princess curtsied deeply in return and gestured for Jalene to go ahead of her. The doors opened before them. The tables were draped in white and gold. The lower nobility was already seated and whispering, but all went silent as the women entered. Sir Wendell stood at attention near the door as trumpets announced royalty.

"The Princess Reyna Brynn Rae, House of Ulmer. The Duke and Duchess of Alain. The Lady Jalene of East Burrow."

The occasion was marked by a collective gasp and silence. Another audible gasp was heard as Benjamin was announced as Lord Benjamin of Gehnry.

Jalene still led the processional. After a few moments of shock, the whispers began without shame. Rebecca kept her eyes on Jalene's dress as they walked to the head table, which was raised above the other tables.

Benjamin leaned in, smiling. "A few were not surprised by your announcement, but I think it's safe to say everyone was surprised to see *me* here."

"That should make you happy."

"Ah, but the question is, will the king be happy about it?"

The flirty blond footman pulled her chair out. Rebecca cringed. *Did he give her a second look?* Benjamin raised an eyebrow. She ignored it. The nobility gaped at her, and her body tensed, ready to run. Perhaps these ridiculous dresses and extravagant hairdos, if nothing else, discouraged nervous young women from bolting at social gatherings. Her skirts alone could tangle and trip her up. She faced the hungry crowd and bowed her head in the stately manner that Dally had her practice. The nobility returned the gesture, and, without the slightest embarrassment, pointed and gawked.

Another royal trumpet blast brought order to the room as Sir Wendell announced King Aldo, lord and master of all of Lam. All bowed deeply as he entered the banquet hall, a triumphant expression on Aldo's face. He smiled at her. She returned it and lowered her head. Branwen followed behind, wearing black robes of a finer material than usual. A single jewel hung from a gold chain around his neck. They all stepped into their places. King Aldo faced Branwen and his escorts, who bowed in deep respect. The king bowed in return to the others at his table, including the princess and Jalene, and finally, to the lesser nobles below him.

He raised a glass by its stem, signaling all eyes toward him. Rebecca gripped her skirts tightly. She focused on keeping her face smooth. Her head felt a little light, so she breathed as deeply as her corset would allow.

"We are here tonight to celebrate the safe return of my niece and heir, the Princess Reyna." Aldo's voice rolled across the great hall, causing all eyes to shift toward her. He held out an expectant hand to her. The sound of her true name pulled off years of disguises. All could see her. A minute ago, she had wanted to run, and now she was unable to move a toe.

Benjamin cleared his throat and then nudged her. He smiled with regal charm and offered his arm, which she accepted. He guided her toward Aldo. Somehow she placed her hand in the king's. Benjamin squeezed her other hand before he let go. Aldo beamed as the crowd bowed deeply to his heir.

"My brother's daughter is home at last. We welcome her!"

The force of the crowd's cheer against her skin released much of the tension that had been building her whole life. She blinked back the stinging in her eyes.

Aldo threw his head back and laughed. This was just the beginning of a list of celebrations. His niece was out in the open, his engagement would be announced next, and one of his most dangerous enemies was in his dungeon. Rebecca could see a weight lifted from her uncle's shoulders. He was truly happy this night, and she could not help but share in his moment of triumph. She grinned at him and then down on those below them. Aldo kissed her hand and sent her back with Benjamin.

King Aldo raised his glass to the room and drank from it, which marked the beginning of the feast. With that, more servants than Rebecca had ever seen began to file in, carrying platters of pigs, birds, bread, and ornate fruits and vegetables. The aroma was intoxicating, and Rebecca was sure that Benjamin would finally have enough to eat.

FIFTY SEVEN

*B*enjamin's smile began to crack around the edges. He could feel it slipping into a smirk as he eyed the shocked nobility. They were beside themselves with all the possibilities of new court gossip. He watched as juicy tidbits passed up and down the tables marked by gasps.

Benjamin lifted his wine glass to his nose to sniff. It smelled right, so he put the cup to his lips but only wetted them; his lips would start burning if there were any poison. With Rebecca and Lady Jalene as possible targets, Benjamin wouldn't be drinking any wine tonight.

He suggested to Branwen that none of the royal party should eat or drink at the dinner. The bent man cawed at that one and admitted that would make his job much easier, but it would also sap all the fun out of the celebrations. He had trusted men placed in the kitchen and hallways to discourage food tampering. It was also standard protocol for the king's wine to be watered down at large banquets and parties.

Jalene's uncle, a duke of some sort, sat next to Benjamin. He choked on his watered-down wine. Lifting up his glass again, he loudly admired it to cover his disappointment. So the aunt was probably the one holding the reins; the uncle was just the horse. The bride-to-be sitting on the other side of Rebecca was too shiny to look at. She had silver and gold woven into her hair, along with ridiculous blue feathers. No bird was that color. At least the lady carried herself with dignity and didn't tittle and guffaw like many others at the banquet. *That* was a point in her favor.

Rebecca sat quietly and watched the servants, especially the footman who had seated her. He made her nervous, but not in a "this guy is suspicious" kind of way. The footman kept glancing at Rebecca the way Benjamin had seen boys at school look at pretty girls. His hair was well groomed, and he filled out his jacket nicely. Surely he could find another girl to be interested in. The room was full of them, after all. *Good luck to you!* Anything the footman tried would probably end with Rebecca holding a knife to his throat, but there was no way to say that with a simple look. If they weren't sitting in the middle of a royal banquet, it would all be very amusing, but right now, it was a distraction.

"What is it?" Benjamin smiled painfully at Rebecca. How could he keep his eyes open for trouble with all this food around him? Even the aroma was distracting. He allowed himself a bite.

Rebecca leaned in, obscuring her mouth as she held her glass up to drink. "I think the footman recognizes me."

Benjamin swallowed. "Isn't that the point of all of this?" He followed this glib comment with a peal of false laughter.

"Is this whole evening's conversation going to be a series of fake responses and comments?" she replied in a singsong voice.

"Only if we live that long."

This bought him a few moments of silence as Rebecca turned to talk to Jalene as if they were friends. He was impressed; he didn't think she could hit it off with anyone, false or not. He watched them chat for a moment. *Are they having a real conversation?* Jalene nodded toward various people and then leaned in to spill their stories. *Well, at least the bride will be informative, if nothing else.*

The dinner passed under the hum of uneventful conversation. Everyone was enjoying themselves—except Benjamin. He scrutinized servants as he ate minimally but savored every bite. Everything was spiced and glazed. *Self-control! I am the master of me.*

From the corner of his eye, he noticed the aunt staring at him. Benjamin smiled back. She leaned over her husband and opened her gold fan.

"Stop being a stick in the mud!" the aunt hissed.

She pulled the fan away in a fit of amusement as if she had been teasing Benjamin, as good friends do. He must have let his smile slip off. Benjamin leered and raised his glass to her. She returned the gesture and joined her husband in talking to some nobody Benjamin didn't care about.

Aldo beamed triumphantly over his banquet. He hadn't unloaded his big prizes yet. His engagement and the capture of one of the greatest threats to the crown and stability of the kingdom would be announced later in the evening. *After the entertainment*, Benjamin hoped. *I just love jugglers.*

The noblemen and their wives who sat on the other side of Aldo displayed a potpourri of shock, awe, and disappointment. For some, the return of the princess was a victory for the future of Lam; for others a disappointment of years of scheming. He scanned the room for outright loathing, but perhaps the shock was still too immediate.

Aldo, and therefore Branwen, had managed to keep Rebecca's presence a secret from even the king's most trusted friends. Branwen assured Benjamin that every few months a girl about the right age would show up with some lord or lady who claimed to have found the lost princess. So Rebecca's arrival to the castle wasn't enough to set off alarms.

A woman in purple, sitting below, caught Benjamin's eye. She watched the king's table thoughtfully behind a silver fan. Her eyes followed the flow of servants in and out of the kitchen. Her eyes flicked to Benjamin's face before she turned her attention to a man in a dark-red velvet coat. Benjamin felt a tinge of familiarity. Her large head covering and sleeves, both laced with sparkling jewels, obscured her face.

Benjamin scowled and took a bite of pork with raisin sauce. The food improved his mood, so he took another bite. The aunt nodded in approval over her husband, who asked for stronger wine. But soon Benjamin was examining servants again. Why was the woman in purple watching the servants? Had Benjamin missed something? Shouldn't the woman be watching Rebecca or the woman rumored to be engaged to the king?

Branwen perched behind the king on a tall stool that the king allowed him. Dally stood next to him. Between the two of them they directed the servants and security, but they were too far away to be helpful. This left the aunt as the closest tool.

"Lady—" Benjamin paused, realizing that wasn't quite right.

"*Duchess!*" she corrected through a tight red smile.

"Yes, Duchess." Benjamin glanced toward the table below. "Do you know who that woman in purple is? The one with the ridiculous sleeves and sparkling head thing?"

The duchess closed her eyes for a few seconds and then peered over to the table Benjamin indicated.

"She does look familiar. Where have I seen her before?" The duchess's smooth face crinkled in thought. "I think I saw her at one of the outer country estates."

"Tunis, that woman with the purple? Was she at one of the hunts? Not the last one, the one before? You know the one where you nearly fell off your horse?"

The duke smoothed his gray mustache as he pointedly inspected the woman. "Unpleasant episode." After a moment he huffed. "No idea what her name was."

"That's right. Later, we wondered if she had even come with anyone." The duchess's voice went cold. "Prickly woman."

A hand reached for the duchess's plate. She nodded, and it was removed, followed by the duke's. Benjamin sampled some of his vegetables before setting his fork down. The hand that removed his plate now exposed, Benjamin noticed that the servant's thin wrist had not been scrubbed as well as his hands had been. Benjamin whipped around to see the backside of a scrawny boy in an ill-fitting uniform.

He spun back around. The woman in purple glanced away and flicked out her silver fan. He glanced over to Sir Wendell, who sat at the table just below the king's. Sir Wendell was nodding along to an old man in gray robes talking while scanning the room. Benjamin caught Wendell's eye. With a small gesture from Benjamin, Sir Wendell pushed his chair back and scanned the table next to his, all the while continuing his conversation. He scowled and then shook his head, returning his focus to his neighbor.

Frustrated, Benjamin turned to Rebecca, who traced the pattern on her plate with her fork. She met his eyes. "Did you see who took my plate?" She shook her head, barely stopping herself from rolling her eyes. "Something is off." She paused at this and scanned the servants around them.

She thinks I'm paranoid, but she is looking.

Benjamin scanned the faces of the nobility below him again, looking for betrayal in someone's eyes. His eyes flicked to the woman in purple again and again. Who was this woman? She didn't belong somehow.

She flipped her silver fan over her face, reflecting light back at Benjamin, blinding him. He turned away to see a small hand drop something into Jalene's cup. The small footman turned away as he scooped up her dinner plate. *How many cups?*

A tingling rang through the hall as the king stood up. He raised his glass of wine. Aldo's triumphant glow filled the room.

Once he announced his engagement, Benjamin realized with a shudder, *everyone would drink. How many from tainted cups?* His whole body grew cold as he met the eyes of the servant who was too small to be a footman. A wicked smile erupted across Baldo's face as he headed to the kitchens. Benjamin slammed his fist onto the table, silencing Aldo just as he pronounced Jalene's name.

"Stop! Poison! The cups! The cups have been poisoned!"

Half of the room stared down at their wine, wide-eyed, while the other half whispered in confusion or cheered the king's engagement. Aldo's eyes uttered all the threats that could have ever been said if Benjamin was wrong.

"Sir Wendell!" Benjamin commanded, waving toward the woman in purple. He did not wait to see if his orders were followed. Benjamin sprinted toward the kitchen. He *would* catch Baldo. He would look him in the eye and see defeat written there. The heavy tread of soldiers followed him.

A scream tore through the room behind Benjamin. Crystal and delicate dishes crashed in every direction. Benjamin parted a cloud of footmen. Guards swore as they collided with the servants. Benjamin followed the stream of broken dishes and food just inside the hallway.

"Baldo!"

The runty brother snaked through the chaos of servants gawking at the upheaval around them. Baldo looked over his shoulder, sneered, and ran. A clash of trays and broken dishes followed his wake.

FIFTY EIGHT

"Did you see who took my plate?" Benjamin's eyes were wide and pleading. Rebecca shook her head. *Is he going to be like this all night?* He had barely touched his food or wine. He was unimportant. No one was trying to kill *him*. "Something is off."

Rebecca reminded herself that she had wanted Benjamin here because he was so paranoid. She surveyed the serving staff. She knew many of the faces, but they often brought in extras for large events. Did Benjamin think she hadn't been watching? Someone likely wanted her or Jalene dead. Of course, he thought he was the only one smart enough to figure that out. If they weren't at such a public event, Rebecca might reach over and smack him upside the head.

She noted the footmen and guards. One servant walked between the tables. He looked wrong somehow—stiff, his gaze locked straight ahead. Benjamin screamed about poison. The servant reached into his sleeve as goose bumps ran down Rebecca's arms. *He was not a servant.* Rebecca reached into her own sleeves for her knives. She pushed off her chair and clambered down the table. Dinnerware shattered with every step. All sound dimmed under her strained breathing.

Curse this corset!

Rebecca thought of Sir Wendell as she let her first knife go. It stuck in the assassin's left arm, slowing him down enough for her to get between him and her uncle. Silver flashed as *his* knife appeared. Rebecca dived from the table and onto a man twice her size, her chin crunching into his nose. Blood bloomed in her mouth as she thrust another knife into the assassin's throat. When they hit the floor, her knife tore through the man's flesh as she rolled away from him, crimson marking her path.

The screaming and clatter returned, just as a force whipped her away. Sir Wendell clenched her to his chest as he repeated that everything was okay. Pain erupted in her left side as Sir Wendell's arms brushed against the assassin's knife that stuck in her corset. She screamed.

Guards streamed toward the bleeding, gasping man on the floor. Aldo, unharmed, stood with his own sword drawn. His face was gray, and his eyes were rimmed in white as he stared at Rebecca. Two guards pulled the king from the room as the lights from the chandeliers glared harshly. Rebecca's hand was covered in blood. Her dress. Sir Wendell. All of it red and hot. Her head floated away. Her body trembled. She had been hurt. Her side throbbed like a second heart. She was bleeding.

"The surgeon. We need the surgeon!" Sir Wendell called out.

"Rebecca!"

Someone lifted her from Sir Wendell's arms. Her arms were too weak to wrap around his neck. Her eyes were open, but she didn't take in any of the events around her. Her arms flailed awkwardly with her head.

"Rebecca! Rebecca!" She focused her eyes on the face next to hers. *Denny?* Why was he weeping?

Dally's voice hovered close by. Rebecca was laid on something hard. Martha glowered down at her and pulled out the knife. Everything in her vision went white as Rebecca screamed until her throat burned. Martha pressed down on the wound, sending another shock of pain through Rebecca's body.

"What have you done? What have you done? And we only just got you back," Martha's voice wavered, but then her sternness returned as she directed guards and kitchen staff alike.

Dally held her hand as something wet was poured over her wound, causing her to thrash and twist. An unholy sound filled her ears. Was that her? A scuffle could be heard somewhere beyond her vision.

"Get him out! Now!" Martha ordered between Rebecca's screams. "It's not so bad. By the Great Wolves! I think she might make it. Bless your royal corset!"

FIFTY NINE

"Someone stop that kid!" Benjamin screamed as he passed bewildered servants. Baldo passed undeterred. "Help!"

Finally, a girl with hair as bright as flame stepped in front of Baldo, and both were knocked to the ground. He bounced up, but she grabbed his leg. It took a kick to her ribs to loosen her grip. Benjamin barely spared her a glance as he ran by. Some of the other kitchen staff were already running to help her, successfully obstructing the guards.

Waves of heat danced through Benjamin's body to the pounding behind his ears. He saw nothing and thought of nothing but the spindly legs that ran from him. Benjamin dodged carts and jumped over flailing maids, who lay bewildered on the ground. The gap was closing. Benjamin could feel power rushing through his veins, as his feet slammed against the floor and pushed him closer to his target. There was nothing else but Benjamin's rage. It grew in him, threatening to burn everything around him.

The hallways grew empty and dark. Baldo slipped invisibly through the shadows, but Benjamin knew he was there. Slivers of light occasionally revealed a spindly leg or arm. Baldo ran a straight line as if he was going somewhere. *This is a diversion.* Benjamin stumbled into a dark courtyard. *Where's Shreb?* The thought slammed into Benjamin, stopping him cold. He scanned the courtyard. Baldo was gone.

"Yes, I'm here," a deep voice crooned from a shadow.

Benjamin panted, his body quivering. Sweat trickled from his hairline. He wiped it away.

"When I heard who you were, I have to say that I was disappointed," Shreb hissed as he stepped out of a shadow. He was wearing a red velvet jacket. "Black-Eyed Barnaby's son? Tsk, tsk." He smiled malevolently. "How I hated that man. Probably as much as my father loved him."

Shreb's eyes flashed dangerously, but he drew a calm breath as he fiddled with his rings. "I'm not the only one disappointed by your *choices.*"

"Choices? Like you hiring Mouthrot? That kind of sealed the deal for me."

"Oh? So you plotted with the king to remove your rival so that you could have his job? That is bordering on grandiose." Shreb tugged on a jeweled cufflink and raised an eyebrow. "I love it! Well, I do have a position available, though Baldo seems ready for a promotion. Should we have a little contest? I would be curious to see who wins. I think Baldo might surprise all of us."

"With a knife in your back, you mean?"

Shreb smiled at this. "No, I have someone watching *my* back. How about you?" He nodded at someone behind Benjamin.

"That's right." A woman's icy voice pierced Benjamin's heart. *It can't be her.* He turned. The woman in purple glistened in the dark like the stars. She was only a head taller than Baldo, who grinned behind her skirt. The world seemed to grind slowly down onto Benjamin's head. His mother stepped out of the shadows.

"No." Benjamin shook his head defiantly.

"I didn't endure years of motherhood so that you could end up *exactly* like your father! I am disappointed." Ursula's eyes narrowed. "I sabotaged, intimidated, and eliminated your competition at school. You think you were the head of your class because you were so good? You can't even defeat a waif of a farm boy!"

"My mother is dead!"

Ursula lifted up a shuttered lantern and opened it. It cast cruel shadows upward on her face. She pushed the jewel-encrusted headdress back from her face, revealing a sneer, which twisted her features into an inhuman expression. "I am glad to know my *demise* worked so well. It was not pleasant to undergo. I wouldn't recommend it, but I had such high hopes for you."

Benjamin tried to fight the desire to approach the woman, but he couldn't. He leaned in closer to her. It was known that some of the greatest villains faked their own deaths. There were ways. Benjamin looked into the woman's dazzling indigo eyes.

"Don't look like a wounded cow! You needed motivation. It got you to make a choice, didn't it? You were always waffling, unable to decide anything. It was the push you needed. You fought me on everything. I saw the only way you'd enter that school was in honor of my memory. Poof. Dead mother, right before you received your acceptance letter."

"I thought Sir Wendell arrested you." He clenched his fists together until he felt his nails cut into the flesh of his hands. He willed himself to stay here in the moment and pushed his dizziness away.

"No, he was busy. In his defense, the banquet was a mess. No good wine to drink."

Benjamin's legs felt weak. *Had he been poisoned?* He glanced behind the woman in purple, looking for the soldiers who had followed him out of the hall. He really needed to sit down, but he willed himself to stand.

"They're not coming. You successfully lost them with a little help from me, *as always.*" She walked past him in measured steps.

"My mother is dead," Benjamin whispered, barely able to hear his own words.

Ursula leaned close to his ear, her large sleeve scratching his jaw. "We can still fix this. Come with me. This is where you are *supposed* to be." She flicked her silver fan open in front of him, reflecting his pale face back to both of them.

"This was where you were always *supposed* to be, but *he* derailed us." Emotion rattled Ursula Black's voice.

Benjamin saw her bat away tears. She collapsed the fan and stepped back to regain command of herself. When she faced him again, she said nothing but stared at him for a long time. Baldo stepped back into the shadows, preparing to do who knows what. Facing two dead parents was too much.

What's next? he wondered. *Not-really-dead grandparents?*

Benjamin's ears steamed as Ursula prowled around him like a wild cat.

"You come from a long line of villains, you know. My father. His father. My *brother.*"

A chill so violent ran through his body that Benjamin's legs nearly buckled. He blinked back at the woman in purple. She smiled but said no more. She circled back around him toward Shreb. Benjamin forced himself to turn, to follow her. She flicked her fan, obviously reveling in the moment. Shreb admired his ring glinting in the moonlight. Meanwhile, a heavy rock was dragging Benjamin under murky water. The villains greedily watched him drown.

"He doesn't look so well," Shreb whined. "I'm not carrying him."

"Of course not! Benjamin needs to walk out of here on his own feet." Ursula slapped her fan against her brother's shoulder. "He knows what he needs to do."

"My mother is dead—" Benjamin said feebly, just to hear it once more. The woman who used to be his mother stared out at him through sparkling jewels and layers of makeup. Her look of impatience shattered the fog in his mind. "You did *all* of this just to get me?"

She smiled. "Not *just* you." He hated when she was condescending.

The sound of broken glass echoed in Benjamin's memory. He thought of Branwen and Rebecca. "My friends!"

"You don't have friends! Only alliances!" Ursula shrieked, pointing her fan at him. "Remember? Did *nothing* I taught you sink in? Well, that alliance is now dead."

She signaled them all to leave. Benjamin stepped back. He clutched one of his daggers. What did she mean? Dead? Rebecca? Ursula reached an arm out as if to scoop him up. *No!* Repulsion tore through his core at the thought of her touch. He slashed through his mother's sleeve and ran. His mother's screams ricocheted through the courtyard. "You belong to *me!*"

"My mother is dead!"

Benjamin regretted every drop of strength he wasted in chasing Baldo. His legs shook as he stumbled across the courtyard. He burst through a doorway, collapsing into a castle guard. "That way!" he gasped. "They went that way!"

"Who?"

My mother. "Shreb and his gang! In the courtyard." Benjamin pointed with his dagger, a glimmer of red visible at the tip.

SIXTY

The guard went white, but gestured for the others to follow him. Benjamin lowered his dagger—unable to look at the blood darkening the blade. He stumbled toward the great hall. Golden light reached out of the open doors. He wasn't sure that he was completely in his body. A cacophony enveloped him as he crossed the threshold.

Noblewomen were clustered in the far corners, fanning one another, as elderly husbands propped fragile wives up. Sir Wendell issued orders from the dais, not far from where the king had been sitting. The golden room dimmed. Benjamin's legs gave out. Suddenly an arm thrust around him, keeping him on his feet. A dirty eye patch looked down at him. *The Lieutenant!*

"She's alive! She was with Shreb!"

The Lieutenant pushed his eye patch back. "She? Shreb? *Who's* with Shreb?" His dark eye pulled Benjamin out of his shock.

Benjamin directed his father's gaze with his blood-tipped dagger. "Mother. She's here!"

His father's jaws flexed. He handed Benjamin over to someone who smelled like goat. Warm, muscled arms wrapped around him.

"Branwen!" Benjamin's scream tore through the chaos of the room.

Sir Wendell's head snapped up. "He's in conference with the king."

Benjamin gasped in relief to hear the king was alive. "Shreb is here!"

With a nod from Sir Wendell, guards cleared the room. A large, bloody mess lay below the king's table. Benjamin dropped his knife and staggered forward. He had to see. All that blood. Broken glasses, dishes, and place settings littered the floor from the bloody heap to where Benjamin had been sitting earlier. Rebecca climbed over the table? Why would she do that?

"Where is she?"

Denny emerged from the kitchens; a mix of dust and blood streaked his shirt and face. He scowled through blurry, fiery blue eyes.

"Where were *you*?" Denny growled, charging across the hall. One of Odie's arms swung out to halt Denny's attack.

"Where is Rebecca?" Benjamin felt his spine and legs fill with strength he did not know he had. Odie let go of him and slipped between the two boys. Benjamin stepped toward Denny and held his gaze. "Where is Rebecca?"

Denny could only glare.

Odie pointed toward the kitchens, while keeping one hand on Denny's chest.

"Benjamin!" Dally stepped out of the doorway and gestured. "I thought I heard you yelling!"

Benjamin met Denny's red glare again. Odie wrapped both arms around his older brother, his eyes also red.

Benjamin headed toward Dally. Her black dress had a dark, wet spot in the front, one of her diamond buttons tinged burgundy. Dally grabbed his arm and led him through the thickness of the room. Her fingernail beds were crusted brown. Fear swelled against Benjamin's heart with every step. Dally looked pale and serious.

Rebecca lay on a large kitchen table. Food and dishes lay scattered under the table. The Lady Jalene's tears glittered off her dark lashes, and she motioned for a tall servant to step aside. Rebecca's hand reached out for him. Relief slammed against him, forcing a cry out of his mouth.

She's alive!

Benjamin grabbed her hand with both of his. Her hand was cold and sticky, and every wrinkle and crease was filled with blood.

Rebecca opened her eyes to look at Benjamin. "Did you catch him?" she rasped.

Benjamin shook his head. Rebecca squeezed her eyes shut.

A muscled woman washed the blood off her face and arms, while a stern woman pressed down on a stack of perfectly white kitchen towels, dark blood seeping through. Both women had tears in their eyes. They crooned comforting nonsense that even Benjamin found reassuring.

Jalene broke through his shock. "There was a footman with a knife. We were all so busy looking at our wine that no one saw him except Rebecca. She pulled out her knives." Jalene gasped and sucked in her tears. Her fingers shook as she twisted them together. "We never thought Aldo was in danger. He has his own bodyguards."

The king's personal surgeon parted the crowd, and Benjamin and Jalene were escorted from the table. Branwen waited by the stoves, his white hair in disarray without his usual black cap. Guards ushered Jalene away; Aldo wanted her with him. Dally took her place beside Rebecca.

"Tell me everything that happened," Branwen said, swooping down on Benjamin and wrapping an arm around his shoulders.

Benjamin blinked blindly. "Is she going to be okay?"

"There is a lot of blood." Branwen glanced over his shoulder at the doctor, biting his lip. "But it's not as bad as it looks. Benjamin, focus!"

He snapped to the present. A chair was brought for him, and he told Branwen all that had happened on his foolish chase. Branwen was not surprised to hear that his mother was still alive. A sick feeling grew inside his chest as he retold the tale, Jalene's words repeating in his head.

"We were all so busy looking at our wine. No one saw him."

"This was my fault," Benjamin tagged at the end of his story.

"Your fault?"

"I fell for their trap. I provided the distraction that they needed."

"No. This was Ursula's doing, not yours." Branwen rubbed his face. Benjamin noticed that his hump was more pronounced than usual. "She spent the last sixteen years planning this. You've been involved for a month with only a glimpse of the whole truth. No one could beat Ursula with those odds, including your father. Or *me*, I might add." Branwen shook his head.

A humorless laugh cut through Benjamin's chest as if severing his heart from his body. The old man's words should have comforted him, but his friend still lay bleeding on a table, and words would not change that. He could not see Rebecca, but he could see Dally's set jaw as she watched the surgeon and knew it would be okay. It had to be.

"What did she mean? Her *father?* Her *brother?*" Benjamin hesitated as he tried force the name out through the swirling mess of his mind. "Not Shr—"

Branwen looked up. His lips drew tightly together and his eyes became stone. "I'll let your father explain that." He bowed and walked away.

Benjamin sank into his chair and swiped his damp hair off his face. The Lieutenant stood just inside the kitchen, watching as the doctor pulled out his thread and needle. Odie slouched beside the Lieutenant. Both looked away, but Dally's eyes stayed fixed on the doctor's needle. Benjamin looked down at the stone floor.

"I can do that for you, if you can't make your stiches smaller," Dally stated forcefully. "I have more experience with a needle than you."

SIXTY ONE

The four of them sat together, feeling miserable. Branwen had tucked them away in a small room. Benjamin sensed a burning on the side of his head. He leaned back to hide behind Odie's thick frame, thereby avoiding the heat of Denny's death glare. He resented that Denny dumped blame on him for everything. It was lazy, in his opinion. But Benjamin didn't have the energy to deal with Denny's petty arguments.

The Lieutenant sat across from the boys. He looked like he'd been smashed in the face by a chair. *I must look like that too.* Benjamin certainly felt that way.

A golden wolf's head stared out from Aldo's royal crest, next to the old man. Benjamin's head swirled, and he dropped his head into his hands. He had been twisted and manipulated his whole life by his mother until he chose to enter the Villains' Academy. He graduated the head of his class by avoiding personal connections. Thoughts of filling Black-Eyed Barnaby's shoes spurred him through those lonely years. *Is that what I'm doing now? Following in my real father's footsteps? Is that what I want to do? Is there a third option?* Benjamin felt nauseated.

He sat up and scrubbed his hair, as if that would force his mind to calm down. Ursula had hinted that Benjamin came from a long line of villains—her father and *brother*. He tried really hard not to understand those words. But the more he shut his mind to them, the more they swirled through his thoughts like a cyclone. His chest tightened as he opened his mouth. "Fa-Lieutenant?"

The Lieutenant's eyes came into focus. His eye patch was pushed aside, leaving an odd circle of white skin around an eye so dark it looked almost black from retina to iris.

"My mo—" He couldn't complete the word, not aloud. *My mother is dead.* "*Ursula* said that her father and brother—"

The Lieutenant motioned for Benjamin to follow him into the hallway. He shuffled over to a quiet niche, his shoulders sagging under the weight of the day's events.

"I had no idea about your mother. I knew even less about her than you did," he pled. "Please believe me. If Aldo or Branwen knew of this, they kept it to themselves for a good reason." His eyes went blank as he sank against the wall. "I can't believe—"

"You saw her?" Benjamin asked.

"A glimpse." The Lieutenant closed his eyes and covered his face with his hands. "I did that to your mother." A dry sob tore from the old man's chest.

They stood quietly for a moment before he opened his eyes.

"The hate on her face. I'm so sorry. I wouldn't have believed it if I hadn't seen it myself."

Benjamin felt a stab of pain in his chest. "Her father and brother?"

"I worked for her father. She actually helped me get my position with him."

"Shreb Senior?"

He nodded.

"So Shreb is her brother? Shreb is *my* uncle?"

"Well, half-brother."

"Is that supposed to make it better?"

"No. Sorry." His father rubbed his face, smudging dirt into his circle of clean. "I just don't understand. She wouldn't have anything to do with her brother. Shreb *hated* me. Oh—" His mouth froze into the shape of a large O.

"This was about revenge?" Benjamin gasped. "My life was revenge against you?"

Benjamin nearly gagged on the disgust that climbed up his throat. He paced back and forth in front of his father, who sparked so much of this misery. All the lies he told had built Benjamin's life.

"Ursula hated her father but loved him all the same. He never had time for her because she couldn't carry on his name. When we fell in love, I told myself that she would be happy to leave it all behind her. When her father discovered that we were secretly married, he was thrilled. She could provide him with a proper heir to his villainy, but then he died."

"What about Shreb II?"

"Shreb never really thought much of the boy who shared his name and even less of the boy's mother. He was always a disappointment. The senior Shreb took me under his wing. He treated me as his son. So, of course, Shreb *Junior* hated me. He tried to kill me after his father gave me the Heart of Darkness, something he wanted more than life."

"The Heart of Darkness?"

"With it comes the power to rule the Thieves Plain. I gave it to the king," the Lieutenant said, tilting his head against the wall. "It was supposed to mark the end of the greatest threat to the crown. Then came the murder of Aldo's brother and my sister—Rebecca's parents—and the rise of Mouthrot, and so on."

Benjamin squeezed his head, trying to push out all the clutter. He had absorbed more information than he could digest in one day.

"Great Wolves! Is my family in the middle of everything in the entire kingdom?" His eyes popped open. "Does that mean I'm related to the king?"

"No, but that makes Rebecca your cousin," the Lieutenant said.

"More family?" Benjamin sighed, collapsing against the wall. "I just had both parents return from the dead. My mother tried to kill the king with my previously unknown uncle. My father is trying to protect the king with my previously unknown cousin." He pressed his fists against his eyes. "I was an orphan not more than a month ago!"

The Lieutenant placed a sympathetic hand on his shoulder and squeezed. And even though it didn't feel very comforting, Benjamin appreciated the sentiment.

Branwen emerged from the shadows, rambling orders, flanked by two guards. His black cap was still missing, but his snowy hair was less rumpled. A clerk attempted to take down the secretary's commands as they walked. He dipped his quill into the ink well that one of the guards held.

Branwen ushered Benjamin and the Lieutenant into their waiting room where Odie stared at his brother Denny, who was a complete mess.

"Rebecca is sleeping in her bed now. The surgeon says she will be fine. Most of the blood was from the assassin when she pulled her knife out of his throat. More kings should wear corsets, it seems."

Denny sank back into his chair in relief, wiping tears away. Odie wrapped a bear-sized arm around him, while Branwen filled them in on the rest. Ursula and Shreb had escaped easily, leaving false trails for the guards. Mouthrot was still safely locked away in the dungeon; the king would set the date for his execution as a gift for his niece.

"How thoughtful," Benjamin said, rolling his eyes.

Branwen barely contained a smile but nodded.

"I'll tell His Majesty that you approve. Though I think he may just be trying to prevent the princess from killing another man with her bare hands." Branwen lifted the corner of his mouth. "I think that we won't have to worry about anyone trying to take advantage of *her*."

Benjamin smirked. The duchess would keep her distance for a while, but it didn't seem to concern Lady Jalene at all. If anything, the opposite was true. She seemed to love Rebecca more.

"How is Aldo taking this?" the Lieutenant asked.

"After having Rebecca in two life-threatening situations in which she came out better than her attacker?"

The Lieutenant swallowed and flexed his jaws.

"I think the king is upset but relieved she was able to defend herself. Though I think he plans to caution the princess against putting herself in direct danger again. She *is* the sole heir at the moment."

"The engagement?" Benjamin just remembered.

"Tomorrow. Now go take care of yourselves." Branwen smiled at him. "You all look terrible."

Benjamin looked down and was surprised to see his new suit torn and bloody. The Lieutenant steered the sad quartet to the kitchens for something warm to eat.

Off in a corner, the fiery-haired maid sat with a cup of tea on her lap and a steak over one eye. A tight frown tugged her full lips down. A tall footman with equally red hair crouched over her, his jaw flexing. Benjamin had forgotten about her. He wasn't sure why she had stepped in front of Baldo, but she was the only person who had helped him.

He pushed his stool back and approached her. The tall man, who must have been her brother, stood up as he approached, his face stony.

"I just wanted to say thank you for helping me."

The girl removed the chunk of meat from her face and smiled faintly. Apricot freckles glistened under her good eye. The purple bruise clashed with her emerald eyes. "A lot of good it did."

Benjamin nodded at this. "We still had to try," he added with a shrug.

Her eyes brightened, and she smiled. "Yes, you're right. We do need to try."

The brother sighed, obviously not happy about the idea of his sister putting herself in harm's way.

"The king will be pleased to know he has such loyal servants. May I ask your name?"

"Molly," she said, blushing.

"Thank you, Molly."

Benjamin shook her hand. Her grip was firm, and he felt heat rise in his own cheeks. He returned to his soup, his hand tingling. The Lieutenant gave him an approving look.

Benjamin ducked his head and ate mechanically, not tasting anything, but at least it was warm. He needed some warming up. His mother's words returned to him, chilling him. *You were meant for villainy. You belong to me.* Ice flowed in his veins. Someone examined and dabbed Benjamin's scrapes and then dismissed him to his room.

Denny and Odie were given their own room, thankfully. Benjamin didn't have the strength to fight with Denny right now. The Lieutenant walked Benjamin to his room quietly, his hands behind his back, his head bent in contemplation.

They paused outside his door. His father struggled with the day's events. He wasn't dealing with Ursula's reappearance any better than

Benjamin was. All of his father's good intentions counted for nothing against all his miscalculations in the end.

"Do you ever wonder if it all was worth it?" Benjamin asked.

"Sometimes. But then I look at you, and I know it is, even if it doesn't feel like it now." The Lieutenant smiled weakly, his eyes focusing on another time. "You were worth it."

Benjamin nodded. The Lieutenant set his hand on Benjamin's shoulder and then wandered off. Benjamin watched the old man for a while, unsure what he felt. His father had showed him more kindness in that moment than he remembered from his entire life with his mother.

He entered his room with a sense of dread. *Sleep.* The one thing that would be the best medicine would probably be the most elusive.

SIXTY TWO

*R*ebecca woke under soft blankets. She tried not to move; breathing hurt. She didn't remember falling asleep or being moved from the kitchen table. A dim lantern burned in the corner behind a shade. A dark form sat by the bed, much too large to be Dally or Benjamin.

The man leaned over with a gasp of relief. "Rebecca!" Aldo grabbed her hand. "I was so afraid that I had lost you before I'd even really gotten you back."

"Your Majesty." Rebecca's voice was rough and broken.

Aldo slid his hand under her neck and placed a glass of water to her lips. She sipped, and he laid her gently down.

"The draught the doctor gave will make you thirsty, but he warned me not to let you drink too fast."

She nodded to this and closed her eyes, feeling the water cool her throat. She had not noticed how dry her mouth was.

"I have faced fear many times in my life, but none compares to the terror I felt watching you throw yourself on my attacker."

A ragged breath stopped her uncle for a moment. Silence filled in his words. Rebecca opened her eyes, shocked at the weariness of his expression. He helped her drink more and pulled the cup away when she began to drink too greedily.

"I would have been anxious if any of my men had acted so boldly. I would have been beside myself if it had been Sir Wendell, Branwen, or even Torrin's son, Benjamin. You cannot imagine how heartsick I felt as I watched, stiff as a rock, as my whole family jumped to her death for my sake. I'm not sure I would have counted it an equal trade. Your life is more precious to me than my own."

He reached out and placed a trembling hand on her head, brushing her hair away from her face. "You must promise me Reyna, to guard your own life with as much fierceness as you have guarded mine tonight."

Rebecca reached up and placed her hand on her uncle's. "Lady Jalene is still young. You will have your own family soon."

"It is *your life*, not my future heir's that I am worried about!" He squeezed her hand too fiercely and withdrew his hand in apology.

The door opened behind him. "I will leave you to Dally. Rest. Your friends will be anxious to see you tomorrow."

He kissed her gently on the forehead, his beard prickling her nose. Smiling, he wished her good night.

Dally cradled her face in her hands. Her tears fell onto Rebecca's nightgown. "You foolish girl!" She planted a big kiss on her forehead. "Don't ever do that again!"

Rebecca reached up and wrapped her arms around Dally. She felt a prick deep in her chest as she saw Dally's composure crumble. It hurt nearly as bad as her injury. "I'm sorry, Dally! I'm okay. Really. I'm sorry!"

They cried for a few moments together and then wiped their eyes and laughed. Rebecca's side burned, and her whole body ached.

"I've never seen Sir Wendell so mad! I think you've just earned yourself a few extra bodyguards." Dally handed Rebecca a beautifully embroidered handkerchief.

Rebecca moaned at this while Dally wiped away more tears. "And the king! I think both of them burst into tears afterward."

She cringed as her nurse adjusted her pillows. Rebecca had just done her duty to her king. How could it end with everyone angry with her? Dally brought over a bowl of broth that smelled wonderful. *I didn't do anything wrong! I'd do it again.*

"I suppose Branwen or Benjamin must have been pleased, at least?"

"Pleased? Pleased you're not dead! Denny was near murdering Benjamin. He acted as if Benjamin had thrown you at that assassin himself!"

"Oh, Denny," she said, accepting a warming spoon of broth. "That's my fault."

"Rebecca?"

"I think he has this idea about us. We've known each other for so long. I always thought he was acting the protective big brother. When he found out who I really was—"

"Ah, his dreams were crushed. He must care for you very much."

She frowned. Dally offered another spoonful of broth.

"He's my friend, Dally. I would do anything for him."

"Then tell him that, but let him find a new path in life." Dally offered more broth. "He just needs time. Too much has happened."

Rebecca closed her eyes, letting her lids cool her burning eyes. She thought quietly as she swallowed the broth. Dally sat the bowl down and pulled the blankets up. "Rest. I'll be close by."

SIXTY THREE

*B*enjamin stared into the dark, unwilling to close his eyes. Every time he did, he saw things he was powerless to undo. He tried pretending his mother didn't exist, even as he caught glimpses of her angry stare in the corner of his mind. Baldo would creep into his thoughts next. Baldo, who was younger, more devious, and more organized, was much more like the boy his mother had tried to make him into. How had they both ended up on the wrong sides? If he had made his interview that day, where would he be now?

Things were supposed to be coming to a close. Mouthrot was captured. Shreb was on the run, and yet it felt like the beginning of something horrible. Was there ever a neat ending? His mother was the reason this couldn't end. She wasn't the type to leave things alone. Neither Benjamin nor Lam would have peace until she either won or was destroyed. And if anyone could help fight Ursula, it was him. He was well practiced.

Ursula's war was not solely about Benjamin or the king; it was about *his* father and *her* father as well. Hadn't she said as much? Perhaps Benjamin could escape to a foreign kingdom while the dust settled. A part of him would love to run away from it all. This war could be another injury to attribute to the Lieutenant, Torrin, or Black-Eyed Barnaby. Benjamin rolled onto his back to stare at the darkness hanging over him.

The Lieutenant, so capable and strong, cowered at the sight of Ursula. How did she have the power to control and frighten so many? *Don't you know who your mother is?* Branwen had asked. Ursula was the daughter of Shreb the First and sister to the idiot Shreb II. She was the most clever and dangerous of them all. His mother had devoured her own heart that had burned with her lover's betrayal. There was no heart left for Benjamin as a child. She only had a hole where she stored all her plans for revenge.

After a time, the night's shadows revealed the serpentine pattern on his pillows. At first, faint lines of gray appeared, and then green vines, leaves, and flowers. Benjamin traced them silently as he lay on his side, waiting for time to pass. Benjamin didn't know what his options were exactly. He had made vague plans to assist Rebecca, to be her personal Branwen, but he wasn't sure he could do it now.

Benjamin pressed the heels of his hands into his eyes, wanting to block out all the thoughts and feelings. He wanted to numb his body. He didn't want to make choices. He didn't want to do anything. He didn't want to think anything. He didn't want to be anywhere. He wanted to be nothing. Hot tears trickled down the side of his nose. Benjamin had cried once because his mother had died…and now he cried because she was alive.

When sunlight filtered through the curtains, someone tapped at Benjamin's door. He got up, thankful for a reason to get out of bed.

Odie slunk in his door, dragging Denny behind him. Denny crossed his arms and glared. Odie slid behind Denny and pressed him forward, prompting his older brother to say something. Benjamin's head throbbed. He closed his eyes and wished he wasn't here. It was too early for hollow apologies or accusations. He couldn't take it.

Not today.

"How about we just skip to the end?" Benjamin said through locked jaws, his chest tightening as he spoke. "You blame me for Baldo's choices, for your lack of fortune, and for Rebecca throwing herself at an assassin."

All the pressure that had been building in him his whole life poured out of him. There was no stopping it. It felt wonderful.

"I don't put ideas into people's heads," Benjamin continued. "And I didn't wake up one morning with an unexpected desire to destroy some guy named Denny." He jabbed the empty space in front of the brothers. Benjamin's face burned, and his head spun with adrenaline.

"I didn't ask for my mother to be the most conniving, evil woman this kingdom has ever known! I didn't *ask* to be Shreb's nephew. I didn't request a father who had taken in a pack of orphans. I didn't *ask* to attract the negative attentions of a hidden princess with a temper that could burn down this whole castle! I never had ambitions so specific or grand."

Benjamin clamped his eyes shut, unable to process the ghostly brothers who stood before him.

"A *crazy* woman raised me! One whose every breath was aimed to make me the greatest villain's assistant that the world had ever seen. Just like my father—a man who never existed. And what kind of mother fakes her death to ensure I followed the path *she* laid out for me?"

Benjamin clenched his fists so tight he thought his knuckles would crack, as if he was trying desperately to hold on to reality itself before it slid away from him. Denny's face was white, his eyes wide. Odie glanced up then tucked his head back down. Benjamin's eyes shifted to the predictable pattern of the wallpaper.

"A man chose to wait for me on that road. He offered me two choices: follow him or let Mouthrot kill me!" Benjamin was screaming now. Blood pulsed behind his ears. "I just stood face to face with my *dead* mother, Shreb Jr., *and* Baldo. *Your* brother lured me into a situation that should have made it impossible for me to refuse to join them!" He jerked his imaginary knife through his mother's sleeve again. "But I severed those ties, literally, running to Rebecca, Aldo, and to all of you, and yet you *still* don't trust me. And what do I have to show for all of this?"

Benjamin sought out Denny's icy eyes as he stepped forward. "*Your* anger! *Your* accusations! I'm *sorry* your brother and I ended up on the wrong sides! I'm not sure how it happened! I thought maybe—"

Odie's fingertips pressed gently against Benjamin's chest. Benjamin was surprised to see that his nose nearly touched Denny's. He turned away, clutching his chest; it felt hollowed out. Did he really just lose it? Benjamin studied his abandoned bed for a moment. The blankets where rumpled, leaving an empty tunnel that marked his sleepless night.

"I thought maybe the hard choices were the right ones. *Maybe* I was wrong," Benjamin mumbled.

He heard the door close behind him before Benjamin realized he was walking down the hallway. Guards saluted as he passed, but no one followed him. Benjamin didn't stop until he found the dusty room full of broken furniture; the giant banquet tables were missing. He didn't want to run into Branwen this time, so he pulled the door closed. Then he screamed and screamed, yanking on his hair to feel the pain. Finally he collapsed to the floor.

Tears blurred his vision as Benjamin realized that he felt worse than before. Anger and confusion pressed inside of him while he sobbed into the floor.

SIXTY FOUR

Benjamin jerked awake, not remembering falling asleep. He heard footsteps approaching.

"Sorry, I didn't mean to startle you."

The Lieutenant stopped a few strides short of Benjamin. The old man was cleaner than he was the night before but still looked no more rested. His eye patch was gone, as well as the circle of dirt that usually marked its absence. He examined the pile of broken furniture and then slumped to the ground and leaned against the pile.

"Odie told me what happened."

That boy chose to speak at the strangest times.

"I don't blame you for being angry. It's easier to lash out at a person rather than cope with a situation that is outside your control." The old man reached for his missing patch and then decided to examine his palms instead. "I spent years being angry with a lot of people—especially myself. It never did me any good."

Benjamin's cheeks burned. He had just done the exact thing he despised Denny for doing to him. It *was* lazy. He pressed the heels of his hands into his eyes. The Lieutenant's voice was empty of anger. No accusation. No scorn. Was it *kindness* Benjamin heard?

"I hardly recognized your mother. Anger has twisted her into something nearly inhuman." He paused to breathe. "I had a part in it, but in the end, *she* chose that path. We all choose."

Benjamin's chest tightened, and he struggled for air. He blinked, unable to say anything. The Lieutenant rubbed his hands together as if he were cold. It was strange to see that one dark eye. *Black-Eyed Barnaby.* His father noticed Benjamin's gaze and rubbed at his eye, smiling awkwardly.

"It does feel strange to be without it after all these years. It tied me to a life of hiding and turned me away from this life." He gestured at their surroundings and sighed.

"You may feel you didn't have much of a choice in all of this, but there were times you could have taken a different path. You could have gone back, but you chose to do what was right over what was easy." Benjamin's father picked up a broken arm of a chair and examined it. "I waited on that road for you because I hoped that somehow we would end up at the same destination in the end."

Benjamin turned his head at this. The Lieutenant shrugged at this confession, one that was a long time coming, making brief eye contact before glancing back at the wood in his hand.

"I just wanted a chance," his father said as he turned his uneven gaze back on his son. "I wanted you to have a chance to make choices with a little more information."

Benjamin sat up stiffly. His head hurt. "You wanted me to know the truth?" Benjamin tugged at his torn cuff, unsure what to do next.

His father stood and offered his hand. "Yes."

Benjamin gripped his father's warm hand and quickly found himself in his embrace, something he'd never experienced in his sixteen years. He was surprised to find it was just what he needed.

Benjamin wrapped his arms around his father and squeezed back. Warmth swelled in his chest, smoothing the sharp edges of the pain there.

"Denny needs time. You gave him something to think about." The Lieutenant stepped back and squeezed Benjamin's shoulder. "I think an apology from both sides wouldn't hurt—eventually."

SIXTY FIVE

*R*ebecca's side burned. Oh, how it burned. She woke up feeling thick headed, and moving felt nearly impossible. *Oh yes, I was stabbed!* She saw the assassin's dark eyes, the stubble on his chin, the throbbing vein she stuck her knife into. She gasped at the pain welling up in her side. Dally's hands were under her head to give her something that smelled overly sweet. Rebecca waved the vial away. "Water," she croaked.

Dally nodded and gave her sweet, cold water. She asked to sit up. What a process that was! Dally promised it would be smoother next time. Rebecca smiled at the old woman, whose face was drawn and shadowed.

"You need to sleep, Dally. Surely you could find someone to help you. What would I do if you were too ill to help me?"

This seemed to strike a chord. Dally nodded, openly acknowledging her fatigue.

Molly soon appeared at her bedroom door. A black eye peered up from behind the tray she set at the foot of the bed. She smiled awkwardly and muttered something about stepping in front of the wrong person. Rebecca felt a twinge of embarrassment as Molly smoothed out her blankets, remembering the jokes and confessions they had shared when she was pretending to be a simple servant.

Rebecca bit her lip. "Molly, I'm sorry I misled you. It was the only way they'd let me out of here."

The maid rubbed the bedspread through her fingers for a moment before responding. "While these rooms are fine, I can't imagine being cooped up in here the whole time." A blush crept up Molly's neck, and she nodded firmly. "You had to get out! Plus, we all knew there was something special about you. We just didn't know exactly *how* special."

Molly rubbed her hands on her skirt as she examined the room. She stopped to meet Rebecca's gaze for a moment with earnest eyes.

"We're all just so happy to have the princess back." She gestured to the tray. "You are forgiven. Henry spent hours making you a sugar butterfly."

Rebecca put her hand to her chest, as warmth spread from her heart. The butterfly was every shade of blue; its delicate wings shimmered in the sunlight. Rebecca remembered a smudge of white faces and strained voices floating around her as she bled on the table. There were a few snatches of prayers in her behalf that stuck out in her mind.

It never occurred to Rebecca what the people felt about her personally. She could never have imagined what her existence meant to them. Rebecca still didn't understand, not really, but she felt more of an obligation to them now. Her view of life had widened enormously as she thought of all the lives that were counting on her.

"Thank you." Rebecca's voice nearly failed.

Rebecca ate and drank obediently, while Molly told stories of upheaval around the castle. The kitchen maid sat next to her on the bed after she finished her tray. Rebecca tried not to giggle as Molly imitated the butler's distress at the shattered dinnerware. Rebecca smiled. She hadn't lost a friend at all. She had gained a devoted ally.

Denny stopped by a few days later. He was dressed in his castle clothes, nearly a new person. His golden waves shone. Molly smiled mischievously as she left the room. Yes, Denny was handsome. He would look fabulous in a uniform. She could probably get him a commission since he was eager to be more than a boy from a farm.

"You look much better," Denny said. He didn't bother to hide his relief. "All that blood. I've never been so scared!"

He looked down at his new boots, and Rebecca motioned for him to sit. He hesitated a moment, but he lowered himself into the chair by her bed. She reached her hand out to him, and he took it eagerly.

Denny's hand was warm and rough, not unlike hers. He had done a lot for her over the years. He looked up into her eyes, nearly blinding her. All of this was new, the touch of his hand, the directness of Denny's gaze. His blue eyes were like the sky on a summer day, bright and full of promise. Warmth ran up her arm to her chest, stealing her breath. She commanded herself to be strong.

"I'm sorry about that. The king has commanded I worry about my own safety and not his. Sir Wendell has given me two additional bodyguards. It will never happen again. They forbid it."

"Why?" A plea layered in Denny's voice as he squeezed her hand. "Why did you do it?"

The room was so quiet she could feel it pressing against her ears. The answer pressed against her tongue, building in her chest like a glowing ember. *The truth?*

"No one's really asked that…or waited for the answer." Rebecca's false laugh crumbled in her throat. She examined the bedposts, the drapes, the walls, and the sleeve of the red silk robe that she wore over her nightgown. She took a deep breath. "I will do *everything* to ensure the safety of the king and any future heir. I will never be queen."

Denny dropped his gaze, and a strand of gold fell over his eyes before he spoke again. "You will be happy to know that the king officially announced his engagement to Lady Jalene. He sent out messengers with his decree this morning." He pressed his lips together. "There will be a court next week to hear Mouthrot's crimes and an execution. A wedding date will be announced soon."

Rebecca smiled and squeezed his hand. She wondered if he could feel her hand trembling. *How easy it would be if I let myself.* "Can we persuade Aldo to get married first?"

Denny laughed as he searched her face. The sun moved out from behind a cloud as he reached up and brushed her cheek. A ripple of expectation and fear raced to her heart.

She remembered the warning Dally had given her about boys. Denny's love was there; she could see it in his face. She wasn't sure she deserved it. She swallowed. There was something she *could* give him freely.

"I want you to do something for me." Rebecca's words crossed her lips more as air than voice.

Denny nodded and traced his thumb across the scabs that had formed over her knuckles and reached for her other hand. She gave it to him freely. It was startling to have him be so open with her. He was so much braver than she.

She licked her lips. "I've talked to my uncle about you and your brothers." She swallowed again. "Would you take a commission if you were offered one?"

"If it would help you," he said, warmly tracing the inside of her palm with his thumb. Her hand tingled and then went numb.

She nodded, not trusting her voice.

"I know I've been a pain lately. I've just been too wrapped up in myself. It's a miserable place to be." Denny leaned into the bed, holding her gaze firmly. "You will always be a part of my plans. I will serve you in whatever way is best."

He raised Rebecca's hands to his lips. They were softer than she had expected. The warmth that passed through her body surprised her even more, and suddenly there wasn't enough air in the room. Only the firm lines of her position and the pain in her side kept her from leaning forward to meet those lips. *Bless that assassin's knife! It had been good for something.* Rebecca pressed her back into her pillow. She ached to feel his arms around her, but somehow that felt dishonest, not to mention physically painful.

"I love you," Denny whispered. It fell like a hopeless prayer from his lips.

How could anyone know that? I'm too young to know about such things. Rebecca's face burned uncomfortably.

"Thank you," she whispered through thick lips.

Denny accepted this and pressed his lips against her hands again and stood to leave. He paused by the door. "I'm sorry about that night by the fire. I just wanted to kiss you, just once."

Not until he left did the air return to the room. Molly returned and fussed with the door, giving Rebecca time to dab her eyes with an extravagantly embroidered handkerchief. "I'm exhausted."

Molly set a glass down next to the sugar butterfly displayed on Rebecca's bed stand, magnifying it through the glass. Molly silently adjusted Rebecca's pillows so that she could lie down, and a fresh handkerchief was left in her hand. It was soft and embroidered with an R that wore a wolf's face. *Princess Reyna. Royalty.*

SIXTY SIX

*B*enjamin poked at his cold breakfast. He chewed a piece of bread and swallowed forcefully. He brushed the crumbs from the new suit brought to him for this morning's special occasion. It was a somber black, like funeral attire. Mouthrot's sentence was being read this morning. Aldo had kept Rebecca away for most of the trial, but this morning, Rebecca insisted on attending. As her friend (or whatever he was), Benjamin would stand by her.

He walked alone to Rebecca's door. There were guards stationed outside and a few more just down the hall. The recent assassination attempts had doubled Aldo's concern for his niece, even with proof of her ability to defend herself.

Dally poked her head out of the door and nodded. Rebecca stepped out wearing a dress the color of cold ash. Benjamin offered his arm, and she took it. Neither was in the mood for conversation. She twisted the ends of her black shawl as they walked stiffly to face her parents' murderer. Benjamin's body moved steadily, but his mind was racing.

This could have been Benjamin's fate. Guards saluted as they walked by, no weapons pointed at him. Princess Reyna casually rested her arm in his. Outside the door, Denny waited in his new uniform. He had been given a commission and would soon leave to fulfill his orders. Rebecca accepted Denny's arm as he escorted her into the courtroom. Benjamin followed behind, scanning the dour faces of noblemen who had spent the last two weeks hearing evidence against the traitor.

The noblemen stood for the princess as the king watched her cross the room. Denny led her to a seat next to the Lieutenant. Torrin. His father. He looked strangely alert with two eyes—one dark, one light—looking out at the world. He took the princess's hand and kissed it. She sat and all sat with her.

The guards slammed their staffs against the floor. The doors opened. Mouthrot entered. He flashed his gold teeth as if he feared no one in this room. His eyes, sagging heavily, rested for a moment on Torrin, his nemesis, but continued to the princess, who sat with dignity under his cold gaze. Rebecca wore no crown, but her royalty could not be mistaken. Mouthrot's smile flickered. He turned and faced the lords, who were visibly bored. The villain fiddled with his chains.

One of the lords cleared his throat and stood. He waited for Aldo to acknowledge him and then spoke. "The list of this man's crimes against the royal family and the kingdom of Lam is long. They include murder, attempted murder, kidnapping, attempted kidnapping, bribery, blackmail, conspiracy, and so forth. Each is serious enough to hold this court, but the one that we will acknowledge at this time is the murder of the king's brother, Prince Evan, and his wife, Brynn, the parents of Princess Reyna, the only living heir to King Aldo, whom he also attempted to kidnap and murder."

"That is two crimes, not one," Mouthrot croaked and sneered at the court.

Rebecca sat straight, face blank. Benjamin wondered how a man so powerful could be reduced so quickly. Mouthrot had lost weight, and the only color left in his face was that of the gold teeth that he was determined to display to the nobility he despised.

The villain played his hand well, but he had lost. The noblemen in this room hadn't defeated him. His own adopted people had done that, people he thought beneath him.

"Last words?" Aldo's voice filled the room, sounding more like a dare than a request.

Mouthrot's smile twisted. He spat in everyone's general direction. Disdain. His last words he wanted to speak to no one in this room. Benjamin remembered Ursula, Baldo, and Shreb standing in the courtyard. Ursula's face had also been filled with disdain. They had expected him to join them. *Would they still let him, even now?*

The rest of it was over quickly. A sack, a large man, and a sharp knife.

It was over.

Rebecca stood, her face like marble, and walked out of the room unassisted. Benjamin followed her out, the doors echoing behind them. She walked straight outside through the main courtyard. The sun was out, but the day was cool. Rebecca peered out the gate for a moment and then climbed up to the watchtowers, Benjamin following her.

Rebecca pressed against the balustrade and gazed toward the forest where Prince Evan's castle would have been. Her castle. Where would Ursula be now? Benjamin then wondered where his father's home was, the home he had been promised. He felt a touch of curiosity. Did he really have a home anymore? He rested his hand on the cold stone, and something wet hit his hand. Tears streamed down Rebecca's face, unchecked. Benjamin put an arm stiffly around her shoulder, and she collapsed in his arms. They cried together for a moment. She handed him a handkerchief when she finally stood back.

"Don't worry. Dally's embroidered loads of these for me. You can keep that one. I have plenty." Rebecca smiled and turned to face the world outside. "It feels nice to be outside and feel the sun on my face again."

Denny and the Lieutenant watched from behind. Rebecca pulled out another newly embroidered handkerchief and wiped her eyes and nose. "I'm done."

Denny offered his arm and eyed the handkerchief in Benjamin's hand as he led Rebecca to the stairs. Benjamin stuffed the handkerchief into his pocket. He turned away, hoping the breeze would dry his face.

The Lieutenant, his father, stood next to him. He gazed into the east.

"After the wedding, we'll have to make a trip to see my estate, Gehnry. I haven't seen it in ages. I was thinking of taking Rebecca and everyone there. Otherwise it really won't feel like home." The Lieutenant pressed his fists into the stone. "I don't know how I'll settle into a quiet life after so many years of dirty work."

"You think the king will let you retire?"

"He agreed to let me try."

"Do you think the king would let *me* retire?" Benjamin tried to laugh but failed.

The Lieutenant turned. He put his hand on Benjamin's shoulder and looked him in both eyes for a long time, trying to read what Benjamin wouldn't say. "Would you want to?"

"I'm not sure. Probably not."

Benjamin sighed, and his father gave his shoulder a sympathetic squeeze. Ursula and Baldo's faces appeared in his mind. They were challenging him, weren't they? A job left unfinished. Benjamin and his father silently looked over Lam until the guard changed.

SIXTY SEVEN

*W*hen Benjamin returned to his room, he knelt in front of the bed that had been his during his short visits to the castle. He tossed back the lace and ruffles and shoved his hand under the mattress, momentarily worried that the maids may have done too fine of a job. But after fishing around, he found them. His villain's suit was properly crumpled. He couldn't risk sending it to the laundry. They'd have gotten it properly clean and mended—or burned. He had washed it himself and rinsed it well enough to remove any obvious signs of mud, but it still felt stiff. After it was dried, he shoved it under the mattress, just in case.

Benjamin stripped off his fine suit and laid it flat on his bed. He pulled on his old suit, rough and gritty. He realized now how poorly his villain's suit fit him and how inferior it was. It scratched against his skin and pinched in a few places. Benjamin looked into the mirror and tried to remember the excitement and confidence he had felt that day he first put the black suit on. He felt none of that now—quite the opposite.

Benjamin slipped his hand into his pocket and pulled out the eye patch that had survived the whole ordeal. It had dried into the shape of a dead blossom. He smoothed it out. It was nothing but a caricature of the one his father had hidden behind for so much of his life. Benjamin tossed it behind him, his eyes locking with Rebecca's in the mirror.

"I know there are rules about entering a lady's chamber. Surely there are rules about the reverse?" he said, ducking his head as he secured his money purse around his waist. "I'm pretty sure I didn't hear a knock."

"You don't have to do this."

"Don't I?" Benjamin looked back at the mirror.

Rebecca stared back, hollow-eyed and pale.

It has to be now. Benjamin felt his stomach twist. Her parents' murderer was not even cold in his grave. *By the Great Wolves, it has to be now!*

He slung the pack he'd paid a stable boy for on his back and walked out the door. Benjamin didn't look back. The brothers were scattered down the hallway, confused. Obviously they'd pursued Rebecca down the hall, not realizing what she had already figured out. He looked past Denny, still in his uniform, who stiffened. Odie locked eyes with Benjamin, read all that was tangled in his heart, and simply nodded.

Benjamin's feet felt heavy. He didn't think it would be this hard. He hadn't realized his exit would leave a wound. He was simply following his story to the close. When did he become interested in the ending to other people's stories? How much of his story was a part of theirs? Benjamin used to think all stories went on, independent of others with main characters and minor characters that came and went, but really they were all main characters whose stories relied on the telling of others' stories.

As Benjamin stepped out into the main courtyard, he caught a glimpse of flaming hair among the bodies coming and going. Molly watched him through her faded black eye and wore a knowing smile, though Benjamin had no idea what she could possibly know. The kitchen maid held out a sack, dropped it into his hands, and walked away. Inside were foodstuffs; alongside the hard rolls, she had packed a pair of worn gloves and a scarf. Summer was over, and the cold weather was coming. Benjamin looked back to thank her but only caught a glimpse of her skirt as she passed her lanky brother. The footman scrutinized Benjamin a moment and then followed his sister.

Benjamin passed through the gate quietly. Sir Wendell did not watch him as he inspected his guard. And with little fanfare, Benjamin set out for his next job interview.

EPILOGUE

The night was unusually cold for so early in the fall. There was a bite to the air, and Benjamin blessed Molly's name again as he rubbed his gloved hands together. The path was dark, but the full moon was quickly rising. He wouldn't get lost in its bright light. He didn't want to sleep in the rough again tonight. Not that his hideout was much better, but at least it had a roof and blankets. The road shone around him like the slow-moving river he'd glimpsed from the upper floors of Rebecca's ruined castle the night before.

The brambles that marked his ill-used path were lit by silver moonlight. The naked branches looked like skeletal sentries posted along the dark path to witness his undoing. Benjamin swallowed the knot in his chest, even as it tore it in two. The broken gate was invisible in the shadows, but he felt its presence all the same. The broken shutter creaked and cast its night shadow onto the bleached walls of the shack.

He was only able to draw a shallow breath as he opened the door. He hadn't thought to lock it in his rush to Shreb's fortress. Inside, moonlight marked a corner of the table that was littered with mugs and plates.

He lit a candle. In three steps, he crossed to the table and flipped it over, scattering broken earthenware across the floor. He leaned in to search out the words written underneath. With a few swift kicks, the top detached from the frame, and he reset the table with the words and a map facing up—a map that would lead him to Ursula. It slipped right into place. The road looked straight for once, without any hidden twists. He pulled out paper and a wax pen and then pulled the table closer to the window to take advantage of the brilliant moonlight. He knew he really should do this in the morning, but he couldn't stop. This task was the one thing that soothed him. And now that he was here, he realized he couldn't sleep here. This place was dead. Another cursed place to avoid at all costs.